Secrets

of the

GOLDEN HOURGLASS

Secrets

of the

GOLDEN HOURGLASS

A MILITARY NOVEL BY:

William H. Christ, Jr.

ISBN: 978-1-63732-246-8   (Paperback Edition)
ISBN: 978-1-63732-247-5   (Hardcover Edition)
ISBN: 978-1-63732-245-1   (E-book Edition)

Some characters and events in this book are fictitious. Any similarity to real persons, living or dead, is coincidental and not intended by the author.

Book Ordering Information

Phone Number: 315 288-7939 ext. 1000 or 347-901-4920
Email: info@globalsummithouse.com
Global Summit House
www.globalsummithouse.com

Printed in the United States of America

For my late Mother, Claire Francis
1920-2000
My Greatest Source of Encouragement.

Man seeks for gold in mines,
that he may weave a lasting chain for his own slavery.
P. B. Shelley, 1818

PROLOGUE

Conditions were awful. Their labor was intense. Twelve men struggled daily during a twelve hour shift deep within their designated mine tunnel. Heavily armed and hooded guards stood nearby ready to trigger the men's common bond - an electronic dog collar. The jolt would bring a prisoner to his knees and remind him that he's enjoying hell on earth.

Red lights hung precariously about in the tunnels. This always created an eerie world for the prisoners. Yet, they labored only thirty feet beneath the beautiful sunshine of Southern California.

Steadily, sand continued to pour in from above onto the prisoners from many small openings in the rock. The men feared it, for when it was cleared away, rocks fell upon them. Sadistic guards laughed as the men cried out.

Suddenly, all personnel paused as they heard a low rumble begin. Soon, their world collapsed and nothing but filtering sand remained in motion...like that found flowing through a golden hourglass.

* 1 *

Architectural drawings and computer plotted prints were strewn all around his work station. Todd Tasselmeyer was completely emerged in his designing work when his partner Larry called from the desk near the window, "Call is for you."

Getting up, made several sheets of drafting paper fall towards the floor. He quickly retrieved them and hastily returned the drawings to the table top while grabbing for the phone that was being thrust at him.

"Tasselmeyer here, how can I help you?"

"Sir. This is Captain Siegewick from Fort Warren outside San Diego, California."

"Captain. Didn't you receive my drawings?"

"Yes, Tasselmeyer, your preliminary drawings have just arrived. My chief construction engineer and I are very impressed with what you have designed,"

Todd, sitting in the office of his architectural firm, six floors above the noises of 14th street in downtown Manhattan, remembered receiving the approval for this project four months before this conversation with Captain Siegewick.

"Is that a go?"

"That's right, Tasselmeyer, the ground-breaking ceremony is scheduled for the fifth of March," the captain continued. "One important point to keep in your mind at all times is your bid. The government will not pay you more than the initial contract," he said strongly.

"I understand, captain."

"You may be called upon to make revisions, once the project has begun, but that provision is in the contract," he reminded Todd. He repeated this point saying, "Of course, Mr. Tasselmeyer, there would be no further expense to us."

Shrugging his shoulders and trying not to drop the phone, Todd replied, "As you say, Captain Siegewick."

"Please make the final drawings exactly to all of the building code information we are sending you. The inspectors here in California are pretty tough."

Todd listened attentively, then stated, "Right, sir, it sounds as though the inspectors left New York, and headed west...."

Captain Siegewick cut Todd's sentence short by saying, "We'll talk in a few days. Goodbye."

Todd thought this man was one arrogant son-of-a-bitch. He hung up the phone, and then began to remember how the preliminary drawings showed the 1ST floor layout: the front, the sides, rear elevations, and a roof design for Herbert Hall.

*   *   *

The Captain, alone in his office, unfolded a map of the Naval Training Center called Fort Warren. The sight of the new building was colored in red pencil on the map. It was located one block inside the main gate. The building will face south. When completed, it would resemble a long two story U-shaped structure.

Fort Warren, established long before World War II as an Army base was turned over to the Navy after the war. The facility now served as both a basic training center for new enlistee's and included several advanced training schools in weaponry and electronics for junior officers.

Herbert Hall, as the new classroom building is to be called, would honor a Congressional Medal-of-Honor winner. Ensign James Herbert had been a twenty-year old ROTC junior officer assigned to active service in August 1941. He had been a division officer aboard the U.S.S. California on December the seventh. During the attack on Pearl Harbor, young Ensign Herbert assisted his men in operating a machine gun turret. Throughout the attack, he helped evacuate wounded men and manned the gun himself until he was mortally wounded. His valor provided him a place among the Nation's finest. He had been posthumously awarded the Medal-of-Honor. After more than forty-five years of obscurity, Ensign Herbert's name had been given its fitting tribute—Herbert Hall.

The commandant of the base was Captain Stanley Siegewick (USN), who was a nineteen-year veteran and a 1970 graduate of Annapolis. He had been decorated in Vietnam and in the 1970's had served abroad in Navy intelligence. He possessed a service record that showed he was an ambitious and hard-nosed individual. He constantly sought perfection and had a habit of overstepping the bounds. The Department of the Navy was forced by subordinate officers' wishes to transfer Stan. Primarily because nobody could stand his arrogance very long. Out of desperation, the high command decided he needed to be assigned some duty where he wouldn't create waves until he retired. They assigned him base commandant about six months before the start of the

Herbert Hall project. Stan was delighted and began making plans to retire to civilian life in about one year.

Captain Siegewick was single. He had dedicated his whole life to the Navy. As the base commandant, he had the responsibility for base security. He knew everything that went on twenty-four hours a day. He ran the base as a *"tight ship,"* and even the military police were under his control. He was respected by his aids who supported and protected him, and he was always chauffeured around. Chief Master-at-Arms Ken Sheppard, who was nearing retirement also, quickly became Stan's trusted assistant. Both men were highly regarded members of the San Diego community.

Captain Siegewick was extremely detail oriented. He overlooked nothing. He saw everything. His only supervisor was an aged rear admiral who spent more time in Hawaii playing golf than in San Diego working for the Navy. Admiral McKinsey owed Captain Siegewick a favor. *"Someday that will come in handy,"* the captain thought.

Stanley Siegewick, the man behind the uniform was tall in stature, had chiseled features, and combed his black hair straight back. He also had piercing dark eyes. Strong, through vigorous exercise, he was also an avid motorcycle rider and a real smash with the ladies. He loathed shortness and weakness in any man or thing. He wouldn't promote people who didn't perform. He was extremely harsh dealing with prisoners when he presided at captain's mast. And he didn't particularly like Mr. George Stands.

George Stands, a forty-year old married engineering contractor, had the task of supervising the construction of Herbert Hall. A native of San Diego and a graduate of Cal Tech, he had worked on many Navy projects over the past ten years.

"You understand, Stands, this entire project is totally under my command. Any changes, any need to requisition for materials or personnel will come through me."

"Of course, Captain Siegewick."

"Furthermore, if any of your men get out of line, they will answer to me directly."

"I'll tell the men that, sir."

"Your job, Stands, as project superintendent, is to keep the project moving forward...no matter what the cost. Is that very clear?"

"Very clear, Captain Siegewick."

The naval contract indicated Todd would obey—no matter what the cost. His job depended on the captain's good graces. This project would not be delayed as others had. The Department of Defense insisted that this project be built with no room for cost over-runs. Together the captain and George Stands reviewed Todd's preliminary drawings with great interest. Stands commented, "Quite good for a young hot-shot architect from New York." Stands said.

"He has a good imagination. This structure should look excellent in that location," the captain replied, pointing to the designated spot on the base map.

* * *

Throughout that month of January, Todd, in New York City, had continued to work long hours on the project. By the first of February, all the preliminaries were approved, and Todd and his two associates had begun what would take nearly another month of data entry to completely digitize over eighty pages of architectural drawings. Each "D size" page measured 24 X 36 inches. All the drawings would be saved on discs and on backup system discs. With the assistance of computer-aided drafting software, each page was entered by digitizing methods into Todd's sophisticated computer which then plotted in multi-colors. Any changes or revisions which might be needed later would only take a few hours, instead of days, since all the information was already stored in the computer's hard drive.

* * *

Todd felt quite anxious as he sent the captain the final set of plans just a week before the ground-breaking ceremony was scheduled to take place. George Stands later called Todd to say that the plans arrived in good condition and again to thank him personally for a job "well done." George confirmed Todd's opinion about the commandant that he had a difficult customer to please. "I can just imagine what you're going through with him. The man comes across so harsh."

"He's all Navy, son."

"Please keep me informed about the building's progress, and you plan to visit the construction site anytime you're in San Diego."

"Thank you, Mr. Stands. I will."

* * *

* 2 *

MONDAY, MARCH 5

The day of the ground-breaking dawned beautifully. As the sun broke over the jagged mountains to the east, the Pacific Ocean, across Pacific Coast Highway, glowed a wonderful golden ocher. Spring in San Diego was not like spring in New York City. San Diego's climate remained fairly constant—always warm and mild, and the flowers bloomed throughout the year. A truly wonderful place to visit or live.

Lieutenant Junior Grade James Lighal (USN), the Protocol Officer, oversaw the details for the day's ceremony. Many of Captain Siegewick's old friends were in attendance. Even the rear admiral had pulled himself away from the golf course to participate.

By 8:30 that morning, about a hundred and fifty people had assembled in the empty lot where the new structure was to be built. The morning sun shone brightly. All the Naval officers wore dress blues with yards of gold piping on their uniforms. About twenty military police directed traffic and conducted weapon searches of each invited guest. The contractor and his family were also present.

Lieutenant Lighal notified the commandant that all was ready by knocking on the office door and saying, "Gentlemen, our guests are waiting."

It was now precisely 0900 hours. Everyone rose to greet the procession of military brass. The wives sat proudly in the front row of folding chairs. Slowly and with dignity, the Navy band began its processional march, "The Navy Hymn."

Once everyone was in place, the base chaplain gave the invocation. The entire company took their seats as the Executive Officer Commander Wilkins, gave the welcoming address. Following that, Rear Admiral McKinsey thanked everyone for coming out to witness such "an historic event."

Little did he know how true those words would be. Finally, the microphone belonged to Captain Siegewick. His strong voice boomed loudly and everyone clearly understood each word he spoke. After explaining the purpose for the new building and introducing Mr. Stands, Stan picked up the gold handled shovel and jammed it into the soil. Raising the shovelful of earth, he exclaimed.

"Let the building begin!"

With that statement, a round of applause echoed throughout the base and everyone then stood proudly as the band played the traditional "Anchors Aweigh."

A brief reception followed, and Captain Siegewick, Commander Wilkins, Mr. Stands, and Lieutenant Lighal greeted their guests. Admiral McKinsey quickly disappeared in his chauffeured car heading back to the greens.

Every day for the last two weeks, Mr. Stands had been watching truckload after truckload of building materials being delivered to the project site. A construction trailer had been setup on the northeast corner. A six-foot high chain link fence had been put in place around the perimeter of the building site. There were two openings in the fence for drive-throughs, and one gate for foot traffic near the trailer.

By 10 o'clock, the ceremony crowd had departed, and Mr. Stands watched as several pieces of earthmoving equipment and backhoes arrived. The workmen soon began excavating the foundation. There were about twelve Hispanic men wearing hard hats within the chain-linked compound.

Several of these men made up the survey crew. They were busy rechecking stakes and bench marks already in place, using their transits and levels. The rod man called back to the surveyor various height readings for them to double check. These readings would determine the depth of the footings and how much earth needed to be removed.

Todd's blueprints specified a two story U-shaped building with a center courtyard. The structure was to have no basement. A monolithic four-inch thick concrete floor would be poured which would encompass the entire first floor and all its footing. It would take about six weeks to excavate, build forms, set reinforcement steel, cover the entire excavated area with gravel, and include the rough-in work for the plumbing and electrical supply conduit. These tasks had to be completed and inspected prior to pouring about forty truckloads of wet concrete.

By noon on that first day, the surveyors reported to Mr. Stands, "Sir, all stakes are in place and are correct."

"Very well, instruct the backhoes to begin digging," said Mr. Stands. Several large dump trucks moved into position to accept the unearthed soil. With a loud clanging noise, the first scoop of soil was lifted and dumped into the truck's empty bed.

The men in the immediate area gave a loud cheer! Their payday would now be next Friday. The project of building Herbert Hall within the private confines of Fort Warren outside San Diego had begun. Everyone present on that job site was excited.

The initial excavation began on the southwest corner of the site. One block away heading due west was the main gate, and beyond it the Pacific Highway ran north and south. Bordering the highway was a fifteen-foot earthen bank leading down to the broad sandy beach.

The Pacific Ocean's pounding surf could be seen about a hundred yards beyond. The beach, at this location was wide and quite empty. The cliff was difficult for people with little children to traverse.

Bathers could go either further north toward San Diego or a mile and a half further south where the cliff diminished to enter onto the beach. The beach in front of the naval base was quite deserted.

Stan finished lunch at the Officer's Club and walked back to his office. Yoeman Roth handed him the afternoon mail as he entered. One letter caught his attention. Closing the door, he quickly read its contents:

"Dear Captain Siegewick, please be advised that your retirement investments with this brokerage have seriously deteriorated due to the continuing downward spiral of the bond market. As of this date your losses amount to $150,000.

We regret this loss, and ensure you that future investments by you will be properly secured."

Stan immediately grabbed the phone and called his broker. "No! You are a theft...You bastard! I need my fucking money for my retirement in nine months!"

"I understand your plight, Captain Siegewick. But there's nothing I can do now. Your money is gone."

Stan sat numb at his desk. Now all that was left was his military pension. That money seemed not to be enough for him to live on until his Social Security began at age sixty-five.

Ground breaking worked ended about 4:30 that afternoon, and Mr. Stands addressed his men, "Thank you each for a good show. We'll begin working again in the morning at 7:30."

"We'll be ready, Mr. Stands," replied the excavation foreman. As the workmen drove away, George Stands padlocked the gate. He then walked over to his pickup and noticed many young recruits preparing to leave the base for an evening's liberty.

Darkness settled over the quiet construction site. Many flood lights glowed. The metal fence surrounding the area was electrified. Two MP's in full camouflage battle gear, carrying M-16 rifles, circulated the perimeter throughout the cool southern California night. All was quiet. The base slept.

* * *

* 3 *

TUESDAY, MARCH 6

About 0945 that morning the sounds of digging abruptly stopped. The men started hollering, "Mr. Stands, come. Come!" said a panicky voice with a heavy Spanish accent, at the door to the construction trailer.

"There's been some sort of cave-in." Spilling his cup of coffee, George Stands and the ten other workers quickly assembled at the southeast corner of the project's foundation. Looking down in horror, George saw before him a large, gaping hole in the ground. Both the operator of the backhoe and the truck driver had fallen into some sort of pit. The backhoe and the dump truck were buried to their front axles, and they were angled precariously on the brink of also being swallowed by this great pit. The men had apparently jumped free when the machine and truck began to sink and were pulled under into a now-open hole and would-be grave.

"What the hell happened? Where's Jose and Alfredo?" George said, not believing his eyes.

"They must have fallen into that hole," another workman shouted.

"Oh, my God! I don't believe this is happening!" yelled George, covering his face and being visibly shaken.

"Quick, let's try to get them out," was the cry from the men. At the opening, other men on solid ground yelled down into the darkness the names of those missing. Only silence came back from below. Seeing the commotion through the chain link fence, one of the MPs hastened to the phone and called Captain Siegewick.

"That's right, Captain, there's been some sort of problem at the construction site. I'll have your car brought around right away, sir." Stan's car drove up within minutes. The paramedics also arrived with sirens flaring. George had towing equipment brought up to remove the backhoe and the dump truck first. The men made a platform and scaffolding to cover the pit. Then they carefully lowered a Navy corpsman from the rig into the darkness. After a brief time, he was pulled up and stood facing Captain Siegewick and George Stands.

"They're dead, sir. They fell about thirty feet into what appears to be some sort of well. There was timber covering it beneath the surface. I suppose the weight of the dump truck and the backhoe caused the timbers to give way. I am sorry, sir, there was nothing I could do for them," he said sadly.

"Understood, well done," said Siegewick to the corpsman. Turning toward Stands, he said, "Have the bodies removed and dismiss your men for the day."

The commandant was visibly irritated at this interruption in the work schedule. "I'll have the base personnel seal off the area. We will investigate this thoroughly."

"I understand, sir," said George dejectedly and left the captain to return to his men. The sun shone brightly that afternoon as the two bodies were recovered from the pit by the paramedics who transported them to an undisclosed location.

*　*　*

The Captain sat in his office behind a large desk with his arms folded. His secretary, Yeoman Roth, buzzed to inform him, "The chief master-at-arms has arrived, sir."

Master Chief Petty Officer Ken Sheppard was short and stocky and weighed well over two hundred and fifty pounds. He always wore a crew-cut and was a heavy social drinker. He had just finished his nineteenth year and planned to retire soon to his boat. He was an excellent sailor and could handle his 30' yacht alone—even in foul weather. Each evening he would leave the base and head for the marina just north of the base. The captain liked him and always trusted him. As chief master-at-arms, Sheppard was assigned responsibilities for base security and the daily operations of the military police. He had the keys to every office, and the combinations to every safe on the base.

Upon entering, the chief saluted and said, "You called for me, Captain?"

"Yes, sit down. There has been an accident over at the construction site. Two workers have fallen into an abandoned well and were killed this morning."

"My God! How awful, sir."

"The bodies have been recovered by our paramedics. I want your people to seal off the area."

"Certainly, sir. How else may I help?" the chief asked.

"I want you to send your best man down into that well tonight to investigate it thoroughly. Once he has finished, have him report to you."

"Naturally, sir."

"It is of the utmost importance that no one other than the MPs on duty see your man going down into that well. Understood?"

The chief replied, "Yes sir."

"Now, if he finds anything of interest, let me know immediately, no matter the hour. I'll be in my quarters. That is all. Dismissed."

Chief Sheppard saluted and closed the door behind him. He liked the captain. He was all navy!

* * *

WEDNESDAY, MARCH 7

About 0200 hours, the chief arrived at the commandant's quarters and was let in by the captain.

"Good morning, sir. I've just returned from the construction site. My assistant reported to me that the underground well is not really a well at all."

"Yes, go on," insisted the captain, anxiously.

"From his report, it is some sort of ventilation shaft to what appeared to be an abandoned mine. He also said that he could see the beginning of three separate tunnels that converge at this site."

"Go on, tell me more."

"Well, sir, each tunnel appears to be carved into the rock, but..."

"But, what!" demanded the captain.

"Well, sir, each tunnel is flooded with sand."

"Damn," said the captain. "How long?"

"How long, what, sir?" asked the chief.

"How long to excavate the sand?"

"Begging your pardon, sir. We're trying to construct a new building here... Not explore someone's abandoned mine tunnel! That could take months."

"Very well, then, thank you for that information. You are dismissed. You are not to tell anyone what we have just discussed. Understood?"

"Of course, sir," the chief replied and saluted. He then left the commandant's quarters.

Stanley Siegewick returned to bed, only to sleep restlessly. He dreamt of exploring the mine. He had visions of diamonds, silver and gold. He also dreamt of finding lots of gold! His dream took him deep under the mountain range to the east of the naval base. When he awoke, the look of determination and greed was permanently etched upon his face. He was certain he would obtain vast wealth from this mine. He thought to himself, it probably was constructed well over a hundred years ago. The owners possibly found some fabulous treasure.

He was positive that, with his access to the latest state-of-the-art mining technology, he could continue the mining operations on a vastly improved basis. Certainly, he could do better than had been done a hundred years ago.

The captain knew he had several major problems to solve. First, who would he get to work for him on this project? Second, how would they be accommodated? And, finally, what percent of the profits would they take? The more he thought, the more obsessed he became with his greed. At 0715 he called the chief master-at-arms to meet him in his office at 0815.

* * *

The California sun broke to the east over the mountains, and it promised to be another spectacular, warm spring day. A gentle breeze drifted across the naval base from the ocean. At 0730, the Captain and George Stands met the now-assembled construction crew. The men looked forlorn and saddened. The commandant, in his usual unemotional manner, addressed the crew. "Gentlemen, yesterday's incident created an unexpected delay. This project will resume today with some changes. To begin with, the area around the cave-in has been designated as '*Off-limits.*' Understood?" The men shook their heads in agreement.

"The entire structure will be shifted twenty-five feet to the north. This will allow the military to continue their own investigation. I will meet with Mr. Stands personally today to discuss some other changes."

"Mr. Stands, inform your survey party to begin to set new corners. That's all." Turning abruptly, he stepped into his waiting car and left.

* * *

At 0800, the sound of the National Anthem echoed throughout the base. American flags were hoisted into position as men in uniform stood silently and proudly saluting.

"The commandant will see you, sir," said Yeoman Roth, the office secretary.

The chief master-at-arms entered Siegewick's Office.

"Good morning, sir," he said saluting.

"At ease. Be seated," said the captain returning his salute. "Listen up, Ken! What we are about to discuss is of the highest priority, and must be held in the strictest confidence. I want the files of all the prisoners that are currently detained in the base brig. I want you to organize a work party of those prisoners. Look here," he said, pointing to a public works' map of the base.

"There's a storm drain beneath the street on the south side of the new construction sight. It extends under the base and the main gate. The drain then continues under the Pacific Coast Highway, and finally empties onto a deserted portion of the beach."

"I see, sir," Ken said, but then added. "The beach entrance is quite secured. You had a new anti-terrorist security system installed only recently."

"Yes, I do recall signing the work order for that," the commandant said, slightly dejectedly. He thought for a moment, then said, "Tonight, turn off the electronic sensor at that beach entrance from your central security command. Tell the duty officer that there has been an accumulation of debris at that entrance, and you have orders to take a work party to clean it out. I want you to personally redirect that sensor, allowing the prisoners and their guards to move in and out of that storm drain virtually unnoticed."

"I still don't understand what this is leading up to, sir," the chief said while still looking at the public works map.

"Tonight, I want your prisoners to begin digging a connecting tunnel between that storm drain and the cave-in site," the captain said, pointing to the map.

"All the debris will be carried through the drain and deposited on the beach. We'll create some new sand dunes there. The tides should wash away all evidence over the next few weeks."

Ken Sheppard was now very interested, but the reason for the connecting tunnel was still unclear to him.

"Once a new tunnel," continued the captain, "has connected the storm drain with the cave-in location, we can then begin the exploration of this mine." The captain looked up at Chief Sheppard and said, "There may be a fortune here for both of us. Are you interested?"

"I am extremely interested, sir," the chief answered.

"It could get pretty involved. Understood?"

"Of course, sir. I believe I can assist you in every aspect of this operation."

"Excellent, I was hoping I could count on you. This investigation that I've initiated will cover a multitude of sins. Besides, there shouldn't be any cost to the taxpayer, and the prisoners need the exercise!" Siegewick said with a sly grin on his face.

"Very well, captain, when should I assemble the prisoners?" "Tonight, at midnight," said the captain.

"They'll work until 0630. Oh, yes, how many 'new miners' do we have on board?"

"Six," the chief replied.

"Refresh me as to what violations of the Military Codes they were charged with."

"Various drug charges, sir," the chief said.

"Yes, they are usually sentenced to sixty days of hard labor," the captain said with a smile. He then told the chief, "See Mr. Stands for any equipment you may require. He'll have my permission to loan it to you. After all, it's part of the... investigation," he said with a smile.

Mr. Stands met Captain Siegewick around 1000 hours that morning of March the seventh. The captain informed George that the chief master-at-arms might require some items for his investigation. Mr. Stands nodded with approval, then asked, "Where are the men who were killed yesterday? Your paramedics removed them, and no one knows where they are."

Siegewick replied, "If any one inquires, tell them the families claimed the bodies and had them cremated. Over the next several days, you are hereby ordered to hire an entire new crew of men."

"What the hell!" George exclaimed.

"Yes, Mr. Stands, you heard me correctly. I want you to give the chief master-at-arms the names and addresses of the men who are on the job now so they can be paid off as they are replaced. By Friday there should be none of the witnesses to the accident left employed there. Understood?"

Thoroughly confused but unwilling to lose his job, George left to place several ads in the local papers. The commandant informed his secretary, "That after the chief master-at-arms has collected the names and addresses of Mr. Stand's current employees, she should type the list and leave it for him."

"Certainly, Captain Siegewick. It will be on your desk." Thinking to himself about how to manage this difficult task, he pondered whether it might be possible to reemploy these ten men for himself. The day was still Thursday. It was high noon. The captain sat at his desk, closely examining the foundation pages of Todd Tasselmeyer's blueprints.

"I've got it!" he exclaimed to the empty office.

He had just had the most brilliant idea in his long military career. He would call the architect and tell him to revise the foundation plans. The changes would provide the captain with room to continue the mining operations. He would have another "*brig*" designed, to be located underneath the new Herbert Hall. Within this holding area, he would confine his six substance-abused sailors, who he had sent to the base brig from his Captain's Mast. When those prisoners are confined there, the Marines naturally worked them hard all day long on their own Marine Corps projects. The Navy seldom used prisoners from the base brig. This way, the captain thought, he could put these unfortunates to his personal use mining his treasure!

Then he plotted to have Stands' ten unemployed ex-construction workers somehow individually kidnapped and forced to become members of his personal labor pool. This project would also require an elite military task force, one that would be sworn to total secrecy and knew they would die if they betrayed him. It would be this group of dedicated bodyguards and henchmen, he thought, who would run the daily mining operations. He knew he might have to share some of the mine's profits with them to keep them loyal. Personnel would need to be carefully chosen. They would need to be the biggest and strongest men to dominate the prisoners. How many would he need? He wondered if such men could be found within a short period of time.

Stan knew that it was imperative that he kept his position as the commandant. He must remain totally visible and in charge of Fort Warren always. But, he decided to delegate more projects to his Executive Officer, Commander Michael Wilkins.

"This operation must have a code name." He pondered the idea some more. "I know. I'll call it *'Operation Sand Dune.'* We'll excavate sand from the tunnels and pile it up on the beach at night. No one should suspect anything."

Nearly all of George Stands' men were Hispanic. Almost daily, Hispanics living in and near San Diego had been rounded up for "Green Card" violations and deported. "Who would waste time hunting for a few missing aliens?" Stan thought.

The captain continued his logic. "Once the new Brig was finished, we'll pour the first-floor slab over it. The only access to the brig would be from the beach through the storm drain into a connecting tunnel that extends to a basement door."

"That door," he thought to himself, *"Must open only from the tunnel side. That way no workmen would accidentally open it and find the mine."*

He decided that he would have Todd design the brig with drawings showing three accesses to the basement from the first floor. Then after the foundation had been properly inspected and the concrete poured, he'd have those entrances closed off so they would not be accessible from the upper floor of the building. The last step in this deceit would be to have those pages removed from the contractor's set of blueprints. This would be accomplished by calling the space *'CLASSIFIED ACCESS ONLY'* and having guards posted at the beach entrance. The only thing left to deal with was his construction supervisor... George Stands. *"Stands can be left alone for now, to get this building underway."*

Reaching for his desk phone, the captain believed it was time to call Mr. Tasselmeyer and ruin his day. "Yeoman Roth, get Mr. Tasselmeyer in New York City on the line."

"TJS and Associates. Tasselmeyer here. How may I help you?"

"Sir, this is Captain Siegewick, at Fort Warren. I'm calling regarding a recent situation that is going to require you to make some revisions to the foundation plans. Listen up, and take notes on your end."

Todd, taken by surprise at the new request, scrambled for his pad and pencil.

"To begin with," the Captain said in a stern voice, "I want a basement brig to be added underneath the entire south section of Herbert Hall. This brig must contain twenty jail cells measuring eight feet square with bars and a bar doors facing a central passageway. Make one cell an isolation cell with only a slot in the door to slid a food tray. There must also be a courtroom."

He continued talking quickly. "Make the courtroom large enough to accommodate a very large rectangular table, four chairs, and a room that could hold up to twelve people at one time."

Todd started to talk but was cut short.

"This brig needs a processing area to prepare prisoners, and a clerical office for records. It also needs a machine shop for repairing broken equipment. I'll need living quarters for one officer and twelve enlisted men."

"How will this area be accessed?" Todd finally interrupted. "Extend the two stairwells at each end of the south wing, and the central elevator of that wing, down to the basement, and put one outside steel door that opens only out, in the far southeast corner of the brig."

Captain Siegewick now made two final additional requests.

"I want this place extremely secure. I want absolutely no escapes. This place must have the most technologically advanced security system available. Is that clearly understood?"

Todd replied, "I believe I have everything noted, sir."

"Good."

"When should I begin these revisions?"

"Right away! It is of the highest priority and this must supersede any other projects you are currently doing. Goodbye."

Todd stared at the silent phone and his hastily written notes. "That arrogant bastard! Now he wants me to design a jail beneath the south wing of Herbert Hall," he thought. "What purpose would this serve? This is a classroom building to train junior officers, not detain them," Todd shouted angrily at the phone on his desk.

"Oh brother, it's only 11:30, and this guy certainly knows how to ruin a perfectly good spring day," Todd said, still shaking his head in disbelief. "Doesn't that son-of-a-bitch know how happy I was when I sent him those completed prints?"

Yelling again toward the phone he said, "Why, you bastard! You didn't even pay for the first set of plans. Now you're ordering me to make a second?" Todd stomped off to discuss this new project with his colleagues Jon and Larry.

* * *

* 4 *

The next three weeks were very hectic for both Todd in New York and George Stands in San Diego. Todd was informed that Mr. Stands had hired a completely new crew and construction had resumed by moving the operation to the opposite side of the construction site. By the month's end, all the foundation work would be completed except where the basement brig would soon be located.

Todd scheduled a tour of the state penitentiary at Attica with its chief architect and designer. The tour provided much of the information he needed to produce the new revisions for the captain. The cost of these new changes alone would run close to three hundred and fifty thousand dollars. Todd was notified the funding for his changes had been approved and that he was to proceed.

* * *

During the same time, the Naval Investigative Service (N.I.S.) completed their work. The final report, which the captain approved, concluded that the two men hired by the original contractor were illegal aliens and that they worked for the Navy with *'False Permits'* which violated military work laws. The report closed by stating that the men were apprehended by military personnel before being deported...not killed by accident.

Following that conclusion, George Stands, having no other recourse for fear of losing his job, instructed his carpenters, "Build a secure cover over the open pit. The area is to be backfilled and graded level."

By the next afternoon, new sod and plants had been installed. The landscaping completely covered the scene of the March 6th cave-in within the construction compound.

* * *

Progress continued being made by the original six prisoners on the connecting tunnel between the street and the cave-in sight at a depth of about twenty-five feet below the surface of Fort Warren. All the digging was done between midnight and dawn.

New dunes appeared to the south side of where the storm drain entered onto the beach. High tides each day diminished these dunes. Everything appeared natural, especially from the coastal highway.

Each morning and afternoon, hundreds of commuters journeyed up and back from San Diego along this stretch of the *Pacific Coast Highway.* They passed the location every weekday and never seemed to notice any of the new activity on the beach in front of the naval base...just as had been predicted by the captain.

*   *   *

* 5 *

By 0630 each morning, all six of the prisoners were returned to the base brig and were handed over to the Marine detachment. They, in turn, continued to use the prisoners on work details throughout the daytime. The men ate well but got little sleep.

Captain Siegewick and the chief master-at-arms recruited ten ex-Marines to serve on their special task force. Not being on active duty and unemployed, they were more than willing to accept this good paying job. The job allowed them to use their muscles and not their brains. They were all expert marksmen. Each man swore an oath to do exactly what was ordered by the captain.

The chief recommended that the captain appoint Sergeant Miller and Corporal Lenert as head guards. Although immediately placed on the payroll by the captain, they knew that they were not to begin actual daily work assignments until after the brig construction was completed. They could, however, be called upon for 'Special Assignments,' at any time.

* * *

WEDNESDAY, MARCH 28

At 0330 that morning, one of the prisoners broke through the wall of the shaft, revealing the sight of the original cave-in and the beginnings of the three tunnels filled with sand.

Later the same day, Todd's preliminary drawings for the new brig arrived and were on the captain's desk by noon. The captain held the set of computer-plotted drawings in front of Stands and said, "You may now proceed to construct the new basement brig."

"The basement what!" exclaimed George loudly.

"You heard me. Look at these pages."

George couldn't believe what was being unfolded before him. The set of plans showed very clearly the configuration of what appeared to be a complete miniature version of the base brig. The access to this space was clearly indicated.

"Well I'll be damned, Captain Siegewick, you have yourself a mighty find looking brig there. You want it build underneath the south wing?"

"That's exactly where I want it."

"May I show these plans to my chief surveyor?"

"Not yet," the captain said sternly. "You'll show him the final blueprints when they arrive. In the meanwhile, continue working on the other side of the structure. Understood?"

"Certainly, sir." George replied as he departed.

The captain then called his secretary, "Reach Mr. Tasselmeyer in New York on the phone."

It was a rainy March afternoon in New York when Todd heard the captain say, "Yes, that's right. We need only two additional revisions." "Change only the name 'Brig' on each page to read, 'COMPUTER STORAGE AREA... CLASSIFIED ACCESS.' This will limit who see these plans. The other change is a short passageway leading to that exterior solid steel door at the extreme southeastern corner of the basement level. That's all. Have the completed set of working drawings sent by courier. Goodbye, Tasselmeyer, it's been a pleasure doing business with you."

* * *

Todd told his colleagues, "I'm so sick of this man's arrogance that I never want to do another government contract again." He reluctantly proceeded to make the requested revisions and to replot the final revisions for mailing. Todd stored the entire project, including the work he did on the computer storage area of Herbert Hall, on several floppy discs and on his computer's hard drive. He thought to himself as he finished entering the last bit of information, "It's only storage area I know that contains twenty jail cells!"

On April 15th Todd sent the final plans. He would hear nothing further until July.

* * *

Between mid-April and the beginning of June, the work proceeded quickly on the underground computer storage area as the blueprints called it. The nighttime diggers continued to extend their tunnel from the cave-in location northwesterly back toward the southeast corner on the building, thirty-five feet. The tunnel was about twenty feet below the surface.

During all of April and May, Captain Stanley Siegewick continued to dream nightly about the discovery and the mining of the three tunnels beneath his Naval base. He became more obsessed and determined that no one would stand between him and the chief and their treasure. He would use any means necessary to protect his claim. He would have his private guards insure its security. He was now fully convinced that he could simultaneously command 'Operation Sand Dune,' and still run Fort Warren as he had done for the previous eight months.

* * *

WEDNESDAY, MAY 30

The connecting tunnel now extended from the storm drain in the street to the cave-in site and back to the solid steel door in the basement. The door remained locked from inside the tunnel. Captain Siegewick and Chief Sheppard had the only two keys. No construction worker could access the newly opened tunnels. The tunnels were about six feet wide and seven feet high, and on the walls, were strung red lamps every eight feet on the starboard side. Inside the storm drain an electric wench and conveyor system was installed. Some fragments of an ancient narrow-gauge railway track were exposed and utilized. Ore cars were loaded by prisoners with sand and emptied onto the conveyor system. That conveyor was designed to pull wheelbarrows full of dirt, sand, and rocks, the 1000 feet to reach the open beach. Once there, the debris was distributed toward the south on the wide beach by the prisoners under heavy guard each moonless night.

* * *

* 6 *

About 1030 hours, the captain and the chief master-at-arms were discussing their next project when the secretary interrupted them. "Excuse me, captain, Mr. Stands and his new assistant are here to see you," she said over the intercom.

Upon entering the captain's office George said, "Good morning, Captain Siegewick. I would like you to meet Paul McCoy. He'll be working as my construction foreman. Paul recently completed the Treasure Island Project up in San Francisco, and I was delighted to get him reassigned to help me out here."

"Welcome aboard, McCoy. This is my chief master-at-arms, Chief Ken Sheppard." Permitting the two men a brief handshake, the captain asked, "Stands, when will the inspectors be finished so that the concrete slab can be poured?"

"They'll be done today, and if everything passed their inspections, we'll start pouring concrete at 0900 hours tomorrow."

"Excellent. You men may return to work. I won't delay you any further."

When the two departed, Chief Sheppard turned towards the Captain and said, "Sir, our six prisoners are scheduled to be released from the base brig in a few days."

"Damn it. I had forgot about the time, Chief."

"Sir, if they are freed, they'll surely tell about our operation."

"Yes, we can't afford to have them expose us." Pausing to think for a moment, the sadistic captain said very unemotionally.

"Ken, assemble those six prisoners at midnight for a final work party. Have two of my guards escort the men down the tunnel and assemble them near the basement steel door. Unlock it prior to their arrival and connect an auxiliary cable from the power generator to the door frame. Notify the guards that they should handcuff the prisoners together after their work is complete. Let the guards lead the prisoners back to the basement door and let the lead prisoner open it. There should be sufficient power to electrocute them."

"That should work fine, sir. But how do we dispose of the bodies?" Stan began writing on some documents, then looking up at the chief, he instructed him,

"Each body should then be carefully carried through the maze of the brig's cement forms and placed along the north wall footing and covered over with just a few inches of dirt," he continued, much to the approval of the chief.

"Tomorrow, concrete will be poured along that formwork on the north side, and it will completely entomb their bodies."

"Understood, Captain. I'll personally see to it," said the chief getting to his feet.

Starting to go, but then turning back, he asked, "Begging your pardon, sir, what will the Marines say about their missing prisoners?"

"Here is the official '*pardon*' for each man," he said, handing the paperwork to the chief.

"You will deliver these documents in person to the sergeant-of-the-guard... once you have the prisoners under my '*protection*.'"

"Very good, sir," said the chief.

* * *

FRIDAY, JUNE 1

Shortly after midnight, the security lights flickered and dimmed briefly in the immediate vicinity of the construction site's southeast corner.

"What the hell's going on with these lights?" asked one of the Navy MPs to his buddy on duty.

"Beats me, but the lights seem okay now."

Neither man appeared to be aware of the cold-blooded slaughter taking place only twenty feet beneath them. No MP that dark night bothered to make note in their daily report.

* * *

By 0945 hours a ray of sunlight managed to slide down the north side forms revealing part of an arm and hand, exposed only briefly as the weight of the pouring concrete quickly filled the form to its top. All the forms now supported the immense weight of the entire first floor slab. By 1630 hours the construction crew was totally exhausted and eagerly gathered outside the trailer for their pay slips. Once their pay was in hand, they quickly headed out the compound exit for a well-earned weekend rest.

Mr. Stands had just handed the last man his check when he noticed the Captain's car parked outside the compound's gate. He proceeded to walk toward it, as the rear window was rolled down.

"The Chief and I," said the captain, "are going fishing tomorrow morning to reward ourselves for a good week's work. We're wondering if you'd like to join us?"

Feeling flattered by the captain's attention, George replied, "I'd be happy to join you, Captain," he said with a smile.

"It's been a long week."

"Good. Meet Chief Sheppard and me at 0900 hours here at the construction site. We'll leave together and drive to where his boat is docked. Then plan to spend a nice relaxing afternoon fishing and having a few drinks. Oh yes, I'll see that you're covered for time-and-a-half for 'working on Saturday.'"

"Sounds good to me," George replied shaking Stan's hand.

*   *   *

SATURDAY, JUNE 2

The captain and the chief decided that Stands had by this time put two and two together. They suspected that he was convinced that the basement brig was designed to hold prisoners who would work in the mine tunnels. They also realized that he could demand payment to keep his mouth shut, or they thought he might use some other type of blackmail technique to ruin their operation.

Saturday morning was slightly overcast, and the sea was relatively calm when the trio reached the marina. Only a few boats remained moored by the time they got underway. Once they passed Point Lomas light, the thirty-foot *"Yankee"* headed on a bearing northwest into the vastness of the Pacific. Fishing was good all afternoon about ten miles off the coast. Ken poured George several strong Scotch and waters while he and Stan only drank a few beers.

Sometime late in the afternoon when everyone seemed quite drunk, George Stands met the ocean. The darkening water quickly pulled him under as the *"Yankee"* sped off for the three-mile return trip.

Saturday evening at sunset, Chief Sheppard's thirty-footer docked at the marina near the naval base. Stan and Ken walked unnoticed to their car. As they were driving away the chief said, "My daddy always said...don't drink with strangers."

Mr. Stands' pickup remained in the parking lot near the construction site.

* * *

MONDAY, JUNE 4

Monday morning's paper contained an article reporting that Coast Guard authorities had recovered a body the day before. The apparent drowning victim was identified as George Stands of San Diego. He had been spotted by a pleasure boating party floating about a mile off shore just north of the San Diego inlet. No other information was available and the article concluded that funeral arrangements were pending.

"I'm sorry to bring you the sad news of Mr. Stands' untimely death, Captain," said Commander Wilkins, while standing in the passageway outside the commandant's office at 0820 hours.

"Yes, it was a terrible shock," said the unemotional commandant. "I saw it in the newspaper."

Looking at his executive officer, he said, "Mike, I've decided to cancel further work on that *computer storage area* in the lower level of the south wing. According to the blueprints, there will be ample space above ground for what the Navy needs. Besides, I'm very concerned about the cost factor, and finishing off that lower level space would be a waste of tax-payer's money."

"I can agree with you there, sir," the executive officer said, "And, I never fully understood why Mr. Tasselmeyer had to make the architectural revisions in the first place."

"I want you now to work closely with Paul McCoy and get those two upper levels of the building completed on schedule. I have other matters to deal with that will require more of my time. I want you to notify the architect in New York that you will be the person-in-charge out here. Don't bother telling him that we just canceled the lower level portion of Herbert Hall. I think he would be somewhat upset with us. Is that understood?"

"Fully understood, Stan. I'll meet with Paul shortly, then call Mr. Tasselmeyer," Commander Wilkins replied.

"Then proceed, Commander," said Stan, as the two men saluted and Stan entered his office closing the door with a slam.

* * *

* 7 *

MONDAY, JULY 9, 1989

It was now more than eight months since Todd Tasselmeyer had signed the government contract to design Herbert Hall. The ground-breaking ceremony had taken place on March the fifth, followed the next day by the cave-in and its resulting two casualties.

Todd's revisions were completed and sent to the commandant of Fort Warren, by the sixteenth of April. Mr. Stands' mysterious drowning occurred on June the second, along with the six original drug user sailors who were executed in the connecting tunnel, then buried in wet concrete.

The commandant and the chief hand-picked local and unemployed ex-Marines to find replacement "miners" during the remainder of June. By this date, however, the newly hired secret guards had already recruited using kidnapping, ten Hispanic men.

Each man was a former employee of the late Mr. Stands, and each had witnessed the cave-in. The ten men were being acclimated in the new, still unfinished, brig below Herbert Hall's south wing by their secret guards.

The hardened ex-Marines enjoyed their new role. They dressed in black uniforms with hoods, and carried the latest military assault weapons. Each night the ten unfortunate prisoners under heavy guard, would deposit more and more sand on the beach. This sand came from only the first of the three tunnels that converged at the sight of the original cave-in. Their nighttime activity continued unnoticed.

Paul McCoy's crew working above ground during the daylight had successfully erected the steel framework for the new building's entire first floor. Everyday more building supplies arrived and were crowding the construction site compound. The compound's original six-foot-high chain-link fence had been replaced by a higher and more opaque fencing material that included an electrified barbed-wire along its top edge.

Captain Siegewick rested comfortably each night in his on-base quarters dreaming about the discovery of gold in each of the three subterranean tunnels.

"Operation Sand Dune" was well underway by this date.

* * *

Earlier that day, Commander Wilkins and Lieutenant Lighal were seen putting on hardhats and entering the construction site. When they did, they motioned to Mr. McCoy for him to join them.

"Excuse me, sir," said Commander Wilkins to Mr. McCoy. "The captain has just informed me that he'll be joining Admiral McKinsey in Hawaii for the next four days to attend a *classified briefing.* He will be departing in two hours and has requested that the Lieutenant and I should conduct a tour of this facility."

Lieutenant Lighal added, "Then we are to make a full report about any discrepancies to him prior to his departure. The captain doesn't tolerate shoddy workmanship nor items that don't *meet naval standards of operation.*"

"Very well then. I have some time to kill before my next delivery arrives," Paul told the officers.

"The captain believes that this building will become a real *'showplace'* among the entire Pacific fleet's training schools," added the lieutenant.

"Good, follow me gentlemen to the entrance of the east wing."

Mr. McCoy spent the next forty-five minutes covering every aspect of the construction to this point by conducting them on a walking tour. He brought to their attention how the concrete slab had been reinforced with number nine-gauge wire, and he pointed out that the monolithic pour was the preferred method for this type of commercial construction. With pride, he also made certain they understood that all the steel beams and cross girders had been manufactured to the architect's exact specifications. He also explained how a typical wall section would be assembled and then attached to the steel framework using bolts. Finally, he showed them all the custom-made, prefinished aluminum windows for the structure's exterior which had just been delivered the day before.

The trio than proceeded to the construction trailer for coffee and to review the plans.

"Do you anticipate any place where the building could experience a significant delay?" asked the commander.

"Only one place...Inspections," replied Paul.

Together they reviewed a set of Todd's architectural blueprints. Paul described the part of the project which would come next.

"Once the steel has been erected over the entire structure, the corrugated metal flooring sections will be installed. From there, more wood forms will have to be built. Then four inches of concrete will be poured over the metal sections to create the first and second deck levels."

"It sounds complicated to me," replied the lieutenant.

"With the excellent crew I've inherited, this project shouldn't have any problems," Paul said with a smile.

"Begging your pardon, sir," the commander said flipping through the set of prints, "I don't see any pages showing the basement construction for the '*classified Computer Storage Area.*' "What the Hell! They're supposed to all be here!" Paul said with a somewhat puzzled look on his face. He then began to open cabinets containing other drawings and to search through a pile of pages over in the corner on his desk.

Beads of sweat started to form on his brow, and the commander and the lieutenant also appeared concerned.

"They have just got to be here. I've looked them over just yesterday," he said, almost in panic.

"Here they are!" said the lieutenant as he turned and noticed the set of plans lying on the floor in the construction trailer's restroom.

"Thank God," was echoed by each man followed by an uneasy laugh.

"Mr. McCoy, the commandant has notified me that this section of the project is to be canceled, and more information will be forthcoming. For now, please concentrate your efforts on the above ground operation," Commander Wilkins said. He then continued, "The architect, and yourself, have been put on notice that I am '*In-Charge*' of this operation. Anything that you need, I'll see that the commandant approves it."

"Thank you, Commander," replied Paul.

The executive officer and the lieutenant then left the trailer to meet with the commandant at base headquarters.

"Everything appears to be in order, sir, and the building is proceeding on schedule," reported the executive officer.

"That's really some complex structure they're building over there, and with that new solid security fencing installed, along with the relocating of the building twenty-five feet further away from the street, no one can possibly decide, just by driving by, how much progress has really been made since we started."

"Is that all, James?" said the captain with a yawn.

"Yes, sir."

"Anything else you two have to report?"

"No sir, not now...only that Mr. McCoy has things very well squared away, and I told him that I had been put in charge of this operation." They made no mention of his misplacing the plans for the basement storage area.

"Very good," said the commandant. "Jim, have my car brought around to take me to the airport. I have one more phone call to make, then I'll be right out."

"It will be waiting, sir." The two officers saluted and departed the captain's office. Stan then picked up the phone and with a big grin called the chief.

"Ken, Stan here. The new training devices have arrived for the prisoners. You'll find the box in the processing room. I believe they'll get a real 'charge' out of wearing them."

"I understand, sir," the chief responded with a laugh.

Then returning to his normal composure Stan continued, "I think it's time to secure the lower level brig access and to make the set of blueprints disappear due to their classified nature." "Will you get the prints, captain?" asked the chief.

"No, chief, I'll be in Hawaii until the fifteenth. You can handle that job. Just see to it that the construction superintendent, Mr. McCoy, understands the reason you need the plans. 'Operation Sand Dune,' must now enter a new phase...and I don't want his people or mine, snooping around downstairs. Is that clear?"

"Yes, captain, I understand my assignment."

"Excellent. I'll talk to you tomorrow from Pearl about 2130 hours. Goodbye."

Late that afternoon, Chief Sheppard met Mr. McCoy in the construction trailer.

"Paul McCoy, I'm Ken Sheppard, the base master-at-arms. We had just met briefly last Friday in Captain Siegewick's office. The purpose of my visit is to notify you that there has been a command change that called for the cancelation of the computer storage area in the lower level of the south wing."

"Yes, Commander Wilkins made mention to that fact. What's the problem, chief. That appeared to be good usable space down there." "Quite so, Mr. McCoy, the captain felt there would be enough storage space above ground, and besides, the finishing of that extra space might cause the Navy to get involved in yet another cost over-run situation."

"All right, what do I have to do now?" asked Paul.

"Please turn over the pages of blueprints pertaining to the lower level, and prepare by this Friday. to close off the two stairwells and the one elevator access to that level."

"In other words, that lower level will have no access from above."

"That is correct, Mr. McCoy."

"Well I'll be a son-of-a-bitch, if that don't beat all."

"Remember, Paul. This building will contain the most highly sensitive electronic equipment, and will also contain many restricted areas. Think of that space as one of them."

"Very well, chief. My men didn't enjoy working there anyway, they considered it dangerous to work underground these days. With earthquake tremors constantly occurring in this area, they've known of construction people who were killed in cave-ins recently."

The chief took Todd's pages of architectural revisions to Herbert Hall back to his office, and put them into his safe.

*   *   *

* 8 *

Upon his arrival in Hawaii, Stan was met at the airport and driven to Pearl Harbor. He was then taken to join Admiral McKinsey for dinner at his residence overlooking the base's golf course.

The following days kept the captain extremely busy attending various meetings. The purpose of this classified conference, held at Pearl Harbor on July eleventh through the fourteenth, was to bring together naval officers who were experts in weaponry and electronics throughout our *'Pacific Fleet'*. Together, they discussed the benefits of the new training center being constructed at Fort Warren. The schedule was hectic and left Captain Siegewick extremely tired. Only after dinner each day did he have some free time to relax.

*　*　*

WEDNESDAY, JULY 11

It was on the evening of his second day in Hawaii while the captain was enjoying a Scotch and soda in the lounge of the officer's club that he noticed the attractive young lieutenant who had sat all day taking notes next to Commander Thomas. The commander had arranged the conference. Captain Siegewick had never been properly introduced to the lieutenant and decided to remedy the situation.

Upon seeing Commander Thomas with his wife and the young lieutenant also in the lounge, he got their attention and said, "Good evening, Commander. And Mrs. Thomas. How good to see you again? Who is your delightful assistant?"

"Captain Siegewick, please meet my bookkeeper, Lieutenant Cheryl Finley (USN)," the commander replied.

"She has served this command for nearly two years, and her skills are quite outstanding."

Stan found Miss Finley an extremely attractive lady. She was twenty-six, slender in build, and about five feet, five inches tall. Her lovely auburn hair and big green eyes fascinated him. She had graduated from Annapolis four years before and had just been promoted to lieutenant the previous month. She had been serving in the supply office as an auditor. She possessed excellent record keeping skills. She had been assigned to Pearl Harbor twenty-three months ago and was anxious to get a stateside assignment. Together with the captain, she conversed and enjoyed another cocktail before dinner. Tonight, the club offered a fabulous *'Luau Buffet'* that featured a pit-roasted pig and all the delicious tropical fruits and vegetables that were produced on the island. The couple ate, conversed and enjoyed the time together.

Captain Siegewick walked to the phone and placed a call to his chief master-at-arms sometime around 2130 hours.

"Ken, Stan here. Did you have any problems with Mister McCoy?"

"Not at all, captain. Paul was most cooperative."

"I see. Put the pages in your office safe until I return."

"Captain, the workers uncovered something I felt was very significant last night. They removed what appeared to be some sort of tool chest from the first tunnel, about a hundred feet from where we first entered the space. There's a large padlock on the trunk, and it'll take some doing to get it opened," said the chief.

"Keep it in a secure location until I return. Understood?"

"Certainly, sir."

"How are the men reacting to their new equipment?"

"They tried to object, but the current was against it."

"I see, how did the control levels operate?" asked the commandant.

"One man experienced cardiac arrest...and we brought him back with CPR. Two of the others just got minor neck burns and should recover shortly."

"Very well then, keep the instruction manual handy. Try to keep things under control, and I'll be back Thursday afternoon." Hanging up the phone, he returned to Lieutenant Finley and said, "Well lieutenant it seems my crew just can't live without me. Now, where were we? Please tell me about yourself."

"Well, sir," she said, but he quickly interrupted her.

"I insist that you call me Stan, and please be at ease, when we're off duty."

Blushing somewhat, she turned towards him and held his hand. "Well, Stan, I come from the New York City area. My twin sister Peggy and my mother still live there. Together they operate an antique shop down in Greenwich Village. I was never much interested in antiques, but I try to keep a lookout in my travels for any unusual items they could use in the shop. Here in Hawaii, I've been able to send them some Polynesian artifacts which brought very high prices in New York."

"Tell me some other interesting things you like to do," Stan suggested as he signaled the waiter for another round.

"I really enjoy biking, swimming, and slow dancing."

"I also enjoy those things, but seldom get an opportunity," he told her as they sipped their drinks.

"The Navy has given me some wonderful experiences. I hope to stay in and make a career of it."

"You seemed to have made a good start, lieutenant." "Would you mind calling me 'Cheryl'?"

"Not at all, Cheryl," the captain replied with a slight smile.

Her big green eyes sparkled in the lights of the club lounge. When the navy musicians began to play around 2200 hours, the couple danced several of the slower numbers.

Around midnight, they walked down the tree-covered pathway to her quarters and gently kissed.

"Well, Cheryl, it's been a lovely evening."

"Yes, Stan, I've enjoyed it very much. Would you like to come in for a night cap?" she inquired.

"I...was hoping you would consider it," he said with a smile.

As she unlocked the door Stan gently took her by the hand and they went inside. He did not bother to turn on any lights. Within only a short time, their clothes were scattered on the bedroom floor.

They held each other close and kissed with longing desires. After she could stand the foreplay no longer, she gave herself to him totally. His weight made her cry out slightly as his hardness penetrated her moist and waiting thighs. The pleasure he gave her was truly unforgettable, and she cried out for more as together they reached their climaxes.

* * *

During the next two days, Captain Stanley Siegewick found something wonderful and charming in Lieutenant Cheryl Finley.

After each day's work, the two of them could be seen on the beach at Waikiki or touring the island of Oahu by bike. They spent late evenings at the officer's club dancing and making love in the darkness of her quarters.

* * *

FRIDAY, JULY 13

When Stan departed for San Diego, he assured her that, "I'll personally find you a billet at Fort Warren."

"Oh, Stan. Please don't forget me here in Hawaii."

"Never Cheryl," and with that they lovingly embraced.

"What are your plans for next year?"

"I'm planning retirement early next year and might relocate out-of-state."

Looking disappointed, she told him, "I really like the San Diego area."

"I just don't want to make California my permanent home after retirement next January. We'll discuss all that later. I must go. Take care."

They kissed tenderly and he was driven to the airport.

*   *   *

* 9 *

Once Stan had arrived back at Fort Warren, he was driven immediately to Base Headquarters. The time was close to 1630 hours when he arrived at his office. Most of the staff were departing for the weekend.

Yeoman Roth informed the Captain, "Sir, there are several messages and faxes waiting for your reply on your desk."

"Thank you. That's all. You may depart," the Captain told her as they saluted and she hastily left to head home. As the Captain reviewed the communiques, one attracted his special interest. It was the schedule and agenda for the next Captain's Mast. It would be held the following Monday, the seventeenth of July at 0900 hours. This meant that he might legally sentence some unfortunate sailors to six months at hard labor, and he could get them to work underground in *Operation Sand Dune.*

The Captain then called Chief Sheppard on the phone.

"Chief," said the Captain. "I'll be in my quarters by 2100 hours.

Plan to bring the 'discovery' by after then."

"Glad you're back, Sir," said the Chief with enthusiasm.

"Please bring the blueprint revisions you picked up from Mr. McCoy, and don't forget to bring something to open the padlock since there are no tools at my place," said Stan.

"No problem, Sir," replied the Chief.

The Captain shortly departed for Fort Warren's Officer's Club to enjoy the 'Happy Hour' and a light buffet supper. Following the meal, he returned alone to his Base quarters. He spent the evening watching television and browsing the pile of San Diego's daily newspapers that had accumulated during his absence.

About 2130 hours that Friday evening, there was a knock at the Captain's quarters.

"Come in, Chief," he said while also admitting two of Fort Warren's enlisted sailors, Petty Officer Second Class Smith and Petty Officer Third Class Davenport.

"At ease, gentlemen," the Captain said, returning their salutes. "Place this trunk over there," he said, pointing to a cleared area in the center of the living room where he had spread newspapers around to cover the carpet. The Chief handed the Captain the rolled-up set of blueprints, and said, "Here are your *'Computer Storage Area'* pages, Sir."

Stan quickly glanced at the roll, took it, and placed it on the top shelf of the living room's closet. After closing the closet door, he returned to the dining room and said, "Well, what have we here?" He looked as greedy as a little child about to open a Christmas present.

"I don't know Captain, but it's certainly heavy," replied one of the enlisted men.

Taking a hack-saw to the ancient padlock, Petty Officer Davenport was finally relieved when the pieces fell to the floor.

"Thank you, Petty Officer Smith and Davenport," replied Stan. "You two men are excused."

"Very good, Sir," the men said in unison as they saluted.

The two enlisted sailors departed for their evening's watches.

Stan and Ken carefully lifted the wooden lid to the old trunk. Cautiously, they slowly lifted and examined each of the buried treasures and displayed each one on the dining room table where the light was best. Neither said a word.

The ancient trunk contained the personal belongings of a California gold rush prospector. There were several picks and shovel heads without handles. Immediately below these tools were three well-worn and rusted shallow pans. Also included in this collection was an apothecary scale with its tiny set of counterweights for weighing gold. There were several now-empty glass viles labeled 'nitric acid' which may have been used to determine the purity of gold.

At this point, there remained in the trunk what appeared to be some sort of dark colored clothing and a hand-made quilt. The clothes simply fell apart when touched; however, it was possible to gently remove the quilt. Unfolding it, they made another discovery inside.

Sitting proudly in the middle of Captain Siegewick's dining room table was a beautiful and slightly tarnished golden hourglass. It appeared to be about twelve inches tall and about five inches around at its top and base. Three slender gold columns stood as sentries in front of the two glass bulbs. Pure white sand filled the lower section half-way up the glass. This certainly was a handsome and rare antique, but they had been hoping for something of more value. No one said it, but they knew they had all been hoping to find some samples of gold.

Upon closer examination of the trunk, Ken said, "Excuse me, Sir, I believe this could be of interest." He handed the Captain several small folded pieces of yellowed paper that had apparently been stuck to the inside wall of the old trunk.

Alone with Chief Sheppard, Stan now looked at the old pieces of paper. Upon closer examination, the first piece contained some sort of inventory list and a request for ten additional 'cars'; whatever that meant. On the second sheet was carefully drawn three lines, almost zig zagged that resembled lightning bolts.

"Chief!" yelled Stan pointing to the design, "I believe we now know the configuration of the three tunnels."

"Excellent, Captain," the Chief replied with excitement.

"But look at this!" exclaimed the excited officer, trying hard to contain his emotions. The last piece of paper appeared to be some type of official document. It was blank except for the type-set letterhead that read: *Dutchman Mining Company*

"Do you have any idea what this means?" Stan asked Ken. "Could it be that this discovery might be the *Lost Dutchman Mine*?" He asked while trying to subdue his feelings of excitement.

"Wow! I'll be damned! I thought that mine was only a legend around these parts," the Captain said with a wide grin.

"We may have just stumbled upon it," said the delighted Chief Master-at-Arms.

"The construction workers did, and it cost them dearly," the Captain reminded the Chief.

"Sir, what would you suggest our next move be?" Ken asked, like a little child asking for directions.

"Now that the lower level has been secured from inquiring eyes, we must employ another contractor to complete the brig," commented Stan.

"I'll find someone, Sir. Someone who can be trusted,"

"His crew would only be able to work at night and must use the beach access. No one would be permitted around the construction site after 1630 hours. The MPs would have their asses put in the brig for trespassing," stated the Captain.

The Chief saluted and left to supervise the night's digging.

The Captain returned to the dining room and poured himself some brandy. He then began to re-examine the contents of the old trunk. He was particularly intrigued by the newly discovered golden hourglass.

As he pondered its history, he noticed some scratches on one side of just one glass bulb. They appeared quite jumbled, and they seemed not to make any sense what-so-ever. He carried the hourglass around his quarters until well past midnight. Setting it on the nightstand by his bed, he fell asleep watching the tiny crystals fall. The Captain began to dream...

There was intense darkness, then he began to see tiny lights. They became brighter as he drew closer. The lights were from burning torches which were mounted against some rocky walls of some sort of cave. He was inside the cave. The torch light made the cave glow a soft orange. The flames occasionally flickered indicating there was a gentle breeze of air coming from the outside.

He then began to hear men talking and the noises from their digging. As he drew closer, he could make out that they were Aztec Indians. They were wearing headbands, loincloths, and sandals. There were about a dozen men in this work party. They were speaking softly when one of them began to yell out in a primitive dialect. Apparently, the Indian had found a treasure. He held up the large dull ocher-colored nugget as the other men began to shout. They had woven baskets nearby. They began to carefully excavate what appeared to be a large vein of gold! One man brought some of the torches closer to the location of the find. The Indians filled their baskets and then departed. It took two men to carry each basket loaded with gold ore. Nearby water constantly dripped off the rocky ceiling.

Outside the cave, the Captain could clearly see detachment of soldiers wearing ancient Spanish Conquistador uniforms. They advanced through the jungle and converged near the foothills of the mountain. The Aztec Indians realized their gold mine might fall into enemy hands.

Beyond the foothills was a large body of water, a lake of some sort. The Indians had already hand-dug a canal to within a few hundred feet of the mine's entrance.

During the night, many Indians gathered to extend the canal. As the new day broke, the lake's water completely flooded the ancient gold mine. When that occurred, sand and silt flowed quickly into the mine's many levels. The Spanish Conquistadors were denied access to the vast wealth of this gold mine.

The Captain remembered that during the previous one hundred and fifty years, the mine was said to have produced enough gold to build seven cities. The Indians in northern Mexico had told the early Spanish explorers about the seven cities of gold that were located to the north. They called it 'Cibola.' The Spanish pursued the legend during the 1530's. They succeeded only in capturing seven Zuni villages. They never located the cities of 'Cibola.'

At this point, the sound of a buzzing doorbell awoke the Aztec adventurer. Shaking his head and trying to fetch his robe, the drowsy Captain struggled to answer the caller.

* * *

* 10 *

"Good morning, Sir." The cheerful voice said behind the screened door.

"Oh, what the hell do you want at this hour?" asked the Captain not hiding his feelings.

"Rear Admiral McKinsey is back from Hawaii this weekend, and he would like you to accompany him this beautiful Saturday morning to the golf course," the driver of the Admiral's car replied.

"Tell the Admiral all right, but first I've got to shower. Go buy him a morning paper or some coffee, and come back in about a half hour. What time is it, anyway?" the sleepy Captain asked.

"It's 0815 hours, Sir," was the response from the other side of the door.

"Very well, be back at 0845," replied the Captain grumpily.

The Admiral as usual had an excellent round of golf, but the Captain had problems concentrating on his game. He couldn't figure out the significance of that unusual dream. He was also very careful not to mention last night's recovered 'lost treasures' from the trunk.

Finally, around noon the Admiral tired, and they returned to the clubhouse.

The Captain finished lunch and was driven back to his office. He entered the empty building and walked past Yeoman Roth's desk. Noticing some mail from yesterday, he picked it up and entered his office. One letter caught his attention. Closing the door, he quickly read its contents:

"Dear Captain Siegewick, please be advised that your retirement investments with this brokerage have seriously deteriorated due to the continuing downward spiral of the bond market. As of this date your losses amount to $150,000.

We regret this loss and ensure you that future investments will be properly secured."

The Captain's face displayed a look of utter disbelief. He immediately grabbed the phone and called his broker at home.

"No! You thief! You bastard! I need my fucking money for my retirement in six months!" yelled the Captain.

"I understand you plight, Captain Siegewick. But there's nothing I can do now. Your money is gone," replied the man on the other end of the line.

The Captain sat numb at his desk. Now all that was left was his military pension which would not be enough for him to live on until his Social Security began in fifteen years.

Sometime later that afternoon, a calmer Captain placed a call to Hawaii to talk with Lieutenant Finley.

"Hello Cheryl, it's Stan," said the Captain.

"Oh Stan! How nice of you to call," replied Cheryl.

"I had a wonderful time with you last week," the Captain told her.

"You haven't forgot about what we discussed?" asked Cheryl. "No, darling," recalled the Captain tenderly. "I'll be certain to see about your new orders. I mentioned something about you to my XO, Commander Wilkins, and he agreed how this base could use such an efficient person as yourself. He always wants the best people on his staff."

"Oh, Stan that sounds terrific," Cheryl exclaimed.

"The other reason I called was...I remembered you mentioning about antiques. Well, I've come across a very beautiful antique golden hourglass. It must be at least one hundred and fifty years old," said the Captain.

Cheryl said, "I didn't think you were the collector type."

"Well, I'm not. But this item seems to date back to *California's Gold Rush Days*," said the Captain defensively.

"It sounds valuable," she replied expressing a more serious attitude.

"That's right. Do you think your family's shop in New York could help me get a handsome price for it?" asked Stan.

"I'm sure my sister and my mom could display it nicely and ask a high price," said Cheryl.

"That would be just fine." He continued, "I'm so glad I found you."

"You're not the only one," she giggled.

Lieutenant Finley gave Captain Siegewick the name, address, and phone number of her mother's shop.

"Cheryl, my love, I must tell you again, I will try very hard to get your transfer orders as soon as possible. I'll talk to you next week," promised the Captain.

"I miss you terribly," she said nearly on the verge of tears.

"I miss you too. Take care of yourself and goodbye," he said, hanging up the phone.

* * *

Late Saturday night, Chief Sheppard knocked at the Captain's quarters.

"Pardon the interruption, Sir, may I come in? I've been doing some serious thinking." the Chief informed him.

"What if we did discover gold down there? Not just a little, but a lot of it. What would we do with the stuff? We couldn't just walk into any local bank or credit union with a wheelbarrow full of gold ore," said the Chief with a concerned look.

"Yes, I've been asking myself the same questions," replied the Captain.

"We've got to exchange it somehow," said Ken.

"We'll have to move it out of this area and work with someone who can handle precious medals. We need to find someone who could quietly exchange what we find for currency," explained the Captain.

"I agree, Sir. It's the only way to prevent any waves," said Ken.

"Check around, would you? But please, be extremely discreet. It's only hypothetical. Perhaps by the summer's end it will become a reality. Goodnight, Chief," said the Captain with a worried look on his face.

"Goodnight, Sir. Pleasant dreams," the Chief said as he saluted then headed into the darkness.

"Uh, pleasant dreams, my ass," mumbled the drowsy Naval Captain, recalling last night's Aztec gold and the flooding mine.

The Captain carefully returned the items to the trunk. He left the set of scales and the golden hourglass sitting out on the dining room table. He turned the hourglass over and then poured himself a brandy. Shortly before midnight, he staggered into bed. The tiny crystals fell effortlessly through the glass bulbs. The July night turned cooler than usual, and at about three A.M., the Captain arose to find a blanket. With the warmth of the blanket, he soon fell asleep and began to dream...

Stan was standing in the middle of some lush tropical jungle. There appeared to be some rays of sunlight streaming through a group of very tall trees. The sounds of exotic birds and parrots could be heard in the distance. He felt the weight of a backpack and then noticed that he was wearing some unusual ill-fitting uniform that included a heavy metal breastplate! He felt very strange and quite lost. He looked around and saw no one. The ground was muddy from a recent shower. This caused his weight to sink in above his ankles. He had on heavy well broken-in leather boots that extended to his knees. He was quickly brought to the startling revelation that he was dressed as some sort of 'Conquistador'! From the look of things, it appeared he was in a place and in an era which was new and strange to him.

"Well I'll be damned! How in the hell did I get here? And how in the hell do I get back?" he exclaimed, as some birds flew overhead.

Suddenly, he heard breaking branches. Looking around, he saw that he was surrounded by what appeared to be a group of young warriors. Each man was dressed in a padded cotton warrior suit and carried a wooden shield. On their heads, they wore wooden helmets decorated with feathers. Some of the helmets resembled what looked like serpent's heads; others were more like tigers. All of them carried some sort of weapon. There were bows, arrows, spiked clubs and lances. One warrior wore some type of gold jewelry that must have denoted his status.

They motioned toward Captain Siegewick. Then one of them proceeded to bind Stan's hands in front of him. They then led him through the jungle. The rain began to fall again. Everything glisten when the sun returned. The men conversed among themselves in some ancient dialect. They seemed to be pleased with their new captive, and they expressed it by patting each other on the back. They seemed to be treating him with some respect. During their walk, they assisted him in removing the backpack and his armor. They carried each item of his with care. Suddenly, the forest ended. Before then was a vast lake with a great city which had been constructed on many islands.

The leader stopped and said, "Tenochtitlan," pointing to one of the three bridges that led into the city. The warriors took Stan across the bridge to the center of the city where there was a gigantic open-air marketplace. It was filled with people who seemed to be of many social classes. Some men wore white cloaks, others simply wore only loincloths. The women, in the market, with their long straight black hair wore ankle-length skirts with colorful embroidered belts. There were also soldiers in the market dressed the same way as young warriors. Men and women of noble status wore jewelry, necklaces, ear rings and bracelets. A few noblemen were dressed in cloaks and headdresses made with brightly colored feathers. Everyone was wearing sandals. The smaller buildings were made of brick adobe and the larger buildings were made of stone. The lower class lived in simple dwellings of mud. All the buildings had roofs made of reeds.

Stan, from his study of American cultures, arrived at the conclusion he was a house guest of the ancient Aztecs and because of his apparel, he must have been included in one of the Spanish expeditions led by Cortez. This totally fascinated and frightened him.

"If they are Aztecs," he thought, "I could be included as the guest of honor, high atop one of those twin pyramid-temples located in the center of this great city."

Shortly, he found himself held prisoner in a small underground cell where he was given a white cloak and some food. As he began to eat, the Captain felt something... something was moving. It was the floor! The floor started to heave. He was thrown back against the wall and parts of broken bricks and mud started falling upon him.

"Oh my God! They're having an earthquake! No one knows I'm down here!"
he yelled as he tried to call for help.

* * *

Deep underground many men labored throughout the night shoveling sand and loading the conveyor. Suddenly, all the red wall lights began to flicker. Men looked at each other with terror in their eyes. Beneath their chained feet, the earth began to heave and shift knocking many of them to the rocky tunnel floor.

Losing their balance and their tools, the chain gang cried out to their guards for help. The conveyor stopped and the guards yelled back obscenities while they quickly fled down the rocking narrow passageway. Sand began pouring from all directions through newly opened fissures in the stone walls and the tunnel ceiling. The escaping guards paid no attention to the fading sounds of screams from the trapped and suffocating prisoners.

* * *

SUNDAY, JULY 15

Suddenly, Captain Siegewick woke up!

Totally surprised and soaking wet from perspiration, he tried to stand. His knees were still shaking as he entered the shower.

The golden hourglass sat on the dining room table where he had left it, but now it was reflecting the Sunday noon's sunshine.

The phone rang...rang...rang...rang.

"Yes, what do you want?" shouted a dripping Captain.

"Sir, there's been an earth tremor and a cave-in," said Chief Sheppard in a shaky voice.

"What? Where?" asked the Captain.

"Inside the first tunnel, Sir. The men working there are gone; there was nothing but sand inside the tunnel. It happened so damn fast," the Chief replied with a still-shaking voice.

"Damn it to hell!" the Captain shouted, "where're you, Sheppard?"

"At a pay phone. Rest Area south," replied the Chief. "You stay put. Give me twenty minutes."

The Captain hastily dressed in civilian clothes, hopped on his motor bike and headed about two miles down the Pacific Coastal Highway. He met the

Chief at a roadside rest area. They sat down at a picnic table. The Chief still had his hands covering his face when the Captain approached.

"How many? How many? Damn you, I said how many? Answer me!" shouted the Captain.

"Ten men and their four guards were killed! How many more lives should be wasted on this operation?" the Chief lamented. "All right, take it easy. Let's reconsider this whole matter," Stan said in a more understanding tone of voice.

"Sir, can we possibility regroup from this disaster?" the worried Chief asked.

The Captain stared at the ocean for a while but said nothing. The two men at the picnic table then decided to swear to each other on that hot Sunday afternoon in July to continue the quest for the treasure. They knew where it was. They knew how to get it. They also knew of the potential wealth it would bring. Now they knew of the danger.

* 11 *

The lost mine traversed a newly active fault line, which unknown to them, ran about ten miles north and twenty miles south into Mexico. Recent earthquake activity along this fault could ultimately destroy the mine and its gold...if the shock-absorbing sand was removed from any of the mine's three tunnels. These two twentieth century prospectors must now pursue this treasure-hunt, no matter how costly the price, before the legend about the 'Lost Dutchman Mine' became only a legend forever.

*   *   *

Later that same Sunday evening, July the fifteenth, the Captain and the Chief were seated in the Captain's living room. Together, they continued to entertain thoughts about the further exploration of the remaining two underground tunnels. They knew that the Captain's Mast scheduled for the next day would provide the needed manpower. They carefully reexamined the contents of the old trunk, and then they proceeded to get very drunk.

"Sir, we have six ex-Marines still on our payroll. We have no prisoners alive now to work our mine and we don't have any money!" the Chief reminded the Captain and added, "we're in one hell of a position, especially if we think we're going to get this job done and retire from active duty next January."

"Yes, I realize the situation seems almost impossible, but that old hourglass may be just what we needed. I've decided to send it to a friend's antique shop in New York City. I've been told it would bring a handsome price," the Captain said feeling good about this idea.

"Now that makes sense, Sir. How about the other items in the trunk?" asked the Chief.

"No, they're really not worth very much being in such poor condition. Of course, those pieces of paper are the most valuable to us," replied the Captain.

"Where should we keep them?" inquired the Chief.

"Put them in your safe. They'll be secure there," replied the Captain.

"Yes, Sir. I'll drop them by the office before I leave the base tonight for the marina," said the Chief.

"How many sailors will be brought up before the Mast tomorrow?" the Captain asked.

"About fifteen, I believe, Sir," replied the Chief.

"Excellent. Are you sleeping aboard your yacht tonight?" asked the Captain.

"Certainly, Sir." the Chief said with a smile.

"That boat could play another important role in our plans. I'll explain it to you later," said the Captain.

"Very well, Sir, have a good night," the Chief said as he saluted and then departed into the darkness.

"Well, little golden hourglass," the Captain said, "I think I'll find you a new home tomorrow. And now, I think I'll retire to the bed. Goodnight. Sweet dreams," the yawning Captain said as he darkened the dining room lights. He set the hourglass on the nightstand beside his bed and then proceeded to fall asleep watching the tiny sand crystals fall. Stan began to dream...

Suddenly, there was a commotion of people about him. He was being dressed in a beautiful white coat and much gold jewelry was being offered to him to wear. He placed several gold rings on his fingers while golden bracelets were being affixed to his wrists and upper arms. The Indian women around him were very beautifully dressed. They wore much gold jewelry. They were preparing him for some sort of ceremony. No one spoke to him, only to each other. It appeared they were pleased with his appearance. The party left the dressing chamber.

They escorted him down a narrow stone passageway and out into the bright sunlight. A loud roar and cheers greeted him as he was presented to the mass of people gathered in the city square. A huge parade of warriors and dignitaries passed in front of him. They were all dressed in their finest. Everyone wore colored feathers and were covered with gold jewelry.

He could hear what seemed to be huge drums being beaten by Indians high upon the very top of one of the great pyramid-shaped temples. It was a spectacle to behold. It made him feel privileged to be there.

He joined the parade and remembered passing a wall of stone-carved serpents. Everyone around him wore gold jewelry of various styles which glistened in the hot sunshine. The crowd continued to cheer wildly. He was then escorted forward until he reached a set of stone stairs. Arms pulled at him from all directions. He was to follow their lead. He then found himself climbing steep stone steps which were narrow where he stepped. The short treads made the ascent extremely difficult. He counted each step while being escorted, on each side, by temple priests and guards.

He remembered one hundred and fourteen steps before reaching the pyramid's summit. As he neared the top, he was panting heavily.

Once he arrived at the very top, he could see for many miles in each direction. The great city of Tenochtitlan lay before him. It contained many splendid palaces and public buildings. It was built in the center of a gigantic lake which had many small islands. They were all connected by bridges. The lake was surrounded by jagged mountains. This great temple, on which he stood, was in the center of the city.

Fear suddenly gripped him as he was turned around to face a horrible looking creature. It was the temple's high priest. The man's robes were covered with blood and his hair was thickly matted, also with blood. The small temple high atop the great pyramid smelled like a slaughterhouse.

He was now being pushed inside past a squat stone temple god, 'Huitzilopochtli' which was covered with gold, pearls and turquoise jewels. It was looking at him with a look of appreciation. He was roughly handled as his arms and feet were stretched to their limits. He was securely bound with hemp rope by several large temple guards. His beautiful ceremonial robes were quickly torn away and tossed onto an altar of embers. Naked, scared and too frightened to speak, he watched as those clothes ignited and lighted up the room. For the first time, he saw a wall on which hung fresh human hearts from the day's earlier victims. The incense, the torches and the flesh made the stench unbelievable.

He began to scream as the stone knife approached his bare chest....

*   *   *

* 12 *

MONDAY, JULY 16, 1989

The alarm clock revealing the time of 0630 hours unleashed its own fury. The Captain couldn't believe the experience he had just had. The whole series of events had been truly realistic and horrifying.

He was still shaking when he put on his all-white uniform with its golden eagles on the shirt's collar, and the rows multicolored ribbons above the shirt's left pocket. Everything reminded him of the dream. As he finished dressing, he glanced at the golden hourglass sitting on the night stand.

"You! You made me dream!" he shouted. "I wanted to dream about my own gold mine not about some Aztecs with their human sacrifice!" He continued with anger in his voice, "I was having excellent dreams about my discovering gold before I discovered you!...You're a jinx in this house! Today you'll be sent away. Is that understood, mister?"

The hourglass sat perfectly still on the edge of the nightstand and reflected Monday's sunrise. The Captain, not receiving a response from the inanimate object, quickly turned and left slamming the bedroom door behind him. A few minutes later, there was a very slight earth tremor. No damage could be noticed but the hourglass had toppled off the nightstand and rolled over against the wall. It pushed the drapery up against an electrical socket's loose-fitting extension cord and shortly the drapery began to smolder.

Within fifteen minutes, the curtain and the upper section of the window casing and wall were burning. Smoke began pouring out of the roof eves and was soon noticed by civilian employees on their way to work. Fort Warren's fire and rescue squad soon arrived at the Captain's burning quarters. The men worked quickly to extinguish the flames. The bedroom and the attic were completely gutted by the flames and smoke.

Yeoman Roth was the person who notified Captain Siegewick that there has been a fire in his living quarters.

The Captain was at his office desk. He was immediately chauffeured back to his quarters. He became extremely upset upon returning to his fire-damaged living quarters.

Trying to calm him, one of the fireman said, "It appears to have been an electrical fire, Sir. There wasn't a lot of structural damage, but you'll have to move out until the Command gets this mess cleaned up and makes the necessary repairs."

Another fireman said to the Captain, "We'll have things under control in a little while, Sir."

The Captain insisted, "Damn it, get out of my way! I've got to get my valuables out of there!"

Reluctantly, the firemen allowed the Captain to walk through his once well-maintained living quarters.

"What a fucking mess!" despaired the Captain. Upon entering the blackened bedroom, he searched around and located the golden hourglass. It had survived the fire. He took it and some other usable items with him and returned to base headquarters.

"Sorry to hear about the fire, Sir," Commander Wilkins said. "Is there anything we can do for you?"

The Captain only turned and asked what time it was.

"0845 hours, Sir," replied the Commander.

The Captain then said, "Call Chief Sheppard and tell him I'll meet him at Mast 0900 hours."

"Understood, right-a-way, Sir," replied the Commander as he saluted.

The morning sun shone brightly and warmly as the Captain briskly walked across the parking lot and entered the next set of buildings. There he was joined by Lieutenant Lighal, Chief Sheppard, and the Provost Marshall, Marine Corps Major Farrell. Together they would preside at today's Captain's Mast.

As the officers saluted and greeted one another, they each expressed their concern over the Captain's unfortunate fire.

"Everything is being handled properly," said Captain Siegewick. "Let's begin these proceedings."

"Master-At-Arms, bring in the first prisoner," Major Farrell said. Slowly and with his head lowered, wearing blue coveralls, with handcuffs and leg irons, the first sailor entered the chamber and stood before Captain Siegewick. All was quiet. Sunlight filtered through the slatted window blinds.

"State your name and rank, sailor," said Chief Sheppard in a loud voice.

"McCaffery, Thomas R., Shipfitter Second Class, Sir," replied the sailor meekly.

Lieutenant Lighal read the following to the young Petty Officer. "Mr. McCaffery, you have been charged with violations of the Uniform Code of Military Justice. You stand accused according to *Article 112a, Section 912* of buying and attempting to distribute drugs and or narcotics, having hallucinogenic effects, to another member of the United States military. In addition, *Article 86, Section 886* states that you are also accused of taking leave without proper authorization, and furthermore, you failed to return to your assigned duties at the prescribed date and time. These failures of yours, according to *Article 87, Section 887*, resulted in your duty officer having to rearrange the watch billet completely and thus created a hardship on his men."

"Mr. McCaffery," said Captain Siegewick. "These are serious charges, and it is my opinion, and that of your superior officers, that you are found to be in violation of Article 35-chapter 12 paragraph 19 and Article 14 chapter 5 paragraphs 10, 14 and 20 of the Uniform Code of Military Justice. You are therefore found guilty before this Mast, and I sentence you to be reduced one pay grade and you are ordered to serve six-months' time in Fort Warren's Brig. While there, you will be required to serve on various work details as your guards see fit."

"Chief Master-At-Arms, remove this prisoner and bring forward the next," requested Major Farrell.

By the noon recess, twelve sailors, most of them charged with unauthorized leave or drug-related offenses, were all similarly convicted and sentenced. They were not represented by legal counsel, which was only required by the Navy for more complicated charges such as theft of military property, helping an enemy agent or murder, at a Court Martial.

"Presiding as the Base Commandant certainly has its privileges," Ken told Stan as they later met briefly in the base headquarters for lunch. There they discussed how to transfer these men to their own base 'brig,' beneath Herbert Hall.

Stan said, "I will personally notify the Marine Sergeant-of-the-Guard that these prisoners are to be transferred to another facility, and I will assume full responsibility for their care. The location will be classified so they won't object. Remember, tomorrow Major Farrell will preside. He'll sentence his own set of Marine Corps men who have been charged as drug users and being A.W.O.L. They will be sent to the base brig for the Marines to supervise."

After the lunch recess, the men returned to the courtroom. The Captain passed similar sentences on the three remaining sailors.

Captain Siegewick returned to his office about 1500 hours and placed a call to New York City to Lieutenant Cheryl Finley's sister Peggy at her antique shop.

"Hello, Miss Peggy Finley?" asked the Captain professionally.

"Yes, this is she," Miss Finley replied.

"My name is Stanley Siegewick from San Diego. I was given your number by your sister Cheryl," said the Captain.

"Oh yes! How do you do. Cheryl called earlier and said that you might be calling," said Miss Finley. Then she added, "What can I do for you?"

"I have an antique golden hourglass that I would like to sell," said the Captain.

"An antique hourglass?" asked Miss Finley.

"That's right, it's a golden hourglass. It's about twelve inches high, has three support columns and is about five inches in diameter at the ends. I believe it dates to the time of the California gold rush. It's quite handsome and is in pretty good shape...considering...," said the Captain.

The voice of Peggy Finley in New York sounded excited, and she instructed the Captain how to wrap and send it. Once she received it, she told the Captain, she would buy it outright–assuming it turned out to be what she expected.

The Captain left the directions and address with his secretary, Yeoman Roth. He then headed out to find lodging for the night. Around 1600 hours, the secretary mailed the parcel to New York City and headed home.

That night Stan slept peacefully in the Officer's Transit Barracks on the base. He didn't even dream.

*   *   *

In total darkness, activity occurred below ground in the partially excavated second tunnel. Another slight tremor caused sand to stream down from the tunnel's ceiling in several locations. Above ground, under a flood of lights, the MP sentries made their rounds behind the perimeter fencing of the Herbert Hall construction site. Waves of the Pacific Ocean pounded harder on the beach that evening suggesting that a storm was approaching from the west. By morning's light, there was little remaining of the dunes that had been built up over the past month. Meanwhile, inside a cargo storage crate at the San Diego airport, the golden hourglass was firmly encased in packing material. Soon it would journey eastward to the delight of its new owners.

*   *   *

* 13 *

"That's right, Sir," Chief Sheppard said. "Mr. Hawkins has a crew of six men and they specialize in finishing commercial interiors. He was a damn good electrician on his own. I believe he could have the lower level completed in no time...for the right price."

"Keep talking," Captain Siegewick told the Chief.

The Chief continued, "I also told him about the limited access to our 'storage area,' and that all the work must be done at night. I reminded him too, if he participated in this project, there certainly would be a bonus at the end if the job is completed ahead of schedule."

"When can I meet Mr. Hawkins?" asked the Captain.

"Tonight, Sir, around 2130 hours on my boat," replied the Chief.

"Fine, pick me up in front of the Officer's Club about 2100 hours," requested the Captain.

The Captain looked at the clock that read 1615 hours. He then placed another phone call, this time to Hawaii.

"Cheryl!" the Captain said with a chuckle in his voice. "I have good news. The Command here did have a billet in the Supply Division for either an ensign or a lieutenant. You should have your orders within a few days. Plan to report for duty here on One August."

"Oh Stan! I hardly can believe it. I'm so excited," exclaimed Cheryl.

"We both will be looking for new quarters," said Stan.

"How come, my love?" asked Cheryl, wondering.

"My quarters on the base had a fire yesterday," replied Stan.

Cheryl said, "Oh my! Was it very bad?"

"Sort of...the damage was confined to only one room and the attic, but it still made quite a mess. I'm now staying in the officer's transit barracks until Navy housing decides what to do for me. Oh, yes, that golden hourglass survived the fire and has been sent to your sister Peggy's antique shop in New York yesterday afternoon. Thank you again for giving me her address," said Stan.

Cheryl said, "When I called her, Peggy seemed quite anxious to receive the hourglass."

"It really was a handsome antique," said the Captain.

"Thank you again for finding me a new assignment," whispered Cheryl into the phone.

"Call me when you get your orders," he told her.

"I will the instant they arrive. I love you, Stan," said Cheryl with her heart pounding.

"Love you too, Cheryl. Goodbye," said the Captain as he held the phone tight in his hand.

He then buzzed his secretary and said, "Yeoman Roth, have my car brought around."

The Captain departed for the *Officer's Club*, had some drinks and dinner, then met Chief Sheppard. He and the Chief drove the short distance to the marina. About 1930 hours that evening, Mr. Hawkins arrived at slip number fourteen and walked onto the deck of the Chief's new 32-foot yacht, *Yankee II*.

Mr. Rodney Hawkins was a tall and muscular black man in his early thirties. He had worked as an electrician with a local construction firm for several years, until recently, when the firm experienced hard economic times. He and his crew had been laid off. The men were seeking employment. He was delighted when the Chief called him. Mr. Hawkins and his men were very eager to get any decent paying local job. Because of being non-union, his company had not bid on the Herbert Hall project.

The three men gathered around the table in the boat's stateroom as the Captain unrolled Todd's set of revised drawings now labeled *'Computer Storage Area.'*

The Captain began by saying, "Since the middle of April, when these revisions to the original set of plans arrived, only the structural, not the electrical, parts of this lower level have been built. None of the interior finish work nor the electricity has been installed. We've been running lamps and a power wench conveyor system since June. These have only been connected temporarily to the base's power supply. This area needs to be on a separate utility must be completed quickly."

"Mr. Hawkins, please note one other thing..." the Chief interrupted, "There's an anti-terrorist security system installed at the beach entrance to the storm drain. Our guards will adjust it to allow your men to pass when they begin work and when they leave. Also, put yourself on notice, that the Captain and I will personally conduct inspections and determine if the work satisfies all Naval requirements."

"I see, gentlemen," Mr. Hawkins said in an agreeable manner. He then looked at the plans that the Chief had earlier taken from Paul McCoy.

Examining the electrical schematic carefully, Mr. Hawkins stated, "This resembles a high-tech prison, Sir. I counted twenty jail cells!"

"Quite so, Mr. Hawkins. There's a classified project underway that required a need for these cells. The other rooms in this space would need only basic finishing...but, the electronic security system must be carefully installed to the architect's exact specifications," said the Captain. "You and your crew will be paid out of a special fund. This is a highly sensitive operation, and absolutely no one must reveal any part of what we're doing. The consequences would be severe. Is that understood, Mr. Hawkins?"

"Very well, Captain Siegewick, whatever you say," Rodney Hawkins replied trying to strongly express to the Captain that he really understood him.

Feeling more comfortable about this situation, the Captain said, "Good, let's proceed. Chief Sheppard, pour our Mr. Hawkins a drink." That evening, the trio spent several more hours discussing Todd's revised architectural plans of the south wing of Herbert Hall. The on-board bar remained opened and each man drank heavily. The boat remained steady until around eleven-thirty that July evening when a very slight earth tremor was felt causing the boat to move.

Around midnight, the Captain and Mr. Hawkins prepared to depart the Chief's yacht. They were holding on tightly to the rope railing of the gangway. They were realizing, each in his own way, the monetary benefits of this business venture.

"Goodnight, Chief, thank you for the drinks and the job," said Mr. Hawkins. Turning to Captain Siegewick, he added, "Captain, where will my crew assemble tomorrow and at what time?"

The Captain replied, "Park your cars near the north side of Fort Warren and walk south on the beach until you are in line with the main gate. There is a storm drain that empties onto the beach at that point. The Chief and his assistants will meet your men there at 2200 hours."

"That's fine with me, Captain Siegewick. I'll be there with my crew at ten o'clock tomorrow night," Mr. Hawkins said excitedly.

"Till then, Mister," the Captain said shaking Mr. Hawkins' hand. After Mr. Hawkins drove off, Chief Sheppard drove the Captain back to his temporary quarters on the base. He returned to his yacht ten minutes later only to fall asleep in his favorite chair.

That night, Captain Siegewick again slept soundly. The golden hourglass had been shipped to New York and no longer caused him to dream about the ancient Aztecs.

* * *

WEDNESDAY, JULY 18

That morning there was a staff meeting in Captain Siegewick's office at 0900 hours. Attending were Chief Sheppard and Mr. McCoy.

"Mr. McCoy, Commander Wilkins informed me that the project has proceeded on schedule. I am very pleased to get that report. I expect Herbert Hall to be ready for the first day of class next January seventh at 0900 hours. Have you encountered any new problems since you last talked to Commander Wilkins?" asked the Captain.

"One, Captain. I'll make every attempt to complete building the forms over the entrances to the south wing's lower level by Friday. I'm just a little shorthanded, Sir," replied Mr. McCoy.

"Very well, I'll authorize you to hire four more labors today," replied the Captain.

"That'll be of great help to me, Sir," said Paul.

"Mr. McCoy, haven't you been around Naval construction long enough?" asked the Captain in a quizzical voice.

"But Sir, I thought we didn't have extra funds available to hire on more help," replied Paul McCoy.

"The Navy will always do what it takes to get the job done right," the Captain said with a peculiar smile, then continued by saying, "The lower level of the south wing has been canceled and it will remain a restricted area. The late Mr. Bennet completed the structural portion of that level and asked no questions as to its purpose. You should do the same. Is that clear, Mr. McCoy?"

"Understood, Captain," Paul said with his eyes looking down at the floor. "Is there anything else you want to tell me?"

"Yes, there is something else. As far as you're concerned, the lower level doesn't exist," the Captain said sternly.

"Really!" Paul said raising his head and eyebrows.

The Captain answered Paul saying, "Each night this next week, classified equipment will be moved into that space and installed by military personnel. Starting today, you will instruct your men not to enter this space. You'll then proceed to have the accesses to that level sealed off with concrete by this Friday. My Naval engineers are highly trained. Once they have finished, that secured area will not appear on any diagram or floor plan of that building."

"What was just mentioned, Sir, is very confidential and must not be repeated to any officer or civilian on this base or outside of it," stated Chief Sheppard emphatically.

Paul turned and exited the room, closing the door behind him. The Captain notified his secretary, "Locate Commander Wilkins and have him report in one hour to my office."

The Captain then instructed Chief Sheppard, "Tonight at 2200 hours, assemble the new former Marine guards at the entrance to the storm drain. They should wear full battle gear and their hoods. Have them escort Mr. Hawkins and his crew into the lower level of Herbert Hall through the steel door. Assure Hawkins' men of their safety. Our guards' identity must never be revealed to anyone."

Returning to his desk, the Captain said, "Before you meet Mr. Hawkins tonight, let our guards move the twelve new prisoners out of their cells and into the mine's second tunnel. Never...never are Mr. Hawkins' men to encounter our prisoners face-to-face. That's all for now, Chief."

"Understood, Sir," the Chief replied, saluting and as he was ready to depart, the Captain suddenly shouted, "Damn it, Sheppard, I almost forgot to tell you that the shipment of more electric collars arrived. Be sure to pick them up today at the base mail room. Just sign for the box and take it with you tonight."

"Very good, Sir. One final question, Sir. What should Mr. Hawkins be told about the sequence he should follow for the completion of the brig?" asked Ken.

"Tell him to start roughing-in the electric. We must get Tasselmeyer's security system installed promptly. I don't like you simply padlocking each cell. That seems extremely primitive and not very secure," replied the Captain.

"I agree one hundred percent, Sir." After saluting, Ken left the Captain's office. On his way out of the building, the Chief saluted and greeted the Executive Officer Commander Wilkins who had just arrived at the base headquarters.

"Good morning, Sir," said the Chief.

"Is Siegewick in?" asked Commander Wilkins.

"Yes, Commander. I've just come from his office," said the Chief.

"Good. Carry on, Mister," the XO replied while returning the Chief's salute.

Upon entering the Captain's office, Commander Wilkins saluted and asked, "Good morning, Sir, you had me paged?"

"Yes," said the Captain. "Listen up. Lieutenant Cheryl Finley will be reporting here the morning August 1st. I want to plan a small reception at the Officer's Club that evening and I'd like you and your wife, Sofia, to join us. Lieutenant Finley wants to meet our Navy family here. I thought your wife would enjoy talking to Cheryl and maybe plan a shopping adventure of some type."

"Very good, Sir. I'll talk to her tonight and I'm sure she'll help the Lieutenant in that department," said the Commander.

"One other thing, Commander," the Captain said in a more serious tone. "I understand that Lieutenant Finley will be assigned to Lieutenant Commander Ellerly's Supply Division."

"Correct, Sir," said Wilkins.

"Ask Ellerly if Lieutenant Finley could handle the accounts payable for the Herbert Hall project," asked the Captain.

"Why would you want her to do that?" asked Commander Wilkins. The Captain answered saying, "I've got a feeling. Should there be any problems with the construction payroll, or any problems with the disbursements of money for materials before that project is complete, I want Lieutenant Finley held strictly accountable. She'll need a difficult project to keep her busy and, if she is as good as the command at Pearl Harbor says she is, she'll complete Herbert Hall's record keeping with flying colors."

"Understood, Sir. I'll talk to Lieutenant Commander Ellerly later today and report back to you with her decision," said Commander Wilkins as he was preparing to leave. Commander Wilkins saluted and departed the Captain's office.

Alone, the Captain opened his calendar to review the next several weeks. He observed that Yeoman Roth had scheduled many things for him before the end of July. He had been invited by the local Chamber of Commerce to be one of the guest speakers at the annual 'Founder's Day' celebration on Thursday, July the twenty-fifth, at noon. The Captain simply was not in the mood to write some stupid speech telling the San Diego community how much he enjoyed living there when he did not. He then wondered if he could get Commander Wilkins to handle it.

Then he noticed that Rear Admiral McKinsey would be joining him for a 'Pass and Review' inspection of a graduating basic training class on Friday the twenty-sixth. The Captain knew the admiral would then insist that he join him on the greens over the weekend.

The Captain couldn't wait until next January when he could retire and leave this place. He took out his pen and circled January the fifth of the next year and wrote, Herbert Hall dedication 1000. Then he made another notation beside the first. 'Change-of-Command Ceremony' 1200 hours. After that day, he would be a civilian!

He hated having to spend the night in transit barracks. He hoped his quarters would soon be ready for occupancy. The fire had taken place on Monday morning and he still had no clue as to how the fire had started in his bedroom.

He was becoming increasingly anxious by the hour over 'Operation Sand Dune' and he was not eating very well either. He knew Cheryl would arrive on August the first and he could not wait to hold her in his arms again.

The Captain then sat back in his chair and stared out the window at the bright early Wednesday morning sunlight and thought to himself, "Wouldn't it be wonderful if I retired from the Navy as a multi-millionaire. I could mine the *Dutchman's* gold treasure and leave the country with it."

But then he became troubled and a frown crossed his brow when thinking to himself about, "How would this goal to achieve that wealth be accomplished? Already, since the beginning of March, two construction workers fell to their death, and six innocent sailors were electrocuted. Mr. Bennet had to be drowned because he understood what the operation was, and now, ten Hispanics and their four guards died in last week's cave-in inside tunnel number one. Twenty-one lives had been casualties of 'Operation Sand Dune,' and the objective of finding the *Dutchman's* gold had not been reached! Now, twelve more new brig prisoners were going to be put at risk by experiencing the danger of working under the threat of a cave-in inside the unsteady second tunnel."

The Captain felt extremely depressed.

"Excuse me, Sir. There's a call for you on line one. It's Chief Sheppard," Yeoman Roth said over the intercom.

"Sheppard! What do you need?" asked the Captain while still in a bad mood.

"Sir" the Chief's excited voice said, "Early this morning, at 0200 hours, the men in the second tunnel uncovered two skeletons! I'm positive those bones have been there for quite a while." "Go on, Chief," said the Captain with great interest.

"Well, Sir, one of the skeletons had what appeared to be a bullet hole in the front of the skull! The other skeleton was holding a Civil War era pistol in one hand and a bag in the other. It's the bag, Sir. That bag is filled with...gold nuggets!" explained the Chief excitedly.

"What!" exclaimed the jubilant Captain, "Repeat what you just said."

"Gold, Sir, and that bag must weigh several pounds!" Ken said with much enthusiasm.

"Excellent, Mister, keep talking," yelled the Captain.

"Sir, it appeared that the first dead man was robbed of his gold and shot in the head by the second man. When the second man fired the pistol, the concussion must have caused a cave-in which allowed part of the ceiling to fall upon him and his mortally wounded comrade," said the Chief.

"Very good detective work, Chief," said the Captain in deep thought.

Chief Sheppard then stated, "I ordered the guards to activate the prisoner's collars and it kept them away from the discovery. The jolt of electricity through their collars really did the trick. Once I had the bag of gold, the prisoners promptly obeyed our orders to remove the two skeletons to the first tunnel and bury then near the others."

"That sounded like a good move," the Captain said.

"The prisoners were then ordered back to the second tunnel, and continued to move more sand and deposit it on the beach. I've just been informed by walkie-talkie that the prisoners are secure in their cells in the basement brig," said the Chief.

"I wish I had been there," the Captain lamented.

"Sir, I think the wait is over. The bag of gold is locked in my office safe. You and I are the only ones who have the combination," the Chief said softly.

"Good thinking, Chief," said the Captain. "Go by my quarters today and get the set of apothecary's scales from the trunk. That trunk is still in the corner of the dining room. The fire didn't bother it. Weigh the gold and report to me later. Thank you, Chief. Your news couldn't have come at a better time."

"Understood, Sir. Oh, yes, Mr. Hawkins and his crew worked until 0530 hours, they were then escorted back to the beach. He and his men appeared to have accomplished a lot of the electrical work last night. I'll meet with you after today's briefing. Till later," said the Chief.

"Fine, Chief. It appears as if we've found the owners of the trunk," the Captain said as he hung up the phone. He then smiled his peculiar smile and before he had time to collect his thoughts, he heard a voice on the intercom.

"Excuse me, Sir. There is a certified letter for you out here. Do you want it brought in?" asked Yoeman Roth.

"Affirmative, Yeoman Roth," the Captain ordered.

His office door opened and the young Petty Officer Second Class handed the Captain the envelope, saluted, and returned to her desk.

Opening the envelope, his eyes widened. "A check for five-hundred dollars from Finley's Antique Shop in New York. How wonderful! That old hourglass must have charmed them too. I'll call Cheryl later and tell her the good news," thought the Captain.

The remainder of the day became very hectic for him. Around 1000 hours there was a staff briefing to review the week's activities. Those in attendance included the Captain, the Executive Officer Commander Wilkins, the Supply Division Officer Lieutenant Commander Ellerly, the Protocol Officer Lieutenant Lighal and the Chief Master-At-Arms Sheppard.

Lieutenant Lighal briefed everyone on the arrangements and preparations that were being made for Admiral McKinsey's arrival the next day. There was to be a dinner and a reception at the Officer's Club beginning at 1830 hours. The uniform was to be dress whites with long pants. The dress parade and 'Naval Review' was to begin at 0930 hours on Friday. There was discussion whether to wear khaki or whites. The white summer uniform won out.

The new boot-camp's non-commissioned graduates on Friday would then be assigned to Pacific fleet operations. Captain Siegewick's job was to approve the orders for ship-duty. Some graduates with proven outstanding leadership or academic abilities would continue their Naval education. They would attend specialized schools at other Naval Training Centers. Fort Warren, had only advanced training for junior commissioned officers in weapons and electronics. Herbert Hall, upon its completion, would contain enough classroom space to house four hundred students at one time studying advanced electronics.

Those attending that Wednesday morning briefing were given an update on the Herbert Hall project by Commander Wilkins. He informed the group of what an outstanding job Mr. McCoy was doing and that everything pertaining to Herbert Hall was on schedule.

Lieutenant Commander Ellerly put everyone on notice, "I expected all the correct paperwork for requisitions of office supplies and any other items to be hand-delivered to my office and not sent through the yard mail. I still suspect someone may be intercepting requisition slips once they have the proper signatures and altering the amounts for supplies. I have not caught anyone yet, but will you please notify your staffs that I am 'on the warpath.'"

"Now, now Denise..." the Captain started to say.

"Don't call me Denise! I hate that name!" Lieutenant Commander Ellerly said angrily.

"Very well, Commander," the Captain quickly interjected while trying to calm this five-foot-tall powder keg.

"You can be assured that all of us will double-check every invoice for its accuracy."

"Thank you, Captain," she said with her usual huff.

* * *

Following the briefing, Chief Sheppard met the Captain in his office behind closed doors.

"The bag of gold weighed a little less than five pounds, Sir," said the Chief.

"Any idea of the current exchange rates?" asked the Captain.

"I believe gold has recently sold for over four hundred dollars a once, Sir," said the Chief with a smile on his face.

"Chief," the Captain said while exhibiting his peculiar smile. "It seems the longer I sit here at the desk this morning, the richer we get. Look at this." He pulled out the check he had just received from Finley's Antique Shop in New York City for our golden hourglass.

"Terrific, Sir," said the Chief.

"Now, we'll have enough money to run the mining operation and keep Lieutenant Commander Ellerly shut up and off our backs," said the Captain.

"Very good Sir. I really began to sweat during her part of the briefing," added the Chief.

"Understood, she made me sweat a little too. Let me know how things go tonight down below," said the Captain.

"We'll have to find someone off the Base within a week or so to get a true value and a fair exchange on the contents of the bag, Sir," the Chief stated while getting ready to leave. "Agreed, but I want to use an unknown third party to exchange the gold," said the Captain.

"May I suggest your new Lieutenant from Hawaii, Sir?" asked the Chief.

"Yes, Chief, Cheryl is quite unknown around here, and she would do anything I asked her. She'll report for duty here in seven days, on August the 1st," said the Captain in an approval of the Chief's suggestion.

"Put this check in your safe with the bag. I'll let Cheryl open a separate account for our '*Operation Sand Dune*' as soon as she's settled in," said the Captain with his peculiar smile.

* * *

Later that afternoon, Captain Siegewick called Hawaii. "Hello, Cheryl," said the Captain seductively.

"Oh Stan, how wonderful to hear your voice again," replied Cheryl.

"Do you realize that in only a week you'll be here with me," he said.

"Yes, I can't wait. I can't thank you enough for getting me transferred off this island and to your Command," she said.

"Listen, your sister just sent me a check for five-hundred dollars for that old golden hourglass," said the Captain in a surprised tone of voice.

"I'm happy for you, Captain."

"You don't seem too enthusiastic."

"Well just before you called I was speaking to my sister in New York and she said that our mother is pretty sick. She's been that way ever since she received the hourglass."

"I'm sorry to hear that, Cheryl. I'm sure she be just fine."

"Will you buy me something nice?" asked Cheryl.

"Of course, I will, once you're Stateside," he assured her.

"Time can't pass quickly enough," she said expressing her impatience.

"I understand, by the way, I've found several interesting projects for you to help me with once you're Stateside," he said.

"What are they?" asked Cheryl.

"Oh, I can't explain now, but I'm certain you're the right person to help me," he assured her while showing his peculiar smile.

"Yes, I'll love working on any project with you, Stan," Cheryl said with enthusiasm.

"Fine, I'll call you on Sunday. Take care, and keep packing," he said as he began to hang up.

"You know I will. Goodbye, darling," Cheryl whispered in the phone. The Captain now felt so much better he could hardly believe it. "Yeoman Roth, find me Commander Wilkins and have him meet me at the *Officer's Club* at 1630 hours," ordered the Captain.

"Certainly, Sir," said Yoeman Roth.

The Captain left his office and walked the three blocks to the Herbert Hall construction site. He admired how the building was taking shape. At the same time, he was thinking to himself about 'Operation Sand Dune.' That secret operation was proceeding around the clock some twenty feet directly below his feet. He flashed his peculiar smile and crossed Fort Warren's *Main Street* and continued walking until he reached the Officer's Club.

Upon entering, the Captain spotted Commander Wilkins at the crowded bar. "I need a favor, Commander," the Captain said.

"Gentlemen, man your battle stations. The Skipper needs something," said the Commander laughing.

"All right. Listen up. I need you to deliver the 'Founder's Day' speech before the town fathers on July the 25th at noon," stated the Captain.

Commander Wilkens quickly replied, "Sure, that shouldn't be any problem."

"Good. Thanks a lot, Commander. Can I buy you another drink?" asked the Captain feeling a little bit better now that that job was out of the way.

Commander Wilkins graciously accepted. The Commander also told the Captain that Lieutenant Commander Ellerly had approved his request to allow Cheryl to handle the Herbert Hall account.

That evening the Captain heard the local extended weather forecast that called for a rainy weekend, much to his delight, and what would be a major disappointment to his golfing Admiral.

* * *

* 14 *

FRIDAY, JULY 20, 1989

At 0900 hours, two large cement mixer trucks arrived at the construction compound. One truck driver carefully positioned himself at the west entrance and the other at the east entrance of Herbert Hall.

Some construction workers and Paul McCoy assembled to position the rear truck chutes. They aimed the chutes so that the wet cement would fill the newly constructed forms that now covered the stairwells to the basement of the south wing. As the two trucks unloaded their concrete, the sounds of 'Anchors Aweigh' and 'The Stars and Stripes Forever' could be heard over the truck noises. The new boot camp graduates passed in review of the Admiral and the assembled guests on the parade grounds near the construction site. The sun shone only briefly on the graduates and, by afternoon, the rain had arrived. The Admiral, deprived of playing a round of golf, departed.

At the end of the afternoon, the cement crew had finished smoothing the concrete slabs that covered, in addition to the two stairwells, the elevator shaft of the south wing. Both the building's metal stairs and elevators would now extend only from the first floor to the second. The computer storage area below was no longer accessible from above ground. The storm drains beneath the street, extending from the foundation's steel door to the Pacific beach, was the only entrance and exit to the brig and the mine.

*   *   *

Each day and night, from then on, heavily armed and hooded guards were posted at the beach's storm drain entrance. The guards were hidden by the high sand dunes that surrounded the entrance.

Saturday, July 21, the Captain called the Chief to meet him on the beach and to give him a guided tour of the operation. The Chief using the walkie-talkie, notified the guards of their arrival time.

On the beach, near the tunnel's entrance, Chief Sheppard said proudly, "Captain Siegewick, I would like you to meet Master Sergeant Miller. He has the most military experience and leads and trains our guards."

"Very good, Mr. Miller. At ease," the Captain said returning the Sergeant's salute. "Sergeant Miller, the Chief and I want a tour of this facility. Please lead on."

"Understood, Sir. Right this way. Here are two hard hats and black hoods you should each put on," said the Sergeant showing he was eager to please them.

"Fine," said the Captain showing his peculiar smile. "Let's see, Chief, what Lieutenant Commander Ellerly's Supply Division has furnished us through our altering of her purchase orders since March."

The Sergeant, wearing his black hood, lead the Captain and the Chief through the small hatchway in the cliffside. They proceeded to walk through the one thousand-foot portion of the concrete storm drain tunnel. Everything was illuminated with red glowing shipboard lamps mounted every six feet or so. The tunnel had a very low overhead and was damp. Beneath their feet was the rubber tread of the conveyor belt.

"This conveyor system really helps the prisoners move the sand, Sir," commented Chief Sheppard.

"This must have cost a small fortune, Chief," said the Captain.

"Not really, Sir. There was a lot of equipment like this requested back in March for our initial investigation. The Navy had almost everything we needed somewhere on Base. The real job, once the equipment was located, was getting it all moved here."

"I'm very impressed, Chief. Carry on, Sergeant Miller," said the Captain anxious to see more of the tunnel.

Upon reaching the location of the original connecting tunnel, they proceeded the twenty-five feet to the ventilation shaft and the scene of the original cave-in on March 6th.

"How deep are we Sergeant?" asked the Captain.

"About thirty feet, Sir. As you can see, the three tunnels angle downward and go below the storm drain. Because they were filled with sand, there was no cave-in, and no discovery was made of the mine tunnels when the storm drain was originally excavated and installed," replied the Sergeant.

"We are truly fortunate to have found it then," said the Captain. The Sergeant proudly continued, "Tunnel Number One runs off to the right and heads slightly southwest, the second heads southeast and the third tunnel runs almost due east, Sir. If you'll now walk to the tunnel on the far left, we will be arriving at the steel door below Herbert Hall's south wing."

Upon unlocking the door, the Captain was utterly amazed at the transformation Mr. Hawkins' crew had achieved in only five days. They had taken the dark concrete walled space and made it into a high-tech command center to monitor 'Operation Sand Dune.'

"Aten-hut!" shouted the Sergeant to the other guards as the party entered the first room.

"At ease, gentlemen. I'm in-charge of this operation and I'm here to look around," said the Captain.

As the Captain toured the facility, he saw that twelve of the twenty cells were occupied because of last week's Captain's Mast. The Captain met the Sergeant's other guards. Each hooded guard saluted him proudly and he exchanged a few words with each man. The Captain and the Chief were then escorted to the courtroom chamber, the records office and the machine shop.

"Chief Sheppard, I owe you my heartfelt appreciation for getting this project so totally well organized. I'm just speechless. Everything appears to be exactly as the architect had specified way back in April," said the Captain trying his best to express thankfulness for a job well done.

"Thank you, Sir. I hoped you would approve," said Ken trying to hide his pride.

"Are the guards satisfied with their pay and duty schedule?" the Captain inquired of the Sergeant.

"Very much, Sir. They make the prisoners perform to their fullest potential. The collar device was simply a brilliant move on your part, Sir," said the Sergeant beneath his hooded face.

"Thank you, Sergeant," said the Captain. "May we proceed back into the mine?"

Sergeant Miller replied, "Certainly, Sir. Tunnel Number One is closed due to the cave-in. Those poor Hispanics and guards didn't know what to do when the tremor struck. The lights went out and all I could hear was faint screams and men calling out for help. By the time the rest of us got the equipment organized, sand had filled that part of the tunnel. There were, of course, no survivors."

"Understood, Sergeant. We were all shocked at the loss," the Captain assured him.

"Is it really worth risking my men, Sir?" asked the Sergeant.

"It is. Continue the tour," said the Captain in a more commanding voice.

The trio now headed into the second tunnel.

"Down here is where the trunk was located. We made a notation on the wall showing where items were recovered," said the Sergeant. "Very well, I've seen enough of this subterranean pit. I'm ready for some fresh air and a stiff drink. How about it, Chief?" asked the Captain.

"Sergeant, you and your men are doing us a very great service. You'll receive special benefits for this faithful service to me. Please pass that information on to your men," the Captain said.

"Allow the prisoners to continue excavating sand from this second tunnel. Mr. Hawkins should be finished with his work by August 1st," the Chief added.

"Carry on, Sergeant. We'll find our way out," said the Captain indicating he was ready to get out of the tunnel as quickly as he could.

*   *   *

* 15 *

WEDNESDAY, AUGUST 1

When the sun broke over the jagged mountains to the east of the San Diego area on the first day of the new month, much had been accomplished above and below the ground at the Herbert Hall construction site.

The second-floor steel framework had been installed and the building was ready for the roofing material. Mr. Hawkins and his crew completed the installation of the security system and made some final adjustments before they activated the system on a permanent basis.

The bag of gold nuggets and the five-hundred-dollar check remained undisturbed in Chief Sheppard's safe. The weight of the bag suggested that the value was at least thirty thousand dollars based on the daily newspaper reports of gold trading.

Twelve sailors, who were recently sentenced from the last Captain's Mast, were being confined in the brig under Herbert Hall. Each of the prisoners, under the direction of the ex-Marine guards, and prodded by the electro-collars, learned how to work more productively. They succeeded in excavating sand from the second tunnel for another two hundred and fifty feet. At that point, the tunnel angled sharply to the northeast and ended abruptly about twenty-five feet beyond.

The prisoners concluded that all indications showed there wasn't any previous exploration beyond that point. All mining activity came to a halt.

This disruption caused the Captain and the Chief to reexamine the yellowed map found in the prospector's trunk. "Sir, the men removing sand inside the second tunnel were unable to proceed. The tunnel just stopped for some strange reason," the Chief explained as the Captain carefully looked at the map found inside the old trunk.

"I'll have to inspect that place again myself," the Captain told him.

"But Sir. Would that be a wise move? After all, it's not too stable a place due to the earth tremors. You could get hurt and, besides, there's still one remaining tunnel to excavate. Maybe that third tunnel would lead us to the mine's treasure," emphasized the Chief.

The Captain thought for a while, then agreed with the Chief's logic stating, "It'd be better if I weren't seen leaving base headquarters for an extended amount of time during working hours. Tonight, have the prisoners begin excavating sand from the third tunnel. Let's see where that takes us."

"Is your Lieutenant friend from Hawaii reporting in today, Sir?" asked the Chief.

"Yes," said the Captain. "Lieutenant Finley is scheduled to meet with Commander Wilkins and me after the 0800 hours morning muster."

"You'll have to introduce me to her since she'll now play such an important role in 'Operation Sand Dune'," said the Chief.

"I've decided on something else she could do," replied the Captain. "I'm going to ask her if she would like to go house-hunting with me tomorrow. I would like her to take up residence with me."

"Begging your pardon, Sir," Ken said almost spilling his mug of coffee. "Is that also part of the operation?"

"On your way, Sheppard! I'll call you later," quickly replied the Captain.

The men departed, saluting. The Captain quickly left for his office on his motor bike. He stopped short of the building to stand at attention and salute as the colors were raised at 0800 hours to the sound of the 'The National Anthem.' The morning sun shone brightly that first day of August. Once the Captain arrived at the base headquarters, he poured himself a mug of coffee and, upon entering his office, was immediately called by his secretary. "Yoeman Roth," the Captain said loudly. "I'm expecting company. Please advise me when they arrive."

"Certainly, Captain," replied the yoeman.

Within a few minutes his intercom sounded, "Sir," said Yoeman Roth in a professional voice. "Commander Wilkins and a Lieutenant Finley are here to see you Captain."

"Good. Send them in," said the Captain trying not to show his inner excitement at the thought of seeing Lieutenant Finley.

They entered and saluted at attention.

"At ease," the Captain said as he rose, returning their salutes. "Good morning, how was your trip, Lieutenant?"

"Wonderful, Sir. It's like a dream come true to be stationed here at Fort Warren," Cheryl said smiling broadly at the Captain.

"Lieutenant Finley has accepted the assignment to Lieutenant Commander Ellerly's Purchasing and Disbursement Division," Commander Wilkins informed the Captain. "She's already checked into the Officer's Transit Barracks and I believe she's ready for some official Fort Warren coffee."

"Oh, thank you, Commander," she said taking the coffee mug from his hand.

"Well, Lieutenant," the Captain said. "Lieutenant Commander Ellerly should be pleased to have such a hard-working assistant. Your service record under Commander Thomas at Pearl Harbor has nothing but the most glowing statements about your performance."

"Thank you, Captain," she said with another smile.

"Well, Miss Finley," said the Commander. "May I escort you to our Supply Office?"

As she began to answer, the Captain turned to the Commander and said, "Commander, may we have a moment alone?"

"Certainly, Sir. Lieutenant, I'll be waiting down the hall in room 103." Upon closing the door, Stan arose and passionately kissed Cheryl.

"Finally, you're here. I couldn't believe how much I'd miss you. You look just great in your white uniform," he said as he hugged her tightly.

"Oh, Stan, I've missed you terribly. When can I see you?" she asked.

"Meet me back here at 1630 hours and we'll go to the Officer's Club for drinks and dinner," he whispered to her.

"It sounds wonderful. Till then, Stan." she said saluting as she left. As Commander Wilkins escorted Cheryl to the building across the street, he pointed to the construction going on down at the far end of the next block. He proceeded to tell her, "The new classroom building is called Herbert Hall. A young New York City architect named Tasselmeyer designed the exterior to resemble the decks of a ship. The building was begun last March and is scheduled to be dedicated on the first Saturday in January."

"It's a beautiful classroom building," Cheryl added.

"I can arrange a tour by the construction superintendent Mr. McCoy after you're more settled in," Commander Wilkins told her.

"It sounds very interesting, Commander. But, please tell me more about Lieutenant Commander Ellerly," said Cheryl.

Commander Wilkins answered by saying, "She's one tough cookie. She knows where every nut and bolt on this base is and how much it cost. Her love life is her work and she's always on duty. She hates kids, animals and house plants! No one even knows where she lives!"

"Are you kidding me?" asked Cheryl, hopping her new supervisor wasn't the 'wicked witch from the North.'

The Commander smiled and said, "You'll work together just fine. Don't worry."

Upon entering the supply office's purchasing division, Lieutenant Finley was properly introduced and said while saluting, "Lieutenant Cheryl Finley reporting for duty."

"At ease, Lieutenant. You're now standing in front of your new home," the short Lieutenant Commander said pointing to Cheryl's desk.

Speaking to Commander Wilkins, Ellerly continued, "Thank you for assigning her here. I need good leadership around this place."

"My pleasure, Commander Ellerly. I'll be available if you have any problems, Lieutenant," said Commander Wilkins directly to Cheryl.

"Thank you," said Cheryl saluting Commander Wilkins.

"Now, Lieutenant, here is your typed job description and a complete listing of the staff members with their telephone exchanges. I advise you to learn these quickly. We'll be having a staff meeting today at 1100 hours and I'll introduce you to everyone then," said the Lieutenant Commander. "My office is through those doors. You are to call me first on the phone before entering my office, and you are never to call me by my first name. Is that understood?"

"Yes, Commander," replied Cheryl in her best conciliatory voice. Cheryl now felt as if Commander Wilkins was right. She was the wicked witch. The staff members Cheryl encountered, her first morning on the job, were very pleasant and everyone commented how lovely she looked.

Around 0915 hours, the Captain was notified by his secretary that the base housing inspector had come with a report.

"Show him in," said the Captain.

"Good morning, Captain Siegewick. All renovations to your quarters have been completed, and you may return there today. All the debris has been removed, and all the ruined items replaced," reported the housing inspector proudly.

"Very good. Thank your staff for me. I didn't realize when it happened what a mess such a small fire could make," said the Captain acting impressed.

"I've seen much worse, Sir," the inspector told him.

"I'm sure you have. Good day, Sir. Thank you again," said the Captain dismissing the inspector.

As the housing inspector departed the office, the Captain reached for the intercom. "Yeoman Roth, have my car brought around."

"Right away, Sir," was the response on the other end.

The Captain departed Base Headquarters and was driven into downtown San Diego. He made several stops at real estate offices to have them keep a lookout for some small out-of-the-way house that Cheryl and he could share. After identifying several interesting listings that sounded as though they would fit their needs, he had his driver pass by the addresses to inspect the neighborhoods. He returned to the base about 1600 hours and waited in his office for Cheryl to arrive.

"Well, Lieutenant, how was your day?" the Captain asked while looking lovingly at Cheryl who had collapsed in the chair in his office and had tossed her shoes off.

"That Lieutenant Commander Ellerly is some tyrant," Cheryl said. "She double checked everything I completed today. Why is she such a pain-in-the-ass, Stan?"

"Perhaps she'll be swallowed up by a black hole tonight, and tomorrow you'll be in charge," said Stan displaying his peculiar smile.

"I wish! Oh well, at least I'm here with you," Cheryl said joyfully.

"Yes, isn't that wonderful. Come here, I want to kiss you again." said Stan with a tone of compassion in his voice.

"Stan, behave, somebody might see us," giggled Cheryl.

"I've invited Mike Wilkins and his wife Sofia to join us at the Officer's Club for dinner tonight. Run along and freshen up and don't unpack everything because we're going house-hunting tomorrow," Stan said tenderly.

"Oh Stan, you're marvelous!" said Cheryl.

During the evening dinner Cheryl found herself liking Sofia. Together they agreed that they would see the shopping district next week. The two ladies excused themselves to leave for the powder room. It was there that Sofia told Cheryl, "I'm a newly appointed assistant bank manager for the '*San Diego Bank & Trust Company.*' The bank was chartered soon after California became a state in 1850. The bank was responsible for most of the growth in the San Diego area."

"How wonderful, Sofia. Your job sounds very interesting," said Cheryl.

Sofia also told Cheryl, "Next year after Captain Siegewick retires, her husband Michael could possibly be promoted to the rank of Captain if the Department of the Navy approved him. He would then stand a better chance of assuming command of Fort Warren before he retired in four years."

"That would keep you two here in San Diego," said Cheryl. "Yes," said Sofia. "Michael and I love living here. Besides, I figured that I'll stand a chance of being promoted to bank manager within that time frame if we continue to live here."

* * *

Cheryl remembered the conversation, and told Stan about it later that night back at his newly refurbished quarters.

"Stan, tell me something wonderful tonight," Cheryl begged. "My dear, there's a safe here on the base. Inside that safe is only the tip of an iceberg," he said.

"I don't follow," Cheryl said bewildered.

"Last week my people discovered a bag deep in the ground. Inside that little bag was...gold nuggets!" exclaimed Stan.

"Really! How many?" Cheryl asked.

"About five pounds worth," he told her.

Cheryl yelled, "My God, Stan! That's a small fortune itself."

"I know, dearest, but the best part is that there may be plenty more where that came from," said Stan.

"Really!" she exclaimed. "How wonderful."

Stan told Cheryl, "There's still a lot of logistical problems that I'm dealing with but things are moving in the right direction. Hopefully over the next few months, we may strike it rich!"

"We?" she asked. "Who's we?"

"So far only the Chief Master-at-Arms, Chief Sheppard and I... and now you, dear," he informed her.

"You want to share your wealth with a little nobody like me?" asked Cheryl still a little overwhelmed.

"Of course, I need your help and expertise and your love and affection," he quickly caught himself. He didn't want to reveal anything further tonight. He talked about house-hunting. Soon they closed the bedroom door and made love in the dark.

*   *   *

* 16 *

SATURDAY, AUGUST 4

The Captain and Cheryl looked at houses that morning and decided on a small one-story stucco with two bedrooms and a red tile roof. It was in the 'Mission Hills District' just to the north of San Diego. The house was about ten miles from Fort Warren. It had a nice view of the Pacific Ocean between two houses across the street. Together they would take occupancy on the fifteenth of August.

They spent the remainder of the weekend inside the Captain's quarters on the base, with the bedroom's new drapery tightly drawn.

* * *

Late Sunday evening Chief Sheppard stopped by to meet Cheryl.

"Lieutenant Finley, this is my right arm around Fort Warren. Chief Sheppard, meet Cheryl," said the Captain proudly. "Welcome to Fort Warren and San Diego, Lieutenant," replied the Chief in his usual military style.

"Oh, Chief Sheppard, Captain Siegewick has told me wonderful things about you," beamed Cheryl. "It's a real pleasure to meet you."

"Well, Ma'am. I think your boss is one-hell-of-a good Skipper," said the Chief with a smile.

"Alright, both of you," replied the Captain.

Chief Sheppard then said, "How's dinner at my place sound for tonight?"

Cheryl turned toward the Captain and he nodded his approval.

"Sounds great, Chief. I believe we're ready to go," said the Captain.

The Chief then drove the Captain and his girlfriend to the marina and fixed them dinner aboard his boat 'Yankee.' They had several drinks and enjoyed a gourmet seafood meal.

"That was delicious, Chief. Cheryl and I really appreciated it," said the Captain expressing his feelings to their chef.

"Well, Sir, I thought it only right. Have you had any time to discuss anything with the lady?" asked the Chief.

"Only a brief mention, and she seemed very interested," the Captain said proudly.

"Do you mind talking about the operation before I return you to your quarters?" asked the Chief.

"Not at all. Cheryl, darling, pour us another drink and come sit down with us," requested the Captain.

The three gathered around the table as the Chief unfolded the map recovered from the trunk. The Captain had given it back to the Chief yesterday morning for safe keeping. Together they revealed the exploration of the tunnels to her, but did not tell Cheryl where the operation was taking place.

"As of yesterday, we've run into a dead end in the second tunnel and now we are turning our attention to the third," the Chief said pointing to the lines on the yellowed piece of paper.

"This map indicates that the second tunnel angles to the northeast, then continues south. But at this point, there is just a rock wall," the Captain told her.

"This map really looks authentic and quite old," Cheryl noted. "Yes, we believe it dates to the time of the California gold rush."

"Well, you boys decide what you must do. I must get some sleep tonight so I can be ready to do battle with that witch Ellerly tomorrow bright and early," Cheryl said with a yawn.

"Very well, Lieutenant. To the car with you," insisted the Captain.

"Sir, I'm going to check on the men tonight after I drop you off," said the Chief.

"That's fine, Chief," said the Captain as the car started.

* * *

SUNDAY, AUGUST 5

Around 0100 hours, Chief Sheppard and two of the hooded guards watched as the men continued removing sand from the second tunnel under the direction of the other guards.

"Take me down to the dead end of tunnel number two," the Chief told his men, "and bring a shovel and a pick."

The trio arrived at the end of the tunnel. There was a single red light that glowed at the place where the prisoners had come to the dead end.

"Start poking around, guys. This tunnel is supposed to continue according to the old map we found," the Chief ordered.

The two guards carefully tapped the rock walls and couldn't move anything.

"That's solid, Chief," the one said as he leaned against the shovel handle. Suddenly, the shovel sank quickly down into the floor of the tunnel and the guard yelled out as the sand beneath his feet began to give way. Within an instant, he had disappeared below through a gaping hole in the tunnel's floor. The horrified Chief and the other guard called frantically the name of their missing comrade. "Corporal Lenert...Corporal Lenert...can you hear us? Are you hurt?" yelled the Chief down into the blackness of the newly discovered tunnel entrance.

"I'm...okay, Chief, just shook up a little bit. Get me a light down here, and I'll give you a report," replied Corporal Lenert still shaking from his fall.

Quickly the other guard summoned help and within two minutes the place was brightly lighted. The report from below was that the tunnel was navigable for several hundred more feet. Three additional guards entered the hole and explored it. When they returned, they told the Chief the tunnel entered a great room with a high ceiling.

The chamber was very large and quite flooded with sand. They had also felt air moving indicating the room was ventilated somehow.

"Excellent, men, split the prisoners and let half of them work in this tunnel. The others can continue in tunnel number three," instructed the Chief.

At 0330 hours, there was a knocking at the Captain's door.

"Pardon the time, Sir," the Chief said. "There's been another major discovery."

"Yes, what is it?" asked the sleepy Captain.

"The second tunnel extends downward to another level and then empties out into what the men called a 'Great Room,'" said the Chief excitedly.

"Oh my God! Chief! I had a dream a while back about Aztec Indians mining gold from the walls of a 'Great Room'! Could it be the same room? Could this lead us to the discovery of the 'El Dorado' that the Spanish explorers had heard about but could never find? Or could it possibly be the mine of the 'lost Dutchman'? They said in the history books that somewhere here in the North American West there was a gold deposit of immense size," said the Captain trying hard to comprehend what he just heard.

"Yes, Captain, but it was only a legend," the Chief reminded him.

"Legend, my ass, we'll prove the history books were right!" exclaimed the Captain again displaying his peculiar smile.

The Chief departed, and Stan returned to Cheryl's arms.

"Who was it, dear?" she inquired.

Stan, trying to hide his total excitement, said, "It was Chief Sheppard with an excellent report on the on-going project that we discussed earlier."

"What time is it?" Cheryl asked.

"It's time we made some money. Go back to sleep, dearest, and dream of soon being very rich," said Stan in a quiet voice as he leaned over and kissed her.

"Oh Stan, I'm already rich, having you here beside me," Cheryl said tenderly.

He kissed her again quite passionately and they continued to make love in the dark.

* * *

Later that day, Stan insisted that Cheryl meet with Sofia Wilkins and enjoy some time together. After scanning the local newspaper, Cheryl decided the best sales were at the downtown mall. She called Sofia and told Stan, "Sounds good for this afternoon. She'll be by around 1600 hours."

Once Sofia arrived, Stan asked, "Cheryl. Pick me up a ledger book at the stationary store, if it won't be any trouble."

"No problem," she exclaimed as she and Sofia departed. "See you in a few hours," shouted Cheryl to Stan as Sofia's car drove off.

Sofia and Cheryl shopped for civilian clothes and looked at furniture for Cheryl's new house. Cheryl almost forgot Stan's request but remembered to buy the ledger on the way back. It was a small green colored book and contained fifty pages.

* * *

MONDAY, AUGUST 6

About 1230 hours, the Captain called Cheryl at the Supply Division office saying, "Lieutenant, I'm having my car brought around to pick you up. Proceed to the bank where Commander Wilkins' wife works."

"That's the *San Diego Bank & Trust* downtown," Cheryl said.

"Affirmative. Tell Sofia Wilkins that you want a large safety deposit box. Then ask her who you could deal with in the assay office of the bank. You'll have some precious metals to exchange. Don't tell her you are talking about gold. I don't want anyone to know our business. Is that understood?" asked the Captain.

"Certainly, Sir. I fully understand the order. I'll be waiting outside," Cheryl said loudly so that Lieutenant Commander Ellerly heard her.

"And where are you going off to in the middle of the workday, Lieutenant Finley?" Commander Ellerly huffed.

"I'm going on an errand for Captain Siegewick. With your permission, Commander," said Cheryl trying to hold back a grin.

"All right, but get your pretty self, back here in a hurry!" ordered Commander Ellerly.

"Certainly, Ma'am. Right away, Commander," Cheryl said as she saluted her and headed for the door.

The Captain's driver took Cheryl to Chief Sheppard's office. While there, the Chief opened the safe and told her, "Lieutenant Finley, the Captain felt that you could be trusted and would work with us just fine."

"Why thank you, Chief Sheppard. I appreciate your confidence," said Cheryl feeling positive of herself.

He handed her the bag of gold nuggets that had been removed from the skeleton in the second tunnel and said, "Listen carefully. Tell the assay officer the contents are from a recent family inheritance and you expect to get more."

"Really!" exclaimed Cheryl not understanding the story she had to tell.

"The Captain wishes you to have the assay officer weigh and appraise this bag," said the Chief emphatically.

"Very well," said Cheryl realizing that this was a favor for the Captain.

"Tell him you want to exchange the contents overseas for U.S. currency. Perhaps on the Hong Kong exchange," said the Chief.

"Will that be a problem?" asked Cheryl.

"No. He should, for a commission, make all the necessary arrangements. Also find out how long the exchange would take," requested the Chief.

"Certainly, Chief Sheppard. Captain Siegewick has asked me to get a safety deposit box," Cheryl informed him.

"Yes, you'll need to keep the cash in that box. Did you pick up a ledger?" asked the Chief.

"Yes, yesterday while shopping," said Cheryl.

"Fine, record all the transactions we make. It will be valuable later. For the time being, you'll oversee the ledger book and that safety deposit box key," said the Chief.

"It all sounds exciting, Chief," said Cheryl who was getting a little more enthused about what she was going to do. He walked her to the waiting car and told her, "Good luck, Lieutenant."

"Thank you, Chief," she said as they saluted and she closed the car door.

* * *

* 17 *

"Let me look at my list of available safety deposit boxes," said Sofia Wilkins to Cheryl.

"Yes, here's one you can rent. Box number 1849."

"That's fine, Sofia, prepare the paperwork, and show me where to sign," said Cheryl.

"Will that be for six months or a year, Lieutenant?" asked Sofia.

"One year would be fine," Cheryl replied.

"Sign here and give this to any one of the tellers. They'll give you the key. Is there anything else I could do for you?" inquired Commander Wilkins' wife as Cheryl signed the form.

"Yes, I've just gotten involved in a family estate settlement and I have some precious metals that need to get appraised and exchanged for cash. Do you have someone here at this bank, or know someone locally who could help me?" asked Cheryl.

"This bank no longer trades in metals. However, just down the next corner on California street, there is an assay office. The strange little man who works there is Henry Mayhen. He's a retired geological researcher and has all types of college degrees in metallurgy. He's something left over from the days of the gold rush. Here's his business card," she said handing it to Cheryl. "Tell him I've recommended you. I must warn you, he's different."

"Thank you, Sofia, you've been such a tremendous help," said Cheryl appreciatively.

"Not at all, Lieutenant. I'll talk to you soon. When can we go shopping again?" asked Sofia.

"Next week will be fine. I'll call you," said Cheryl.

Cheryl picked up the golden safety deposit key and walked to the car to collect the bag of gold nuggets. She told the driver that she had to make another stop and would not be much longer. She then proceeded to walk down the street to Mr. Mayhen's assay office. It was another beautiful sunny August afternoon in San Diego. In her mind, she tried to compare this place with downtown Honolulu which she missed. Once at the address on the card, Cheryl peeked through the old beveled glass panes of the ancient shop's front window. The interior was dark and gloomy. The 'Open' sign was displayed, so she entered.

She felt like she had just stepped back in time. The tiny mildew-smelling shop was filled with unusual items. Many of them pertained to geology, mountain climbing, and cave exploring. She even noticed some Indian artifacts. Everything was covered with a thick layer of dust. At the rear of the shop she found a caged-in area. Within it was a huge safe and some office furniture.

"Is anybody here?" asked Cheryl timidly.

"What's your business, Lieutenant?" was the reply coming from behind a large rolled-top desk in the corner.

"I'm looking for a Mr. Mayhen. Mrs. Wilkins from the bank sent me over here," replied Cheryl.

"What for?" said the voice.

"I have some gold nuggets," replied Cheryl.

With that, a short old gray-haired man with a large handle-bar moustache walked over to Cheryl.

"Henry Mayhen, Lieutenant. At your service," said Mr. Mayhen.

"Hello, sir. My name is Cheryl Finley and I'm stationed at Fort Warren." said Cheryl not knowing really how to act.

"You say you have some gold?" he asked with the look of greed in his eyes.

"Yes, I do, sir. It's part of an estate. Can you examine it and tell me its purity and perhaps its worth?" she said showing him the bag.

"I have been told that more gold will be sent to me soon as the estate becomes settled," Cheryl informed him.

"Bring it over here, and lay the gold in this tray," ordered Mr. Mayhen.

Upon doing as she was instructed, the old-timer closely examined all the nuggets and put some drops of chemicals on a couple of them. He also used an ultra-violet light for his examination.

"These nuggets are the purest I've seen in these parts for some time. They'll bring you a top price. Did you realize you had four pounds and seven ounces of nuggets here?" asked Mr. Mayhen excitedly.

"Not exactly, sir," Cheryl replied.

"There should be at least thirty thousand dollars' worth of gold here, based on today's market. That's quite a nice inheritance for you, Lieutenant."

"Where can I sell my gold?" asked Cheryl.

"Foreign investors are your best bet," replied Mr. Mayhen.

"Will you put me in touch with someone from Hong Kong?" asked Cheryl.

"My fee is ten per cent for each transaction," said Mr. Mayhen.

"I understand," Cheryl told Mr. Mayhen.

"One minute, please let me place a call, and I'll find out who is available to exchange with you, and when," said Mr. Mayhen.

He returned to his desk and made his call. Shortly he came back to talk to Cheryl.

"There is a Mr. Lee from Hong Kong who is currently visiting San Diego on business. He could meet you tonight at eight-thirty here at my shop," said Mr. Mayhen.

"Fine, I'll be back at that time," Cheryl said as Mr. Mayhen handed her back the bag with the gold nuggets inside.

"If he buys, I'll expect payment," Mr. Mayhen reminded Cheryl.

"Very well, Mr. Mayhen. I'll see you and Mr. Lee tonight," said Cheryl while leaving the shop.

Once he saw that Cheryl's car had left the area, Mr. Mayhen went back to his deck and placed another phone call.

"That's right, operator. I want to talk person to person with Senor Raul Gartez, at the '*Central Congress Building*' in Mexico City," said Mr. Mayhen.

"Your Excellency, Buenos Dias. I'm Senor Henry Mayhen, from the assay office in downtown San Diego, California. I have some important news that I believe would be of interest to you and your staff," said Mr. Mayhen quietly into the phone.

"Si, Señor Mayhen, please continue," said His Excellency.

"Gracias, Your Excellency. I have just spoken with a beautiful young female Navy Lieutenant named Finley. She left my shop a few minutes ago. She had a bag of gold nuggets; almost five pounds in weight. She referred that she would get even more. The gold was of the highest quality and will bring her a top price," said Mr. Mayhen now showing a little excitement in his voice.

"Por favor, Senor Mayhen, continue to let me know of the Lieutenant's activities. I am very interested. Gracias," said His Excellency as he hung up.

"Not at all, Your Excellency, adios," Mr. Mayhen replied.

* * *

Lieutenant Finley returned to Fort Warren and gave Chief Sheppard back the bag which he returned to the safe. She told him of her appointment later that night.

"Excellent, Lieutenant, I'll pick you up at 1930 hours and take you to town. I think we should both wear civilian clothes for the appointment," the Chief added.

At 1630 hours, Cheryl met Stan at his office.

"Lieutenant Commander Ellerly suspects something is really wrong with the Herbert Hall account, Stan. She has ordered me to start a thorough investigation of the people making material requests. Also, particularly, there's a major discrepancy with the electrical usage for that building. Ellerly also told me that over the past two months, the electric bill for that construction site has tripled. Can you help me?" requested Cheryl.

"I see, Cheryl. Together, we'll work on answering the lieutenant commander's questions. How much is the utility usage overrun?" asked the Captain with that peculiar smile.

"She claims it's fifteen-thousand dollars, Stan," said Cheryl.

"All right. Listen up. Tonight, if this Mr. Lee buys the gold, take what you need to replenish Lieutenant Commander Ellerly's account and deposit it tomorrow in her disbursement account. Any money left, you can put into the safety deposit box," the Captain instructed her.

"Where do I tell disbursement, I got this money?" asked Cheryl with a concerned look.

"Tell them extra material from the job site had just been returned, and that was the refund," said the Captain.

"Wonderful, Stan," said Cheryl.

"I can then report to the lieutenant commander that those utility figures were incorrect, and as soon as she would check with her dispersing people, she'll find that the money is available!" Cheryl said much relieved.

"Chief Sheppard will pick me up at your quarters at 1930 hours. Shall we go have dinner at the Officer's Club?" asked Cheryl.

"Of course, my darling Cheryl, tonight we'll celebrate," replied the Captain.

* * *

After a wonderful seafood dinner of *Alaskan King Crab* legs, Cheryl and Stan walked to his quarters.

"You don't know how much I appreciate your getting involved with this gold exchange business. I couldn't figure out how I was going to exchange it for cash since everyone around here knows me," the Captain tried to explain to her.

"I can understand, Stan. It would seem odd if you walked around with gold nuggets and a large bank roll," Cheryl said.

"Since you're unknown in this area, no one knows your business. And as soon as we move off base into our house on the fifteenth, no one will know my business either," said the Captain as he gave her a tight hug.

They quickly went up the front steps of his quarters, and once inside they embraced and kissed passionately.

Within half an hour, Chief Sheppard arrived.

"Howdy partners," the Chief said dressed in blue jeans, cowboy boots and a western shirt. "Is the young lady ready?"

"Sheppard! Are you going to a round-up or the assay office?" asked Stan.

"Both, Sir. Once we finish downtown, I'll come back and pick you up. I've got three tickets for tonight to a night-time rodeo event being held on the outskirts of town," said the Chief while holding the tickets up in the air.

"Whatever you say, Chief. Do you hear that, Cheryl?" the Captain asked while displaying his peculiar smile.

As the two departed for downtown San Diego, Stan picked up the green ledger book. Already Cheryl had begun to make entries in the accounts payable column.

"Utility bill, fifteen-thousand dollars." Thinking to himself that the true figure was more like three hundred thousand dollars. Together with the Chief, they had redirected funds from the Herbert Hall project. They used the money to complete the brig, and fund the mining operations since last March.

Tasslemeyer's architectural revisions for the lower level brig were completed at no charge to the Navy as part of his original government contract. The construction of those pages of revisions cost over two hundred and fifty thousand dollars. Additional money was needed for the initial investigation, recruiting and training of his special guards, the payroll, all the necessary mining equipment, all the electronic gear for the brig's security system, and Mr. Hawkins' crew's payroll came out of the building budget for Herbert Hall.

The Captain realized the importance of replenishing that disbursement account as quickly as possible. At least, he thought, with Cheryl working on the inside, he could stall Lieutenant Commander Ellerly's investigation and keep things running smoothly.

Now that the great room had been located, the Captain was certain that more gold would be found and could be mined from that location.

* * *

When the Chief and Cheryl approached the assay office, there was a stretched black limo parked out front. After they had entered Mayhen's office, two Oriental bodyguards escorted Mr. Lee into the shop. He was carrying a black briefcase.

For many years, Mr. Lee had worked closely with Henry Mayhen. This small Oriental gentleman was truly a man of great wealth and influence in the business community. His many industrial interests allowed him to travel world-wide to satisfy his companies ever-increasing thirst for new technology and natural resources. Whenever he saw an opportunity to obtain raw materials, no matter the source or the price, Mr. Lee always was interested in buying.

Recently Mr. Lee had been experiencing poor health as he rapidly approached his eightieth birthday. Wherever he traveled, he was constantly protected by a highly trained staff of bodyguards. Most of the time, he lived in absolute luxury with his faithful wife aboard the flagship of his fleet of freighters, The 'Dragon Lady.'

Once everyone was assembled, Mr. Mayhen made the introductions. Cheryl told them, "Mr. Sheppard was a cousin who was supplying her the gold."

Mr. Lee asked, "May I see the bag of gold?"

Cheryl handed Mr. Lee the bag upon which he said, "Mr. Mayhen, tells me these nuggets are of the purest quality. I have trusted his expertise for many years." He looked at each nugget closely and said, "They're truly exquisite. Please, let me weigh them."

"Four pounds and seven ounces. May I offer you thirty thousand in U.S. currency?" Mr. Lee asked with a slight smile.

"Of course, Mr. Lee," the delighted Cheryl said.

"Mr. Mayhen has done you a great service and must be paid his commission first. Mr. Mayhen, hand me my briefcase," requested Mr. Lee.

Upon opening the case, the Chief and Cheryl saw it was filled with stacks of one hundred-dollar bills.

"Ten thousand in each stack," Mr. Lee told the group.

Once the money was paid, and Mr. Mayhen received his ten per cent commission, Mr. Lee took the gold. Then he said, "I travel here from Hong Kong twice each month to meet my West coast connections. If you have further need to exchange more gold, Mr. Mayhen will know my schedule.

Everyone stood, then bowed to each other in the oriental custom. Mr. Lee and his bodyguards departed first. The Chief and Cheryl stayed for a moment longer.

"Mr. Mayhen," The Chief inquired, "What happens to the gold now?"

"Mr. Lee owns a shipping firm. The gold will be put into one of his ship's safes. From there, it will eventually end up in Hong Kong. Mr. Lee owns several manufacturing plants there that use gold in their operations. He constantly requires more gold and will travel world-wide to meet sellers. You were fortunate he was available to meet with us. Usually he requires more notice.

"We understand, Mr. Mayhen. We'll give you more notice for the next exchange. Thank you for all that you've done," Cheryl said as she and the Chief departed the tiny assay office.

They picked up Captain Siegewick around 2100 hours. The Captain, Chief and Cheryl enjoyed the rodeo event that night.

*   *   *

* 18 *

TUESDAY, AUGUST 7

Cheryl made her deposit in the Herbert Hall account during an early morning coffee break. Once back at her desk, she called Stan to advise him that everything seemed to be in order.

"Lieutenant Commander Ellerly, may I see you for a moment?" asked Cheryl.

"What is it, Lieutenant?" snapped Ellerly.

"The utility account for Herbert Hall appears to be under control, funds were impounded under another entry in the account ledger. I saw to it that the money has been transferred to the utility account," explained Cheryl.

"Very well," she huffed. "But I still think something is going on here and if there is, I'll be the one to discover it. Anything else, Lieutenant?" again snapped Ellerly.

Cheryl decided it was time to leave Ellerly's office, so she saluted and said, "Nothing else. Good day, Commander Ellerly."

During the lunch hour, Cheryl was driven into town. She put the remaining currency into her safety deposit box. Upon returning to Fort Warren, she stopped at the Captain's quarters to make the entry into the green ledger.

"Fifteen-thousand back to the Navy, three-thousand commission paid to Mr. Henry Mayhen, and twelve-thousand balance on-hand. "Four August," read the entry.

"There's only one thing I don't like about this ledger," Stan told Cheryl that evening. "This Mr. Henry Mayhen will become very wealthy if we produce a lot of gold."

"I know, Stan, but we need him to arrange the exchanges with Mr. Lee," Cheryl reminded him.

"Why do we need this middle man? How can we deal directly with Mr. Lee?" Stan asked Cheryl.

"Maybe the next meeting, I'll try to get Mr. Lee's number or address or something. I think if Mr. Mayhen gets cut out of the action, he may cause us some real problems, dear," Cheryl said with a sigh.

"All right. We'll pay Mayhen his commission for the time being, but we'll make sure he doesn't increase his per cent," said the Captain reluctantly.

* * *

WEDNESDAY, AUGUST 8

Around 0330 hours, two of the prisoners working in the mine's great room with their guard watching removed enough sand from against one wall to reveal the true depth of the room. Upon doing so, they were surprised to find several picks and shovels. These ancient tools were worn down in several places, yet they still were in usable condition. Soon more lights were brought into the area. With bright illumination, a vein of gold extending perhaps ten feet in length and up to six inches in width, was seen clearly embedded in the rocky wall.

The Sergeant of the watch immediately phoned Chief Sheppard. "That's right, Chief, a huge vein of gold in the wall!" exclaimed the Sergeant.

"Was Mr. Hawkins' crew working tonight?" the Chief asked.

"They did earlier but finished their final work and were escorted out of the tunnel about twenty minutes ago," the Sergeant replied.

"Fine, cease further mining operations for tonight. Return the prisoners to their cells. The Captain and I will inspect this discovery within the hour," ordered the Chief.

"As you wish, Chief," replied the Sergeant.

The Chief called the Captain and picked him up at his quarters. He then parked on the north side of Fort Warren Naval Training Center.

As they walked down the beach towards the storm drain entrance, the eastern sky glowed a golden ocher color.

"Look there, Chief, even the sky is gold this morning," said the Captain pointing to the sky.

The two men were met by Sergeant Miller who escorted them to the sight of the discovery.

"I knew the gold was here. I saw this room in my dreams, sometime last month prior to the fire in my quarters. In those dreams, I saw Aztec Indians finding gold in a great underground room, perhaps three hundred years ago! But, I had no idea about where on this planet that great room of gold was located," the Captain told the amazed Chief and Sergeant.

"Finally, this hole in the ground is going to pay off," replied the Chief.

"Look here, Sir. The vein of gold starts there and extends down to that point," said the Sergeant pointing toward the floor.

"Sergeant, as the prisoners remove this gold, place it in the storage cabinet in the record office next to the brig area. Then activate the electronic surveillance system and post an around the clock guard in that room. The gold will have to be prepared for shipment, since we can only exchange small amounts at a time for security reasons," ordered the Captain.

"Understood, Sir," replied the saluting sergeant who remained standing at attention.

"Of course, you and your guards realize that anyone who tampers with the gold, or even mentions anything about this operation, will be dealt with harshly, perhaps even eliminated! Is that quite clear, Sergeant?" threatened the Captain.

"Quite clear, Sir. My men are totally committed to your service, and we'll do everything you ask of us," said the sergeant in a voice trying to convince the Captain of his loyalty.

"Fine, carry on Sergeant. Keep Chief Sheppard informed of your progress. Have all twelve prisoners work in the great room and take twelve hour shifts to keep this mine in full operation," said the Captain sternly.

"Sir. The Corporal here will escort you gentlemen outside," the Sergeant told him.

"Good day, Sergeant," said the Captain saluting as he left.

* * *

WEDNESDAY, AUGUST 15

Early in the morning the moving van approached the Captain's quarters. Both Stan and Cheryl had put in for several days of vacation leave. They needed the time to get settled into their Mission Hills residence. As usual, the San Diego weather was warm and sunny for their moving day.

The enlisted sailors who were ordered to move the Captain's things did an excellent job of packing and crating up each possession. Everything was handled with care. The movers checked each room and closet for leftover items. However, they overlooked the set of rolled up blueprint pages labeled, 'Computer Storage Area', which were on the back of the top shelf in the living room closet.

After Stan's personal belongings were loaded, the van stopped at the officer's transit barracks. There the men loaded the few boxes Cheryl had brought from Hawaii.

The six-month lease for their rental house in Mission Hills would expire the following February. This would give Stan enough time, once he had retired, to plan which direction he and Cheryl would take.

The white stucco house with the red Spanish tile roof contained a large Livingroom with a view of the Pacific, three small bedrooms, a vaulted ceiling family room, and a modern well-equipped kitchen with a separate dining room. The house had a private courtyard enclosed by a six-foot-high stucco wall. The building also included a double car garage.

The entire housing development had been built about fifteen years before and the palm trees and shrubbery were nicely developed and well maintained. Their real estate broker met them at the property, let them have the keys and sign the lease.

Finally, the couple could enjoy a separate life away from Fort Warren Naval Training Center. Stan felt relieved to know that the mining operation would continue around the clock. He held Cheryl close and whispered gently in her ear. "Come, darling, let's take a break from all this moving. I'll darken the bedroom," replied Stan with his peculiar smile.

As the hot August sun set over the vastness of the Pacific, Stan began to make passionate love to Cheryl in their new residence. She eagerly accepted his invitation.

*　*　*

Together with Chief Sheppard, the Captain closely monitored the daily mining activity. The work of extracting the gold ore from the vein took an exceedingly long time. Only small amounts of gold could be removed due to the hardness of the surrounding rock formations. The miners removed much gangue, or worthless material mixed with the ore.

The Captain did some research and found out that gold lode deposits were always associated with acidic igneous intrusive in rocks. The Sierra Nevada and California Coastal ranges were formed about fifty-million years ago during the Jurassic Period and many of their formations produced gold of varying amounts and purity.

Many types of gold veins were caused by mineral-containing solutions that flowed through passageways between rocks.

Upon reexamination of the old yellowed map recovered from the prospector's trunk, the Captain now understood that the lines drawn on the map represented tunnels. These tunnels angled back into the great room by way of winzes, or passageways dug downward from one level to another.

He theorized that the *'Dutchman Mining Company'* must have explored this underground area and dug many of these tunnels. He also concluded that the company's employees must have reached the great room and exploited the gold resources, thus gaining their legendary fame.

The *'Lost Dutchman Mine,'* was rumored to be the biggest gold claim of the entire gold rush era. Under mysterious circumstances, possibly by an earthquake, it had been lost to the ages only to be recalled and talked about as a legend.

Captain Siegewick and Chief Sheppard hoped that their initial investigation, that had begun that previous March, was about to be realized now by mid-August. As they saw it, there existed only one more major obstacle to overcome.

Each evening when the mining occurred in the great room, about a hundred-wheel barrow of sand would first have to be removed. By the next working shift, the entire work area would again be covered with sand which continued to fill the room from many locations. Over the next several weeks, the sand dunes on the beach nearly doubled in size.

"Captain, the sergeant reports that we simply must have more men to move the sand," said the Chief.

"When will that damn sand ever stop long enough for us to excavate the rest of the gold?" the frustrated Captain asked. "Sir, we'll just have to enlarge the number of men. That way, the first group of prisoners can deal with the sand problem while the second group gets the mining operation back on schedule," said the Chief.

"All right, Chief. You tell me where we can come up with more bodies?" Stan said in frustration. "I'm not scheduled to conduct a base Mast until twenty-one September. That's three weeks from now!" he angrily yelled, hitting his fist on his desk.

"Understand, Sir, I may have a solution," said the Chief with a sly look on his face.

"Name it, Mister," said the Captain looking curiously at the Chief.

"Send our guards down to Tijuana, Mexico, this coming weekend at night and kidnap a few of our drunken sailors. Our guards could pose as Shore Patrols. The cafe owners that I know would gladly give us these patrons," the Chief said with pride.

"Sounds good, Chief. But how are you going to get those sailors and our people back through the border without official documents?" the Captain inquired.

"Sir, we'll use my boat to evacuate them and deliver the new prisoners directly to the beach storm drain entrance," explained the Chief.

"Very well, organize this search and rescue expedition to Tijuana over the coming weekend."

"Fine, Sir. I'll call you Monday morning with the results."

"Monday afternoon, we'll conduct an unofficial Captain's Mast in the basement of Herbert Hall's brig and give these chaps something to really help stop their drinking problems."

"Did you forget that Cheryl planned to meet Mr. Mayhen and Mr. Lee tonight? Are the packets of gold ready to transport?" the Captain asked the Chief.

"Yes, Sir, everything's set. I'll get the packets after work, and pick her up at your house at 1930 hours," replied the Chief.

"Oh, Chief, yesterday Cheryl and I bought a car out of the 'profits.' Simply plan to meet her at Mayhen's shop tonight at 2000 hours," said the Captain while watching the Chief's reaction to this admission.

"That'll be fine, Sir. Till then," said the Chief saluting the Captain.

"Carry on, Chief," the Captain said as he returned the Chief's salute.

After a moment, the intercom sounded.

"Excuse me, Captain, Commander Wilkins is here to see you. May I send him in?" said Yeoman Roth.

"The door's unlocked, Yeoman," said the Captain.

"Good day, Sir," the commander said in a rather cheery voice as he entered and saluted. "I've just finished another tour of the construction site. Mr. McCoy informed me everything is proceeding on schedule. However..."

"What is it, Commander?" the Captain said returning his salute and then looking down to the items on his desk.

"Well, Sir. Yesterday one of his men accidentally cut a power cable," said the commander again hesitating to speak further.

"Go on," insisted the Captain.

"The men hooked up an auxiliary generator to complete the day's work, and then shut the system down for the night," said the Commander.

"So, go on," said the Captain looking up with interest.

"It seems that the generator was turned back on and continued to run through the night producing power for something," said the commander in a quizzical voice.

"Something like what, for an example?" asked the Captain.

"Mr. McCoy wondered if something was in operation in that abandoned lower level of the south wing, Sir," said the commander finally.

A frown crossed the Captain's face. His voice became angry. "My, aren't we noisy this morning!"

Then he regained his composure and jokingly said, "You tell Mr. McCoy that I've personally set up an un-manned earthquake monitoring station from Cal-Tech University in that space and their equipment must remain on-line twenty-four hours a day. And furthermore, it's none of his God damned business what we do around here. Is that understood, Commander Wilkins!" the Captain shouted. "Now get out, you're bothering me!"

"Sorry, Sir. Begging your pardon, Sir," the very surprised Commander said as he hastily saluted, then closed the door and quickly left headquarters.

"Excuse me, again, Captain Siegewick," the intercom interrupted, "Lieutenant Finley is on line two."

"Hello, Cheryl," his voice still sounding harsh.

"Stan, are you, all right?" she asked.

"I'm okay, just had a few problems to deal with, and I'm ready for a drink!" replied the Captain.

"But dear, it's still morning!" exclaimed Cheryl.

"When you come by later bring me something from the commissary," requested the Captain.

"What do you need?" she asked.

"Pick up a packet of rat poison, we have some pests around here," said the Captain again displaying his peculiar smile.

"All right," she replied hesitantly, "I'll be by at 1230. I hope the rest of your morning goes better. Good bye, darling."

* * *

After meeting Cheryl for lunch, the Captain returned to his office and made several calls.

"Hello, Mr. McCoy, this is Captain Siegewick. May I meet with you this afternoon in the construction trailer at 1330. I'd like to review the second-floor plans for equipment placement," said the Captain.

"Certainly, Captain. I'll be expecting you, "replied Mr. McCoy.

"I'll see you then," said the Captain as he hung up the phone. The Captain again picked up the phone and said, "Operator, give me the base hospital."

Within a moment the operator asked who he was calling. "Corpsman Taylor, please." When the Corpsman came on the line, he said. "This is Captain Siegewick. I need a favor."

"Yes, Sir. How can I help you?" asked the Corpsman wondering.

"This afternoon at 1330 have one of your medic units arrive at the Herbert Hall construction site near the construction trailer's entrance," requested the Captain.

"The gate on the west side, Sir?" asked Corpsman Taylor.

"That's right," said the Captain.

"Now listen up. I don't want any sirens. I don't want to attract unnecessary attention. Have your man park nearby on the street outside the construction compound. Someone will call for him when it's necessary," ordered the Captain.

"As you wish, Sir, said the Corpsman."

"Thank you, Mr. Taylor," replied the Captain.

When the corpsman hung up, the Captain made another call. "Operator, get me the Chief Master-At-Arms," said the Captain.

"Hello, Chief. Meet me at the construction trailer at 1330," said the Captain without any explanation.

Finally, the Captain notified his secretary ordering, "Yeoman Roth, have my car brought around."

"Right away, Sir," replied the Yeoman.

When the two met at the gate they saluted and the Captain instructed his Chief, "I'm going to upset Mr. McCoy a bit. Would you kindly distract him long enough for me to 'doctor' his coffee mug?"

"Certainly, Sir," Chief Sheppard replied.

Shortly after the two men entered the trailer and began to talk, Paul spilled his mug of coffee and struggled out the door only to fall flat on the ground.

"Somebody get a medic! There's a man down over here!" yelled the Captain.

Quickly the Corpsman arrived to give aid to the stricken Mr. McCoy who was put in the ambulance just as Commander Wilkins arrived.

"What happened here?" the Commander asked as he saluted and approached the Captain, the Chief and the assembled construction crew.

"We were going over the second-floor plans when he suddenly became very sick," the Chief said.

The Commander turned and said, "You men may return to work, we'll handle this."

Captain Siegewick turned toward Corpsman Taylor and said, "I insist that you report back to headquarters about Mr. McCoy's status as soon as you've learned it."

"Certainly, Captain," the Corpsman said while saluting.

"Well, Chief," said the Captain. "We'll just have to plan another meeting with Mr. McCoy once he recovers. Carry on Commander. Chief, I'll catch up with you later this afternoon."

The men saluted each other and the Captain entered his waiting car. Chief Sheppard walked back to his office. Once back at the base headquarters, Stan flushed the remainder of the rat poison crystals down the toilet in the men's room.

Within the hour Corpsman Taylor called the Captain and said, "Sir, Mr. McCoy had suffered from some type of poisoning. His system has now been thoroughly cleaned out and he will remain hospitalized over the weekend for further observations."

"Thank you, Mr. Taylor. Please relay my appreciation to your staffers for saving that man's life," said the Captain kindly.

"Thank you, Sir. I will," replied the Corpsman.

"Good, and I'll notify the XO and the other workers at the job site about Mr. McCoy's status," the Captain said through his peculiar smile.

*   *   *

* 19 *

That evening, a little before eight, Cheryl parked her car across the street from Mr. Mayhen's assay office on California Street. Mr. Lee's black stretch limo was also parked in the vicinity. Cheryl waited in her car for Chief Sheppard to arrive.

The car radio was on, and she heard a spot announcement about a special on TV tonight at ten. The show would cover recent happenings from Mexico City. Also scheduled would be exclusive coverage about a newly emerging political force. It was being led by the political opposition leader and presidential candidate, Señor Raul Gartez.

As Chief Sheppard drove up and parked, Cheryl left her car and walked over to him. She picked up the gold packets and said, "Chief, Stan wants me to handle this exchange alone."

"All right," he said. "But be careful."

She left the Chief, and crossed the street to enter the small dark office.

"Welcome, Lieutenant Finley, Are you alone?" Mr. Mayhen asked.

"Yes, I am, sir."

"Mr. Lee has another appointment tonight, so we must not keep him waiting. Come, right this way." requested Mr. Mayhen.

The interior of the cluttered shop was dimly light by an antique kerosene chimney lamp. Cherly felt as if she was being transported back in time. She heard an old Regulator style wall clock chime gently. Out of the shadows stepped a small statured Oriental gentleman with black hair and wire framed glasses. He motioned to Cheryl to come and sit with him at the table.

"Lieutenant Finley, please meet Mr. Lee," said Henry.

Once everyone was seated, Mr. Mayhen brought out the scales. Cheryl carefully opened each package and put the nuggets carefully on the scales. Mr. Lee sat patiently waiting for Mayhen to finish weighing all the nuggets.

"All together the gold weighs twenty-one pounds and two-ounces. This gold is of the purest quality," Henry said.

"Is there any more?" Mr. Lee asked, smiling with approval.

"Perhaps by next month, we'll be able to supply you with even more," said Cheryl on the advice that Stan had given her. "Lieutenant Finley, you do me and my Hong Kong manufacturer a great service by allowing us the use of your gold. I promise to continue to meet you and to purchase whatever amount you can furnish," said Mr. Lee presaging much satisfaction with the relationship.

"Thank you, Mr. Lee," Cheryl said, "You'll be my only point of exchange."

Henry now interrupted saying, "Lieutenant Finley, as of tonight, my commission has increased to fifteen percent due to the larger amount of gold exchanged."

Before she had time to protest, he promptly pulled out a contract from the rolled-top desk.

"Please sign here, or leave without the currency," was his demand.

Wishing Stan was available to handle the sudden increase, Cheryl reluctantly agreed and signed the document.

Turning to Mr. Lee, she said, "My gold supplier wishes to know more about your interests and would like to arrange a private meeting with you at your convenience."

Cheryl turned toward Henry and said, "Nothing will be bought or sold without you. You can have my word that you will not be excluded from any future gold transactions."

Turning back to Mr. Lee, she asked, "Is it possible to make that meeting happen?"

"Of course, my pretty and rich Ms. Finley," said Mr. Lee. "Here's my business card. My personal secretary arranges all my appointments, and his number is on that card."

"Thank you, Mr. Lee," Cheryl said. "My supplier will definitely be contacting your secretary to arrange a mutually convenient time to meet."

Eight bundles of ten thousand-dollar bills were given to Cheryl for the gold packets. Once she had counted out Mr. Mayhen's commission, she put the money in her brown briefcase. The group bowed, then Mr. Lee and Cheryl departed.

Cheryl waved a sign to Chief Sheppard that the exchange had gone smoothly. She quickly drove to Mission Hills to see Stan.

Henry remained behind to close his office. Before he left, he placed another phone call to Senor Gartez. This time, Henry called Gartez's vacation villa overlooking the Pacific. The villa was about sixty-five miles south of San Diego, on the Baja peninsula, and was located just on the outskirts of Ensenada, Mexico.

"Buenos Noches, this is Señor Mayhen from San Diego," he told the housekeeper. "Please leave the message for His Excellency that the young lady Lieutenant has just made another gold exchange with Señor Lee of Hong

Kong, tonight, here in my office. Tell his excellency that future exchanges are anticipated. Gracias. Adios."

* * *

FRIDAY, AUGUST 17

Stan held a briefing in his office at 0900 hours and told his staff that he had just been informed by the Department of the Navy that Captain Douglas Howerton (USN) would be his successor here at Fort Warren.

"Captain Howerton will report for duty on 12 December 1989 and will take full responsibility at the Change-of-Command ceremony on Saturday, 5 January 1990 at 1200 hours." Stan also reminded to group that, after that day, he would become a civilian.

"I can't believe that your two-year tour of duty as Base Commandant is nearly completed," said Commander Wilkins.

With a broad smile, the Captain said, "Mr. McCoy will be returning to work on Monday."

"Recent reports showed that Herbert Hall was now seventy percent complete," Lieutenant Commander Ellerly informed the group. She continued saying, "Lieutenant Finley and myself are still investigating the discrepancies in the Herbert Hall account. Some of the missing funds seemed to have been recovered since the lieutenant has come on board. The lieutenant's excellent accounting skills found that some of the money had been put under wrong entries."

Before the assembled group, Commander Wilkins thanked Cheryl for her assistance on that account saying, "Yes, Cheryl, you've helped us a lot in the short time that you have been here."

"Why, thank you, Commander. I see it as just part of my job," said Cheryl smiling.

Lieutenant Lighal startled the group by saying, "Attention, please."

"What is it Lieutenant?" mumbled the Captain.

"Sir. There will be visitors on base this weekend for a Parent's Open House. The new recruits will pass-in-review on Saturday beginning at 1100 hours. Following that, there will be base tours and several afternoon sporting events," replied Jim.

"Thank you, Lieutenant, and this concludes my briefing. You're all dismissed," said the Captain with authority.

* * *

Later that afternoon on the way home from the base, Stan drove Cheryl into town to put the money into the safety deposit box.

"I must tell you again, Cheryl, what a wonderful help you've been to me in the last two weeks," the Captain said tenderly with his peculiar smile.

"Oh dearest, so have you." Suddenly, a serious frown crossed Cheryl's brow. "But you know, once I had a chance to closely examine those ledgers that Ellerly was keeping, it showed that nearly three hundred thousand dollars had been appropriated for some computer storage area."

"Really!" he said acting his usual unemotional self.

"I even overheard Wilkins telling Ellerly that the area doesn't even exist on the original set of blueprints!" she said.

"Listen to me," said the Captain. "I'll tell you later about that storage area. For now, just focus on the fact that all further gold exchanges must replenish the building fund. Yes. It must be our top priority."

He parked and watched Cheryl enter the bank with her brown briefcase. Her summer white uniform sparkled in the San Diego afternoon sunlight.

"Lieutenant Finley, how nice to see you again," said Sofia Wilkins. "How may I help you?" she asked, seeing that Cheryl was carrying her brown briefcase with both hands.

"Mrs. Wilkins, I would like to access my safety deposit box, please," said Cheryl.

"Certainly, Lieutenant Finley, step right into the exchange room," instructed Sofia.

"May I have your key?" asked Sofia.

"Yes, it's here on my dog tag chain," said Cheryl as she laid down the briefcase to unfasten her chain.

"Come with me to the vault and I'll unlock the box for you," said Cheryl.

Leaving the brown briefcase of money in the small room, Sofia locked the door as they walked to the vault. Once inside the bank vault, she quickly found Cheryl's box number.

"Here it is, number 1849," said Sofia.

"Thank you, Mrs. Wilkins," Cheryl said as she reached in and pulled out the large, but not very heavy, box.

When she returned to the room, Sofia unlocked the door and prepared to leave the room to give Cheryl privacy.

"Call me when you're finished so I can return the box to the vault and have you sign the log at the reception desk," said Sofia.

Stopping and turning back towards Cheryl, she said, "I'm free Sunday afternoon. Let's meet at the Mall."

"Sounds fine," Cheryl smiled. "Shall we meet around two in the Mall's center court?"

"Wonderful, I'll be there." With that, Sofia left Cheryl to her business.

Cheryl closed the door to the room and began quickly to unpack the stacks of dollars. Since she had bought the car, the box was quite empty when she opened it. Once she finished, it contained sixty-eight thousand dollars.

Sofia Wilkins silently watched on a closed-circuit monitor in another room, as her new girlfriend put the cash into her box and then prepared to leave.

"Now where did all that cash come from?" she wondered.

* * *

That same Friday afternoon, Chief Sheppard briefed his men for their first mission into the wild weekend nightlife of Tijuana. The four secret brig guards were dressed as *Navy Shore Patrol*. They wore SP helmets, SP arm bands, and night sticks. When they assembled at 1800 hours at the marina's dock each man was given a pistol.

Within twenty minutes the *Yankee* was underway and heading past Point Lomas. They entered the vastness of the smooth Pacific and headed on a bearing of due South toward Mexico.

The boat moored about two hours later in a small inlet. The men proceeded to hire a taxi to take them into Tijuana. The Chief remained on his boat and finished off a few strong drinks before preparing himself some dinner.

The sounds of the music and people in the distance filled the summer evening air. Around 2200 hours, two guards returned carrying a very drunken sailor between then who was passed out. Shortly after that, another taxicab arrived with the other two guards and their unconscious sailor.

Just before Friday midnight, the *Yankee* got underway for home. Staying about a mile offshore on a heading of due north, they could see the lights of Imperial Beach and San Diego which twinkled like stars on the horizon. The air had turned warmly humid and the sky was somewhat overcast.

* * *

SATURDAY, AUGUST 18

Around 0200 hours, the boat was parallel with the storm drain's beach entrance The Chief dropped the anchor. More guards hurried out into the shallow water to assist in unloading the two drunken sailors. While they were being escorted into the basement brig, the Chief raised the anchor and returned to the marina, passing the *Point Lomas Lighthouse.*

The Chief and his men relaxed that afternoon. On Saturday night, they and made two more trips south. They returned with six more sailors from their drunken liberty in Tijuana. The basement brig's twenty cells were, for the first time, now fully occupied.

*   *   *

* 20 *

MONDAY, NOVEMBER 5

At 0815 hours that morning, Commander Wilkins was standing before Stan's desk.

"Sir, there seems to be a new development with the Herbert Hall account," he said nervously.

"What's the problem, Commander?" asked the Captain. "Lieutenant Finley. She may be stealing money from the Herbert Hall account, Sir," said Wilkins.

"Really, Commander. What makes you say something like that?" asked the Captain.

Not wanting to mention that his wife had spied on Cheryl, the Commander said. "I... I don't know, Sir. I guess because she was new here and worked on the inside of the supply division with all that money," replied Wilkins.

"I see, well, when she comes into the briefing in a few minutes, I'll let you discuss that with her personally," said the Captain. He then asked the Commander, "Since your wife works in the *San Diego Bank and Trust*, does that make her a bank robber?"

"But, Sir, you know Sofia is an honest person. We don't know anything about Lieutenant Finley," replied Wilkins.

"Get out of my office, Mister!" Stan said with anger in his voice.

"Yes, Sir, right-a-way, Sir," Wilkins said while saluting and he quickly closed the door behind him.

Once the briefing started, the Captain allowed Lieutenant Commander Ellerly to open with the first item. She turned to Cheryl and said, "Well Lieutenant, the Herbert Hall books appear to be in harmony with the budget requests and Department of Defense's cost recommendations for this project. You have really straightened out a major mess for Fort Warren."

"Why, thank you, Lieutenant Commander Ellerly, your comments are very much appreciated," Cheryl said with a smile and a sigh of relief. Commander Wilkins remained silent throughout the briefing and never mentioned anything further about Cheryl.

Nearby neighbors near the Wilkins' quarters heard loud quarreling voices throughout the evening and night.

* * *

Although Cheryl never actually knew where the gold was being mined, she decided that once Stan retired from active service in January, she would ask him to explain the source of the gold. She was extremely curious to know the entire story.

She hoped that together they would be set for life with their vast cash reserve. As Thanksgiving vacation approached, their nest egg had grown to be nearly two million dollars from the gold exchanges with Mr. Lee. Henry Mayhen was delighted to assist Cheryl each time he evaluated and weighed her gold packages. Sofia Wilkins no longer talked to Cheryl, nor did she continue to monitor Cheryl's activities in the vault or the small room for box holders.

* * *

Each day the Captain and the Chief would closely follow the activities in the mine. Stan began to pay Chief Sheppard his percentage from the mine. That allowed him to purchase a new car and a new luxurious ocean-going sixty-five-foot yacht that he christened 'Yankee II.'

Mr. Mayhen continued to call Señor Gartez after each gold exchange between Cheryl and Mr. Lee. Señor Gartez remained very curious about where Cheryl was getting all that gold. Mr. Mayhen remained totally at a loss as to who her supplier was. Mr. Lee also revealed nothing about his meeting with the Captain to Mr. Mayhen.

* * *

FRIDAY, NOVEMBER 30

Herbert Hall was now entering the final phase of construction and proceeding rapidly to completion. Mr. McCoy knew of the deadline to have the project completed and ready for occupancy by seven January. He received authorization from Commander Wilkins to hire several additional men who would assist in the interior finish work.

The building's exterior was covered with battleship grey siding panels with aluminum trim around black glass windows. Everyone agreed that the building was excitedly contemporary. All the exterior handrails on the two-story building were painted red. The building contained no interior hallways except the central open-spaced two-story lobby. Each classroom was entered from an outside covered walkway. Todd Tasselmeyer's design allowed the structure to blend extremely well with its surrounding architectural companions.

* * *

SUNDAY, DECEMBER 2

On a cloudy and cool Sunday evening, Chief Sheppard and Captain Siegewick met on board the Chief's new yacht. The men poured themselves drinks, then returned to the stateroom and sat down at the table.

"Listen, Chief," said the Captain while stirring his drink. "So far everything has moved according to plan. There is only one area of discrepancy that I can see."

"What's that, Sir?" asked the Chief.

"Henry Mayhen," said the Captain.

"Yes, I agree, Sir. He's become quite wealthy from us," said the Chief expressing contempt in his voice.

"According to Cheryl's green ledger entries, she's given that bastard over three hundred thousand dollars just for letting her use his office," said the Captain speaking louder than normal.

"It's sure a high price to pay when such a little bit of time is required to exchange the gold packets," replied the Chief.

"I think it's time we convince Mr. Mayhen that his price, or rather his extortion has just ended," said the Captain again displaying his peculiar smile.

"You mean we should kill him?" asked the concerned Chief.

"No, let's have a little 'convincing' fun with him," Stan suggested with an evil look in his eyes.

"What do you have up your sleeve, Captain?" asked the Chief.

"I believe two of our top guards should pay Mr. Mayhen a visit tomorrow at closing time. Let them somehow kidnap him, blindfold and cuff him, and bring him into our holding cell. There he'll be processed and brought before us in a 'fake mast'. With our hoods on he'll not know us nor even where he is," said the Captain while rubbing his hands together.

"I'm certain of that, Sir," said the Chief.

"We'll convince him of his wrong-doing and threaten him with bodily harm if he doesn't cooperate with us," said the Captain.

"No more commissions, right?" the Chief asked.

"That, and pay us back what he already stole!" exclaimed the Captain.

"Oh, brother, Captain, is he ever going to be pissed!" said the Chief laughing.

"I tell you, Chief. When I retire in five weeks, Cheryl and I are planning an extended world tour just to house hunt. And, you should never have to work another day if you live," said the Captain joyfully.

"It really does sound wonderful," the Chief said as he proposed a toast to the continuing success of 'Operation Sand Dune.'

"Without any doubt, Sir, you're truly a genius. Just to figure out this whole gold mining scheme and have it take place directly underneath the ever-watching eye of the Navy!"

"Thank you, Chief," said the Captain as he clicked his glass and drank up.

"Tomorrow I'll notify the guards and have everything ready," commented the Chief.

"Fine," asked the Captain. "Plan on the mast around midnight. That way Mr. Mayhen can be safely returned home before dawn."

A slight frown appeared on the Chief's brow and he said, "Sir, what about Mr. Lee? He's a very good friend of old Henry Mayhen."

"I know," the Captain replied then added, "do you recall when you took me out to meet with Mr. Lee on the freighter?"

"Sure," said the Chief. "I remember you spent about an hour talking to him about something."

"Among other things I mentioned that Henry Mayhem was getting in my way," said the Captain.

"Please, Sir, tell me more," the Chief said expressing great interest. "It seems that a while back Mr. Mayhen did a double cross and made Mr. Lee lose out on some sort of large shipment headed for Mexico. Mr. Lee warned me that Mr. Mayhen might try something similar with Cheryl," stated the Captain. Then he continued stating, "I really didn't know how to deal with this problem until recently."

"Of course, Sir. I think the sooner he gets our message the better," said the Chief.

"I agree, Chief. Mr. Lee's loss amounted to over four hundred thousand from Mayhen's double cross. If we can recover a large amount of cash from him, I will present it to Mr. Lee as a good will gesture," said the Captain.

"What do we get in return?" asked the Chief.

"Within a few weeks, Ken, we'll exchange gold with Mr. Lee on his freighter. Henry Mayhen will be completely cut off and penniless," advised the Captain.

"Have another drink, Sir. You have amazed me again with your logic," said the Chief.

"Thank you, Chief. Here's to you too," he said as their glasses again clicked together.

* * *

MONDAY, DECEMBER 3

The first week of December was very wet. Almost daily the sky opened, and the heavy rain caused many outdoor events to be postponed. However, the inclement weather posed no delay at the building site since all the activity was being done indoors. Each night the military sentries patrolled the perimeter of the construction site, and the flood lights provided them with clear vision of any activity within the construction compound once the workmen had departed each afternoon at 1630 hours.

Monday afternoon, Chief Sheppard met with Master Sergeant Miller and Corporal Lenert in the underground brig beneath Herbert Hall. They were the most qualified of the ex-Marines that had been chosen to serve in, *'Operation Sand Dune.'*

"Men, we have new problem to deal with. Listen up carefully," requested the Chief.

"Sure, Chief," they replied.

"There's a certain individual named Henry Mayhen who has been actively involved in our gold shipments. He has become a middle-man and the Captain wants him brought here to the brig tonight for some special instructions," the Chief informed them.

"Does he know where we are?" asked Sergeant Miller.

"No, and he must not find out under any circumstances," replied the Chief.

"What should we do, Chief?" asked Sergeant Miller.

"Follow my instructions to the tee. Do not do anything that would attract attention," the Chief told them.

"Certainly, Chief," they replied.

"The Captain and I decided that you, Sergeant Miller should enter Mr. Mayhen's assay office on California Street shortly before closing today and pose as a potential seller of precious metals. Show Mr. Mayhen a single gold nugget to get his attention and then invite him to accompany you to the location of more gold. Let the old man leave and lock his office," said the Chief.

"Where do I fit in, Chief?" asked Corporal Lenert.

"Corporal Lenert, you'll wait in the car hidden from view in the rear seat until the car leaves the vicinity. Then use this hypodermic containing a mild sedative," instructed the Chief.

Ken then handed the young Corporal an envelope containing the syringe and said, "this is provided to us complements of Corpsman Thomas, the Captain's friend."

"No problem, Chief," said the Corporal.

"After you park the car on the beach, carry Mr. Mayhen to the storm drain entrance. Our guards will assist you carrying him into the basement brig. He should recover from the injection around midnight. At that time, you two may escort him, in handcuffs and leg-irons, down the passageway and into the Brig's Courtroom," said the Chief. Continuing, he told them, "the Captain and I will be waiting there to interrogate Mr. Mayhen while wearing our black hoods."

"No problem, Chief, the plan sounds excellent," Sergeant Miller said with a broad grin.

"You men have a good evening downtown on California Street, and I'll be at the storm drain entrance to over-ride the surveillance system when you arrive back with your guest," said the Chief.

"Thank you, Chief. You can count on things going smoothly," said the Sergeant.

* * *

Mr. Mayhen was very interested in the gold that the sergeant showed him that Monday evening before closing. He agreed to accompany the Sergeant on the trip to see the remainder of the gold supply. It didn't take Corporal Lenert very long to have Mr. Mayhen totally unconscious in the back seat of their car by using the injection. The trip was successful. When he awoke from his sleep, Mr. Mayhen found himself handcuffed from behind, wearing leg-irons and gagged. He soon realized he was inside of a small jail cell. As he struggled and attempted to call out for help, the hooded guards watching on the closed-circuit monitor notified the Captain and the Chief that their new prisoner was ready to stand at Mast.

Mr. Mayhen's eyes widened as two hooded guards entered his cell and pulled him out into the passageway. Handling him roughly, he tried to protest but was unable to make a sound with the guard's hand over his mouth. After he was slapped and had sustained a few blows to his midsection, he became very cooperative. The door to the dimly lighted courtroom was opened and he was made to stand facing a long table. Seated behind it were the Captain and the Chief. They wore black hoods and coveralls. He struggled to protest and was hit again by another hooded guard.

"Henry Mayhen. May this serve as a warning to you," the Chief said in a deep voice.

"You are interfering with my operation by requesting that the Lieutenant pay you fifteen percent commission each time she exchanges her gold with Mr. Lee," the Captain said in his usual straight forward tone since he had never met Henry Mayhen before. He again tried to argue, but to no avail. Stan then told the prisoner, "You are hereby ordered by this court to cease charging the lieutenant further commissions and are hereby ordered to return to Lieutenant Finley all the commissions that you extorted from her."

He shook his head sideways in protest towards the prosecuting bench meaning that he would not accept their conditions.

"Very well then, you will suffer bodily harm and your business will cease to exist if you fail to obey my order," the Captain said as he rose from the chair and approached the prisoner. Backing Mr. Mayhen up against the wall, the Captain could see that the old man's eyes were full of terror. He soon shook his head in agreement and behind the gag, pleaded not to be hurt.

Through the hood, the captain saw the man's will to fight diminish. The Captain then called the guards, "Remove him and return the prisoner to his cell."

Once he was taken there, he was again injected. Within a few seconds he passed out cold and was placed on the cell's cot.

* * *

TUESDAY, DECEMBER 4

It was morning when Henry Mayhen awoke. He was lying on a park bench near his California Street office. His cloths were quite rumpled and his wrists had red lines from the handcuffs. He staggered to get up but a tremendous headache made him fall back down on the bench.

After a brief rest, his eyes focused better and he managed to return to his shop. He struggled to his desk and picked up the phone to place a call to Señor Gartez.

"Si, Señor Mayhen here. I'm calling about a most urgent problem that has developed regarding the gold supply. I must meet with you, Your Excellency, at your villa. Si, tomorrow afternoon would be perfect. Gracias. Buenos Dias."

* * *

* 21 *

Captain Siegewick watched as his beautiful lieutenant girlfriend with the brightest smile and flashing green eyes called Henry Mayhen on the phone to tell him she had more gold to exchange with Mr. Lee. "Hello, Mr. Mayhen. This is Lieutenant Finley calling."

"Please, leave me alone. I'm very angry at what just happened," said Mr. Mayhen.

"Mr. Mayhen, you seem upset to hear from me. What's the matter?" Cheryl asked.

"Well, Lieutenant, there's been some recent developments that may prevent me from working with you in the future," Mr. Mayhen informed her.

"What happened?" Cheryl inquired.

"I'd rather only say that I was threatened last night and told to return my commissions to you from all your exchanges," said Mr. Mayhen solemnly.

"I... I don't understand, Mr. Mayhen. You earned them by allowing me to use your office for my exchanges," Cheryl said in bewilderment.

"Well, I've agreed to do that. Please come by this afternoon, and I'll have your check ready. I really am not up to being hurt or losing my business by dealing with you," said Mr. Mayhen.

"I'm sorry you were threatened. My sources don't inform me of their intentions," said Cheryl.

"Just come by, and forget we ever worked together," said Mr. Mayhen as he hung up the phone.

Hanging up the phone, Cheryl glared at Stan, "What the hell did you do to that poor old man?"

"I simply put him on notice that he should return the commission and no harm would come to him," said Stan showing his peculiar smile.

"Oh, Stan!" Cheryl said in disgust.

"Listen up, dear, that man has cost us over three hundred thousand dollars in extortion money commissions, and I want it back!" exclaimed the Captain.

"You're a greedy son-of-a-bitch! You only have about two million dollars at the other end of this key!" She pulled her dog tag from her blouse with the safety deposit key attached.

He quickly yanked it from her neck. She screamed and ran crying into the bedroom. He held the key for a moment, then put it safely into his wallet.

Knowing he still needed her to do his dirty work, he quickly changed face and entered the bedroom. He approached saying how sorry he was and that he would not lose his temper with her again. He held her hand and dried her tears with his handkerchief.

"Cheryl, darling, the money that Mayhen is returning will be given to Mr. Lee," Stan said as tenderly as he could.

"I... I don't understand," she sobbed.

"It seems that old Henry Mayhen owed Mr. Lee that money, and I told Mr. Lee that as a favor I would get it for him," said Stan.

"What's...the favor," asked Cheryl.

"You and I can now exchange the gold directly with Mr. Lee. Mayhen is completely out of the picture," Stan informed her.

"Are you sure, Stan?" Cheryl asked.

"I'm sure, "said Stan.

* * *

When Cheryl departed from their Mission Hills home for her final meeting with Henry Mayhen, Stan reached for the phone. "Hello, Chief Sheppard, please. This is Captain Siegewick."

"Yes Captain," said the Chief.

"Chief, listen up. I have some new instructions I want you to pass onto the secret brig guards," said the Captain.

"Excuse me Sir. I can't talk right now, there are too many people here in my office. Call me later aboard my boat after 1700 hours," said the Chief apologetically.

"Very well, Chief. Goodbye," said the Captain trying to conceal his agitation.

The Captain now placed a call to Base Headquarters.

"Yeoman Roth, Captain Siegewick. Is Commander Wilkins around?"

"Yes Captain. He's in his office," replied Yoeman Roth.

"Fine, transfer me. I'll hold," said the Captain. After a brief pause, the Captain continued, "hello, Commander. I need a status report on the condition of the base security. With Christmas vacation time coming up, and the visit from Rear Admiral McKinsey in three weeks, I need to know who will be available for what duties,"

"Certainly, Captain. I'll meet right away with Chief Sheppard and the new Sergeant Major of our Marine detachment," said the Commander.

"Fine. When can I expect your report?" asked the Captain.

"That status report will be on your desk in the morning." "Very good, Commander. Carry on," said the Captain.

The Captain hung up the phone and thought to himself, "I need some sort of practice drill to test how good the base security system really is."

Suddenly, the phone rang.

"Excuse me, Sir. Sergeant Miller, here."

"Yes, Sergeant. What is it?" asked the Captain.

"Sir, there's been another cave-in," replied the Sergeant.

"What! Where?" asked the anxious Captain.

"In the second tunnel, Sir. There are ten men trapped beyond the cave in within the great room. There's another very serious problem, Sir," said Sergeant Miller.

"What is it, Sergeant?" asked the Captain in an anxious voice.

"Sir, I think those men might find a way to the outside through the ventilation shaft and escape!" exclaimed the Sergeant.

"All right, listen up. Have some guards take the ten prisoners and clear out tunnel number two, and shore it up with timbers," ordered the Captain.

"Very good, Sir. But what about the ten prisoners trapped in the great room?" asked the Sergeant.

"Let's wait until we reach them. They may not have been too lucky. It seems that every time there's a tremor, sand continually pours into that space. I really don't think we have to be concerned with survivors, only finding their replacements," said the Captain with his peculiar smile.

"Yes, Sir. Understood. I'll report back as soon as I have some more information," said the Sergeant.

"Carry on, Sergeant Miller, I'll be calling the Chief in a few minutes. I'll tell him everything," said the Captain.

"Thank you, Sir," the Sergeant said as he hung up.

"I'm home," Stan heard Cheryl call from the other side of the house.

"In here, dear!" Stan called to Cheryl.

"Mayhen gave me the check and told me to be careful," said Cheryl grinning.

"Fine. Endorse it, and give it to me. Mr. Lee will take care of cashing it," said Stan while in deep thought.

She did as she was ordered and then left the room to prepare supper. The Captain now placed a call to the *"Yankee II."*

"Chief. Problem down below."

"What is it, Sir?" asked the Chief.

"Sergeant Miller called a little while ago to report that there was another cave-in, in the second tunnel," the Captain informed him.

"Oh, shit! This project always has complications," said the Chief angrily.

"Agreed, I instructed him to use the other prisoners and reopen the tunnel. You probably ought to check it out tonight. If there were casualties, see that our guards get some more local help," said the Captain.

"How local, Sir?" asked Chief.

"I don't care. Perhaps find some drunks among the bars to the south of Imperial Beach, along the Pacific Coastal Highway," said Stan in a frustrated tone of voice.

"Are you talking civilians, Sir?" asked the Chief.

"I am, Chief," replied the Captain.

"As you wish, Sir. I'll report back later. Oh, yes, Commander Wilkins called me to snoop about base security systems," the Chief said as an afterthought.

"Yes, give him whatever he needs. I'll meet with you later to discuss a little security drill that I'm planning," said the Captain.

"Whatever you say, Sir," said the Chief.

"Thank, you, Chief. Till then," said the Captain as if in deep thought.

"Dinner's ready, dear!" Cheryl called to Stan.

*　*　*

WEDNESDAY, DECEMBER 5

Mr. Mayhen crossed into Mexico around noon. He drove the sixty-five miles south along the Baja Peninsula's Coastal Highway until he reached the town of Ensenada. On the southern edge of the town was a side road, and he turned onto it and drove about four more miles. At the end, along the rugged coast was a magnificent Spanish style villa belonging to Señor Raul Gartez. Heavily armed guards were posted at the main entrance and at various positions along the courtyard walls.

Mr. Mayhen was welcomed by the head housekeeper and escorted into a patio covered with lush tropical plants. In the patio's center was a handsome three-level running fountain with a lovely view of the Pacific beyond.

"His Excellency will be right out, Señor," said the housekeeper.

After being seated and given a tropical drink by the housekeeper, Henry arose to greet Señor Gartez.

"Your Excellency, how good of you to meet with me," Henry said while slightly bowing his head.

"Señor Mayhen, the information you have already furnished me has caused great interest among my followers and supporters," said Señor Gartez as he carefully watched Henry's reactions.

"Sir, I've been threatened with bodily harm, and business ruin by the Lieutenant's gold supplier," replied Mr. Mayhen.

"Por favor, continue, Señor Mayhen," said Señor Gartez showing great concern about what he had just heard.

"Sir," continued Mr. Mayhen, "under the direst threats to me, I was forced to return the legitimate commissions that I had charged the lieutenant for exchanging her gold."

"I see, Señor Mayhen. You also wish to recover your losses?" asked Señor Gartez.

"Yes, Your Excellency," replied Mr. Mayhen.

"My secret army here needs the proceeds from that gold. If we are to become an influential force in Mexico City, then this gold money is needed to bring down the current regime," Señor Gartez informed Mr. Mayhen.

"There is much gold, Your Excellency. Already the Lieutenant has exchanged many troy ounces amounting to a large fortune," stressed Mr. Mayhen.

"That would be an excellent boost to the moral of my troops," said Señor Gartez. Continuing, he said, "I could then pay them to fight for me. Now they only protect me."

"What action would your people take to secure the gold?" asked Mr. Mayhen.

"Señor Mayhen," Gartez said with a smile. "First my people in San Diego will tail the lieutenant and find out where she lives, and whom she sleeps with. Then, when the time is right, she will be invited here as my special guest to discuss a business venture."

"What makes you think that my Lieutenant will want to do business with you, Your Excellency?" asked Mr. Mayhen.

"I have many convincing ways, Señor Mayhen," said Señor Gartez expressing a sinister grin on his face.

"And what about the source of her gold, Señor Gartez?" asked Mr. Mayhen.

"Ah, si, the gold. I'm positive that your Lieutenant will tell me of its location...and then my people will take it away from the Gringoes!" he said with an evil laugh.

"I see, Your Excellency," commented Mr. Mayhen.

"What's your Lieutenant's name, Señor Mayhen?" asked Señor Gartez suddenly.

"Finley, Your Excellency, Lieutenant Cheryl Finley, U.S. Navy," replied Mr. Mayhen quickly.

"How may I identify this Lieutenant Finley?" Gartez pressed. "She's in her mid-twenties, about five feet five, and has auburn colored hair with big beautiful green eyes. That's all I can tell you now...because...Your Excellency, I need to be paid my commission today...for all this information that I have given to you," said Mr. Mayhen meekly.

"Ah, si, Muchos Gracias, Señor Mayhen. Your commission will be paid by me personally," assured Señor Gartez.

Suddenly there was a loud burst and Mr. Mayhen fell backwards into the flower bed. Handing the small caliber revolver to his servant, Gartez said, "Pedro, have Señor Mayhen's body removed to a better grave site than my patio. Gracias."

*   *   *

* 22 *

The Captain and the Chief met Sergeant Miller later in the basement brig area and were told by the Sergeant of the effects of the most recent cave in. "All ten of the dead prisoners have been recovered and buried near the others in the first tunnel, Sir. Here are their dog tags," Sergeant Miller said as he handed the Captain the group of metal tags and chains.

Taking the items, the Captain said, "Thank you, Sergeant, I'll put them in my desk drawer with the others."

"Sir, that second tunnel still is not one-hundred percent stable," stated the Sergeant.

"Use what you need to shore it up and to make the passageway usable," said Chief Sheppard.

"Understood, Sir," said the Sergeant.

As the men continued talking, they were suddenly interrupted by Corporal Lenert. "Excuse me, gentlemen, I've just returned from the great room. There seems to have been significant movement of the southeast rock wall from the last tremor, and now there is exposed another large vein of gold!"

"How wonderful!" exclaimed the Captain.

"Nothing appeared to have been damaged here in the brig," the Corporal told the Captain.

"One problem, Sir," said Corporal Lenert.

"I knew it! What?" shouted the angry Captain.

"Water is now being mixed with the sand, Sir. It will take twice as long now to move on the conveyor due to its weight," replied the young Corporal.

"Chief, let's get the guards out recruiting right-a-way," ordered the Captain.

"Agree, Sir," replied the Chief.

"Sergeant Miller, you and Corporal Lenert work with the Chief. I must get back topside before I'm missed," said the Captain.

"We'll take care of this new development, sir, and notify you as to when another group of gold packets are available for exchange," said the Chief.

"Carry on, men," the Captain said as they saluted each other. The Captain walked down the dimly lighted red colored passageway to the record office of the secret brig. There was no guard posted since all the gold packets had recently been exchanged. He entered the room and unlocked the desk drawer. He removed the green ledger that Cheryl had been keeping for him and closely read the most recent entries.

Two million dollars was now in the safety deposit box. He really did not comprehend how many actual stacks of money the box could hold. Cheryl said that the stacks were bundles of ten thousand dollars each. The box now contained two hundred bundles. The Captain took out his wallet. Reaching inside, he removed the safety deposit box key, and Mr. Mayhen's check for three-hundred-thousand dollars. He put the check inside the ledger and slipped the key under the plastic covering of the book. Then he thought, "I must not forget to tell Cheryl that her book and key are down here. Oh...she still doesn't know about this brig or the mine...so I guess I should only tell the Chief."

He returned the ledger to the desk drawer. Turning towards the hat rack, he grabbed his cover and left the underground space through the steel door. The Captain quickly passed through the connecting tunnel and followed the storm drain back to the beach.

THURSDAY, DECEMBER 6

When the Captain arrived at the Base Headquarters, Commander Wilkins immediately called at his office door. "Good Morning, Sir. Here's the status report of the base security system," he said as he passed the Captain's desk and headed for the coffee.

"This doesn't look too encouraging, Commander," the Captain said as he examined the report.

"Any foreign spy would have a field day in this place. Herbert Hall alone has few provisions to protect the millions of dollars in electronic equipment now being installed," the Commander told the Captain.

"When is Rear Admiral McKinsey scheduled to arrive here again?" the Captain asked.

"Fortunately, not until five January, Sir, to attend your retirement dinner and Herbert Hall's dedication ceremony the following day," replied the Commander while drinking his coffee.

"We really should beef-up the base security, and maybe plan some sort of mock security breech prior to his arrival," said the Captain.

"That shouldn't be a problem, Sir. I think the Admiral would be pleased to know that the team at Fort Warren is committed to maintaining top base security," said the Commander proudly.

"All right, Commander. You set something up, and we'll address it at the next briefing on twelve December," ordered the Captain.

"Very good, Sir. Oh, by the way, I told Mr. McCoy that his people could begin disassembling the fencing around Herbert Hall. The landscaper wants to start final planting toward the end of the week," said the Commander as an afterthought.

"That's fine with me, Commander. Is there anything else?" the Captain asked.

"Well Sir, my wife, Sofia, informs me that she sees Lieutenant Finley come into her bank a lot. Each time the Lieutenant has a brown briefcase containing cash," said the Commander hesitantly.

"Do you suspect something, Commander?" asked the Captain remembering what the Commander had said.

"I did a while ago, Sir. I thought she may have been stealing money from the Dispersing Office," said the Commander with a frustrated look on his face.

"What changed your mind, Commander?" the Captain asked with much curiosity.

"Well, I checked with Lieutenant Commander Ellerly and she assured me that everything was in order. She even showed me the ledger books that contained all the entries for the Herbert Hall accounts. Each entry appeared to be correct, Sir," replied Commander Wilkins.

"I see, Commander, since the Lieutenant has been staying with me, she has received some money from an estate settlement back East somewhere. That is what she is taking to the bank. Rest assured that Lieutenant Finley is just conducting family business," said the Captain.

"Very well, Sir. Thank you for removing my suspicions about her. We all really like Cheryl and I'd feel bad if she got herself tied up with some wrong-doers," said the Commander.

"Yes, I feel the same way, Commander," added the Captain.

* * *

Señor Gartez instructed his agents in San Diego to begin tailing Lieutenant Finley. He wanted to know everything about her. He must find out what her source of gold was.

Within the week, the first agent reported by phone and reached him while he was attending a political rally in Mexico City. The agent said, "Your Excellency, the Navy Lieutenant lives in the Mission Hills district with a Naval Captain. He is the commandant of Fort Warren. They rented the house on a six-month lease beginning August the fifteenth. They drive to the base together and return home together each evening around six."

"Excellent work, gracias, Señor. Continue to make your reports," Señor Gartez told his agent.

*   *   *

Because of the most recent earth tremor, a new vein of gold was revealed on the wall in the great room. Ten civilian *miners* wererecruited locally and forced to labor long hours to free only a mere fraction of the gold. The workers had to constantly move the shifting sand that steadily poured into the great room. At one point the conveyor broke from the sheer weight of the wet sand. It took three days to repair the conveyor.

*   *   *

TUESDAY, DECEMBER 11

The Captain now had enough gold to set up another exchange between Mr. Lee and Cheryl. He called Mr. Lee's secretary and said, "Yes, tell Mr. Lee that Lieutenant Finley and I will come aboard his ship tomorrow."

The secretary replied, "The freighter will be docked at the Marine Terminal downtown. See Mr. Lee at 10 P.M.."

"Very well, 2200 hours will be fine," said the Captain.

The Captain then called Chief Sheppard. "Chief, there's to be an exchange. Bring me the gold tomorrow after work."

"Very good, Sir," replied the Chief.

"Oh, by the way, Chief. Do you have anything to share at tomorrow's briefing about a test of the base security system?" the Captain asked.

"Yes, Sir. I've been working closely with Commander Wilkins, and we've come up with an interesting situation for the security forces to deal with," said the Chief.

"Sounds good, Chief. How are the new '*miners*' working out?" asked the Captain.

"The civilians were a bit confused to begin with and tried to fight with the guards, but they got their new assignments straightened out real soon. They seem to be accepting military life well with their new collars as part of the regulation uniform, Sir," said the Chief grinning.

"Excellent. Have there been any more tremors down below?" asked the Captain.

"Sir, that's got to be one of the most dangerous places to work in that I've ever experienced," said the Chief.

"Well, after next month when I retire, I'll personally supervise the operation daily and determine what will be the best way to continue the mining," said the Captain with a faraway look in his eyes.

* * *

WEDNESDAY, DECEMBER 12

The morning was cloudy and wet as the staff assembled in the Commandant's Office for their briefing at 0900 hours.

"Officers, I would like you to meet my successor, Captain Douglas Howerton," Captain Siegewick said as he introduced the newly assigned Commandant-to-be to the group.

"I believe you already know Commander Wilkins from a previous Command," Captain Siegewick said to Captain Howerton.

"Yes, Commander. Good to serve with you again," said Captain Howerton smiling.

"This is Lieutenant Commander Ellerly and her assistant in the Supply Division, Lieutenant Cheryl Finley," Captain Siegewick said with pleasure.

"Ladies," Captain Howerton said as he shook their hands.

"Welcome aboard, Captain," they replied.

"This is our Public Affair's Officer, Lieutenant Lighal," said the Captain.

"Lieutenant," Captain Howerton said as he shook his hand. "And here is the backbone of the entire operation, Chief Master-

At-Arms, Sheppard," said Captain Siegewick proudly.

"Howdy, Captain Howerton, welcome to San Diego and Fort Warren," the Chief said as he shook the new Captain's hand.

"Thank you, Chief. It is a real pleasure to be here. Please consider me as strictly a casual observer for the next month. When I assume command on five January, I'll decide what changes may be in order," said Captain Howerton trying to put the Chief at ease.

"As you wish, Captain Howerton," Captain Siegewick said offering him a mug of coffee. "Thank you, Captain Siegewick," said Captain Howerton who added, "please continue with your briefing."

"Chief, I believe you may proceed with your information,"

"Thank you, Captain Siegewick. I'll be coordinating with base security to inspect all existing systems. They should make full reports to me regarding their status and condition of security."

Commander Wilkins said, "I've been notified by the Department of Defense of possible terrorist threats to military installations because of recent activities south of the border. The Mexican Government is having internal problems. Some groups might resort to terrorist tactics. They would like to provoke our Government to support their new liberation front instead of the current regime."

Captain Siegewick then notified his staff, "The new security guidelines will be strictly enforced. I certainly don't want any God damn terrorist getting on base and planting an explosive device, especially with the new class of junior officers starting their training at Herbert Hall on the first Monday in January."

The officers all agreed to do their part.

"I'll now turn the meeting over to Lieutenant Lighal who has an additional item of interest to everyone," said the Captain as he sat down.

"Thank you, Captain Siegewick," said Jim. "Our Christmas office party has been scheduled for the twenty-fourth at the Officer's Club, 1600 hours."

"That's all. You're dismissed. Good day," replied Stan to the assembled group. Following the briefing, Cheryl and Captain Siegewick walked outside, and then Cheryl departed with Lieutenant Commander Ellerly to return to the Supply Office. Captain Howerton and Commander Wilkins also left for a tour of the training center.

Captain Siegewick came back inside Base Headquarters and met Chief Sheppard alone in his office. "Listen up, Chief. I've determined that our Mr. Lee wants direct access to our mining operation, and he's looking for a way to find it. Right now, he's probably tailing us to find out the mine's location. Tonight, I'm going to invite Mr. Lee to allow some of his people to join us in our little security breach."

"Begging you pardon, Captain," the puzzled Chief asked. "You want to invite his private body guards to attack our Base?"

"Not the Base, the storm drain," said the Captain.

"But, Sir, if the sensor indicated that the storm drain was being invaded, that would bring the entire Marine detachment to the front door of our mine!" the Chief insisted.

"Well, they still would be one thousand feet away from our tunnel," the Captain noted. Then he added, "Listen, if Lee's men are apprehended or killed by Fort Warren's Marines, that would eliminate him from trying to gain personal access to our gold. Our people would not be involved at all and would remain hidden throughout the invasion. This possible threat to our mine could be legally eliminated."

"Do you think he'll agree to it?" asked the Chief.

"I have a check for three-hundred-thousand that says he'll send us his men," the Captain told the Chief.

"Can we find someone else to exchange our gold with after next month?" the Chief asked.

"Of course, we haven't contacted anyone outside the San Diego community. There must be others who will eagerly exchange with us," replied the Captain.

Captain Siegewick's remaining workday was hectic and towards late afternoon Captain Howerton and Commander Wilkins came by. The Commander informed him, "Sir, Captain Howerton and his wife will be in your old headquarters tomorrow."

"Very good, Commander," Captain Siegewick replied, then turned to Captain Howerton and said. "I hope you and your wife will like our little home here."

"Yes, Captain, everyone seems to be most friendly," said Captain Howerton.

"Carry on, gentlemen, I've had a busy day, and I'm out of here," Captain Siegewick said saluting them both.

"As you say, Sir. We're out of here too," said the Commander saluting.

* * *

Captain Siegewick departed his office around 1630 and met Cheryl. On the drive home, he told her, "We'll meet with Mr. Lee tonight."

After dinner both Stan and Cheryl changed into civilian clothes and drove to the marina to meet Chief Sheppard. He gave them the two new packets of gold, the safety deposit box key, and Mr. Mayhen's check from the green ledger, which he had recovered from the secret brig's record office.

Stan gave the gold key back to Cheryl who then attached it to her dog tag. She put the packs of gold into her briefcase while Stan put the check in his wallet. He then drove Cheryl downtown to the city docks. After passing several freighters, Stan recognized Mr. Lee's ship.

"The *Dragon Lady, Hong Kong*. Remember that name, Cheryl. Mr.

Lee travels aboard her when he visits San Diego," said the Captain.

"That's some ship, Stan," she said eyeing the huge length of the freighter. It was docked alongside a smaller ship of Panamanian registry. Stan parked the car and escorted Cheryl. Together they approached the ship.

Pulling in behind a low dock shed, a white car with black windows came to a quiet stop near a phone booth. A dark figure emerged and placed a phone call. "Si, Your Excellency, the commandant and the lieutenant have gone aboard a freighter. The ship is registered in Hong Kong. The ship is moored and not getting underway. I'll wait until they depart. Then I'll find out who they met with."

Stan and Cheryl walked up the gangway and were met by the officer-of-the-deck.

"We are here for our 2000-hour meeting with Mr. Lee, sir," said Stan in his best formal voice.

"Yes, may I inspect the lady's brown briefcase for our security?" the officer requested.

Cheryl opened the case and showed the officer that it was empty except for two packages containing the gold ore.

"Mr. Lee will be pleased," he reported. Just then, a young Oriental sailor approached.

"Follow this man. He'll take you to Mr. Lee," said the officer politely.

Their escort was armed with a sub-machine gun and a side arm. They were lead up several ladders on the superstructure to a cabin near the bridge. Their escort knocked on the hatch and then opened it.

"Welcome, Lieutenant and Honorable Stan," Mr. Lee stated as they entered his stateroom. The gold exchange took place first, and Cheryl put the stacks of money into her brown briefcase. Stan then told Cheryl, "Please wait in the other cabin. What I'm going to discuss with Mr. Lee is confidential."

"Very well, darling. I understand. See you in a bit," she said. When Cheryl left the stateroom, Stan said, "Mr. Lee, I know that you must be extremely curious as to where I am getting this gold that the lieutenant has been exchanging with you."

"Yes, Mr. Stan," said Mr. Lee. "I have been most curious ever since my first meeting with Lieutenant Finley."

"Mr. Lee, the lieutenant does not know where I am getting the gold and I need to keep it that way."

"I see," said Mr. Lee looking at Stan. "That's why you asked her to step into the other cabin."

"Sir, my source is located near the Naval Base where the Lieutenant works. She could get herself into trouble with the Navy if they knew of its location," said Stan.

"Very interesting, Mr. Stan," commented Mr. Lee.

"Mr. Lee, I need your assistance in recovering the gold. I cannot continue the mining operation alone and have decided that I must find additional help," Stan informed him.

"Why, certainly, Mr. Stan. My staff could easily assist you in your mining operation. However, this could cost you a percentage for their labor," said Mr. Lee smiling.

"Yes, I'm willing to pay you for this service. Oh, to begin with, here's a check from Henry Mayhen for three-hundred-thousand," said Stan showing the check to Mr. Lee.

"Mr. Stan, how did you ever convince Henry to pay you back his commissions that he collected from the Lieutenant?" asked Mr. Lee.

"After our last meeting, you said he had double-crossed you and made you lose money. Well, I'm helping you recover it. All I need is for you to loan me your best men for a while, and we'll both become richer," replied Stan.

"You may use ten of my men to help mine the gold, Mr. Stan," said Mr. Lee.

"Fine, Mr. Lee. May I instruct them where to meet me?" asked Stan.

"Please, tell me, and I'll make the arrangements. The *Dragon Lady* is scheduled to get underway on Monday, December the seventeenth at 0600 hours. The men would be available to you on the sixteenth. I'll be returning here at the end of January," Mr. Lee informed Stan.

"I can provide them housing and safe working conditions until you return. Within that time, your men will be able to mine more gold then you can imagine," said Stan.

"Excellent, Mr. Stan. My men will be waiting your pick up next Sunday night," said Mr. Lee trying to hide his excitement about the new adventure.

"Thank you, Mr. Lee," Stan said as he handed him the check. Both men bowed. Stan left to get Cheryl and to head home.

* * *

* 23 *

THURSDAY, DECEMBER 13

During her lunch break, Cheryl drove herself to the bank and put the cash into her safety deposit box. She quickly left and returned to the Base before she was missed. She failed to notice the white car with the black glass windows continuing past the main gate of Fort Warren just as she turned onto the Base.

"Señor Gartez," the voice said. "Today the Lieutenant paid a visit to the San Diego Bank and Trust at lunchtime. She carried a brown briefcase with her. She was seen going into the vault. The tellers in the bank talk friendly to her like she comes there regularly. Last night she and the Commandant went aboard the freighter, *'Dragon Lady.'* The ship belongs to a Mr. Lee from Hong Kong. He is very rich and buys gold for his overseas factories."

"Gracias, Señor. Continue to follow the Lieutenant and report everything to me," requested Señor Gartez.

*   *   *

FRIDAY, DECEMBER 14

The Captain had met with the Chief and laid out the strategy for the so-called security breach using Mr. Lee's men. The Chief put the base's Marine detachment on notice to be prepared for a possible terrorist attack.

The Chief then met with Sergeant Miller and informed him, "Your prisoners are to remain in their cells Sunday until the security breach operation is completed."

"Yes, Chief. That can be arranged," said Sergeant Miller.

"Sergeant, have your men disassemble the conveyor system in the storm drain section tomorrow and seal off access to our tunnel. We're expecting some unfriendly guests Sunday night to trespass our working space. They shouldn't be aware of our presence," said the Chief.

"Understood, Chief. Are we to cease mining operations?" asked the Sergeant.

"Only cease depositing sand on the beach. Have the prisoners put the sand in another location until we can resume normal operations next week. This exercise is really to let Commander Wilkins experience a real-life terrorist threat at Fort Warren," the Chief advised him. Feeling very pleased with himself, he added, "those assholes still won't find our mine."

"But, Chief, if we remove the conveyor, and seal up the tunnel leading to Herbert Hall's basement this weekend, how are we to enter and exit ourselves?" the Sergeant asked.

"I guess you won't, Sergeant. Tell your men to prepare to spend the weekend here," ordered the Chief.

"We'll bring in supplies enough for the twenty prisoners and for ourselves tomorrow," said the Sergeant.

"That will be fine. Carry on," said the Chief as he saluted and departed.

* * *

SUNDAY, DECEMBER 16

At 1800 hours, Captain Siegewick watched as Mr. Lee supervised his ten sailors. They loaded all their gear into the van the Captain had provided. Mr. Lee, before departing in his limo, instructed his men, "You've been personally selected by myself to participate in this great opportunity for my company. What you will learn and the many benefits from your hard work will be generously rewarded by me."

The assembled men smiled and bowed to their boss.

"Mr. Stan, these are my most trusted men. They have been instructed by me to follow your directions closely," said Mr. Lee assuring the Captain of the caliber of his selected men.

"Thank you, Mr. Lee, for allowing me to use your staff on this project. They should really be able to expiate matters. I will personally guarantee the safety of each man." Turning towards Lee, he softly promised that, "The gold will be ready for export to Hong Kong upon Lee's return the following month."

The men shook hands and Lee entered his limo.

"That man suspects nothing," thought the Captain as he drove the van away from the pier. Within a half hour, the van was parked off the Pacific Coast Highway just north of Fort Warren.

"Mr. Chan, have your men walk down the beach along the ocean-side of those dunes. About a half mile down the beach, there's a storm drain on the left that empties onto the beach from the cliff. Lead your men into that storm drain and travel about two thousand feet. There you'll meet my people who will escort you into the gold mine," said the Captain.

"Mr. Stan, the mine is under Fort Warren?" Mr. Chan asked.

"No, the mine is under those hills to the east of the base. This is the only way to get into the mine," the Captain reassured him. Then he added, "my people will pick up these personal belongings of your men and store them in the Base accommodations we have readied for you."

"Very well, Mr. Stan, Mr. Lee told us that you were to be trusted, and we were to carry out your instructions exactly. I have no further questions, Mr. Stan. Thank you," said Mr. Chan who then bowed and led his men down the darkened beach.

Stan drove the van to a nearby phone booth and called the Chief at his on-Base Security Office.

The Captain told the Chief, "Tell Sergeant Miller to have his people sit tight. When the Asians set off the storm drain alarm in your office, instruct the Marine detachment to enter the manhole in the street a thousand feet from the corner of the Herbert Hall construction. Tell our Base Marines that this is the real thing and to use live ammo."

"Understood, Captain. We're ready for these Oriental terrorists. Our Base Marines will take them out in short order," the Chief assured the Captain. As the first man entered the storm drain, the silent motion light sensor was tripped. However, as Chan's men proceeded down the darkened tunnel, they heard no sounds. They took their time getting accustomed to the darkness and walked slowly past the real mine's entrance.

The Marine detachment, being already on an alert status hustled to meet the Chief Master-At-Arms at the correct manhole location to enter the storm drain from the street. Their M-16 rifles were ready for action. Twenty Marines wearing night camouflage quickly disappeared down the manhole with their orders. Within a moment, the Chief heard a burst of gunfire emerging through the opened darkness of the manhole from deep underneath the street.

* * *

* 24 *

MONDAY, DECEMBER 17

By 0815 hours, Commander Wilkins had already notified the Commandant about last night's terrorist attempt on the Base through the storm drain tunnel. Answering one of the Captain's questions, Commander Wilkins said, "Correct, Sir. All ten Asians were taken out by our base Marine detachment. The Asians carried weapons."

"See that those Marines are properly recognized for their brave actions in the defense of our base," ordered the Captain.

"Certainly, Sir. I'll be forwarding a final report and their recommendations to Admiral McKinsey later today," replied Commander Wilkins.

"You do that, Commander. Please inform Captain Howerton of your actions," said the Captain.

"Certainly, Sir," agreed Commander Wilkins.

Each man saluted. The Commander left the Captain's office closing the door behind him. The Captain then proceeded to call Chief Sheppard. "Chief, I must congratulate you on a job well done."

"Thank you, Sir, I couldn't have done it without you," said the Chief.

Each man laughed, feeling much relieved over lessening the threat to their mining operation while giving the base marine detachment some target practice.

"How's the crew down below, Chief?" the Captain asked.

"They did fine, Sir, according to Sergeant Miller who told me that everyone really jumped when the shooting began," replied the Chief.

"I guess we all did," laughed the Captain.

"Sir, he did report that the gunfire caused more sand to enter our workspace," advised the Chief.

"That infernal sand. Where the hell does it all come from?" asked the Captain.

* * *

THURSDAY, 0430 HOURS, DECEMBER 20

The ten miners stopped digging sand when one of the group noticed that the guards were nowhere in sight. The prisoners carefully removed each other's electric collar. The men decided the time was right to attempt to escape and expose the mining operation to the authorities.

The band of prisoners slowly and carefully crawled on their hands and knees. Red lights glowed in the narrow passageway when they entered from a side tunnel. The leader of the group was an older, higher-ranking petty officer. He had been kidnapped and brought back in September from his Tijuana liberty weekend.

They stopped when they heard voices approaching from another tunnel. The group instantly sought refuge in many of the smaller and non-illuminated sidewall niches. As two guards approached, one guard was talking back to the brig on his walkie-talkie. Suddenly, two of the prisoners threw rocks that struck each guard directly in the head. Once the two guards had fallen to the tunnel floor, the unrestrained prisoners quickly finished off the guards with their newly acquired M-16s and pulled their bleeding bodies into a dark tunnel. When the brig command called the guard names and got no response, they knew there was trouble and that possibly prisoners were loose. Two prisoners now carried the M-16s and led the others through the red lighted tunnel.

Back at the command center, the remaining guards decided to cut the electric power to the mine. They proceeded to assemble and use their night scopes to hunt down the freed prisoners.

When the escaping prisoners were plunged into the eternal darkness of the mine tunnels, they cried out to each other for help. Even their leader was totally at a loss for helping his men.

The armed guards entered the black tunnel and proceeded without hamper to the area of the prisoners. Understanding their inability to capture all ten prisoners at once, they elected that each guard be responsible for one man.

Moving silently behind each prisoner, the night vision equipment allowed the guard to hit their victim over the head and carry the man back to the brig unconscious. After five prisoners had been recovered, there was an exchange of gunfire.

Five prisoners lay dead on the floor of the tunnel. Then came the low rumble below the floor of the tunnel. The three guards quickly scrambled through the tunnel just as it collapsed and filled with oozing wet sand.

Sergeant Miller called the Chief before he left the marina for the base. "Yes, Chief, five were killed this morning in an escape attempt and five were recaptured."

"Shit! the Captain isn't going to be very pleased," said the Chief.

"I understand. There is another problem, Chief," said Sergeant Miller.

"What's that, Sergeant?" asked the Chief now becoming very upset.

"Their escape route caved in again. I'm afraid the survivors who took part in the escape will refuse to cooperate and force us to stop mining all together," explained the Sergeant.

"I see. I'll talk to the Captain and give you his decision," said the Chief.

"Fine, Chief. We'll wait to hear from you," replied the Sergeant.

The Chief called the Captain and reported the latest mining situation about the attempted escape. Later after speaking to the Sergeant, the Chief again called the Captain saying, "Hello Sir. Sergeant Miller believes that the five prisoners who were recaptured refuse to cooperate with us."

"It sounds like the five survivors actually didn't survive after all," replied the Captain in his usual tone of voice and peculiar smile.

Knowing what the Captain really meant, the Chief said, "I understand, Sir. I'll give Sergeant Miller the order to dispose of those five before they have a chance to upset us anymore."

"We'll find some new help, Chief. I'm certain of it," said the ruthless Captain.

* * *

FRIDAY, 1330 HOURS, DECEMBER 21

Shortly after lunch, Commander Wilkins and Lieutenant Lighal invited Captain Howerton and Captain Siegewick to tour Herbert Hall with Mr. McCoy. The men assembled at the construction trailer.

"Mr. McCoy," Commander Wilkins said, "I would like you to meet our new Commandant designate, Captain Howerton."

"Pleasure, sir," said Mr. McCoy.

"Mr. McCoy has overseen the construction since early June, Captain," Lieutenant Lighal told Howerton.

"Well, Mr. McCoy, I can't wait to see what you've accomplished since June," Howerton said.

"Would you gentlemen care for some coffee?" Mr. McCoy asked.

"Well thank you, Mr. McCoy," Captain Siegewick said accepting the mug, considering how Mr. McCoy didn't even greet him as he entered the trailer.

"When this project began last March, nobody ever realized how wonderful a structure this would turn out to be. Mr. McCoy, you've worked wonders here," Captain Siegewick told the other officers while attempting to shake

McCoy's hand, but Mr. McCoy quickly pulled it away with a disgusted look on his face.

"Oh, cheer up, Mr. McCoy, the late Mr. Bennet would have been as proud of your accomplishments as I am," said Commander Wilkins.

"I'm certain of that," Captain Siegewick added.

"Lieutenant Lighal has been keeping us informed of every detail concerning the building's progress. You've showed him a lot about construction, Mr. McCoy, and we appreciate your telling the Lieutenant about your procedures," Captain Siegewick added with a smile.

"Yes, Lieutenant Lighal seemed very interested in how everything was assembled, sir," McCoy said as he opened the trailer's door. "Come, gentlemen, we'll begin on the second deck and work our way down to the main lobby where the men are laying tile today."

* * *

Sofia Wilkins made a call to Cheryl that evening, to see if she would like to join her for some last-minute Christmas shopping at the mall. Cheryl was delighted to be on speaking terms again with Sofia. She still didn't know why Sofia had stopped talking to her at the bank. Cheryl never bothered to ask why.

"Stan, I'd like to go shopping with Sofia Wilkins at the mall tomorrow. Will that be all right?" asked Cheryl.

"Certainly, tell her I'll look forward to seeing her and the Commander at the Christmas party on the twenty-fourth, said the Captain."

"Sure, Sofia, I'll meet you in center court at noon. Goodbye," said Cheryl feeling good about going shopping.

As she hung up the phone, Stan took hold of her dainty hands and kissed her. "You know, darling," he said, "this Christmas will be the best one yet. We have accumulated a fortune in cash, and we have each other. As soon as I retire in two weeks you can resign your commission. We'll head so far from San Diego you won't believe it."

Feeling so happy, Cheryl said, "oh, Stan, it truly sounds so incredible. I could never have dreamed we would be so fortunate nor so rich from Naval life."

Stan said, "dear, I've not let anything or anybody come between what Chief Sheppard and I found last March."

"You've certainly struck-it-rich from what you both found. Will the Chief continue mining gold after we leave?" she asked.

"That's up to him. I've gotten all we'll ever need," replied Stan.

Stan helped Cheryl finish decorating the Christmas tree in the family room. He then went through the rest of the house turning out the lights while Cheryl prepared herself for him. Together they made passionate love on the sofa in the family room, their naked bodies became illuminated by the many-colored lights of the tree. They gently kissed and caressed each other. He had experienced Cheryl's desires before, so he knew where to touch her. Her large nipples became immediately hard as he touched them with his tongue. She moved her soft hands over his chest and lowered herself to better consume his hardness. She panted and moved her hips to allow his entry. Together they became one. Around midnight, they rose to enter the darkened bedroom. Falling on the bed, they continued their romance.

*   *   *

* 25 *

SATURDAY, DECEMBER 22

Saturday afternoon at the mall was worse than being at the *San Diego Zoo* on half-price Kid's Day. Thousands of frantic shoppers jammed into every tiny shop. Sofia and Cheryl met in the mobbed center court near where the line of anxious children stood to visit a besieged and beleaguered, slightly tipsy, Santa.

The two women shook their heads and laughed at the whole crazy scene. Cheryl noticed two tall dark Spanish men wearing sunglasses and standing against the far wall. When the Cheryl and Sofia approached, the two men disappeared into a crowd of shoppers.

"I would like to check out this boutique," Sofia said, and pulled Cheryl with her into the festively decorated shop. The two men, having lost the girls in the crowd, left the mall and found a phone booth near their parked white car. The one man placed a call, "Si, Your Excellency, her commandant allows her to travel alone or with a girlfriend. Maybe soon, she'll be ready to visit with you."

"In a few more days things should be excellent, Señor. Gracias, and Buenos Dias," Señor Gartez told his agent.

* * *

New York City
MONDAY, NOON, DECEMBER 24

"I really want to get my boyfriend Todd one more gift, something unique," Janet Derr said to her senior editor in the press room as she put on her luscious mink hat and coat. "I'm going down to *Greenwich Village* this afternoon to see what I can find. Have a Merry Christmas, Mary, and I'll see you next Thursday."

"You have a Merry Christmas too, Janet, and best of luck finding that gift for Todd. Enjoy your vacation," her editor called as Janet happily scurried through the doorway looking the picture of youth and beauty.

"What a time to still be shopping!" thought Janet as she was pushed and pulled by the multitude of people on each sidewalk and cross-walk she encountered. She squeezed on the downtown "A" train at Times Square and soon got off at Christopher Street. Once she climbed the stairs to the street, the crowd had thinned somewhat. Now she could find her bearings. Janet proceeded down several short side streets filled with antique and curiosity shops.

"New York does have everything anyone could possibly want," she thought to herself. After about an hour of intense browsing, the afternoon sunlight brilliantly glared off something across the street in a shop window. The gleam from this unknown metal object immediately caught her attention.

Crossing the street for a closer look, Janet was delighted to find that the reflecting object was a beautiful golden hourglass. 'Finley's Antiques,' the sign over the doorway read. Janet wondered if the shop belonged to her old college roommate who was an avid antique collector.

Once inside the tiny shop, she was pleasantly surprised by a familiar voice.

"Janet Derr!" the excited voice said.

"Peggy Finley!" Janet replied. "Merry Christmas, and, how are you?"

"Just fine, Janet, and Merry Christmas to you. What brings you down here to the Village?" asked Peggy joyfully.

"Oh, I'm trying without much success to find my boyfriend a special gift," replied Janet.

"I see," said Peggy. "There are some unusual things still left. Was there anything he could use?"

"Yes," said Janet. "Todd has a time piece collection and that golden hourglass in the window really caught my attention."

"Mother just put it in the window yesterday. She bought it during the summer from someone in San Diego. It's been in a storage trunk until I found it and made her put it on display. Mother told me it dated back to the days of the California gold rush," explained Peggy.

"Really, now that would make him a wonderful gift," said Janet.

"I'll check with Mother about the price. She's upstairs. We run the shop together," Peggy said as she disappeared up the stairway. Upon returning, Peggy said, "the price is six hundred dollars."

"Do I have a choice?" thought Janet as she pulled out her charge card and handed it to Peggy.

"May I gift wrap it for you, Janet?" asked Peggy.

"Please, however much six hundred dollars will buy!" Both girls laughed. "How is your twin sister Cheryl doing these days?" asked Janet.

"Oh, haven't you heard? Cheryl is being very successful in her Navy career. She recently was promoted to the rank of lieutenant and she's stationed at Fort Warren in San Diego," Peggy said as she handed Janet the attractively wrapped box.

"Isn't that something - my boyfriend Todd is an architect, and he'll be flying out to San Diego after New Years to attend a ribbon-cutting ceremony at Fort Warren. Last year he designed an award-winning classroom building for the Naval Command there. The building has just been finished," Janet said proudly.

"Well, I'm jealous, my boyfriend only drives a cab, and me, a bit crazy!" Peggy said laughing.

The girls exchanged addresses and promised to keep in touch.

* * *

MONDAY, DECEMBER 24

In the early part of the afternoon on Christmas Eve, Cheryl took a long-distance phone call at her desk in the supply office.

"Thank you, operator," Cheryl said.

"Merry Christmas, Sister," said Peggy.

"Peggy! Merry Christmas to you dear," Cheryl said excitedly. "I was planning to call you and Mother a little later."

"Mother and I hope you are enjoying your time off," replied Peggy.

"Oh, Peggy, I am fine and always happy to hear your voice," said Cheryl happily.

Peggy said, "I called to tell you that I just sold that golden hourglass that your friend had sent us last July."

"Yes," said Cheryl. "I remember Stan sending it to your shop."

"Well, I'll bet you a million dollars you can't guess who bought it," said Peggy.

"All right, you can keep the money and tell me," said Cheryl.

"My old college roommate, Janet Derr," said Peggy excitedly.

"Oh, I remember meeting Janet several times a long time ago. Why would she want an old hourglass?" asked Cheryl.

"She bought it for her boyfriend, Todd Tasselmeyer," replied Peggy.

"Wait, I know that name," Cheryl told Peggy.

"Janet said he was the architect who designed your new classroom building out there," said Peggy.

"Why, yes! He designed our building, Herbert Hall! Isn't that a small world," stated Cheryl.

"Janet told me that Todd collects old timepieces and that the golden hourglass would be something he would really treasure," added Peggy.

"I believe Mr. Tasselmeyer is on the guest list for the dedication ceremony here the fifth of January," said Cheryl.

"Yes, Janet said he would be out there for it," said Peggy.

Cheryl then quickly became very concerned and asked. "How's Mother?"

"She's doing just fine. She still blames her condition on that mysterious hourglass. Once it left the shop, Mother seemed to be completely cured."

"It's a miracle," cried Cheryl out of sheer joy.

"It'll be a blessed Christmas now that Mother's health is fine."

"And you're sure she survived with no apparent permanent damage."

"None. Mom is fully recovered. She believes that just by handling that thing it made her sick. Like it was cursed or something."

"I just don't know. It didn't seem to effect Stan when he had it." "Didn't you tell me his quarters caught on fire?"

"Oh my! You may be right about that thing."

"Well it's your architect's problem now."

"Please tell me how's the love in your life doing, Peggy?" Cheryl asked.

"The company's giving Tommy a new taxicab for Christmas. He'll 'break-it-in' on the following day!" exclaimed Peggy.

"Those poor riders!" Cheryl said laughing.

"Well, dear Sis, Mom's here now so take it easy, and visit us when you're on leave. Merry Christmas," said Peggy.

"Merry Christmas, Peggy, thanks so much for calling," said Cheryl.

"Wait! Hold on. There's someone who wants to say hello."

"Merry Christmas to my darling daughter in California," said her mother.

"Merry Christmas to you, Mother. I'm so glad you're feeling better," replied Cheryl.

"You know darling in this business you get to examine and handle lots of items that you do not know their real origins. That golden hourglass was one of those pieces. It's as if it was cursed. I never felt so completely disconnected from reality as I did after handling that hourglass. I've been sick before...but for nearly five months!"

"I know, Mother. Peggy and I have been so concerned for you. My prayers seem now answered. You're better and Stan is just wonderful toward me. I've been helping him on a special project that will give us plenty of money for our lives together."

"Oh Cheryl. That sounds so good."

"Mom, I couldn't be happier. Stan and I are going to get engaged shortly and after he retires next month, we may plan an early wedding."

"That sounds wonderful, Cheryl," said her mother.

"Peggy sees that I take my pills and eat regularly. She's such a wonderful caring daughter to me."

"I'm glad. I love you too, Mom. I'll call again before the New Year to tell you about my holiday plans."

"Please don't forget to call, Cheryl. Goodbye," said her mother a little sadly.

"Goodbye, Mother," replied Cheryl also feeling a little sad.

* * *

Shortly thereafter, Cheryl joined Stan and the rest of the staff and their mates for the Christmas party at the Officer's Club. Stan took advantage of the festive gathering to make the announcement, "Ladies and gentlemen, Cheryl Finley and I are now engaged and we plan to wed in the early spring."

The group certainly was surprised by the announcement and immediately began to extend the couple their best wishes.

"So, the old man really will marry," said Lieutenant Lighal to Lieutenant Commander Ellerly.

"I really don't see what all the fuss is about," she barked.

"I suppose you'll never trap a man, Commander?" Lighal inquired.

"If I did, he'd better know checks and balances and never mention kids or pets!" Ellerly replied.

"Attention everyone," Captain Howerton said loudly. "May I propose a toast to the new couple. Health, Wealth, and Happiness." Everyone rose to their feet and clicked their glasses together. Stan moved quickly to the club's bar and was given one drink after another by his subordinates. Cheryl was somewhat embarrassed over the whole scene but continued to smile and exchanged pleasantries with the other officers' wives.

"Congratulations, Lieutenant," Ellerly told Cheryl. "I guess you'll leave Fort Warren when the Captain retires?"

"Oh, no, Commander. I'll be staying on for a while, at least until Stan decides where we should live and what type of work he wants to pursue," said Cheryl with a sly grin on her face.

"Very good, Lieutenant. Enjoy your nine days of vacation leave. I'll see you at your desk at 0800 on three January," said Ellerly sharply.

As the Supply Officer left, Cheryl thought, "I didn't think the witch would approve of me taking all that time off. Oh well, maybe the holiday spirit got to her."

"Oh, Cheryl. I was so happy to hear about your announcement," Sofia Wilkins said. "I do hope you two will be happy with all that..."

"That what Sofia?" asked Cheryl who knew she was going to say money.

"Oh...that time that you two will have together," said Sofia quickly.

Feeling her secret was secure, Cheryl said, "Yes, Stan and I do plan to spend a lot..."

"Cheryl, darling, do step over here for a moment," called Stan. She excused herself from her table guests and walked into the bar area.

"Since Chief Sheppard didn't attend tonight, he asked us to drop by the marina on our way home. Would that be all right?" asked Stan.

"Of course, darling. We both need to wish him a Merry Christmas anyway," replied Cheryl.

"I'm ready whenever you are," Stan told Cheryl.

"Let me use the powder room, and I'll meet you in the front lobby," said Cheryl.

* * *

* 26 *

MONDAY EVENING, DECEMBER 24, NEW YORK CITY

As Janet Derr handed her fiancé Todd Tasselmeyer the last gift, she smiled. He was somewhat startled by the weight of the small rectangular present. The paper and ribbon showed that she had taken extra care in wrapping the gift and the joy in her face showed she was excited to see his reaction. The time she had spent preparing for this moment had been worth its weight in gold.

He took his time, admiring and commenting on the beautiful wrappings. Todd, feeling as anxious as a small child, wanted to open the package and learn of its contents, but he also wanted the feeling of the moment to last if possible. The wrapping fell and the box lid opened. He pushed the insulation aside and finally the treasure was revealed. He was totally overcome with joy. He jumped up to kiss her and nearly spilled her glass of wine. It was such a fantastic gift. With great care, Todd carefully removed from the box what would become the focal point of his collection.

Janet had given her lover the ancient golden timepiece. It was twelve inches tall and five inches in diameter at both base and top. In front of the two glass orbs were three slender gold columns. The purest white sand filled half the lower chamber, indicating that yet another hour had passed into history.

"Where did you ever find such a beautiful hourglass?" he asked.

"Yesterday I went down to shop in Greenwich Village. That hourglass attracted my attention by reflecting the sun in the little shop's window display."

"Really caught your eye?" he said with a chuckle.

"I discovered that my old girlfriend from college, Peggy Finley, runs the antique shop," she added while taking another sip of wine. Then she said, "We exchanged addresses and information about our boyfriends. Peggy told me that her twin sister Cheryl is a Navy Lieutenant stationed at Fort Warren in San Diego. I told her about you and that you'll be out there after New Year's Day to attend the dedication of the building you designed for the Navy. Boy, was she ever impressed!" Janet continued, "I then inquired about Peggy's mom and she told me that she and her mother ran the shop. They had received the hourglass from San Diego last July as a consignment piece. Peggy said that her mom told her it was a real curiosity piece, and that it gave her a bad feeling. She believed it was a souvenir of the 'gold rush days.'"

Upon closer examination of the ancient hourglass, Todd noticed many signs of wear and tear and said, "This hourglass must have done some traveling in its day."

"Todd, I do hope you like it. It was the only one available," said Janet lovingly.

"It's just wonderful!" he replied. "It's truly a magnificent gift. I'm so pleased to add it to my collection."

Todd had been collecting timepieces and time-related items since his childhood and his collection contained about one hundred clocks, watches, and other unusual items. Among these were furniture and stuffed or ceramic animals with clocks "built right in," as he would say. All the timepieces were proudly and carefully displayed throughout Todd's Riverside Drive apartment in New York City.

He had spent a lot of time apartment hunting throughout lower Manhattan before he ventured uptown and fell in love with the classical looks of this fifty-year-old all-brick lady overlooking the Hudson River. The fifteen-story building had just undergone an extensive facelift and the work was done by true professionals who were sensitive to maintain the *Art Deco* exterior with its rounded corner windows.

Todd Tasselmeyer was a thirty-year-old registered architect who was six feet in stature with light brown hair and dark brown eyes. He was somewhat muscular from his days in college sports and his occasional workouts.

He had been born and raised in Queens, a borough of New York. He was of German heritage. His great-grandparents had arrived at *Ellis Island* in 1895. Being very pleased with the place– having no sense of direction, as Todd had said– they journeyed only as far as Queens. He had attended New York University and completed his two-year apprenticeship with a local architectural firm. Three years ago, he joined with two other architects and created the firm of TJS and Associates. Todd met Janet Derr two years ago while skiing in Vermont during a Christmas vacation. She moved into his Riverside Drive apartment about six months ago after they announced their engagement. They enjoyed each other's company and eagerly looked forward to their springtime marriage.

Janet Derr, a striking beautiful twenty-seven-year-old with Nordic heritage, was tall, slender, and had fine features that included bright blue eyes, and long blonde hair that she wore up. She had a well-toned figure and was very far from being "flat chested," much to Todd's enjoyment. She had been a journalism major in college and now professionally wrote 'Current Affairs' articles for <u>The Daily Times</u>. She had recently received a top award for an article on Central America. Everyone at the newspaper agreed that Janet really knew her trade and how to get the most information from her sources. She enjoyed this work that allowed her to travel and occasionally rendezvous with Todd in some far away and romantic location. Together, they tried to arrange their schedules to see the most of each other. Both called New York City home.

Janet poured Todd another glass of Chablis and together they surveyed the aftermath of their gift exchange for this year. She had received some new clothes that included a two-piece suit, a leather jacket, a handsome scarf, gloves, and some lingerie. For him, a sweater, cologne, wallet, and the hourglass. They were both very pleased with each other's gift selections. They continued to talk and share with each other stories of past Christmases and family traditions. Sitting silently on the teak coffee table with its handsome brass trim, the golden hourglass reflected the many-colored lights of the Christmas tree. After a time, the hourglass reflected the images of two naked young lovers on the overstuffed sofa. Sounds of love-making could be heard throughout the darkened apartment.

The superbly appointed apartment contained a gas log fireplace in large living room with two picture windows overlooking Riverside Drive and the Hudson River. The dominant feature of the room was the fireplace with a carved mantelpiece and an overhanging large gilded mirror. A generous size eat-in kitchen was situated to the right of the living room. The master bedroom, measuring eighteen by twenty- two feet, contained a king-size bed with a handsome teak headboard. To the side of the bedroom was a dressing area with a full bath. The smaller den was located off the living room and contained a single window that afforded a brief glimpse of downtown Manhattan.

The apartment's interior design was truly elegant because Janet had insisted they work with a professional decorator. Although she was difficult to understand because of her thick French accent, Michelle transformed his bachelor's pad into a comfortable place of peace and harmony using many pastels and brass trimmings.

Michelle enjoyed helping Janet, who thought that many of the decorator's ideas wouldn't work. However, Michelle showed her how they could improve the apartment and at the same time not cost a fortune. Michelle took great care to display Todd's timepiece collection in a decorative and tasteful way. She even used track-lighting to accent his antique grandfather clock and to highlight the numerous gold and silver pocket watches he had displayed on glass shelves.

Every hour throughout the day was a festival of chimes to welcome the passing of time. At bedtime, Todd turned many of the larger clock chimes off. Having put the chimes to rest and darkened the apartment, he and Janet retired to the bedroom. They both seemed especially tired. He was sure she would not ask him for an encore love-making performance after the session on the sofa. He was wrong. Their love-making continued for another forty-five minutes.

Todd always considered himself a light sleeper. He could quickly muster a strong "Who goes there?" sitting upright in bed ready to tackle any intruder.

"Living in the city, one must always be on guard," he told Janet. Never having been assaulted or robbed, he knew of those who had become the city's victims. Tonight, was somewhat different. Tonight, he would become a different sort of victim thanks to the invisible but powerful energy radiating from the golden hourglass. He would be both witness and victim to a bizarre plot, that would all but encompass every minute of his sleep, even though he was home in his Manhattan apartment.

The plot would be revealed slowly in his dreams. Only bits and pieces of information, destined to confuse and propel him into one of the greatest adventures of his life, would be experienced over the next week and a half. Tonight, Todd was restless and couldn't seem to get comfortable.

Janet, lying next to him, never had any problem falling asleep, staying asleep, or waking up totally refreshed. She told him how important rest and sleep were to allow one's body to rebuild itself. Janet enjoyed life and was aware of what was essential for good nutrition and proper exercise. She would often drag Todd...kicking and screaming...for a before dawn workout and run in Central Park. Todd believed the best exercise was just to keep the refrigerator door well-oiled so no one would hear him.

* * *

MONDAY EVENING, DECEMBER 24, SAN DIEGO

When the Captain's car left Fort Warren, another set of lights followed closely. The white car passed them as they turned into the marina parking lot. The Captain and Cheryl walked up to the pier and approached the Chief's spectacular new yacht.

"Permission to come aboard, Skipper," asked the Captain.

"Permission granted, and Merry Christmas to you both," the Chief replied as he handed them each a drink.

"We got engaged tonight, Chief," Cheryl said excitedly.

"Well, isn't that just terrific. You two have my congratulations. Please, come into my stateroom and make yourselves comfortable," the Chief said as he bowed when they passed him.

The trio drank and conversed until well past midnight. The Captain told the Chief, "I still had to get home and play 'Santa' for Cheryl."

The Captain then added, "She's been a very good girl this year. I just know that this old Santa has something special for her."

"You two be off then, and I'll call you on Wednesday the twenty-sixth for a status report. Merry Christmas," said the Chief with a sleepy yawn.

"Have a Merry Christmas too, Chief," Cheryl said as she gave the Chief a kiss for his hospitality.

Once they had left the Marina, the white car again followed them at a distance. When Stan entered the garage, he noticed the white car was gone. Closing the garage door, he and Cheryl entered their darkened house. Just as Stan reached for the light switch, Cheryl took his hand.

Together they walked silently through the house in the dark. When they reached the bedroom, they quickly began to undress. Cheryl had become accustomed to slipping off her dog tags and the safety deposit box key that was attached to the same chain before having sex with Stan. Tonight, as usual, she put the unattractive necklace on the night stand beside the bed.

"It's been a wonderful evening, darling," she whispered in his ear. "Let's save our gift exchange for the morning."

He passionately kissed her and held her close in his arms. He continued to touch her where she was most sensitive and she massaged him in a way that brought total arousal. Deciding that the foreplay was complete, he easily penetrated her. Together they found the most comfortable position and continued their love-making. After both had experienced sexual climaxes, they each fell into a deep sleep.

* * *

NEW YORK, DECEMBER 25, 1989

Around two o'clock on Christmas morning Todd arose from Janet's arms and went into the kitchen for a "refrigerator raid." After about five minutes of trying to get tops off and cling wrap opened, he settled for some sliced apples. He fixed a Bloody Mary and sat at the table staring out the window. The many lights from the New Jersey side of the Hudson seemed bright.

He thought, "*how many Santas were still losing sleep, frantically decorating trees and assembling toys from impossible to read instructions for their early young risers. These dear little children eager to disassemble and dismember the toys in front of their parent's blood-shot eyes even after their parent's nocturnal accomplishments.*"

Todd's own blood-shot eyes reflected a longing for children in his world. Someday, he'd be that proud parent losing sleep on Christmas morning. A distant siren could be heard, suggesting to him that some parent needed additional help. Traffic still zoomed below on Riverside Drive. The sky seemed hazy; perhaps tomorrow it would rain or snow.

He sat there for a brief time and then walked silently over and picked up the golden hourglass from the top of the teak coffee table. He held it up to the lighted picture window and watched as the tiny crystals fell effortlessly through the center into the waiting tomb below. The entire unit fascinated him. The gold seemed to glow a warm ocher color. Its heaviness suggested it was very well made. He pondered who was its previous owners, and what stories or secrets it held.

Returning to bed, he placed the hourglass close by on the night stand. He proceeded to fall asleep watching the tiny sand crystals fall.

*   *   *

Suddenly, he was walking across a sand dune. He could hear the roar of the surf, but he was unable to see it. It was daylight. The sand sucked at his shoes and was firm until he approached the dune's summit. Then, the sand just gave way. He felt he was being pulled down. It was a terrible feeling. The sand was covering him. Sand was crushing him. The unrelenting sand was devouring him. He cried out for help...

He awoke... covered with sweat and wrapped tightly in the bed linens with Janet looking at him sternly.

"What the hell are you doing?" she asked. "Go back to sleep, you must have been dreaming."

"I was dying," he said. "The whole damn thing felt so real! The sand was so cold; the ocean surf pounded so loudly." Then he kissed Janet and straightened the bed clothes. He attempted sleep but was unable. Soon though his mind allowed him a brief respite.

*   *   *

* 27 *

Christmas day arrived grey and blustery. Both Todd and Janet prepared to attend Morning Worship. Later, they would go off to visit family members.

Shortly before eleven o'clock, Todd and Janet quickly covered the two blocks in the cold to reach Riverside Church. The Church was very crowded and they had to sit near the back. Hundreds of red poinsettias and lighted candles made the Gothic Cathedral wonderfully festive. The Reverend Doctor Mettingly delivered an inspirational homely and the music was performed by a brass ensemble and pipe organ with a fifty-voice choir. When the final 'Gloria in Excelsis' sounded, they rose to leave. Upon passing one of the many niches in the Church, Todd noticed the Nativity.

He gave special notice to the statue of the Wise Man presenting his gift of gold to the infant Jesus. Todd wondered where this ancient king had obtained the chest of gold. He was certain that the king must have had more in his treasury. What wealth, he thought.

Their next assignment was to load the MG with gifts and head out for the Bronx. Both seemed specially to enjoy this holiday and the chance to compare adventures with relatives.

Janet wore her new outfit, jacket, scarf and gloves that Todd had given her the night before. She looked terrific. Todd warned her that his little brother would surely not stop pestering her for kisses and then he said, "Please don't use them all up on a ten-year-old." She charmingly laughed and called him "Jealous."

Todd had bought his little brother, the young future architect, a new-type of building block set that allowed the creator to first see his design on a computer screen. The computer then printed out a materials list for the young builder. It told exactly what blocks would be needed to recreate his design in 3-D. Upon seeing it in the toy store and the price, Todd had lamented that he didn't own stock in that company.

Janet's parents lived alone in the Bronx. Her older sister, with her husband and four adorable hellions, lived a bit further to the north.

Todd said, "Maybe this year Santa took the real kids away and left, in their place, some cute and well-mannered children."

Janet looked at him with a frown and said, "Behave, we'll only be there a short while." Then with a big grin she added, "I'll make sure the little darlings return any missing parts of your car before we leave."

"Thanks," he replied as he closed the trunk lid.

"We'll see them first, then end up at my parents' house later in the afternoon," he told her as he started the car. "I enjoy city life, but it doesn't give me much time for driving my MG."

"It seems to be running great and I can't wait until nice warm weather arrives so we can put the top down," she said.

*   *   *

The Christmas morning sun was high in the sky over San Diego's Mission Hills district when the lovers arose and entered the family room. Stan turned on the tree lights and they handed each other a gift. "Merry Christmas, Cheryl," said Stan smiling. I hope this is the first of many Christmases together. Here's a little something for you, with love."

She eagerly unwrapped the small beautifully wrapped package. Stan's gift was a magnificent engagement ring with a two-karat diamond handsomely mounted.

"Oh Stan! It's the most gorgeous thing I've ever seen!" exclaimed Cheryl.

"Only the best for my girl," he told her with a smile and a kiss. She presented him with two tickets for an all-expenses paid ski vacation to Beaver Creek, Colorado. They would depart the day after Christmas and return on the thirty-first.

"Will you have any problem getting leave?" Cheryl asked, a bit concerned because she had already gotten approval from Lieutenant Commander Ellerly.

"Not at all. Because I'm so close to retiring, Commander Wilkins and Captain Howerton can cover for me. The trip sounds wonderful. I've heard a lot about that place but never had the opportunity to visit. We should have a ball!" said Stan Joyfully.

"I hope you didn't mind if a few dollars didn't make it into the safety deposit box," she told him with a smile.

"Of course not, darling. That money is for our dreams," Stan said also smiling.

"Come, let me fix us something to eat," she said taking his arm and pulling him close enough to kiss, she led him into the kitchen. Stan assisted Cheryl in fixing brunch. They didn't travel anywhere Christmas day since both of their families were from back East. They spent the evening talking about their future.

*   *   *

By four-thirty that afternoon in the *Borough of Queens*, everyone had assembled at Todd's parent's house. The Christmas dinner was spectacular and everyone liked their gifts, especially baby brother. Todd had brought his newly acquired timepiece to show his family. Once Todd opened the box and the assembled gathering were surprised.

"So, son, this is what Janet gave you?" Todd's father remarked. "It is very handsome. A truly wonderful antique. Where did you ever find it, Janet?"

"I was down in Greenwich Village on Christmas Eve when I spotted it," she replied with a proud smile.

Todd's little brother carefully held the hourglass with fascination and asked, "How does it work?"

"The sand in the glass orb will flow for one hour into the other side and then must be turned again," Todd told him.

Their father then said, "Hourglasses were used in ancient times. Often a prisoner had only until the sand ran out to confess or be killed."

Todd's little brother's eyes widened and he became very interested, so his father elaborated, "Did you know that a lot of gold was stolen from the Americas in the 1500's and taken back to Christian Europe?"

"No, Dad. I didn't know that," replied Todd.

"There, the gold was melted down and re-cast into items for the Catholic Church or the royal families." Continuing, he said, "I once saw a craftsman hand-blow the glass, and how the sand was measured out and inserted. The glass was then melted shut. Glass-blowing is really an art that goes back many thousands of years."

Todd told everyone, "It certainly adds another dimension to my already interesting collection of timepieces."

He did not mention the first dream to his family. The remainder of the evening passed quickly. While driving back to the apartment, Todd asked Janet, "How about our future?" He knew she enjoyed children. Perhaps in springtime they would get engaged and marry by summer's end. Janet lovingly said, "We really don't need to rush things. We each need to better establish ourselves and save harder. I think we'll run in the morning-if it's not too cold."

*   *   *

"Stan, darling. I've been wondering for a long time where all those packets of gold nuggets come from. Now, could you please tell me the real story?" Cheryl asked as her big green eyes sparkled with the Christmas tree lights and she held up her empty glass. Heaving a sigh and handing her another drink, he figured it was safe to tell his future wife the truth.

"You know, darling, whatever I tell you, must be held in the strictest confidence. It has become a very involved and potentially deadly business," said Stan now looking very serious.

"Really, dear. You mean someone had died over this gold!" asked Cheryl hesitantly.

"Probably over the past four hundred years, since I believe it was first discovered by the Aztecs, this gold has led many a man to his demise," replied Stan.

"Oh my, please continue," she implored him, as she poured herself another drink.

"Since the beginning of last March, I've been convinced that Chief Sheppard and I have found what has turned out to be the 'Lost Dutchman Mine'," Stan said proudly.

"Wow! I thought that was only a legend, "said Cheryl almost in disbelief.

"You know this part of the country is full of stories and legends. I have come to believe that the 'Lost Dutchman Mine' was the 'El Dorado' that the Spanish Conquistadors sought in the 1500's. The gold from that mine was said to have built the famous 'Seven Cities of Cibola,' which Francisco Coronado and his Spanish expedition unsuccessfully sought for many years," Stan tried to explain.

"Yes, go on," insisted Cheryl.

As Stan continued, he said, "well, on the second day of March, the construction crew over at the Herbert Hall site experienced a cave-in near the southeast corner of that foundation. Two workers fell into what we thought was an abandoned well and were killed."

"Oh, my, how terrible!" she said putting her hands to her chin.

Stan continued saying, "Chief Sheppard and his men explored the well and discovered it was some sort of ventilation shaft to an old mine. There were three tunnels carved in the rock which converged at that location. He and I decided to somehow continue exploration without telling the Navy."

"I see," she said sternly. "And I suppose your 'exploration' cost the three hundred thousand dollars that was missing from the Herbert Hall account when I arrived her in August?"

Sheepishly Stan said, "In a way...yes, but you remember by the end of October all the money was paid back."

"Lucky for you. Ellerly was right all along! She would have skinned you alive if I hadn't covered your ass!" exclaimed Cheryl angrily.

"Yes, and I'll be forever grateful, darling," Stan said holding her hands in his while looking deep into her green eyes.

"I've passed the Herbert Hall construction project many times and I've not seen any evidence of people mining. How did you pull that one off?" she inquired, handing him another drink.

"Let me back up a moment, please," requested Stan.

"As you wish," said Cheryl trying to be patient.

"Remember I told you the tunnels converged at the cave-in site?" asked Stan.

"Yes, I remember," Cheryl replied.

"Well, although the tunnels were carved into rock, they were filled to the top with sand. It took many hired men to help me get the sand removed enough to find out what was there. All the sand had to be taken through the storm drain that runs under Fort Warren's main street. Over the months, the sand was deposited on the beach in front of the Naval Base. Most of it has washed away and no one ever suspected anything because nothing ever looked different." Taking a sip of his drink, Stan continued the interesting adventure.

"Early in July, the men that I hired to work in the mine tunnel found this old trunk buried beneath the sand. In that trunk were prospector's tools, some documents that belonged to the 'Dutchman Mining Company,' and the golden hourglass."

"That hourglass! The same one you sent to my sister Peggy in New York?" asked Cheryl.

"Yes, that was the one I had found in the trunk," replied Stan.

"Listen to this," Cheryl eagerly said. "Peggy called me yesterday to wish me a Merry Christmas. During the conversation, she told me that her college girlfriend, a certain Janet Derr, had just bought the hourglass that afternoon,"

"That's nice," Stan said with a yawn.

"Janet Derr is the girlfriend of Todd Tasselmeyer, the architect of our Herbert Hall project!" exclaimed Cheryl.

"Well, isn't that a coincidence. Maybe his heart will be cut out by the Aztecs and he'll stop bugging me for his payment," said Stan with that peculiar smile on his face.

"What did you say?" asked Cheryl.

"Oh, nothing, my love, nothing at all," said Stan not wanting to tell her about his bad experiences with the golden hourglass.

"Peggy said that Janet told her Todd would be out here next week to attend the dedication. Maybe you two could meet? After all, he did one hell of a job designing that beautiful structure," Cheryl exclaimed.

"Yes, he did," Stan thought to himself, then replied, "Herbert Hall is the pride of our Pacific Fleet's training facilities."

"So, dearest, the mine lies somewhere under Fort Warren?" asked Cheryl wondering.

"Heavens, no, the actual mine was located about a mile east, under those jagged mountains. See there," Stan said as he pointed out the family room window.

"Yes, we see those mountains each time we drive to Fort Warren," stated Cheryl. She continued to look out the window and, after a while, she said, "Well, it's been a wonderful and relaxing Christmas day, sweetie. I'm about to take a bubble bath and hit the bed."

"Go on, dear, I'll finish my drink and join you in a little while," said Stan approvingly.

Stan sat and stared at the lights on the Christmas tree. The many drinks that he had consumed now made him a bit dizzy. Suddenly, he began to see the face of each man who had been killed in his *"Operation Sand Dune"* reflected on the many Christmas balls and tree ornaments. He imagined seeing the two workers falling from their heavy equipment into the black pit below and screaming. Stan then saw George Bennet drowning as Ken's boat pulled away on the open ocean. Stan clearly recognized the young sailors who were electrocuted after digging the connecting tunnel. Stan's eyes blinked as he saw other faces of his prisoners contorted in pain and fear as they called out for help as tons of sand caved-in upon them and they gasped for air. Stan then envisioned Mr. Lee's men and those six innocent sailors being ruthlessly shot in the darkness of the tunnel.

"Oh, my God!" he screamed, spilling his drink and falling head first into the tree! Everything came smashing down with a loud crash.

Cheryl, hearing the noise, quickly grabbed her bath robe and rushed to aid her now stricken and crying fiancé.

"Are you all right!" she screamed. "What the hell happened?"

"I...I don't know what came over me," he uttered as she gently wiped his tears and held him close.

"Oh, Cheryl, I have the blood of many men on my hands from my own greed and obsession with the *Dutchman's* gold," he cried.

"Hush, hush, now, don't worry...your secrets are safe with me, my love. And besides, only you, me, and Chief Sheppard really know where the mine is located," she said trying to comfort him.

"Please, please, Cheryl, promise me that you will never enter that mine. There must be some sort of earthquake fault in the area and it makes the mine tunnel extremely unstable. It is an unbelievably dangerous place to be," he pleaded.

"As you wish. Come, lay down in bed. I'll take care of the mess," Cheryl said while helping him into the bedroom.

Cheryl helped Stan to his feet and put him into bed. She kissed him gently as he quickly dozed off.

*   *   *

* 28 *

Christmas Day had come to an end. Todd and Janet arrived back home from their relatives shortly before eleven. They caught <u>The</u> <u>Evening</u> <u>News</u> and retired to their bedroom.

Sometime after midnight, the only light on in the apartment came from the open refrigerator. Todd returned to bed and quickly fell back into a deep sleep. The golden hourglass sat silently on the nightstand.

* * *

From the eternal darkness, he found himself in his second dream seated in some sort of canteen or cafe. The place was busy. All around him sat foreigners speaking to each other. No one noticed him. Festive music played in the background. Cigarettes and cigar smoke drifted upward from each table. He had just eaten some sort of spicy food, and his mouth burned. He felt somewhat drunk but couldn't remember what he'd been drinking nor how to reorder another. Before long, the manager appeared, and demanded payment. Todd began to fumble for a non-existent wallet. His heart began to pound. Suddenly, there was a hand on his shoulder pulling him upward.

He was quickly turned around to face two very large, and very well armed military policemen. Together, they landed some painful blows to his face and midsection. Todd crumpled beneath the onslaught. He then felt himself being quickly bound, blindfolded, and gaged.

He soon realized he was being carried outdoors. It was raining very hard. The rain pelted him like tiny needles pricking his skin. After a short while, lying helpless in the rain, he heard a vehicle approach. Again, he felt himself being lifted and put down again, and he heard the trunk lid close above him. At least the rain was no longer pelting him. His clothes were soaking wet, and his hands, being secured behind him, began to hurt. His guts ached, and naturally, he had to urinate. Well, he thought, he'd solve that problem, and did.

With the release of his bladder, he was immediately brought back to the reality that he had just wet his bed in his Riverside Drive apartment with his beautiful girlfriend sleeping soundly next to him.

Todd cursed, trying desperately to think of an excuse other than the ridiculous one that he had been kidnapped by some foreign hit squad.

"What is it dear? What's wrong?" Janet whispered still half asleep, then totally woke in the commotion. "Todd! I don't believe my eyes! A grown man wetting his bed! You have no self-control?"

"I'm so sorry about the mess," said Todd trying to hide his embarrassment.

"Well you should be!" exclaimed Janet.

"Please forgive me, darling. My dream..." Todd tried to explain.

"Your dreams! Get up and launder these bed clothes. I'm going to the sofa," Janet said angrily.

For the second night he stared, perplexed and confused, at the golden hourglass that had been added to his timepiece collection.

* * *

WEDNESDAY, DECEMBER 26

Both Janet and Todd enjoyed another vacation day away from their offices. When Todd finally got up, he began to work on his home computer system. Any architectural revisions he made could be phone modemed to the office plotter. He enjoyed the relative ease compared to the older way of drawing plans by hand on the drafting table which now sat useless in the den, covered over with pages of computer plots.

Janet also awoke from her recently disturbed sleep. She prepared some brunch. Todd purposefully diverted the conversation away from any thoughts about a run in the cold. He then called to her from the den, "Have you seen that set of prints for Herbert Hall?"

"Last time I saw them, they were on that old drafting table," she replied.

Looking up at the 'Felix The Cat' clock which hung above the drafting table, Todd smiled and said, "Stupid thing!"

"What did you call me?" she asked from the kitchen.

"Oh, not you, darling. This clock is stupid looking," he quickly responded, not wanting to create any more confrontations.

Todd turned and walked over to the drafting table and proceeded to sort through the drawings. Toward the bottom of the pile, he finally came across the set for Herbert Hall. Unfolding the drawings, he began to reflect about the building he had designed nearly two years earlier.

The multi-million-dollar structure contained the most up-to-date naval training equipment available to Junior Officers outside of Annapolis. Following the dedication scheduled for next Saturday, he had been informed that the commanding officer would give him a personal tour of the completed project.

He still thought the Navy had some strange ways of getting this classroom structure built. To this day, almost sixteen months later, he continued to question why it was necessary to include within a 'Computer Storage Area'; a twenty-cell brig, a holding area, a processing room, a records office, and a machine shop underneath the south wing of the training center. After all, the purpose of the building was to train junior naval officers in advanced weaponry and electronics, not to detain prisoners of war!

Todd remembered how he had been "ordered" by Captain Siegewick, the commanding officer, to make the revisions for this new "Storage Area", after the initial drawings had already been approved and completed. Todd also recalled the urgency in Stan's voice demanding the changes be made "right away, and to tell no one of these revisions. It was a matter of top priority." Todd thought later that the Captain acted as though he were paying for these revisions out of his own pocket. Todd had never been requested to design a jail or 'Brig' before. This new addition to the original plans required extensive research on his part and it was to include the latest technology in prison security systems.

This information was provided to Todd when he toured the state penitentiary with its architect and designer shortly after he received Captain Siegewick's order. Todd could not explain to the architect and designer exactly why he needed the details of this assignment. He said that he had a client in San Diego who had requested a similar security system to be included in the lower level of their new building.

He had yet to be paid in full for his work. Todd stopped daydreaming and returned to the computer on which he was working. Janet was content reading articles on Mexico as December 27th slipped by like sand sliding through the hourglass.

* * *

On this same beautiful day, Chief Sheppard could drive Stan and Cheryl to the San Diego airport for their trip to Beaver Creek, Colorado. While walking through the terminal, Cheryl noticed the two Spanish men wearing sunglasses that she had seen at the Mall last Saturday with Sofia.

"Stan, do you see those two men over there?" she asked pointing.

"Yes, darling. What about them?" asked Stan.

"I've seen them before. I wonder if they're following me?" asked Cheryl as she moved closer to Stan.

"Are you sure? I personally have no dealings with the Mexicans, only with Mr. Lee's people from Hong Kong," said Stan.

"Possibly I'm just overly nervous about all that money we have," said Cheryl still feeling uncomfortable.

"Don't worry, the money is secure in the bank. Let's hurry so we can make that flight," urged Stan.

No sooner had Stan and Cheryl passed through security and boarded their plane than one of the agents phoned Mexico.

"Si, Your Excellency, the Commandant and the Lieutenant have left San Diego on a flight to Denver," reported the agent.

"Damn it! Do nothing further until they return," Señor Gartez instructed his man.

"Very good, Your Excellency. Buenos Dias," said the agent.

* * *

Shortly after eleven that night, with the chimes turned off and the lights out in the apartment, Todd and Janet kissed each other goodnight. Within a brief time, Todd's third dream began.

* * *

Now he was somehow floating in the air looking down on a yellow colored car that appeared to have its front section buried in a sand dune. The trunk lid was open and two figures were unloading what appeared to be a body. They placed the body face down on the sand. It lied there motionless while they continued to cover the remainder of the car with sand. They also carefully covered the tire tracks. From his vantage point, Todd could not see their faces nor the identity of the body on the sand. They then turned their attention to their cargo, cut some bindings, and raised the figure up between them. The three dark shapes approached some sort of hatchway in the earthen embankment. As they entered the hatch, suddenly his alarm clock went off.

"Good Morning, sweetie," Janet said, rubbing her eyes and yawning. "You didn't wet your pants or get killed in your dreams last night. Did you?" asked Janet a little sarcastically.

"No dear. I was merely a spectator and not the center of attraction of the dream this time," replied Todd.

"What did you see?" she inquired. "Can you remember any of the details?"

"It was some sort of kidnapping; then everyone disappeared through a hatchway," said Todd.

"Really. It was that clear?" asked Janet.

"That part was, but I can't remember much more about the action nor where it took place," Todd lamented.

She looked at him with those big blue eyes and reassured him, "Everything will turn out fine."

"I hope you're right," Todd said with a deep breath.

The hourglass sat patiently on the teak coffee table reflecting a bright Thursday morning sunlight. The tiny sand crystals lay motionless in the lower glass orb. They were always ready to flow in the opposite direction.

* * *

THURSDAY, DECEMBER 27

Today, both Todd and Janet were required to make appearances at their offices. After a hurried breakfast, they swung open the apartment house front door and ventured out into a frigid New York morning. Together they quickly covered the three blocks that separated the apartment from the subway. Both took the same "A" train downtown. Janet got off at *Times Square*, while Todd watched; then he was swiftly taken to his 14th Street station. The 8th Avenue Subway covers the sixty blocks in about ten minutes.

Once at her desk, Janet reviewed the stack of correspondence that had accumulated during her absence. Janet's co-workers began drifting in. By 9:00 A.M. the office appeared as though nothing such as a Christmas Vacation had ever taken place. The newspaper office buzzed with phones ringing off their hooks, computer screens bulging with information, and the smell of coffee and cigarettes hung heavy in the post-Christmas air.

It was 9:30 A.M. when Janet called her travel agent to confirm her booking. "Hello, Mrs. Snead. This is Miss Derr. I was wondering if you had my reservation specifics?"

"Yes, Miss Derr," said Mrs. Snead. "Your flight leaves New York next Thursday, January 3rd, for Mexico City and Ensenada on the 4th. On to San Diego the 5th and return to New York on the 6th."

"Thank you, Mrs. Snead," said Janet. "My fiancé, Mr. Tasselmeyer, will be leaving on the 4th for San Diego to attend the dedication of a new building that he designed. He's to call you later to confirm."

"Fine, Miss Derr," said Mrs. Snead. "I'll wait to hear from Mr. Tasselmeyer."

Janet had been given the opportunity to conduct an exclusive interview with the Mexican Opposition Leader, Raul Gartez, at his private villa just outside of Ensenada which was about a hundred miles south of San Diego on the Baja Peninsula. It had taken her three months to make all the preparations needed. She was to meet the newspaper correspondent, Roberto Perron, at the Mexico City airport upon her arrival. She reminded herself to dig out her passport.

"I know where it is," she thought. "It's in the drawer below Todd's Panda Bear clock!" That thought brought a smile and a soft chuckle to her lips.

Janet was very excited and pleased that her managing editor had allowed her to go unaccompanied to Ensenada, Mexico. Of course, she knew of the danger involved in traveling alone in a foreign place. She also knew she would be constantly under surveillance from the time she stepped off the plane until she departed again.

Much activity had been going on there lately. A new *'Liberating Army'* of rebels under the direction of Raul Gartez, seemed to have emerged. He had also found a money source to buy arms and supplies. There were strong denials from the State Department that our government was involved in the building, training, or supplying this new army. Janet felt this money source could provide the necessary boost the *'Liberators'* needed to take over the existing Mexican Government and perhaps several surrounding vulnerable countries. If this occurred, she suspected, it could place this new government in a major conflict with our own foreign policies toward that region. The possibility of a new cartel emerging to control all the drug shipments heading north could result. "Now that would be some story to bring back to my boss," she thought to herself!

She departed from work around four o'clock and arrived home before Todd. She examined the very empty refrigerator and decided to venture out again into the cold to get some Chinese food for dinner. Todd had three favorite things in his life. Janet appeared to lead the list, next came his collection of timepieces and lastly was Chinese food.

* * *

Todd Tasselmeyer, Jon Jacobs and Larry Stevenson had formed their architectural firm called *'TJS & Associates'* three years earlier. Jon and Larry concentrated on shopping malls and customized apartment renovations in high rise structures. Todd usually worked on school and church designs. Because of his impressive portfolio in school and classroom designs, he had been selected a year and a half ago to produce the drawings which, would result in the new classroom building for Fort Warren Naval Training Center outside San Diego. He had signed the government contract in September the year before.

Todd, who usually took an active role during the actual construction of all his projects by making on-site inspections, was informed by the Naval Command in San Diego that any visit he made would not be paid for out of government funds. He decided the further he stayed away from Captain Siegewick the better off he would feel. He was also told that once the project was underway, the naval contractors would rely on their own inspectors and building codes and had highly skilled professionals doing the entire project.

After six months of drawing, the final set was sent to California this past February. The building was started on the March 5th, and was just about complete except for some last-minute punch-out work. The actual time of the construction had taken a full nine months. Todd was called on the phone from California several times during the construction for revisions, but he never made an appearance during the construction due to a backlog of new projects at home. During that time, he submitted many bills for payments, all of which went unpaid by Stan.

Todd was surprised and delighted to receive a complementary V.I.P. guest pass to the dedication ceremony on January the fifth. He was also invited to stay at the new on-base Transit barracks and attend the retirement banquet for Captain Siegewick at the Officer's Club. Todd decided to accept and fly to San Diego and see for himself what's been going on at Fort Warren. The first day of classes in the new Herbert Hall classroom building was scheduled to begin the following Monday morning the seventh at 0900.

* * *

THURSDAY, DECEMBER 27

On his first day back at the office, Todd also contacted their travel agent to confirm his flight next week to Southern California.

"Yes, Mr. Tasselmeyer," said Mrs. Snead. "You're booked on Centennial flight 136 next Friday at 2:30 P.M. Have a pleasant trip."

"Thank you, Mrs. Snead," said Todd. "I appreciate your kindness but I still dislike flying."

Todd's partners came into his office shortly thereafter, and the three of them exchanged stories of Christmas family adventures. It seemed that Jon had gone to Upstate New York and had gotten caught in a nasty ice storm. He was forced to spend agonizing hours listening to his mother-in-law tell stories of Christmas in the "Depression Years of the 1930s." Todd kidding him said, "Depression years? Oh, you mean the time since you met her?" They all laughed.

Larry had traveled South, somewhere near Atlanta. He said, "The weather was mild, the food was truly Southern fried, and the Southern bells were balling!"

Knowing exactly what Larry meant, Todd and Jon laughed again.

"Hey guys, Janet gave me a great gift. It was an antique golden hourglass," said Todd excitedly.

"Now that's something you don't find every day," replied Jon. Todd continued saying, "it's really neat and looks terrific in my time piece collection." He did not mention his three dreams.

Each of the trio was presently involved in his own separate project. If the trend continued, Todd thought, the firm might have to find larger quarters. The current space was adequate for them, but there was not much storage space. Each project required dozens of architectural plotted drawings and many pages of notes.

Todd was unable to concentrate much in those days due to his new nighttime activity. The images he dreamt seemed so real. He had no leads, nor any prior experiences to draw from or to make any connections. He decided to try and schedule an appointment with a friend who was an excellent psychologist.

"Dr. Hardesty will be out of the country until January the eighth. Please leave a message at the tone..." the answering machine informed Todd. Todd did not leave a message on his friend's machine. He only said to himself, "shit, wouldn't you know it. Oh, well, maybe Janet knows someone."

Upon arriving back at the apartment, the aroma of the Chinese food, which Janet had just brought back, drove him into a feeding frenzy. Together they enjoyed the wonderfully prepared dishes of Sweet and Sour Pork, Moo Goo Gai Pan and Egg Rolls.

"There's absolutely nothing in the way of leftovers to put into the refrigerator dear," she informed him.

"Fine. Let's move to the overstuffed sofa and the remote control," suggested Todd.

Together they spent the evening trying to stay awake watching television. They both stirred enough to catch some information on The Evening News about activity going on in Mexico City. It appeared some high-ranking government officials had not been seen for some time and were feared to have been kidnapped.

"Love, it sounds very unstable down there," he said in a concerned voice. "Are you still sure you want to go to that place?" "I've just got to go and get my interview," she replied then continued by saying, "everything will go as planned. They're expecting me to set the story straight. They need the favorable press coverage here in our country and they want me to come."

She was squeezing his hand tighter now. He could tell she was feeling tense. He bent forward and kissed her tenderly. She closed her eyes and let his lips cover hers. She hugged his neck. Gently lowering her arms, he proceeded to lead her towards the bedroom while he turned off the chimes and the lights.

"Chinese food does make me feel more romantic," he whispered to her. Her lips met his and they held each other close again. Their clothes fell to the floor and he tenderly laid her back into the pillows. Kissing her nakedness all over only caused her to want him even more. She caressed him and fondled him. He massaged her back and legs which made her even more eager for him. Their passionate lovemaking continued well past midnight.

* * *

* 29 *

Sleeping soundly, Todd found himself entering the fourth dream, He was sitting on a stool in the center of a small room with one door and no windows. He was wearing some sort of coveralls, army combat boots and, for that added accent, leg irons and hand-cuffs. A single red-light bulb glowed overhead and made seeing details very difficult. He no longer had his wallet nor his gold watch. He felt a tightness around his throat, and he realized he was wearing one of those dog-like collars. He tried to get up and was immediately jolted by an electric shock that stunned him. He could not move from his place!

"Oh God, please help me!" *he prayed.*

Suddenly, the door swung open with a loud crash. It startled him. Todd's eyes widened as two hooded henchmen approached him. Together they lifted him and one removed the electro-collar.

"Who the hell are you and where are you taking me?" *asked Todd angrily.*

They mumbled beneath their hoods, "Mast, buddy boy, you're going to Mast."

Not understanding what they meant, he struggled as they forced him down a short passageway to another room. The trio entered the chamber. They positioned Todd standing and facing a long table. Behind it were seated two additional hooded figures. The one on the right spoke first.

"Your name is Tasselmeyer?" *asked the figure on the right.*

Todd said, "Yes, so what about it?"

A hard slap across his face indicated he had answered incorrectly.

"Yes Sir, would be acceptable. Understood?" *came from behind the table.*

Todd replied softly, "Yes sir."

Again, another slap!

"We didn't hear you!" *the voice said loudly.*

"Yes Sir!" *yelled Todd on the verge of tears.*

"You have been found to be a trespasser. Is that correct?" *asked the voice. Todd decided to agree to the charges and simply said,* "Yes Sir."

The other seated figure said in a much deeper voice, "Trespassers found here are always detained."

"How wonderful," thought Todd.

"This mast finds the defendant...guilty of criminal trespass, and sentences Mr. Tasselmeyer to six months at hard labor. Take him away!" said the deep voice.

Todd, shocked at this whole scene, was led kicking and shouting insults back down the passageway. The cuffs and leg irons banged against the walls and floor as they went. Everything was bathed in that eerie red light.

Arriving at his would-be cell, the door opened, and he was pushed into the interior's eternal darkness. The door slammed shut.

He let out an ear-piercing scream and woke up soaking wet.

"Thank you, God!" he sighed, feeling much relieved. He then called to Janet who was already in the kitchen fixing Friday morning's breakfast. "Oh darling, I just had the most terrifying dream."

"What did you say? The water was running and I didn't hear what you just said," replied Janet.

He went to her open arms and they gently kissed.

"These weird dreams have got to mean something, dear," said Todd still shaking.

"Maybe when you leave for California you'll forget all about them," said Janet trying to console him.

"I sure hope so. Come on, let's get dressed," said Todd giving Janet a hug.

*   *   *

Todd picked Janet up from her office later that day. Together they drove the MG the three hours to reach Vermont for a weekend of skiing. Both enjoyed the exhilaration of the slopes.

"It's great exercise," Janet said pulling Todd to his feet. Janet had much more experience skiing than Todd. Of course, what Todd lacked in training on the mountain, he made up once they returned to the bedroom in the lodge. Janet was a wonderful, sensitive and caring person. She was beautiful to make love to. She wanted his hardness penetrating her innermost desires. She never tired of him and often accomplished several heights of ecstasy during a single session. Todd loved to kiss her constantly. Anywhere and anytime was acceptable for him to show her how much he truly loved her with all his passion.

That weekend, however, Janet felt anxious about her upcoming trip on Thursday to Mexico. Todd held her, kissed her, and said, "Get your story and get back to San Diego to my hotel bedroom as quick as you can. I just can't stand to be separated from you too long."

Todd was extremely pleased not to be bothered by nocturnal brain disturbances throughout the entire weekend. "Maybe it's over," he thought to himself.

* * *

Stan and Cheryl thoroughly enjoyed their get-a-way vacation. The Colorado mountain scenery was spectacular and the weather conditions were perfect for skiing. They ate at all the most popular places and spent each romantic evening in the comfortable surroundings of their mountainside, multi-level villa.

By the fifth day both had really skied and partied enough. They were ready for New Years and Stan's last week as commandant of Fort Warren.

* * *

MONDAY, DECEMBER 31

Todd and Janet arrived back in New York City early that morning. Parking the MG in the underground garage, they quickly dashed upstairs to change clothes. They were both back at their office desks by 9:00 A.M. but soon realized that working on New Year's Eve didn't accomplish much for either of them. Most of the other employees had left early after bidding everyone a "Happy New Year!"

They each dressed in their finest that special evening. He wore a tux. She wore a stunning evening gown with a fur wrap and the beautiful set of pearls which Todd had given to her last Christmas. The taxi was waiting downstairs and took them quickly to Times Square about 10:00 P.M. The evening was a truly magnificent one. All the glamour and makeup New York could apply was used this night. Close to midnight, Todd and Janet stepped outside the hotel lobby to party with the throngs of happy spectators there in Times Square indulging in a ritual many years old. As the lighted ball began its slow decent, the crowd went wild! Thousands of happy people united for a singular countdown, four...three...two... one...Happy New Year! Horns blew, kisses were given even to strangers, and the party continued for hours.

* * *

Chief Sheppard picked Cheryl and Stan up upon their return to San Diego that afternoon. "How about you two love-birds joining me and some of my friends aboard 'Yankee II' tonight for a New Year's Eve celebration?" asked the Chief.

"Oh, Chief that sounds marvelous. What do you say, Stan?" asked Cheryl pleading.

"Sure, why not," he replied.

"The party should be underway around 2200 hours, Sir," said the Chief.

"Can we bring anything?" Cheryl asked.

"Just yourselves, there will be plenty of booze and eats," replied Chief Sheppard.

Once Stan opened the front door of their Mission Hills house, he stood there for an instant in horror.

"What's the matter, dear?" Cheryl asked.

"We've been broken into! This place is in shambles!" replied Stan.

"Oh, God, no!" Cheryl yelled as she ran crying into the bedroom.

Stan found the phone and called the Marina saying, "Chief, our house has been broken into. Notify Base Security and have some personnel assigned over here to investigate this."

"Certainly, Sir, but it's going to be a hard thing to do tonight. Everyone's out partying," said the Chief sorrowfully.

"Oh yes, damn it, I forgot it's New Year's Eve. I suppose we should call 911," said the Captain in an uncertain voice.

"Stan," Cheryl came running back into his arms crying, "they've ruined everything!"

"Can you tell if anything is missing?" asked Stan quickly.

"Yes," she said, sobbing. "My dog tag chain and the safety deposit box key!"

"Oh, shit, not that!" exclaimed Stan in a rage.

"I had put it on the nightstand on Christmas eve before we made love. I never put it back on afterward," sobbed Cheryl.

Stan called 911 and asked the Mission Hills police to come and investigate the break-in. He then called Chief Sheppard back and said, "the police should be here shortly and we'll catch up with you later tonight after this mess is squared away."

"Are you sure, Sir?" the Chief asked.

"Yes, we'll be all right. Till later," Stan said as he hung up the phone. He then turned and walked into the destroyed living room.

The Mission Hills police soon arrived and filed a complete report. The house had sustained substantial destruction to its contents. All their personnel belongings had been dumped out of each drawer, cabinet, and closet.

"Any idea what they were looking for, Captain Siegewick?" the City of San Diego Police Officer asked.

"So far, my fiancé said that her set of military dog tags were missing. I am missing a safe deposit key from the *San Diego Bank and Trust*."

"Stan," Cheryl called from the bedroom.

"Excuse me, Officer. I want to join her," said Stan.

Walking into the bedroom he saw Cheryl and the other Police Investigator looking at a note left beside the bed.

The note read, "Gringos, we want what you have, and we're going to get it."

"Any idea, folks, what the hell this means?" the officer asked Stan and Cheryl.

"Not really, we don't know of any Mexicans locally," replied Stan.

"All right, but you two shouldn't stay here. Whoever they are, they will probably be back now that you're home," advised the officer.

Stan said, "Yes, you're right, Officer." Then he turned toward Cheryl and said, "Let's pick up a few essentials and head over to the marina."

"That's fine with me, darling," said Cheryl, feeling relieved that she would not have to stay in this house.

"We'll remain here for a while longer dusting for fingerprints," replied the Police Investigator.

"Thank you, Officer, have a successful evening," Stan said as they were leaving.

"Yes, thank you, too," said Cheryl "And have yourself a Happy New Year!"

"Yes Ma'am, you try to do the same," said the Officer smiling.

Their car, fortunately, had been safe inside the garage. Stan did manage to have the car key on his ring along with the house key. Together they drove to the Marina, and the Chief's party. Everyone there was very sympathetic toward the couple's plight. The guests attempted to cheer up Stan and Cheryl, but that did not stop everyone onboard the luxurious yacht from eating and drinking throughout the evening. At midnight, all the other occupied party boats in the marina blew their whistles and horns.

Many lights from the other yachts sparkled on the water. In the distance, the party guests could see beautiful fireworks exploding over San Diego's harbor area.

"Happy New Year, darling," Stan told Cheryl, as he gently hugged and kissed her tears away.

"Oh, Stan, I'm so worried about your money. How will we gain access without the key?" asked Cheryl.

"Don't worry, we'll get the key and the money. I promise," said Stan staring into the night sky.

* * *

TUESDAY, JANUARY 1

It must have been sometime after four A.M. when Todd collapsed into bed, only to be immediately ejected into what would be the fifth bizarre dream since Christmas Eve.

* * *

With his eyes wide opened and his hands cuffed behind his back, he was being forcibly and roughly pushed through what seemed like an endless tunnel. Two hooded figures carried him forward without stopping. It was very dark and cold. Along the way, he heard what sounded like machinery in full operation. Red lights appeared lining the walls.

"Right this way, asshole!" the lead guard called.

Todd felt very much afraid.

"What's that?" the other guard said. "Listen..." The trio stopped abruptly. A low rumble could be heard and even felt. The red lights flickered and went out! Todd was immediately dropped.

"What about the prisoner?" yelled the one guard.

"Forget him, you jerk. Run for your life!" yelled the other guard running.

As his captors fled into the darkness he heard what sounded like men's voices crying and calling out for help. Then another rumble made sand start pouring down from above him. As the sand began to cover him, he started crying out for help... when he awoke.

"Help me, someone. I can't breathe!" He called out while still shaking from the cave-in experience.

"What is it Todd? Another nightmare?" Janet asked looking very concerned.

"I guess I've got to stop eating and drinking before bed if it kills me...Oh no,...Oh Janet! If only I could make the connection about these dreams," Todd lamented.

He proceeded to the bath room and took a long shower. After that, Todd spent most of New Year's Day holding the golden hourglass and turning it every hour once the sand had run its course. Todd examined the scratches on the glass. He thought it was interesting that they appeared only on one side of one orb. He could not discern any pattern in the scratches. He laughed once to himself, thinking that the scratches were probably from a price tag placed there long ago, and an eager gift-giver couldn't get it off without scratching the glass.

Janet was relieved to find her passport. The Panda Bear clock, sitting on its base above the drawer, seemed to smile at her after she whispered, "Thanks for standing guard over it."

With no stores or restaurants open, dinner was limited to a frozen pizza and some left-over Christmas cookies. They did manage to locate an unopened bottle of *'Cabernet Sauvignon'* and a VHS tape they hadn't yet viewed.

*   *   *

New Year's Day was spent putting their Mission Hills house back together. As Stan and Cheryl worked inside, the white car with the black windows cruised through the neighborhood and passed their house several times that morning. The white car proceeded to downtown San Diego where the driver got out and placed a phone call at a gas station.

"Señor Gartez, the Lieutenant and her Commandant are at home today for New Year's cleaning up," the agent reported.

"Excellent, I'm having Miguel bring my yacht to San Diego tonight. It will be at Marina del Rey by midnight. Meet him there and he will give you further instructions," ordered Gartez.

"Si, Your Excellency. Is there anything else?" asked the agent.

"Si. Don't harm the Lieutenant! Your people must not create a disturbance. Understood?" asked Gartez sternly.

"Si, Your Excellency, no harm will come to the Lieutenant," replied the agent obediently.

"Gracias, Señor. Carry on. Buenos Dias," said Gartez.

*   *   *

* 30 *

"Cheryl, there's a call for you, I think it's Commander Wilkins' wife," said Stan. As Cheryl reached the phone, Stan instructed her, "don't mention anything about the break-in."

"Hello. Sofia, Happy New Year!" said Cheryl. "How were your holidays?"

"Fine, Cheryl. For Christmas, Michael bought me some lovely things. However, the blouse didn't fit and I've been wanting to exchange it. Would you be interested in meeting me tomorrow for lunch at the mall?" asked Sofia.

"Sure, I hate sitting around a messy house on a day off anyway. I'll meet you in center court at noon," replied Cheryl.

"Great, Cheryl, I'll see you then. Bye," said Sofia.

"Stan," Cheryl called. "Are you going to the office tomorrow?" "I was planning to, why?" he asked.

"Would you mind very much if I dropped you at base headquarters, then drove over to the mall and had lunch with Sofia. I promise to be very careful," explained Cheryl.

"That will be fine, darling," replied Stan.

* * *

That evening, Stan and Cheryl stayed at home and comforted each other. They hadn't found anything else missing. Stan was relieved to once again locate the prospector's trunk that came from the mine tunnel. The trunk had been put up into the attic by the movers and had not been disturbed by the intruders.

They couldn't help but laugh at the sorry state of their little Christmas tree. A few lights still twinkled and only half a dozen balls remained unbroken. Even the star on top of the tree was bent out of shape. Stan promised her that next Christmas would be simply spectacular. Around 11:00 o'clock they called it quits and headed for the bedroom. They wanted so much to make love but felt that their privacy had been invaded by the intruders. The bedroom would never feel the same.

They finally managed to fall asleep in each other's arms about 0100 hours, but Stan was called to the ringing phone shortly before 0400 hours.

"Captain, there's been another cave-in and we've lost five more prisoners and no guards," reported the extremely upset Chief.

"Good God, Chief! Will this problem of losing personnel ever cease?" asked the Captain who was feeling very concerned.

"I can't imagine why each time we find a gold vein to mine there is always a cave-in. It's like the place is spooked," replied the Chief.

"Now who's left, Chief?" asked the Captain.

"There should be five prisoners remaining along with our eight guards," replied the Chief.

The Captain still standing in his underwear said, "I'll tell you what. Let's begin a taxi service at night towards the south and Imperial Beach."

"Tell me more, Sir," said the Chief.

The Captain began saying, "buy an old used taxi and have our guards offer drunken sailors and Marines rides back to Fort Warren. They're all along the Pacific coast highway in bars by the dozens."

"Every night that they have liberty, Sir," said the Chief.

The Captain continued saying, "see that our new guests are dropped off at the beach entrance and escorted below."

"No problem, Sir. But what do we do about the taxicab?" asked the Chief.

"Have the guards cover it with sand behind a dune during the day for safe keeping," said the Captain.

"Excellent, Sir. You're truly a Master problem solver," said the Chief now feeling better about the whole situation.

"Goodnight, Chief," said the Captain.

Stan returned to Cheryl's waiting arms. "Who was on the phone, darling?" she asked.

"It was Chief Sheppard. There was a problem below ground and now he needed my permission to hire some new employees," said the Captain trying to avoid the subject.

"Oh, I see. Well, I'm sure you boys will work everything out all right. Good night, again," said Cheryl understanding Stan's feelings.

*   *   *

WEDNESDAY, JANUARY 2

Shortly after 1:00 A.M., Todd entered the sixth dream.

He was standing alone in a tunnel. The ceiling was low. The rock wall was lined with red glowing lamps. He was wearing black coveralls and army boots. His hands were once again secured in front of him with handcuffs. Leg-irons hung from each ankle and that electro-collar was secured about his neck again.

He timidly called out, "is anybody there?"

Quickly, two hooded henchmen approach him. They roughly grabbed him and then escorted him further down the tunnel to the end. Suddenly, appearing before them was a huge underground room. Todd looked around and determined the size to be close to one hundred by at least another hundred feet. The ceiling must have risen thirty feet above him. Within this large room, there was much activity. He saw many men, dressed as he was, pushing ore cars over a narrow-gauge railroad track. The ore cars are filled with sand! He was escorted to a slow-moving conveyor belt.

"Listen up, asshole. Your job is to take the sand from the car and load it onto the moving conveyor."

The dumped sand disappeared on the conveyor through another tunnel. Not a single word was spoken by the workers. Todd quickly found out why. He attempted to call out to the other men and was instantly jolted with electricity from the collar. The shock sent him reeling forward and he fell with a loud "thud."

Janet gently lifted her hero and helped him back into bed. "There now, everything will be all right," she said as she held her trembling and sobbing lover close to her bosom. The smell of her perfume and her gentle kisses assured him that he had only been dreaming.

The golden hourglass had interacted with Todd's life for seven days and six nights in the apartment. Its shiny surface reflected the dreary morning, the second day of the New Year. Both Todd and Janet left for work about eight-thirty.

*   *   *

Around 2:00 P.M., Todd sat staring blankly at the flicking computer screen in his office. Larry called him to the phone saying, "It's some Lieutenant Lighal. He says he's the Protocol Officer from Fort Warren in San Diego. He wants to talk to you."

Todd, still not one hundred percent together, answered the phone. "Yes sir," said Todd. "I'll be arriving about 4:30 P.M., or should I say, 1630. That's right, Centennial Flight 136 from New York. I'll meet you at the baggage claim area on the lower level. I'll be wearing my brown sports jacket and a red tie."

"That will be just fine, Mr. Tasselmeyer. We'll look for you there," stated Lieutenant Lighal.

"Thank you, sir," Todd said. "I look forward to meeting all of you, and touring the completed building. I'll call if there are any changes."

"Have a good flight on Friday, and Happy New Year!" said the lieutenant.

"Oh yes, have a Happy New Year. Thank you, sir, and goodbye," replied Todd.

Todd hung up his phone. Shortly, he left the office and took the "A" train back uptown.

* * *

The alarm sounded at 0700. Stan and Cheryl woke to a dull grey January the second. She dressed in jeans and a blouse with a light jacket. Stan wore his winter blue uniform.

Cheryl drove the Captain to Base Headquarters and went inside with him to wish everyone a Happy New Year. After drinking a mug of coffee, prepared by Yeomen Roth, she kissed him in his office and left. Cheryl drove past the beautiful newly completed edifice of Herbert Hall. She noticed a lot of activity going on near the front lobby. She parked her car along the curb and walked over for a peek.

"What seems to be the problem, Mr. McCoy?" asked Cheryl.

"Oh, Lieutenant Finley. I hardly recognized you in civilian clothes," said Mr. McCoy.

"Yes, today I'm still on leave," said Cheryl smiling.

"The sidewalk at this location appears to be settling. This makes an unsafe condition," Mr. McCoy told her.

"Yes, I can see that. Do you have any idea what's causing the problem?" asked Cheryl now becoming concerned.

"This place always has earth tremors," replied Mr. McCoy.

"With the dedication ceremony on Saturday, will you have enough time to fix it?" she asked him.

"I suppose so. I'll add it to my punch out list."

"Oh, what's that mean?" asked Cheryl.

"That simply lists all the final little painting and cleaning-up projects that must be addressed throughout the building before Saturday's dedication," replied Mr. McCoy.

Cheryl bid him good day and then drove her car off the base to meet Sofia at the mall. She failed to notice the white car that followed several car lengths behind her. The morning sky remained gloomy. She figured it would rain before noon. Since she had only her light-weight jacket on, she wished she also had her umbrella. Traffic slowed on the northbound side of the San Diego Freeway prior to the mall's exit. She hoped it would not make her late.

Once at the mall, she circled through the parking lot looking for a space near an entrance door. Finally, she settled for a space that was quite far from where she had planned to park.

She noticed a lot of cars parked in her location but failed to see any other people. She turned off the ignition and unbuckled her seat belt. Just as she opened the driver's side door Cheryl heard a man's voice. "Lieutenant Finley," the voice called with a Spanish accent.

"Yes," she replied, as she quickly turned around to see who had called. When she did, two large men, with dark clothes and hair, grabbed hold of her. Before she could scream for help, a large hand covered her mouth. She was instantly pushed into the back seat of the white car with the black windows. In the struggle, her car keys fell to the ground and landed under her car, completely unnoticed. The white sedan quickly left the mall's parking lot and headed back South on the San Diego Freeway.

* * *

* 31 *

Sofia walked outside to see if she could find Cheryl.

She was certain that Cheryl had only gotten held up in traffic, so she decided to wait a little longer. After waiting nearly an hour, she gave up on the idea of meeting Cheryl. She slowly walked back inside the mall and had lunch alone. After shopping and exchanging her blouse, Sofia left the mall and walked outside toward her car.

Not believing her eyes, Sofia saw Cheryl's car parked there alone in the far corner of the parking lot near her own car. "Oh, good, maybe she's in the vicinity," Sofia thought to herself. Just as she got a little closer to the car, she saw Cheryl's car keys lying on the ground.

Sofia thought, "Oh, poor Cheryl! She'll be so upset when she discovers she's lost her keys. I know she'll come out here to her car and look for them. I guess I'd better wait here a little while for her." Sofia waited and wondered why Cheryl didn't return to her car. The more time that passed the more worried Sofia became. By nearly four o'clock that afternoon, Sofia walked back inside the mall and called the Captain. "Hello, Captain Siegewick, this is Sofia Wilkins."

"Yes, Mrs. Wilkins," the Captain replied.

"Sir, Lieutenant Finley never showed up to have lunch with me," Sofia informed him.

"What!" said the Captain in a concerned voice.

"Your car is parked here at the mall and her car keys were lying on the ground when I approached," said Sofia.

"There's no sign of Cheryl?" the Captain asked.

"None, Captain, I've been waiting here by your car for well over an hour, and she's nowhere around," replied Sofia now becoming concerned about Cheryl.

"I can't believe this!" said the Captain seemingly angry and very concerned for Cheryl's well-being.

"What can I do, Captain?" asked Sofia.

Thinking for a moment, he said, "Please leave her keys at the mall's office. I'll get a ride over there right-a-way with Chief Sheppard."

"As you wish, Captain. I'm sorry I don't know any more," Sofia said as she started to cry.

"Thank you, Mrs. Wilkins, I'm sure no harm has come to Cheryl," the Captain said as he also held back his tears.

Hanging up the phone, he hit his fists on the desk.

"Damn it! I told her to be careful," he said to himself.

Reaching for the phone, the Captain called the Security Office. "Chief Sheppard, please. This is Captain Siegewick. Yes, I'll hold."

After what seemed like forever, the Chief answered the phone.

"Chief! Something's happened to Cheryl," the Captain said quickly.

"Say that again, Sir," asked the Chief.

"Cheryl has disappeared from the mall this afternoon. Commander Wilkins' wife just called me to say that Cheryl didn't meet her for lunch," said the Captain while pacing.

"Are you positive, Sir?" the Chief asked.

The Captain continued his explanation saying, "Cheryl had driven my car to the mall to go shopping with Commander Wilkins' wife. Sofia Wilkins found my car still parked there about 1600 hours along with Cheryl's keys on the ground near the car."

"Oh, my God! Captain, do you supposed Cheryl was kidnapped?" asked the Chief in disbelief.

"It's hard to tell at this point. Please come over here," requested the Captain.

"Certainly, Sir, right-a-way," replied the Chief.

Chief Sheppard quickly drove over to the Base Headquarters and picked up the Captain. Together they drove to the mall parking lot where Sofia had found the empty car. They immediately proceeded to the mall's security office.

"I'm Captain Siegewick. A set of car keys were found in the parking lot and left here for me," stated the Captain firmly.

"Yes, Captain. Please sign here that you claimed them," said the pretty young receptionist.

"Much obliged, Miss," said the Captain.

"No problem, Captain," she said, flashing him a beautiful smile. The Chief left the Captain and returned to Fort Warren. Stan drove his car from the mall' parking lot and went home to sit by the phone.

*   *   *

Janet was busy packing for her trip the next day when Todd opened the door and stepped inside the apartment. Later that evening, Todd continued to re-examine the blueprints of Herbert Hall. He was closely tracing the electrical schematic of the lower computer storage area's *"brig"* with a pencil, when suddenly, something dawned on him. Above the ceiling light fixture in the cell area was a pulsating electronic device. If that device ever got itself shorted out, it would automatically open all the cell doors!

"Someday," he thought smiling, *"That could come in handy for some unfortunate prisoner looking for a way out."*

Todd still tried to make a connection between his dreams and the new *"brig"* he had designed. He began to review out loud his many dream sequences: "Walking on the dunes...being kidnapped in a foreign canteen...the taxi buried in the sand dune...being dragged through red-colored underground tunnels... wearing the electronic dog-collar...having the sand cave in on me...being taken into the great room filled with men and machinery...and, the sand, always the damn sand...just like inside this golden hourglass."

Nothing suggested to him any connection to the Navy nor to his building design. Todd stared blankly at the many pages of drawings. Both he and they reflected in the golden hourglass, now sitting on his desk.

Todd became angry. He thought, "damn it all. There's got to be a connection." He pounded his fists on the drawing board to vent his frustrations. He turned to Janet, whose, large and sympathetic, blue eyes gently beckoned him, "Come, darling. Come to me."

He quickly moved through the apartment turning off the lights and the chimes and placed the golden hourglass upon the mantel. He then caught a glimpse of Janet who was standing naked in the bedroom doorway. Her soft and delicate hands pulled him toward her. They passionately kissed, then fell on the bed entwined and longing for each other. Janet knew she would leave tomorrow and would not sleep with Todd again for at least the next five nights. She would miss him terribly. She became more aroused as he lifted her upon himself. She let out a moan from the sheer pleasure. Together they each reached emotional climaxes.

Their love-making did not leave many hours for sleeping that night. When Todd finally sunk into semi-consciousness, he dreamt not of beautiful lovemaking but rather of hearing rumbling sounds inside a black void...

*   *   *

The seventh adventure began with men calling out for help, trying to run, unable to move, and that terrible feeling of being smothered by sand pouring down from above your head.

He suddenly awoke. He was choking and gasping for breath. The look of pure terror in his eyes was too much for Janet.

"There, there. You're only dreaming again," said Janet as she again tried to console him after another dream.

"Oh Janet. I'm so lucky to have you. You're such a help," Todd told her as he clung to her tightly.

She continued to hold him and reassured him it was only a dream. It was only his imagination. Todd did manage a few brief hours of undisturbed sleep.

* * *

As the white sedan with the black glass windows approached the border crossing into Mexico. The driver's side window lowered enough for the driver to tell the policeman, "We have a special gift for His Excellency, Señor Gartez."

With that information, the policeman quickly waved them through. By five o'clock on that overcast Wednesday afternoon of January the second, the white car passed through downtown Ensenada. Turning onto the small road that led to Señor Gartez's villa, the car came to a halt once it was inside the high security walls. Several other villa guards came running to greet the white car's arrival. They assisted Miguel and his partner getting Cheryl out of the car. Cheryl had been blindfolded and gagged. Her hands were tied behind her and she had endured the bumpy Mexican roads lying across the rear seat.

She panicked when she was abducted in the parking lot. She continued to remain scared and very confused throughout most of the ride. When the car stopped, her heart once again began to pound.

The two men in the front seat continually spoke Spanish. She understood little of what they said. Cheryl did hear the name of Señor Raul Gartez and remembered seeing him on a television interview the week before. She understood that he was some sort of major political force in the Mexican government. She also recalled hearing the television commentator say, "Gartez was a ruthless man who was power hungry and had obtained his status through violence."

Suddenly, Cheryl was grabbed and pulled out of the car. As she struggled to her feet, she heard several doors creak open. She remained blindfolded and was led into a space and positioned against a wall until the door was closed behind her. The blindfold was finally removed. Her eyes at first saw nothing, then shapes emerged from the shadows. Someone roughly pushed her forward through a low passageway as two escorts walked behind her. There was total silence except for the sounds their footsteps made on the tile floor. The trio descended a flight of steps to a lower level. There she was untied and her gag removed.

"Who the hell are you people? What do you want with me?" came immediately from her now opened mouth.

"Calm down, Señorita Finley, you are the guest of honor of His Excellency, Señor Raul Gartez," the taller abductor told her.

"You go tell that son of a bitch that if I don't report for duty tomorrow the entire *U.S. Pacific Fleet* will be down here looking for me!" said Cheryl with eyes glaring with anger.

"Oh, yes, you are so very sure of yourself, Señorita. I think His Excellency does have other plans for you tomorrow," said the abductor.

"I am a United States citizen. I demand to see Mr. Gartez now," Cheryl shouted, almost in tears. She was then led into a tiny sunless room. The other man spoke directly to Cheryl, "His Excellency is not here now - he will see you in the morning. We have been instructed to put you here for safe keeping."

Calming herself somewhat, Cheryl realized they did not wish to harm her if she agreed to stay in her place.

"The house servant Pedro will bring you supper in a short while," said the same man.

"Adios, Señorita Finley," the two henchmen said as they closed and bolted the door behind them.

Cheryl looked around the room. There was a small table against the far wall with two plain wooden chairs. On the table was a small dimly light kerosene lamp. It provided the only light in this windowless space. A set of two bunk beds were against the opposite wall. The floor was dirt and the ceiling was made of beams and planking. Obviously, she was in a basement room below the main part of the villa.

After about an hour sitting alone, there was a knocking at the door. Cheryl heard the bolt being slid, and as the door opened, she was delighted to see the housekeeper with a large tray of Mexican food.

"Buenos Noches, Señorita. I am Pedro. His Excellency has instructed me to feed you and to provide you with some reading material for tonight," he said to Cheryl in very clear English.

"Thank you, Pedro," said Cheryl. "I was very hungry since my luncheon date was canceled by Mr. Gartez's men."

"Si, Señorita," said Pedro. "I will return in the morning with your breakfast. Enjoy your meal."

"Gracias, Señor," Cheryl said as he quickly left and bolted the door.

Cheryl proceeded to eat every tasty morsel. When she had finished her meal, she found some propaganda pamphlets about the *New Liberation Front* that was headed by Raul Gartez. Fortunately for her, some of the brochures were written in both Spanish and English.

"That's quite an extensive operation he's running," she thought to herself. "I wonder where he gets his money to mount such an elaborate campaign?"

Her living quarters were not the most comfortable, but at least she had made it through one of the most harrowing days of her life. After having freshened up in the small bath facility in the corner of her room, she returned to the lower bunk, and quickly fell asleep.

*   *   *

* 32 *

THURSDAY, JANUARY 3

Morning soon broke. Todd left Janet's tender arms and proceeded to make coffee in the kitchen. Somehow the last few days had passed quickly. Todd couldn't believe it was time for her departure for Mexico. A few quick phone calls and completion of the packing were all Janet needed to do. Todd planned to drive her to *Kennedy Airport*. Around 11:00 that morning, Todd took the elevator downstairs to get the car. Janet looked around the apartment for the last time. She had a strange feeling something was missing.

She did not see the golden hourglass on the coffee table nor on Todd's desk. It wasn't on the night stand either. She didn't have the time to hunt for it, so she decided simply to leave that job up to Todd.

*   *   *

Cheryl was awake when Pedro delivered her breakfast.

"Buenos Dias, Señorita," said Pedro politely. "During the night, Señor Gartez arrived. He wishes to meet with you after you have eaten. I'll be back in an hour."

"Thank you, Pedro. I'll be ready to meet the Señor," said Cheryl while watching him leave.

When Pedro returned, another armed henchman joined them. The trio made its way through a maze of passageways and finally entered on to the lush tropical patio. Once there, they tied her hands behind her. Cheryl was then secured with rope to the chair. She was left to wait in the bright sunlight for His Excellency.

As the armed guard suddenly came to rigid attention, the tall uniformed figure of Señor Gartez emerged from a doorway on the opposite side of the patio. Cheryl remained defiant and her ropes kept her seated.

"Ah, Señorita Lieutenant Finley, how nice it is to have you come and visit me," said Señor Gartez as he approached her.

"You had me kidnapped, you son-of-a-bitch!" Cheryl screamed.

"Oh, my, our Lieutenant is sensitive," said Señor Gartez with a big grin on his face.

"What do you want with me?" Cheryl cried.

"I want nothing...except your gold!" said Señor Gartez, now changing his facial expressions.

With that he held out his hand and showed her the chain with her dog tags and the safety deposit box key.

"You...you bastard! Your people broke into my house and stole that," Cheryl yelled at him.

"Yes, Señorita," said Señor Gartez. "Now I'm going to steal all your gold!"

"Never, you'll never find out where it is," said Cheryl defiantly.

"Really! Come Lieutenant Finley, be reasonable," said Señor Gartez.

He moved closer to Cheryl and said, "I want your gold, and you want to live, correct?"

With that she spits in his face. He slapped her for her defiance and said, "When your Commandant gets my ransom demands, he will follow my instructions or you are history, Lieutenant."

"He'll kill you first before you will ever see any of the gold," she said as she started to spit again.

Señor Gartez looked at Cheryl and said, "You are one tough bitch, Lieutenant. I have ways of dealing with you...but, I will do nothing but keep you here under my protection until I hear from your Commandant boyfriend."

"I won't help you and neither will Stan," Cheryl shouted.

"Guards, remove the Lieutenant to her basement room," ordered Señor Gartez.

"As you wish, Your Excellency," they said as they hauled Cheryl kicking and biting down from the patio level. When Señor Gartez left the patio area, he headed for his study. There he laid Cheryl's dog tags and key in his desk ashtray. He then proceeded to write the ransom note. When he had finished, he called for Pedro.

"Si, Your Excellency, you called?" said Pedro.

"Give this ransom note to Miguel and have him deliver it to Lieutenant Finley's Commandant boyfriend at his Mission Hills home tonight," ordered Señor Gartez.

"Very good, Your Excellency, I'll see to it right away," said Pedro.

* * *

While driving to *John F. Kennedy Airport*, Janet told Todd, "I couldn't locate your hourglass in the apartment."

"Oh," said Todd. "I remember placing it up on the mantelpiece next to the candle in the glass holder. I thought they balanced each other since together the two objects were nearly the same size."

"Well, aren't we the decorator in our old age. Michelle must have done something right while redoing our apartment," laughed Janet.

Arriving at the airport with not much time to spare, Janet gave Todd a loving farewell kiss before hundreds of spectators.

"Goodbye, darling," Todd said. "Keep safe, call me when you get to Mexico City, and don't forget I'll meet you Saturday afternoon at five o'clock in San Diego."

"Will the main lobby of the *Hotel Del Coronado* do?" she asked.

"That will be just perfect. Maybe we could spend the weekend there?" he suggested to her.

"Yes, it's a lovely old-time place and I'm sure there would be a room with an ocean view. Goodbye, Todd, enjoy your flight tomorrow," said Janet with a mischievous grin.

"Sure, you know how much I hate to fly," said Todd.

"Oh, yes, try not to think about being thirty thousand feet up, rather only five and a half miles away," she said with a smile.

"Oh, go on," he said as he handed her the carry-on bag. She then quickly proceeded through the terminal, and boarded her flight to Mexico City. "This flight is quite full for this time of year," she thought. Janet got a window seat next to a nun who she recognized as a Sister of Charity. The two women spent the remainder of the flight discussing world hunger and the problems associated with the current regime in Mexico City.

The hour was early afternoon when Todd arrived back at his Manhattan architectural firm. Jon and Larry inquired as to Janet's departure.

"She's gone. Her flight was on time," Todd told them.

"Oh Todd. You'll see her in a couple of days, and who knows, you might have an interesting weekend out on the coast," Jon said smiling.

Already, Todd felt lonely. He just said goodbye to the love of his life. He secretly wanted her to stay home with him, but he understood the importance of this interview with the opposition leader, Raul Gartez. If anything, unusual was going on, certainly Janet's ability to use tactfulness would help expose, to her readers and to congressional leaders, the truth about that place.

He had told her many times to be constantly on the lookout for danger while in Mexico and for some bargains in the little shops along the Main Street Marketplace in the center of Ensenada.

* * *

* 33 *

THURSDAY, 1500 HOURS, JANUARY 3

Janet Derr stepped off the plane in Mexico City almost twenty-four hours after Cheryl Finley had been taken to the basement of Gartez's villa outside Ensenada. Janet immediately was greeted by another newspaper journalist who helped her with customs and transportation.

"Welcome to Mexico, Señorita Derr, I am Roberto Perron," he told Janet.

"Thank you, Señor Perron, I am delighted to be here to attend the press briefing with you this evening at the National Palace," said Janet in her most business manner.

"Please call me Roberto," said Mr. Perron.

"Fine, Roberto. I can't believe all the media coverage lately about Mexico," said Janet.

"Si, Seniority. There have certainly been some new and exciting developments going on around there," said Roberto smiling.

"Almost every night on the news in New York City, there's something about Mexico and its political doings," she said.

"Por favor, Señorita Derr, follow me, I'll take you to my car," Roberto told her.

"Please call me Janet," she asked with a smile.

"Si, Janet, that's a lovely name," said Roberto shyly.

The airport was very congested, and there were people with crying babies everywhere.

"Is this place always like this, Roberto?" Janet asked.

"Si, many of these people have relatives in the States, and they are trying to leave the country before any fighting breaks out," replied Roberto.

"Oh, my, is the situation that serious, Señor?" asked Janet in a concerned tone of voice.

"Si, Señorita Janet," replied Roberto.

Upon reaching the car, he loaded her suitcase into the trunk and said, "I truly believe that if Señor Raul Gartez gets his hands on enough money, he'll turn this country upside down with his ever-increasing Liberation Army."

"So, who's giving him support now?" Janet asked Roberto as they buckled their seat belts.

"No one actually knows for sure. He must be using drug money or some other illegal source because the CIA, your State Department, and the other foreign governments constantly deny supporting him," replied Roberto.

"Well, maybe tomorrow when I meet with him at his villa, he'll answer my questions," stated Janet.

Hearing that Janet was going to Gartez's villa so startled Roberto, that he nearly drove off the road. He said in an excited voice, "Señorita! I had no idea that you were personally going to conduct that interview. Señor Gartez speaks to no reporters. Never!"

"Well, I've got a special invitation to conduct my interview," Janet assured him.

"That will be excellent, Señorita. We'll look forward to what he has to say to you," said Roberto in a serious attempt to be convincing.

They drove through the center of the city, and Roberto pointed out several new archeological digs.

"Did you know that Mexico City was built over the ancient Aztec city of Tenochtitlan?" asked Roberto.

"I understood that the city was built in the center of a lake," replied Janet.

"Si, legend tells us that the *Aztec Indian King Quasamodal* believed he should build his capital city at the place where his people found an eagle perched on a cactus with a snake in its beak. They found the conditions of his belief on a small island in the center of a lake surrounded by steep mountains. It took quite an engineering feat for the Indians to build this city. Today, the lake is gone and Mexico City stands on that site," explained Roberto.

"Doesn't your national crest on the flag show that eagle?" asked Janet.

"Si. You know much about Mexico." Then pointing he said, "near this location stood two immense stone pyramids."

"Really," Janet said with great interest.

"After the Spanish conquered the Aztecs, the tribes scattered. Most of their civilization lay in ruins," said Roberto.

"That's such a terrible thing to have happened," said Janet sympathetically.

"But," said Roberto. "What is so terrible is that it still could happen today with madmen like Gartez in control."

Roberto continued warning Janet, "You should be careful because your hotel room may be bugged. You should just put your things inside the room and freshen up quickly."

"Thanks for you tip, Señor," said Janet in deep thought.

"I'll be back in one hour to pick you up for dinner and the press conference," stated Roberto.

"Gracias, Roberto. You've been most kind," said Janet politely.

As they arrived at the hotel he handed her the bags. Once inside the lobby, Janet registered. She then immediately made a phone call to Todd in New York City to tell him of her safe arrival.

* * *

Bringing his thoughts back to his work, Todd wondered if he would need to take a set of the architectural drawings to Herbert Hall in San Diego. He reassured himself that wouldn't be necessary because he would have access to the contractor's plans if any problems arose. Todd still thought he would have liked to have more input into the actual construction by visiting San Diego. Todd then remembered again how shortly after the construction began last March, he was ordered to immediately begin the additional plans for the basement computer storage area design. It took him six weeks to complete the design changes. Todd also recalled talking to the original contractor, George Bennet. Mr. Bennet told him it shouldn't take much more than nine months to get her "usable."

Todd was informed that Mr. Bennet had been replaced by a Mr. Paul McCoy after only about two months into the project. Todd had been told only that Mr. Bennet had suffered an unfortunate experience and was unable to continue working there. Todd disliked doing government contracts. They were so involved, and the government always took its time making payments to sub-contractors like himself.

Five o'clock rolled around. Jon told Todd he had been invited back to his mothers-in-law for the weekend. It seemed she was moving and needed his truck the next day. Todd shook his head and gave Jon his blessings. "See you when I return from San Diego next Tuesday," said Todd.

As Jon was leaving the office, the phone rang. Todd accepted the long-distance call from Mexico City.

"Hello, dear," said Janet joyfully. "I had a wonderful flight. I'm now in the lobby of the Imperial Hotel in Mexico City."

"Janet!" Todd replied, "I'm so glad your flight went well."

"A Señor Roberto Perron met me at the airport and plans to pick me up shortly for my press briefing tonight."

"Sounds good," he said, "Now you be careful down there. I'll meet you Saturday at five at the Hotel Del Coronado."

"Si, Señor," she chuckled. "I'll be expecting you. Have a good flight tomorrow, Todd."

"I'll try to stay calm, and enjoy my Bloody Mary's," said Todd with a nervous laugh.

"You do that," she told him with approval. "I've got to go. Take care, and love you."

"I love you too, dear. Good bye," Todd told her.

Once he had finished talking to Janet, his other partner, Larry, who was getting ready to depart for the night, asked him, "how was Janet's trip?"

"She just told me everything was fine," Todd told him.

"Good. I'll see you tomorrow before your flight," said Larry.

Once Larry left, Todd sat in his empty office. Eventually, he shut off the computer, the lights and headed for a nearby Chinese restaurant. He ordered Sweet and Sour Pork, Moo Goo Gia Pan and an Egg Roll.

*   *   *

As Janet hung up the phone from talking to Todd, the bellhop escorted her to her room. Within the hour she returned to the lobby to meet Roberto.

Roberto said, "Ah, Señorita. You look most lovely tonight."

"Thank you, Señor," said Janet. "Shall we have supper together?"

"Si. I know just the place," replied Roberto.

Together they dined at one of the nicer restaurants in the downtown area. Following dinner, they drove across town and entered the grounds of the National Palace. Both showed their press passes and walked through the metal detectors. All around were heavily armed security guards. They were ushered through the grand foyer into the great ballroom where they took their seats on the side. The crystal chandeliers were beautifully reflected in the gold gilt mirrors.

The audience rose when the announcement was made, *"His Excellency, the Minister of State Affairs."*

The tall, dark, handsome man entered the room wearing a black suit and a wide red sash over his shoulder. Attached to his coat were various medals and honorable decorations. He spoke in Spanish. Janet and Roberto followed the English translator carefully.

After his prepared remarks, he opened the floor to questions. Most of the other reporters were interested in how the current regime was handling the tough economic conditions from generally wide-spread unemployment and poverty that existed throughout the country. There was also mention about supporting rebels in San Sable and other hot spots in Central America.

The Minister of State Affairs at one point became very annoyed with one reporter's question and called for the security guards to remove the man.

"I guess free speech has a different meaning down here?" Janet quietly whispered to Roberto.

Finally, Roberto got the opportunity to ask a question. "Your Excellency, Roberto Perron, correspondent for the <u>Daily Times</u>. Sir, my question has to do with what direction your government will follow to avoid a direct confrontation with the *Liberation Army?*"

Total silence fell over the room as all eyes eagerly turned toward the Minister as he began talking, "Por favor, Señor Perron, my government will not negotiate directly with Señor Gartez's underground party. In the past when he has requested a meeting to discuss his intentions, our representatives have often been kidnapped or killed. This man only talks of violence and not of peaceful reforms. I'm afraid we may shortly need to apply a greater force to put down his activities."

"Gracias, Your Excellency, for your honest answer," said Roberto bowing.

During the drive back to Janet's hotel, Roberto commented on how wrong the Minister was saying, "That man underestimates the popularity among the people that Señor Gartez enjoys. He is extremely well armed and could possibly destroy Mexico's military power. He is an expert at guerilla warfare and terrorist tactics."

"I see," Janet replied and continued, "why did the Minister lie about the situation, Roberto?"

Roberto answered, "I personally think they are all afraid of what Gartez could do if he had more money. The politicians agree that without outside financial aid or internal embezzling, Gartez would amount to nothing more than hot air." Roberto pulled up in front of the Imperial Hotel and parked.

"Well, I hope he never finds a source for the money he wants," Janet said. "Tomorrow morning I'll have a column written for you to fax to New York."

"What is 'Fax,' Señorita Janet?" he asked.

"Oh, my, this is a primitive country! You can wire it, can't you?" asked Janet.

"Si, we can wire it," Roberto said with a reassuring smile.

Smiling back, Janet asked, "my flight to Ensenada leaves at 9:30 tomorrow morning. Would it be inconvenient to come by and pick me up, Señor?"

"Not at all. Fridays are usually easy for me, I'll be waiting in the lobby at 8:30," replied Roberto.

"Gracias, Señor. I really do appreciate the lift. Buenos Noches.

Adios," said Janet as she began to walk away.

"Buenos Noches, Señorita Janet. Sleep well. I'll see you at 8:30. Till then," said Roberto.

Janet went to her room and had room service bring her a snack. "Since living with Todd, he's taught me well about eating before bedtime," she laughed to the non-English speaking attendant.

Meanwhile downstairs at the front desk the hotel manager placed a phone call to Señor Gartez's villa saying, "Hello, Señor, this is the night manager at the Imperial Hotel in Mexico City. Inform His Excellency upon his return tonight, that Señorita Janet Derr will be picked up here at 8:30 tomorrow morning and taken to the airport. She should be arriving in Ensenada about noon."

"Gracias, Señor," Pedro told the manager. "Buenos Noches."

* * *

Back in San Diego that same Thursday afternoon of January the third, final landscaping and painting were being done at Herbert Hall's construction site in preparation for Saturday's ribbon cutting ceremony. At 0800 Thursday, the Captain notified the Supply Division that Lieutenant Finley would not be at her desk that day. He told the yeoman that the Lieutenant had taken 'Emergency Leave,' and he would advise them when Cheryl would return. The remainder of the day proved disastrous for Stan as he knew nothing about Cheryl's mysterious disappearance. He had not heard from her for over eighteen hours and was totally unable to concentrate on anything at work.

Finally, at 1630, he left the base headquarters and had dinner with Chief Sheppard aboard "*Yankee II.*" The two men sat and talked. The Captain said, "I honestly have no clue where she is, Chief."

The Chief replied, "If she was kidnapped, we certainly should get some sort of phone call or ransom demand."

"I know, Chief, it's been more than twenty-four hours and we've heard nothing. Thanks for the meal, but I've got to go. I'll call you if anything new develops," said the Captain as he prepared to leave.

When Stan arrived home about nine that evening, Miguel was waiting in a parked car across the street. He had placed the ransom note in Stan's screen door.

Seeing the envelope, Stan jumped out of his car and ran to the door. Grabbing the note, he quickly went inside and called Chief Sheppard at the marina and said, "Hello, Chief, the ransom note about Cheryl was in my screen door when I got home."

"Fine, Sir. Tell me what they want," said the Chief anxiously.

"The note says that Cheryl is in the protective custody of His Excellency, Señor Raul Gartez," replied the Captain.

"Who the hell is he, Sir?" asked the Chief.

"I don't know," said the Captain who then continued, "the note goes on to say, 'that she will be harmed if I don't immediately turn over all the gold mining operations and all the money that has already been made from my gold exchanges.' Isn't that something, Chief?"

"I wonder where this character and his operation are located?" asked the Chief.

"I'll contact my friend tomorrow morning at the CIA and have him dig up some interesting facts on Señor Raul Gartez," replied the Captain.

"Very good, Sir. Please tell me what you find out," said the Chief.

"I will, good night, Chief, and thanks," said the Captain.

"Don't worry, we'll get her back," the Chief assured him. As soon as Stan hung up the phone, he heard tires squeal on the street outside as the white car quickly drove off. Sometime later Miguel stopped at a nearby phone booth and called Señor Gartez and said, "Si, Your Excellency, the Commandant has the note. Buenos Noches, Señor."

"Miguel, return immediately to the villa tonight," ordered Señor Gartez.

* * *

Stuffed to overflowing from his Chinese meal, Todd entered his deserted New York apartment. He turned the golden hourglass over. He watched how effortlessly the tiny sand crystals fell. Soon he was fast asleep on the sofa in the dimly lighted living room. The sound of cars could be heard zooming down Riverside Drive four floors below. The snow started to flurry outside, and the wind blew a little stronger off the Hudson River. The night sky was overcast, forcing the building lights to glow softly like smoldering embers. Todd slept as the last grain of sand fell downward onto the accumulated sand pile in the lower orb. Clock chimes echoed softly throughout the apartment at midnight. Thursday had come to an end. Todd was now ready for some well-deserved sleep.

* * *

Darkness surrounded him. He could hear the conveyor in the distance. He began to see the red lanterns against the rocky walls. There were shadows of men on the walls. He could feel the collar around his neck, but he knew he dare not touch it. He could also hear men talking about the daily quota. They mentioned troy ounces and he heard them say, "Motherload!"

He seemed to be inside someone's gold mine. Where was it? How did he get involved in this? Who was running this operation? Maybe he was even having a vision from a past-life experience.

He thought, "am I dreaming or not? This seems too real!" He could feel it and hear it. Was he a captive working here in this mine or not?

"Oh my God! What the hell is going on here?" he yelled.

Just when Todd began to get hold of his emotions, there came a low rumble. This time it didn't seem too far away.

"What's happening?" Todd cried out as he fell to his knees. Everything around him started to shake. Sand began to pour down over him and he heard running water. He scrambled to his feet and started to run through the rocking tunnel. Behind him were the screams of other men trapped in the cave-in. His heart was racing; his head was throbbing.

He reached for his neck when a jolting shock of electricity ripped through him. Everything became quiet and still...

*   *   *

* 34 *

FRIDAY, JANUARY 4

Todd opened his eyes. The morning sunlight filled the apartment.

The time was 7:45 A.M. as Todd crawled into the shower to recover. He fixed himself a Bloody Mary to recover some more.

He began to do a load of laundry since he and Janet had long ago agreed to share the household duties. He thought he would take light-weight suit, some summer-type clothes and some junk food to nibble during the flight.

Todd disliked flying. Since he had gotten sick at Coney Island twenty-five years ago on the little airplane ride, just the mention of airplanes made him whiten. His associates took full advantage of this story from his childhood, much to Todd's embarrassment at dinner parties.

"Just a few more items and I'll be on my way" said Todd making one last final tour of the apartment to collect his brown tweed sports coat, red tie and airline ticket.

"What's this?" he said glancing at the golden hourglass sitting on the mantel. It seemed that the gilded mirror above the fireplace was reflecting those scratches on the hourglass.

"*Shit, would you get a load at that!*' he thought. It looked like some sort of map upon closer examination. Looking at the reverse figure in the mirror, Todd quickly sketched on a small piece of paper the lines and letters he could make out. He folded the paper and put it into his wallet. He locked the apartment door and headed for the downtown "A" train, suitcase in hand.

As the noonday sun shone into the empty apartment, a strand of sunlight hit the mirror. The slanting laser's angle illuminated the etched word "*Dutchman's.*" The letters were only about one-eighth inch high. The simple lines and dashes represented tunnels.

* * *

Knowing that Eastern time was three hours later, Stan called Washington shortly after 0500 hours, Pacific time.

Pacing the floor Stan said, "This is Captain Siegewick at Fort Warren in San Diego. I would like to speak with Mr. Farrell. Hello, Mr. Farrell, Stan Siegewick."

"Captain! What brings your call first thing this morning?" asked Mr. Farrell.

"Sir, my fiancé was kidnapped Wednesday afternoon from a local shopping mall here in San Diego by a group of Mexican terrorists led by a Señor Raul Gartez," explained the Captain excitedly.

"Oh, Captain, you're dealing with some serious shit," said Mr. Farrell.

"Who is this asshole, and where does he live?" asked the Captain.

"Listen, Captain. Give me about a half hour and I'll Fax everything we have on him," said Mr. Farrell.

"He's pretty big, huh?" asked the surprised Captain.

"Well, let me just say, if he ever gets to be Mexico's President, we're all in deep shit!" exclaimed Mr. Farrell.

"Fine, I'll deal with this son-of-a-bitch on my terms. I'm leaving for Base Headquarters now," said the Captain.

He gave Mr. Farrell the base's Fax number and thanked him for everything.

"Good luck, Captain, and when you get your special girl back, congratulate her for me for trapping you into marriage."

"Ha, sure thing. I'll see that you come to our wedding," said the Captain as he hung up the phone.

* * *

"Buenos Dias, Your Excellency," Pedro said as he handed Gartez the morning paper and his coffee. As Gartez began to read the paper, Pedro said, "Excuse me, Your Excellency, late last night the manager of the Imperial Hotel called from Mexico City. He informed me that this morning at 8:30, Señorita Janet Derr from New York would be picked up there at his hotel and taken to the airport for her flight here."

"Si, she is a newspaper reporter that I'm allowing to interview me. See that she's picked up at the Ensenada airport at noon. Then, have her brought here to my villa. I will receive her in my study," said Señor Gartez.

"Fine, Your Excellency. As you wish," replied Pedro.

* * *

By 0730, the Captain had received about fifteen Fax pages from Washington. He called Chief Sheppard and asked him to drop by before heading for his security office. The Captain proceeded carefully to examine each sheet. A ruthless tale unfolded.

"Excuse me, Captain, Chief Sheppard is here," Yeoman Roth said over his desk intercom.

"Good morning, Chief, have a seat and get a load of this," the Captain said, returning the Chief's salute.

"This Gartez is the leader of Mexico's 'Liberation Front' and has his eyes on the Presidency," the Captain told the Chief.

"Does it say where he operates from?" asked the Chief.

"Yes, Gartez has a seaside villa on the outskirts of Ensenada, south of here on the Baja Peninsula," replied the Captain.

"Do you suppose that's where Cheryl is?" asked the Chief.

Looking at the documents the Captain said, "I'm certain, it appears to be about a hundred miles from here."

"How far by boat, Sir?" asked the Chief.

"Why, yes! Of course, the distance would be much less. We could plan a rescue by boat!" exclaimed the Captain showing his peculiar smile. "Here's a CIA aerial reconnaissance photo of Gartez's villa," he said as he handed the Chief the photo.

"May I take this with me?" the Chief asked.

"After work, today and before the reception tonight for my retirement, let's meet in the basement brig and plot our next move," said the Captain.

"Fine, Sir. I'll be there at 1630," replied the Chief while saluting.

* * *

Soon after Cheryl had a simple breakfast of toast and coffee two armed guards unbolted the door and entered her room followed by Señor Gartez.

"Buenos Dias, Lieutenant Finley, I hope you slept well." Gartez said.

"Please go away. Leave me alone," she pleaded.

"Not until you tell me the location of your gold."

"Never, you bastard!" she screamed.

The two guards quickly grabbed her and held her tight. Gartez then approached her, and took a firm grip on her chin.

"You listen to me, Lieutenant," Señor Gartez said loudly. "I don't want to hurt you."

"Fuck you," she said, spitting in his face.

Outraged at Cheryl's defiance, he slapped her face. The guards pushed her hard to the dirt floor. They tied her hands behind her and wrapped the cord around her ankles. Gartez pulled out a riding stick and began to whip her back.

"Stop, stop," Cheryl pleaded, "Please don't hit me again."

"All right," he yelled, "Tell me where the damn gold is!" Cheryl then decided to tell what little she could remember from Stan's drunken explanation on Christmas Eve. She said, "The gold is under Fort Warren Naval Base."

"What!" he said surprisingly. "And how does one get it?"

"Ask the Marine sentry at the main gate," Cheryl replied.

He became angrier and hit her several more times with the stick as his two men stood there enjoying the scene. "Get her up," Gartez commanded.

"Si, Your Excellency," the two said as they lifted Cheryl.

"Now, for the last time, where's the gold, and how can I get to it," yelled Señor Gartez.

Coughing and hurting tremendously, Cheryl managed to say, "There's a tunnel that is under Fort Warren. The entrance is from the beach. Somewhere in that tunnel, is the source of the gold."

"Anything else, Lieutenant?" asked Señor Gartez.

"No, I swear it. I know nothing else," cried Cheryl.

"And the key? What does that go to?" inquired Señor Gartez.

"Nothing," she answered softly. "It unlocks my storage trunk of uniforms. Honest, Señor Gartez."

"Huh," sighed Gartez. "Untie her and keep her here."

The trio departed and bolted the door. Cheryl sat at the small table and cried hysterically.

*   *   *

Todd's 2:30 P.M. flight to San Diego was delayed for twenty-minutes on the runway. It seemed there was some unwanted smoke in the cockpit. Todd nervously sipped on his second Bloody Mary shortly before liftoff. Once airborne, he finally fell asleep. The small piece of paper remained safely tucked away inside his wallet.

*   *   *

Shortly before noon Pacific time, Janet's small chartered plane touched down at Ensenada, Mexico, where the jagged mountains abruptly end at the coast. The starkness of the Baja Peninsula struck Janet as she disembarked the plane and a tall man wearing sunglasses stood on the runway. Being the only passenger with blond hair, Janet was easily identifiable.

"Señorita Derr," the driver said. "Please come with me for your meeting with His Excellency, Señor Gartez."

"Gracias, Señor," Janet replied. "It is such an honor that his excellency has agreed to an interview with me."

"Si, Señorita, His Excellency will not interview with Mexican news people due to their misunderstanding of his intentions."

"I see," Janet said.

"Señor Gartez wants the people of the United States to better understand our struggle for liberation," said the driver.

Janet rode through a small seaport town full of working people and loads of darling little children. When the car stopped for a traffic light, many of the children ran toward the car begging for money and food.

"Driver, give the children what they need," said Janet sadly.

"No, Señorita, we ignore then. They're too young to work or fight in our army!" With that statement, he blew the horn and proceeded through the juvenile crowd.

Janet saw the look of hunger and despair on many of their young faces. "Damn it," she thought, "These people have so little and we have so much. What a shame."

Turning into the road approaching the villa, Janet saw what had to be one of the most spectacular houses she had ever seen. The villa sat high in the edge of a cliff with a sweeping view of the ocean.

"My God, Señor, His Excellency's villa is immense!" she exclaimed to the driver.

Janet saw the surrounding high white stucco wall. There were armed guards posted everywhere. The multi-level red tile roofs covered many interior structures and connected then into one.

As the wrought iron gate was opened, one of the guards stepped forward. "May I see your papers, Señorita?" asked the guard.

Janet handed him her passport, press ID and her invitation. She could clearly see that the villa looked more like a military headquarters than a comfortable oceanside retreat.

"Very good, Señorita Derr, now please step out of the car and open your suitcase for a weapons search," ordered the guard.

Following his directions, Janet did as was told.

"Señor Gartez will meet you in his study now. You may enter the villa's grounds," said the guard now being more pleasant.

* * *

* 35 *

FRIDAY, 1300 HOURS

"Hey Doug, come look at what I found this morning on the top shelf of the living room closet," Pam Howerton told her Commandant-to-be husband, who had dropped by for lunch.

"What have we here?" he asked her, as she handed him the rolled-up set of architectural revisions stamped *"CLASSIFIED – COMPUTER STORAGE AREA, HERBERT HALL. FORT WARREN N.T.C., SAN DIEGO, 15 APRIL, 1989.'*

"I'll take this over to Base Headquarters and ask around," said Captain Howerton.

"What else do you want on your sandwich?" his wife called from the kitchen.

"Lettuce and tomatoes would be fine, dear," replied the Captain.

* * *

The Spanish driver took the car around the circular driveway and parked it close to the front entrance of the villa and said, "You may leave your suitcase in the car. It will be safe."

"Señor, may I freshen up from my travels before I meet with His Excellency," asked Janet.

"Certainly, Señorita, right this way," said the driver.

When they left the hot Baja sunshine and walked under a covered arched walkway, a cold chill went up her spine. When Janet returned to her escort, he directed her to the study. She took a mental note that room after room was filled with beautiful antique furnishings and crystal. Many of the rooms were adobe with beam ceilings and tile floors. Skins and wall tapestries hung everywhere. Every window provided a gorgeous ocean view. As Janet entered the study, Gartez arose from his huge intricately carved desk and extended a warm welcome. Thinking to himself of an excuse to put her down below with Cheryl, he nevertheless said, "Welcome, Señorita Derr. Welcome to my casa."

"Your Excellency, it is truly a pleasure to be here," said Janet in a business manner.

Pedro returned and served them drinks as they took their seats. Janet removed her note pad and pencil from her purse and began her interview.

"Sir," said Janet, "I've just come from Mexico City where I attended a news conference last night given by the Minister of Internal Affairs who said, when asked about you, that you are a strong political force, and the government feels it will shortly be in direct confrontation with you."

"Si," said Señor Gartez, "Those currently running the government are idiots! They accomplish little and are ruining this country. They cannot deal with me directly."

"Why is that, sir," asked Janet.

"Each time they send someone to negotiate with me that person turns out to be an assassin!" exclaimed Señor Gartez.

"Is that why all the security?" asked Janet.

Señor Gartez replied, "Si, everywhere I travel, I must provide my own security."

"Don't the taxpayers pay for that?" asked Janet.

"No, Señorita, at least not until I'm elected President," replied Señor Gartez.

Seeing that her interview was going well, Janet asked, "how do you plan to run for the Presidency, Your Excellency?"

"I have access to money from my sale of Pre-Columbian artifacts," replied Señor Gartez proudly.

"How interesting," she said while thinking about his current Columbian drug dealings instead of antiques.

"The money is made slowly, one piece at a time," explained Señor Gartez.

"In other words, you have to rely on the black market to sell those pieces?" asked Janet.

Catching Gartez off guard and trying to get him to admit to illegal dealings, she sat back and waited for his response.

"My, my, Señorita Derr, you do ask some probing questions," said Señor Gartez trying to remain courteous.

She looked at him, and smiled.

"If you could find me another source of money, I would be very grateful," said Señor Gartez. Then, remembering the contents of Cheryl's ransom note, he said, "perhaps, though, I may in a short while inherit some property on which there is a working gold mine."

"A gold mine! Oh my." said Janet who then thought to herself, "That bastard could really complicate matters and make himself quite rich and powerful."

She then asked him, "Your Excellency, tell me about your army."

"My Army!" he laughed, "I have no Army. Only a few bodyguards. I have good friends who are high-ranking officers in the Mexican Army. When the time is right, they will support me and convince their troops to do the same."

"I see," said Janet who continued, "and I suppose with your wealth from this new gold mine, you'll be able to pay their salaries."

"Double their salaries, Señorita. Is there anything else you would like to ask? I'm rather busy this afternoon," said Señor Gartez preparing to leave.

"One final question, sir. Who's set of dog tags are those in your ashtray?" asked Janet.

Suddenly, Gartez leaped to his feet and began acting crazy. He yelled, "Guards! Here! Get this stupid bitch out of my sight! Already she knows all my plans."

The two men quickly grabbed Janet, and one put his hands over her mouth to prevent her from screaming.

"Put her below with the other one," screamed Gartez.

Janet had dropped her purse and note pad. Once the guards had taken Janet away, Gartez picked up her things and placed them on the corner of his desk next to the ashtray.

* * *

Cheryl heard the commotion outside her door. Suddenly the dead bolt slid back and Janet was roughly pushed inside. She lay on the dirt floor as the door quickly shut and was bolted.

"Who the hell are you?" Janet sobbed, not having remembered meeting Cheryl before.

"I'm Cheryl Finley," she replied.

"Cheryl Finley!" exclaimed Janet as she got up from the floor and brushed herself off. "I'm Janet Derr from New York. I went to college with your sister, Peggy!"

"Oh, my God! Janet, of course. Peggy introduced us years ago," said Cheryl bewildered.

"Why are you here?" Janet asked.

"First, Janet, please tell me where I am. I was kidnapped in San Diego Wednesday afternoon and brought here blindfolded," said Cheryl.

"Oh, you poor dear. You're...rather we're South of Ensenada, Mexico, on the Baja Peninsula. Probably about sixty or seventy miles South of the U.S. border," Janet told her.

"I was invited outside early yesterday morning to meet His Excellency, Raul Gartez," said Cheryl.

"Yes, I just left him also. I was conducting an interview for the <u>Daily Times</u>," said Janet.

"I guess the bastard didn't like what we said," said Cheryl.

"It's now Friday afternoon, how long do you think we'll be detained?" Janet asked Cheryl with tears in her eyes.

They both started to cry and held each other for comfort. The two young women were very much afraid. Cheryl knew she was being held for ransom for her gold but what did Gartez want with Janet? "How can we escape from here?" Cheryl asked. "Have you seen the layout of this place?"

Janet stopped crying and attempted to recall what she had noticed and said, "Plenty of armed guards about and only one road comes to the villa. There is a steep cliff with the ocean beyond."

Cheryl said, "Well, have a bite of leftover breakfast and let's sit tight until an opportunity to escape presents itself." Cheryl continued to inform Janet, "Later tonight there'll be a retirement dinner and a reception for my fiancé, Captain Stan Siegewick, at the Officer's Club of Fort Warren." She started to cry again.

Janet tried to be reassuring saying, "It'll be all right, and besides, my boyfriend Todd Tasselmeyer should be landing at the San Diego Airport about this hour. I think Todd was going to be at that retirement dinner tonight."

"Oh, Janet, how I so looked forward to being there with Stan," said Cheryl sobbing.

"I know, Cheryl," Janet said sobbing, "I had planned to meet Todd tomorrow at five in the lobby of the Hotel Del Coronado."

* * *

Meanwhile, upstairs in the villa's study, Gartez informed Pedro, "Miguel and I are leaving for Mexico City to meet tomorrow with several of my Generals to tell them about my new source of gold!"

* * *

* 36 *

Captain Doug Howerton returned to Base Headquarters and asked Yeoman Roth who was in their offices.

"Commander Wilkins, Sir, is down the hall in room 105," replied Yoeman Roth.

"Thank you, Yeoman," he said as he proceeded down the passageway carrying the roll of drawings.

"Excuse me, Commander. May I see you for a moment?" asked Captain Howerton.

"Of course, Captain. What do you have?" asked Commander Wilkins as the men saluted each other.

"Sir, my wife discovered this roll of blueprints in our new quarters and asked me to return it here. It's stamped '*Classified*', and I thought you might know where it belongs," replied Captain Howerton.

"Let's see. Oh, yes, this is the set of revisions that Captain Siegewick had requested from the architect of Herbert Hall last spring. He and I decided we didn't need any more additional computer storage space after all and just to '*shit can*' that part of the construction project to save the taxpayers' money," explained the Commander.

"So, these prints were never built?" asked the Captain.

"Correct, Sir. We had Mr. McCoy close off the access and just continued building," explained the Commander.

"Did these revisions cost anything?" the Captain asked the Commander.

"No, Sir. Our contract with the architect had that provision," said the Commander.

"Shall I dispose of them?" asked Captain Howerton.

"Sure. Yeoman Roth has a burn bag started. Let her put them in there," said Commander Wilkins.

"Very good, Commander. There for a minute, I thought I may have stumbled on something," said the Captain grinning.

"Everything's fine, Sir. I'm sure of it," said Commander Wilkins trying to reassure the Captain.

When Captain Howerton gave the blueprints to Yeoman Roth, she crumpled each page separately to insure they would burn completely in the incinerator. Smoke from the incinerator chimney could be seen, as Lieutenant Lighal rode by the building on his way to the airport.

* * *

FRIDAY 1600 HOURS

Todd Tasselmeyer, feeling extremely nauseated from his five-hour bumpy flight and half dozen Bloody Mary's, walked slowly through the San Diego International Airport terminal to the lower level where he claimed his suitcase.

"Mr. Tasselmeyer," the friendly voice of Lieutenant Lighal called.

"I'd recognize your red tie anywhere!" he laughed.

The two men shook hands and headed outside to the waiting car with its Navy driver.

As the car began to move, Lieutenant Lighal said, "We're delighted that you were able to join us for all these special happenings."

"Thank you, Lieutenant." Todd answered, "How far is Fort Warren from here?"

"Actually. It is only about fifteen miles, but it'll take a while getting through the Friday afternoon rush hour," replied Lieutenant Lighal.

Looking out the window, Todd said, "Of course, just like back in New York. It'll be good to see how much this place has grown."

"Oh, you've been to San Diego before?" asked the lieutenant.

"Yes, we visited here about twenty years ago when my parents were on vacation," replied Todd.

Peering through the front window, Lieutenant Lighal said, "Once we leave this airport congestion, we'll hit *Interstate 5* and pass through downtown. Then we'll go across the *San Diego-Coronado Toll Bridge*."

"Good, I still remember how beautiful Coronado was with all the palm trees and marinas. I plan to meet my fiancé there tomorrow afternoon at the *Hotel Del Coronado*," Todd said boastfully.

"What's her name?" asked the Lieutenant Lighal.

"Janet," Todd fondly replied as he watched the palm trees pass by along the highway.

"Where's she today?" inquired the Lieutenant.

"She's somewhere in Mexico, sir, conducting some interviews with Mexican government officials. She writes for the <u>Daily Times</u> in New York City," replied Todd.

"That's some prestigious newspaper to be working for," said Lieutenant Lighal.

"Yes, and she's good at her job as a reporter," Todd said beaming proudly.

Passing through the downtown section of their trip, the lieutenant pointed out some of the sights. They passed near *Balboa Park* and the *San Diego City College* buildings, when Lieutenant Lighal pointed saying, "There's the newly restored *Gaslight Shopping District* and the new *Seaport Village* with its spectacular view of *San Diego Bay*."

Once they crossed the toll bridge, Todd saw the red Victorian roofs of the *Hotel Del Coronado*. Beyond the hotel and to the right was *North Island Naval Air Station*. They then turned left and headed southwest past the many sail boats and luxury yachts tied up at the marina on *Glorietta Bay*.

Soon they headed straight south on the *Coastal Highway*. Todd enjoyed the evening sunset over the Pacific and commented on the beach saying, "There doesn't seem to be any access to the beach here, Lieutenant."

"No, Mr. Tasselmeyer," replied Lieutenant Lighal. "The population must go further south towards Imperial Beach to enter. That leaves the beach in front of Fort Warren quite deserted most of the year except for occasional surfers."

Todd then asked the Lieutenant, "Sir, I have never been paid by the Navy for this building project. I've submitted bills many times over the past several months. Who should I see regarding this matter?"

"Lieutenant Commander Ellerly oversees disbursing and she's the one you'll need to see," said Lieutenant Lighal with a smile.

Their Navy car again turned left and passed through the Main Gate. The driver slowed for Todd to get his first look at the magnificent new structure of Herbert Hall.

As Todd was looking at the building, Lieutenant Lighal said, "That's some beautiful building you designed, Mr. Tasselmeyer."

"Why, thank you, Lieutenant," said Todd trying not to show how proud he was.

"I've taken a personal interest in its construction since Mr. McCoy took over as Construction Superintendent," said the Lieutenant.

"Yes, I heard that Mr. Bennet had been replaced," said Todd.

"Mr. Bennet was found floating in the ocean...an apparent drowning victim," said Lieutenant Lighal sadly.

"Oh my!" Todd exclaimed, "Commander Wilkins didn't tell me that one."

Todd was assigned a room for the night at the eight-story high-rise on the base that was used as transit barracks.

While Todd was getting out of the car, Lieutenant Lighal said, "Be outside at 1830, and the car will pick you up for dinner."

"Thank you, Lieutenant," said Todd as he closed the car door.

* * *

When Captain Siegewick reached the main entrance of the storm drain, Corporal Lenert was standing the watch.

"Good evening, Sir. Chief Sheppard and the other guards are assembled inside." the young Corporal said coming to attention and saluting.

"Excellent, Corporal. After the meeting, I'll see that you're instructed as to your roll in the mission," the Captain said returning his salute.

"Thank you, Sir," the Corporal said saluting again.

Remaining at his post, he allowed the Captain to enter and pass the temporarily deflected light sensor. This way he would not alert Fort Warren's Marine detachment of a security violation.

"Captain Siegewick is headed in," called the Corporal over the walkie-talkie.

"Very good, Corporal. Carry on," a voice responded.

The Captain proceeded slowly and adjusted his hard hat while his eyes adjusted to the red wall lights. When he reached the steel door, Sergeant Miller greeted him.

"Welcome, Sir, we were very sorry to hear about Lieutenant Finley," said Sergeant Miller trying to show sincerity in his greeting.

"Yes, that's primarily why I'm here. We're going to plan a rescue of her tonight," said the Captain.

"Fine, Sir. My men are in top condition to kick some asses!" exclaimed Sergeant Miller.

Just then, Chief Sheppard approached in his dress blue uniform and saluted.

Returning his salute, the Captain said, "Chief, I decided to let you take six of our best men and head south tonight after midnight to assault Gartez's villa."

"Excellent, Captain. The men should have no problem since the Mexicans are not suspecting such a daring rescue," said the Chief feeling the urgency of this mission.

The Captain said to Sergeant Miller, "I want your men to take out as many of his body guards as possible. Leave Corporal Lenert here in charge of mining operations tonight."

"Understood, Sir," said Sergeant Miller saluting.

"I've got to get back to the Officer's Club for my retirement dinner, so you men work out all the rest of the details. Come, Chief, our staff and their guests await us topside," said the Captain as he returned the Sergeant's salute and started to leave.

"Right this way, Sir. Men, meet me at the Marina about 2330. Wear black uniforms and carry your M-16s. Don't forget to bring some delayed-action explosive devices and all of the night vision equipment," said the Chief as he and the Captain left through the steel door and proceeded to walk through the connecting tunnel.

* * *

FRIDAY, 1930 HOURS

Todd stood outside the transit barracks waiting for his ride. He wondered if anyone at the dinner would even speak to him. The snack he had eaten onboard the flight didn't last very long, and he was extremely hungry. Just then, the gray car pulled up.

"Mr. Tasselmeyer, I'll take you to the Officer's Club," said the Petty Officer driver.

Feeling somewhat apprehensive, Todd decided to go for at least the food. He knew he would finally meet the infamous Captain Siegewick.

The car pulled up at the front entrance to the Officer's Club. Todd was directed to the main dining room. Once inside, the affair seemed like a class reunion, and Todd, not knowing anyone, felt like a dropout!

"Mr. Tasselmeyer, I'm the Executive Officer, Commander Wilkins. Welcome to Fort Warren. I hope you had a pleasant flight," said the Commander while shaking Todd's hand.

"Yes, Commander, and thank you." said Todd. "It was nice to have been invited tonight."

"Come, meet the staff. The guest of honor hasn't arrived yet," said Commander Wilkins.

Todd spent the next twenty minutes being introduced as the architect of Herbert Hall. The Officers and ladies were all very impressed with his building design. Todd was introduced to Admiral McKinsey, who gave him an, "Outstanding design, Mr. Tasselmeyer. She's the best-looking classroom building in the entire Pacific Fleet's training centers."

"Thank you, Admiral," said Todd. "Your words are appreciated." Todd finally managed to be served a Bloody Mary, and some hors d'oeuvres.

"Attention everyone," Commander Wilkins announced. "Our guest of honor has arrived. Would you all give a round of applause to our Commandant and soon-to-be civilian, Captain Stanley Siegewick, USN." With that the room burst into loud clapping and hollering as the Captain made his way to the head table. Captain Howerton and his wife were seated to Captain Siegewick's right. Admiral McKinsey and Commander Wilkins and his wife, Sofia, were seated on the left.

"Thank you, everyone, you're most kind," the Captain said appearing slightly choked up but thinking, "I can't wait until this is over with." Then he said, "Please, everyone be seated, and let's eat." Another round of applause followed.

Todd was seated near the head table. He watched as Mrs. Wilkins whispered something to Captain Siegewick, "You surely must have heard from Cheryl by now, Captain."

"I haven't heard directly from her, but I have a good idea where she is. If you'll excuse me, Mrs. Wilkins, I really must meet my guests," said the Captain feeling on edge.

"Of course, Captain. Just let me know if there is anything I can do," said Sofia.

"Just one thing. Don't mention Cheryl's disappearance to anyone, because it could hinder our efforts to get her back," said Stan almost whispering.

"As you wish, Captain," she said. Sofia turned and continued to talk with her husband.

Todd eventually was introduced to Captain Siegewick.

"Mr. Tasselmeyer, of course, our famous architect from New York. I hope all's well with you." the Captain said.

"Yes, Captain, I'm doing fine. Everything seems to have gone well with the construction. I'm looking forward to touring the facility tomorrow and finally receiving payment from your disbursing people," said Todd with a look of determination.

"Yes, you do that. Thank you for joining us this evening," said the Captain.

"Pleasure, Captain," said Todd then he quickly added, "enjoy your retirement, sir."

The Captain, showing his peculiar smile, then said, "Oh, I will, be assured. Mr. Tasselmeyer, meet Captain Howerton, my replacement."

"How do you do, sir," said Todd.

"Nice job, son, on Herbert Hall. The Navy needs more good designers and architects like you," said Captain Howerton.

"Thank you, Captain. Begging your pardon, I think I see my table being served," said Todd excusing himself.

"Please, go right ahead," said Captain Howerton.

The evening concluded about 2200 after Stan had opened many gifts and read notes from his friends and associates. Todd couldn't wait to get back to his room and into bed. The Bloody Mary's worked their magic. By 2230, he was fast asleep.

Meanwhile, Captain Siegewick and the Chief drove separately off Base. They followed each other's car back to the marina.

*   *   *

Down in the cellar of Gartez's villa, Janet and Cheryl spent the evening talking and trying to understand their serious predicament. They heard many sounds upstairs and constantly sat in fear of being dragged off somewhere to be tortured. Suddenly, there was a knock on their door. The voice said, "Señoritas, it's Pedro, I've brought some food."

The grateful women appreciated his concern for their welfare. "His Excellency has left the villa for Mexico City. He will return tomorrow. I will come back in the morning with breakfast," said Pedro.

"Gracias, Señor Pedro, Gracias," they both said at the same time.

"Buenos Noches, Señoritas," he said as he left and bolted the door.

"Oh, I feel so relieved knowing that horrible man has left for the night," Cheryl told Janet.

Janet had told Cheryl earlier why she had visited the villa, but she still didn't understand why Cheryl had been kidnapped. Cheryl was reluctant at first but then figured Janet could be trusted to keep the secret. She said, "Stan found a treasure buried under Fort Warren last March. Nobody connected with the Navy except the Chief Master-At-Arms knows the exact location."

"What kind of treasure is it, Cheryl?" Janet asked.

"There must have been some sort of old gold mine located down there," replied Cheryl.

"Of, course," said Janet. "Señor Gartez told me about his acquiring gold to finance his military take-over of the Mexican government."

"Yes, that bastard wants to steal the gold from Stan and me," said Cheryl angrily.

"Is there a lot of gold?" Janet inquired.

"I believe there is. So far, Stan has collected a little more than two million dollars from the sale of his gold," said Cheryl proudly.

"Cheryl! That's fabulous. You are so lucky. I can't imagine that much money. What does it look like?"

"We have a safety deposit box that is nearly full of stacks of ten thousand, one hundred-dollar bills," replied Cheryl.

"Wow! Can Gartez get to it?" asked Janet.

"Maybe, the key is on my dog tag chain," said Cheryl.

"Yes, I saw it lying in his ashtray on his desk," said Janet.

"Oh, thank God! It's still here. I told him that the key unlocked my trunk of uniforms," Cheryl said with a grin.

"Did he believe you, Cheryl?" asked Janet.

"I think so, but if we ever get out of here, I must take that key back to Stan!" said Cheryl emphatically.

"How did Gartez get your key?" asked Janet.

"His people ransacked our home in Mission Hills on New Year's Eve and took the dog tags and the key off the night stand by my bed," replied Cheryl, the memory making her feel ill.

"I hope you'll get it back soon," said Janet encouragingly.

"Yes, Janet, so do I," Cheryl said, bowing her head into her hands.

* * *

* 37 *

The Captain and the Chief assisted Sergeant Miller and his four-fellow former Marine guards to load their gear aboard the yacht, *Yankee II.* It was a moonless, overcast night. The chilly January air forced everyone to wear some type of jacket. After the gear was stowed, the Chief instructed the men to cast off the lines.

The Captain told the assembled men shortly before midnight, "Good luck, men. You will be paid well for tonight's exercise."

"We'll make every attempt to return by early morning, Captain," the Chief told him.

"Very good, carry on, Chief," Captain Siegewick said while saluting for another time. At noon, tomorrow his retirement would take effect.

The Captain disembarked the yacht and stood on the pier watching his friends sail out of sight. Then he got in his car and drove home.

Knowing of the danger involved in such a rescue attempt, the Captain realized that if they failed, he would be left alone to defend his claim against Gartez's wrath. The whole idea made him wish tomorrow's ceremonies didn't require his presence. He longed to be aboard the Chief's yacht and to lead the rescue.

"Damn it, all of it," Stan said angrily as he hit the steering wheel. "Cheryl, darling, I miss you so much. They'll be there soon to get you and bring you home to me."

* * *

The four-hour journey south to Mexico's Baja Peninsula passed quickly. The ocean remained relatively calm. The lights along the shore helped in navigation. The sixty-five-foot yacht was fully outfitted with the latest state-of-the-art sonar and radar equipment. The ship maintained a constant twenty knots and passed no other ships.

"I suspect the villa is heavily fortified, Chief," Sergeant Miller said.

"Plan on it, Sergeant. We also know from the CIA photos, that the Captain gave me, that the villa sits on a cliff which appeared to be close to forty feet high," the Chief told him.

"Understood, Chief. We brought the grappling hooks and plenty of rope," said Sergeant Miller.

"Good, Sergeant. That'll help things," replied the Chief.

"Do you think we should cut the power to the villa, Chief?" asked Sergeant Miller.

"Yes, and phone lines if possible. That'll enable us to use the night vision equipment easily," replied the Chief while watching his navigational instruments.

Close to 4:00 A.M. the *Yankee II* dropped anchor about a mile off shore. In the distance, the faint lights of the lone structure could be seen.

"I see it perfectly," the Sergeant told the Chief, looking through his special pair of night binoculars.

"You men prepare the dingy for launch," ordered the Chief.

"Right, Chief," replied Sergeant Miller.

Each man took a backpack full of equipment and his M-16. The Chief carried the explosive devices. They pushed silently away from the darkened yacht and proceeded to row towards the shore. The tide assisted and quickly pulled the dingy onto the deserted beach below the villa. Once everything was unloaded, the six men, wearing black coveralls and hoods, began the assent of the cliff.

The grappling hooks assisted the men in their climbing. Soon they were looking over the top where they could plainly see two guards patrolling near the front entrance gate. The Chief and the Sergeant affixed silencers to their rifles. Each took aim and fired once.

As the guards fell, the other men ran toward the villa's stucco walls. Two of the men quickly pulled the dead bodies off into the bushes. One man traced the villa's electric power source and another the phone lines. Both men succeeded in cutting the wires. The villa fell into silence and complete darkness. Now they heard several more voices on the inside of the walls. They figured these guards would come out to check the power loss.

The Chief and his men hid as the main gate was manually pushed open by the guards from the inside. When two more guards appeared by the opened gate, the Chief's men ambushed and killed them. The Chief then led his five men through the main gate and around to the front entrance of the villa's main structure.

Pedro watched the whole event from an upstairs bedroom and focused on the shapes of the black figures as they advanced. He quickly put on his robe and reached for the dead phone. Throwing the useless phone to the floor, he went to a trunk near the side wall of his dressing room and got out a hand gun. He proceeded downstairs and entered Gartez's study. There he hid under the massive wood desk.

Within a few minutes, he heard the Chief and his men enter the room. Just as they approached the desk, he jumped out with a yell and fired three quick rounds. Sergeant Miller instantly cut him down with a burst of gunfire.

Chief Sheppard fell backward from one of Pedro's bullets which had entered and exited his shoulder. Immediately, one of his men yelled, "damn it! Chief, how bad are you hit?"

"I'll live, Mister. How's the Mexican?" the wounded Chief asked the Sergeant. "He's still alive, Chief. But I don't think he's going to be for long," replied Sergeant Miller.

"Chief, over here. It's Lieutenant Finley's dog tags and her purse," said one of the men.

"Good, she must be here," Sergeant Miller said while holding a handkerchief to the Chief's bleeding shoulder.

"Cheryl, ask him where's Cheryl?" yelled the Chief.

"Señor, where is Señorita Lieutenant, por favor?"

"Si, the Señoritas, they...are...below," said Pedro who pointed downward, then died in the arms of one of the Chief's men.

"Chief, the Lieutenant must be down in the basement. He's gone, Chief," said Sergeant Miller.

"Come on men, let's find the cellar and blow this place," ordered the Chief.

Chief Sheppard was assisted to his feet, and he said, "give me Cheryl's personal items."

"Here you are, Chief," Sergeant Miller said as he handed him Cheryl's dog tag chain with the safe deposit key still attached and Janet's purse and note pad.

The men, still carefully watching out for more guards, moved quickly and silently through the dark passageways. They finally located the stairs.

Cheryl and Janet were awakened suddenly when the dead bolt was slid and the door was quickly pushed open. Both girls screamed when they saw the men wearing black hoods coming into their little room. Upon entering the space, each man pulled off his hood. Cheryl, recognizing Chief Sheppard, immediately realized they were being rescued. Each girl embraced their liberators.

"Oh, Chief Sheppard, how did you ever find us?" asked Cheryl ecstatically.

"Don't worry, I'll explain later," replied the Chief. "Men, help the ladies' topside."

"Chief, you're wounded!" cried Cheryl.

"I'll be all right. Who's your friend?" he asked, as they all quickly went up the steps.

"She's Janet Derr," said Cheryl. "May we take her back to San Diego with us?"

"Fine, you men go ahead and set the charge in the hallway of the main house. Set the timer for forty-five minutes," ordered the Chief.

"Right, Chief," replied Sergeant Miller. Turning to Cheryl he said. "We're going to leave Gartez's house like his men left yours. Only we'll be a bit more thorough."

Soon all the Chief's men returned and everyone headed for the cliff. The descent was treacherous, and Chief Sheppard had an especially difficult time.

Once they were all safe aboard the dingy Cheryl and Janet thanked all the men for their heroic rescue. Janet, feeling secure fell back to sleep.

"Chief Sheppard! Thank you for recovering my chain and Janet's things. She's a newspaper reporter for the New York <u>Daily Times</u>, and her note pad contains her interview with Gartez," Cheryl said.

"That should be interesting reading, someday," replied the Chief. As the dingy approached the yacht, an explosion could be heard in the distance. The Saturday morning Eastern sky glowed with an orange tint as the *Yankee II* raised anchor.

The wounded Chief said, "Sergeant Miller, take the helm."

"Certainly, Chief. You go on down below and rest," replied Sergeant Miller.

After cruising in a northerly direction for about twenty miles, the Sergeant had one of his men go below to notify the Chief that a fog bank lay dead ahead.

"Damn it! Now we'll be delayed for our return. Help me up," the Chief asked his man.

As the Chief approached the helm, he saw the fog and instructed Sergeant Miller, "Reduce speed to ten knots and hold her steady on the current course."

"Chief, San Diego radio reports the fog bank extends about fifty miles up the coast," said Sergeant Miller.

"We'll be all right. We'll be free of this shit in about four hours. This is not a major shipping lane but go ahead and activate the fog horn. The switch is somewhere under the control panel," instructed the Chief.

By 0900 hours Saturday morning, they still were not half way back to San Diego and home.

* * *

* 38 *

EARLY SATURDAY MORNING, JANUARY 5

Todd awoke earlier than usual. He tossed restlessly in bed, half asleep and half awake, and wondered if it were the three-hour time difference or the anticipated excitement of the day ahead.

His room on the eighth floor of the Navy transit barracks was furnished stylishly modern with a lovely green plant growing peacefully in the corner. A large window near his bed afforded a spectacular view of the ocean. The dark of night was fading and the sky had begun to glow in anticipation of the coming day.

"Hurry up Sun, your light's already three hours old in New York City."

Todd put on his bathrobe and walked towards the window. He stared out through the vertical blinds. Although looking like prison bars, they were only plastic panels that swayed gently with his touch.

"Ah, the mighty Pacific. It's been a while since I last saw you," Todd said as he stretched and yawned. Looking out the window, he noticed the horizon to the left resembled that of torn paper. The dark jagged shapes of the mountains loomed at him, as they had for others through the generations. In striking contrast to the irregularly shaped mountains, the smooth flat ocean on his right almost beckoned to be explored.

Todd noticed what appeared to be a thick bank of fog lying several miles off the coast. It extended southward the entire length of the horizon.

Tiny lights from the fading night still twinkled from the city of San Diego along the base of the mountains. He saw that the bay separated Fort Warren from the city. "Each light represents a life story," he thought.

It was still too early for him to see any details from the eighth floor, but he observed how the morning's activities began to grow. Todd's attention was drawn to a distant pair of headlights approaching from the south along the Coastal Highway. The lights took a sharp left turn onto the beach and disappeared behind some sand dunes.

Todd thought, "Maybe a couple of young lovers wanted to have an early morning dip before breakfast." Continuing to stare out the window, he watched the approaching dawn.

Suddenly, the few dull grey clouds drifting effortlessly above him changed to the color of glowing embers. Surrounding clouds seemed to congregate and welcome the new day. Todd was extremely impressed with the silent light show taking place just outside his window. Splendid golds, yellows and oranges appeared in brilliant contrast to the nearby black mountains.

Having nothing on his agenda before 10:00 A.M., he decided to take a stroll on the beach before breakfast. After dressing in casual clothes, he took the elevator to the lobby. Venturing outside, he found a tropical world that felt quite chilly.

To reach the beach, Todd first walked through Fort Warren's main gate and crossed the Coastal Highway. Because it was Saturday, the usual line of commuters heading towards downtown San Diego failed to appear.

Todd carefully climbed down the twenty-five-foot cliff to the beach, noticing, as he went, how bulldozers had apparently piled up the sand to make artificial dunes about a hundred yards beyond the highway.

"I'll have to climb these damn man-made mountains before I can get a good view of the Pacific," he said to no one.

Within a few more minutes he was eyeing the crashing surf and rediscovering emotions that he had felt as a small boy. His parents had spent a summer vacation in Southern California when he was ten. Todd always wanted to return.

"The surf is pounding particularly hard for only a slight breeze," he thought. Glancing back and forth along the foaming shoreline, he could not make out any sign of the vehicle he had seen earlier.

Proceeding casually down the hard-packed dune to the water's edge, his eyes squinted as the bright sunlight shone on the waves and sparkling surf. It reminded him of the beaches Janet and he enjoyed visiting along the New Jersey coast. The morning sun was now illuminating the edges of the fog bank that was maintaining its distance off shore.

It made Todd feel good to be back in San Diego even though it was winter. He continued walking along the beach for about a quarter of a mile, looking at everything he passed.

Round pebbles by the thousands littered the beach and came in an endless variety of sizes and shapes. He gathered a few small stones that he thought would look excellent in his little brother's aquarium. Soon, his jacket pocket bulged with about a dozen shaped stones.

As he walked up the beach, the dunes continued to stretch out in front of him for some distance. They appeared to be between fifteen and twenty feet higher than the cliff and were much lower closer to the water's edge. When he walked in the shadow of one of the tallest dunes, the lack of sunlight and the chill morning air made him shiver.

After about an hour of exploration, he felt he'd visited the beach long enough. He decided to begin climbing over the dunes towards the cliff. Each step seemed to be much more difficult than earlier. The sand dissolved beneath his feet and, with each step, he began sinking up past his ankles. Todd became frightened when he realized he could get stuck here and he was totally alone.

Suddenly, he felt something solid only a few inches below the soft sand. He reached down to investigate. Pushing the sand aside, he saw that the buried object was colored yellow. Soon, the sun reflected off a chrome strip. To his surprise, he was standing on the roof of a taxicab!

The taxi somehow had gotten buried in the dune. Todd wondered how it got there and where its passengers were. Scooping away more sand revealed that the passenger compartment was quite empty. Much to his relief, there appeared no indications of foul play. The sand covered the windows and doors making it nearly impossible to investigate further.

"I wonder what's the story?" he thought. From the looks of things, he speculated that the cab had been driven here and covered over to conceal it from the view of passing motorists along the *Pacific Coastal Highway*.

He thought, "Sure, just like in my dream the other night in New York City!" He spent a moment trying to remember some of the dream's details, but couldn't. He glanced around to see if anyone else was in the vicinity. Quite far in the distance he saw a couple of joggers running in the opposite direction, away from him. He could also just about make out the shape of a person holding a metal detector.

Todd had to laugh at the metal object he'd just found...a complete taxicab! Then he observed the watermark on the dune. It was low tide, and the roaring surf was about fifty feet away.

"I'll bet that by high tide this cab will be washed out to sea and no one would ever know...if the owner doesn't come back soon." Glancing at his wristwatch, he noticed it was 8:00 A.M., so he'd better return to his quarters for breakfast. After all, this was California and an empty taxicab stuck in some sand dune didn't seem to be out of the ordinary nor create any security crisis. Todd decided that later this afternoon, after all the naval stuff was finished, he'd have some free time to explore this area before meeting Janet at 5:00 P.M.

When Todd approached Fort Warren's main gate, the Marine sentry said to him, "Good morning, sir. State your business."

"I'm an invited guest for this morning's dedication of Herbert Hall," replied Todd.

"Do you have your invitation, sir?" asked the sentry.

Being somewhat embarrassed, he was momentarily nonplused. Finally, he remembered he'd brought his transit barracks key. When the sentry saw Todd's key, he permitted him back into Fort Warren.

"Huh, I forgot they'd beef up security this morning," he thought to himself. "I could have missed all the fun!"

As he walked past Herbert Hall, Todd noticed two workmen installing the letters which gave the structure its name. He liked what he saw and returned to his temporary quarters for a light breakfast of eggs, bacon and a Bloody Mary.

About 9:45 A.M., Todd headed out the door of the high-rise and proceeded across the street towards the dedication ceremony site.

Civilians and military brass were assembling in front of the beautiful all-glass lobby. Folding chairs had been set up in the central courtyard of the structure. The front section was reserved for some of the junior officers. They would begin attending class here on Monday morning and had already arrived for the special occasion.

*   *   *

SATURDAY, 1000 HOURS

The Navy band began to play as the officers, all in dress blues, paraded down the center aisle. Several admirals had been invited along with the staff officers assigned to Fort Warren.

Many flags flapped in the light breeze and cameras clicked everywhere. Everyone rose as the base chaplain delivered the invocation. Following that, Commander Wilkins welcomed everyone and introduced Captain Siegewick and his successor, Captain Howerton.

Captain Siegewick spoke first saying, "*Admiral McKinsey, Admiral Haley, Admiral Lloyd, Officers, Ladies, and honored guests. Over the past ten months many people have labored long and hard to build this magnificent structure. We are assembled here today to dedicate this classroom building as a living memorial to a brave young twenty-year-old Ensign who, in the height of battle, so nobly distinguished himself and perished while doing so. This building will stand to serve, train and educate the fleet in which he so proudly served. Ensign James Herbert, we with great reverence and honor to your memory do hereby this day dedicate this structure and place upon its walls your name.*"

There was a round of applause as Captain Siegewick, surrounded by his staff and admirals, cut the ribbon and unlocked the front door. The Navy band played *Anchors Aweigh* and *The Stars and Stripes Forever.* The whole short ceremony made Todd very proud of his role in designing the newly dedicated building.

In what seemed like an instant, Captain Siegewick, Captain Howerton and their admirals left for Base Headquarters. About hundred-people entered the lobby where coffee and doughnuts were being served. Looking around, Todd felt as though he was experiencing a dream. Everything he'd envisioned gleamed and sparkled.

Todd's eyes were particularly drawn to the tasteful way the interior designer had displayed various personal items that belonged to Ensign Herbert. There on one wall was a painted portrait of him next to a framed Congressional Citation signed by President Franklin Roosevelt.

Everywhere gray tones accented with red reflected in the black tile floor of the vast open lobby. A historical forty-eight-star flag, that flew defiantly throughout the attack on Pearl Harbor, hung from the ceiling rafters.

"It's certainly an impressive lobby," Commander Wilkins said as he approached Todd. "How long did you spend designing her?"

"Four months, Commander," said Todd. "Everything these days certainly cost's a lot and open space helps save dollars."

"Are you ready for your grand tour, Mr. Tasselmeyer?" asked Commander Wilkins.

"Certainly, sir. Please lead on," replied Todd anxious to get started.

After only a short distance, the Commander spotted Mr. McCoy in the crowd and introduced him.

"Mr. Tasselmeyer, this is Mr. McCoy, our Construction Superintendent," said Commander Wilkins and, "Mr. McCoy, he's our architect."

"Well, you designed one hell of a beautiful building, Mr. Tasselmeyer," said Mr. McCoy.

"Thank you. And you did one hell of a good job putting her together," Todd replied.

"Mr. McCoy, would you like to join our tour?" inquired the Commander.

"I'd be delighted Commander Wilkins," Mr. McCoy said with a smile.

"Gentlemen, kindly step this way," said the Commander acting as a guide.

As the trio climbed the open, free-standing and very wide metal stairs for the main lobby, Todd now understood the need the Navy had for such a large facility.

"Nearly four-hundred Junior Officers will train here every fifteen-weeks," the Commander told his tour guests. As the men moved through each classroom they inspected everything from trim molding to lighting fixtures.

"Mr. Tasselmeyer, your use of so much prefabricated materials certainly made my job a hell of a lot easier," Paul added.

They walked outside the building onto the upper deck and examined the exterior window panes and door jambs of several of the twenty-four classrooms contained within the building.

"You know, from the street the structure's low profile and these exterior covered walkways really make it resemble a ship," said the Commander to Todd.

"Sounds like an approval rating of satisfactory, aye, Commander?" asked Todd.

"No, Mr. Tasselmeyer. More like outstanding!" exclaimed the Commander.

"Thank you, sir," Todd replied smiling.

"Well, gentlemen. This place and its schedules requires us to proceed across the street and find a seat in the reviewing stand," said the Commander.

Mr. McCoy replied, "I'm afraid, Commander, I'll pass for the moment, since some of my men are still punching out."

Turning toward the Commander, Todd said, "I'll also be along shortly, Commander Wilkins. I just wanted to check out a few more items."

"Very well. I've reserved you two seats across from the reviewing stand," said Commander Wilkins.

"Thank you, sir," the men responded.

Todd thanked Mr. McCoy for doing such a fine job of supervising the whole project. Todd then decided to investigate, by himself, the entire south wing's lower *"Computer Storage Area."*

Todd quickly approached the wing's southwest corner stairs and flung open the exit door to go downstairs. "What the hell!" he exclaimed. "Where's my down steps?"

The concrete floor in front of him revealed nothing below the first-floor level. The metal stairs only rose towards the second level. He then left the stairwell space and made off for the central elevator.

"This will surely take me below," he thought while waiting for the doors to open. Once the elevator arrived, he stepped inside to discover that the buttons were labeled "1" and "2."

"All right. Where the hell's the 'B' button?" he asked himself. Becoming more upset with the sudden realization that the elevator only went up, he walked to the other remaining stairwell.

"Well, I'll be damned!" exclaimed Todd. "Nothing goes downstairs here either."

Todd then clearly remembered that his final revised plans called for an outside entrance to the lower level. "I'll check that way next. Surely, that must have been built," he thought as he walked away from the elevator.

After walking around almost the entire length of the south wing complex, Todd could find no visible sign of anything leading down below grade. "I can't believe there's no access to that lower level," he said to himself. He shrugged his shoulders and headed across the street to the reviewing stand where he found his reserved seat.

As Todd surveyed the crowd, he realized that it had increased substantially since the 10:00 o'clock gathering for the dedication. Todd saw many squads of graduating recruits eagerly taking their assigned places on the parade ground. The sun, reflecting Todd's happy mood at having his building design completed, finally decided to shine again as the Navy band began to play. Nevertheless, Todd still found the stairway construction situation very perplexing.

* * *

* 39 *

SATURDAY, NOON, JANUARY 5

Todd rose to his feet and stood in silence as the Navy Band began to play the "*Star Spangled Banner*." He watched the huge assembled crowd of civilians and uniformed sailors in their dress blues. The sun shone off and on throughout the song and reflected off the color guard holding the flags.

The crowd remained standing while the Base Chaplain delivered the invocation. The entire company gave a resounding, 'Amen,' and the civilians sat while the companies stood at 'Parade Rest.'

Commander Wilkins again welcomed everyone and stood directly in front of Captain Siegewick on the reviewing stand. When he stepped aside once, Todd clearly saw that the Captain's face was full of anxiety. The Officers seated near him simply thought he was eager to get the ceremony finished. Throughout the ceremony, Todd watched as Captain Siegewick continued to scan the crowd of spectators as though he were looking for someone.

Then Commander Wilkins invited Admiral McKinsey to the dais, who then greeted the guests and talked about Captain Siegewick's accomplishments since becoming Commandant two years ago at Fort Warren. He finally asked the two captains to step forward. Captain Siegewick was presented a token gift plaque for his outstanding service record over the past twenty years of military service. Then Captain Siegewick presented Captain Howerton with the ceremonial Sword of Command.

The audience applauded their approval, and all the Officers congratulated each of the Captains. Captain Howerton signaled to the band conductor their readiness to proceed. The ranks of young uniformed recruits snapped to attention. The first company led the parade as the band played "*Anchors Aweigh*." The two Captains and the Admiral proudly saluted the marching sailors as they passed the reviewing stand.

Todd had found his reserved seat on the bleachers directly across from the reviewing stand. Mr. McCoy had joined him. When the pass and review began, Mr. McCoy turned to Todd and said, "That Captain Siegewick is one hard-ass son-of-a-bitch." He always gave me a hard time."

"I can imagine, Mr. McCoy," said Todd. "The few times I personally had to deal with that man by phone were unnerving enough. After talking with him, I'd often wished I had never even taken on the project."

"The man always wins," Mr. McCoy noted. "No matter what sort of misery he causes others."

"Yes, I'm sure he has some real schemes set in motion for the world now that he's a civilian. I've been invited to join Commander Wilkins for lunch somewhere later. Would you care to join us?" Todd asked.

"No, thanks anyway, I'm leaving for Hawaii this afternoon for a week's vacation," said Mr. McCoy smiling.

"Oh, that sounds great," said Todd.

"Yes...unless Stan Siegewick has planted a bomb on my plane!" he said in a nervous laugh.

"Well, Mr. McCoy. It's been nice to meet you. I want to say, that from the looks of things, you really did a great job of supervision for Herbert Hall's construction," said Todd.

As the last Company passed, Todd glanced over at the reviewing stand and saw that Captain Siegewick had gone. Todd left the bleachers and walked with Mr. McCoy to meet Commander Wilkins.

The Commander said, "My car is waiting behind the bleachers, Mr. Tasselmeyer. I'll meet you at the car shortly after I see that the admiral is taken care of."

"Very well, Commander. Take your time." Turning to Mr. McCoy, Todd told him, "Have a great trip, you've earned it."

1300 HOURS

During lunch at the Officer's Club, Todd asked Commander Wilkins, "Sir, is the beach in front of the *Fort Warren Naval Training Center* a secure area or are vehicles permitted to travel on the beach?"

"Our Base security ends at the main gate on the *coastal highway*. The beach is open to the public, but due to the cliff, the public must enter the beach several miles further south where the cliff ends," replied the Commander.

Commander Wilkins then told Todd, "This training center has three watchtowers where the marine sentries can get a good view of the base, the bay, and the ocean simultaneously. The Navy has invested heavily in base security. I can assure you that we are well protected."

Todd thought to himself that, only a few hours before, he had discovered the taxi buried in the dune only a half mile from where they were seated. Following lunch, Todd walked back past Herbert Hall and noticed some of

Mr. McCoy's men still working on the telephone switching equipment on the outside of the building. As Todd approached, the men quickly shut the cover to the panel box and disappeared inside the building through a side entrance door.

"In this place, everything looks suspicious," he thought to himself. He soon returned to the high-rise transit barracks and took the elevator to the eighth floor and entered his room for a brief rest.

*   *   *

1330 HOURS

As retired Captain Siegewick drove up to the marina, the *"Yankee II"* was just nearing the docks.

"Over here, Captain," the voice of Sergeant Miller called. "Please take hold of the line."

"What delayed your voyage, Sergeant?" the Captain called, as he secured the line.

"Fog, Sir, the damn stuff followed us almost the entire trip back from Mexico," said Sergeant Miller in a frustrated tone of voice.

"Stan!" Cheryl yelled and waved half hysterically. "The Chief's been wounded and will need medical help."

When Stan finished tying the lines and the ship was secured, he hastened aboard to embrace Cheryl. "Oh, darling, I'm so happy to see you," he said as he kissed her. She quickly pulled away, and said, "Chief Sheppard was shot in the shoulder by one of Gartez's men. He's resting down below and probably shouldn't be moved until he gets his wound patched."

"All right, Sergeant, notify the Base Hospital and have Corpsman Thomas come here and take care of the Chief," ordered the Captain.

"Right-a-way, Sir," replied Sergeant Miller saluting.

After climbing the ladder topside from below, Janet approached the Captain and Cheryl. "Well, who have we here?" the surprised Captain asked Cheryl, eyeing Janet's beauty. "Hello, sir, I'm Janet Derr from New York," Janet replied avoiding his look at her.

"How do you do, Miss Derr?" said the Captain coyly.

"Very well, Captain Siegewick. Cheryl told me that you've just retired from the Navy today, and that you two are engaged," said Janet.

"Yes, that's correct," he replied. He then pulled Cheryl quickly aside and asked with a stern voice, "Did you tell her anymore?"

"Just girl talk. Nothing else, darling," Cheryl said with her loving smile and her big green eyes sparkling.

"Good," he huffed. Turning back towards Janet he asked, "Well, how did you get to be rescued with Cheryl?"

"Let's see, Captain," replied Janet. "I went to the villa yesterday morning to conduct a personal interview with Raul Gartez. During our conversation, he got mad over something I asked and he ordered his guards to throw me into the same basement room where Cheryl was being kept."

"Are you, all right?" the Captain asked Janet.

"Yes, Captain. I'm fine, and I can't wait to find my boyfriend this afternoon," replied Janet.

"Is he here in San Diego?" asked the Captain.

Just then, the Navy ambulance pulled up to the dock. Everyone ran to assist the corpsman to go below with his gear.

"Right this way, Corpsman Thomas. The Chief was shot in the shoulder early this morning," said the Sergeant.

Entering the Chief's cabin, he stirred enough to say with a groggy voice, "Oh, what's all the commotion about?"

"Just lay still, Chief," said the Corpsman. "I'll give you something for the pain and clean your wound."

Corpsman Thomas returned topside in a short while and told the Captain and the others, "Chief Sheppard will be back on his feet in a few more hours once the sedative wears off."

The Captain then ordered, "You girls go and gather up your things and wait for me on the dock."

Once Janet and Cheryl had left, Sergeant Miller approached the Captain and mentioned, "I'll stay here with the Chief, Sir."

"Yes, that'll be fine, Sergeant," said the Captain.

The Captain then instructed his men saying, "The rest of you need to return to the underground brig for a good meal and some well-deserved rest."

The four men saluted then drove away from the marina.

"Go ahead, Sir. Take the young ladies, and I'll call you later when the Chief's up," said Sergeant Miller.

"Fine, Sergeant," said the Captain realizing he no longer had to salute, being a civilian, gave the Sergeant a warm handshake and a sincere, "Thank you for a very successful rescue mission."

"I appreciate that, Sir. We kicked some ass and left his villa burning," said Sergeant Miller.

"Did you kill Gartez?" asked the Captain.

"No, Sir. We killed four of his body guards and his house servant. According to Lieutenant Finley, Gartez had left the villa for Mexico City before we stormed the place," said Sergeant Miller.

"I see. I feel we haven't seen or felt the last of Gartez," said the Captain.

"I think you are correct, Sir. He's going to be one pissed-off S.O.B. when he gets back to what's left of his house," said Sergeant Miller proudly.

"We probably should expect him to continue his terrorist tactics with full vengeance," said the Captain.

Sergeant Miller then told him, "Sir, we'll take appropriate action to protect the mine."

"Do that, Sergeant. Carry on," said the Captain as he walked away.

* * *

1400 HOURS

Cheryl and Janet got into Stan's car. Cheryl told her, "Don't say anything about what we discussed during our captivity to Stan. I'll have him drop you off downtown and you can kill a few hours before you meet up with Todd."

"Yes, Cheryl, that would be fine. Since I left my luggage in Gartez's car, I do need to pick up some new clothes," said Janet.

When the Captain approached the car, Cheryl said, "Janet would like to be dropped off downtown."

"All right, ladies, right this way," said Stan smiling. He closed the car door and drove out of the marina to head across the toll bridge. He let Janet off near the downtown shopping area along *Market Street,* and together he and Cheryl proceeded to their *Mission Hills* home. "Oh darling. I was so scared after I was abducted from the Mall last Wednesday and taken to Mexico," Cheryl said as she hugged his neck.

Stan told her, "Yes, Sofia Wilkins found our empty car and your keys lying on the ground nearby. She called me to say that she was afraid for your safety."

"I suppose I should call her once we get home," Cheryl said.

"I don't know if you should call her just yet. Everyone around this place believes that you took emergency leave and will be back next week. I simply don't want anyone right now to know you're home," said Stan.

"Gartez's men might return if they knew we're back home," Cheryl reminded him.

"That's right, Cheryl," Stan agreed.

"Where can we hide and be safe?" asked Cheryl still worried.

"Don't worry, darling. I know of a very safe place," replied Stan trying to soothe her feelings.

* * *

When Stan and Cheryl arrived home, he parked in the garage and closed the overhead door. Once they entered the house, Cheryl took the key off the dog tag chain and slipped it under the plastic cover of the green ledger. She then placed the book on top of the dining room table.

Together they embraced and quickly left for the bedroom to get undressed. Over the next several hours that afternoon, their passionate love-making continued in the darkened room.

* * *

1430 HOURS

Raul Gartez and his assistant Miguel returned to the Ensenada airport. Since Pedro was not waiting for them, they hired a local taxicab to take them to the villa.

"Something is wrong, your excellency," Miguel said as the taxi turned into the road.

"Oh no, stop the car! Driver! Wait here," yelled Gartez.

"Si, Señor," said the driver nervously.

Leaving the cab, Gartez and Miguel approached the main gate of the villa and carefully walked among the smoldering ruins.

"They have come here and destroyed my house and killed my men!" he yelled.

"Your Excellency, come over here, quick," Miguel called from the outdoor patio.

Upon entering the passageway off the patio, they headed for the basement.

Miguel, who was walking in front of Gartez, replied to him, "the Señoritas are gone, Your Excellency!"

"Si, and now I must seek revenge on the Gringoes!" Gartez said hitting his fists together. "Come, we will take the cab back to town and reorganize our forces."

* * *

1500 HOURS

Todd awoke from his nap and noticed he still had a couple of hours before his planned rendezvous with Janet, so he decided to take a brief walk down the beach. He didn't pack his clothes figuring that he would return later. He went downstairs and proceeded to walk down the street. Passing the Marine guard at the Main Gate, he said. "I'm a guest of Commander Wilkins. I'll be back in a little while to pick up my baggage from the transit high rise."

"Very good, sir," the Marine sentry replied.

The sky had clouded over and there had been a brief shower earlier in the afternoon. After some difficulty climbing the wet rocks on the cliff, Todd soon stood near the spot where he had found the taxicab that morning.

Only a slight depression in the sand remained where the taxi had been buried. The watermark was well over the cab's roof, and no trace of the vehicle was visible. He kicked the sand and began to turn away when he heard voices.

"You, down there, halt!" said a commanding voice.

Todd, pretending not to hear their call began to slowly walk toward the North. Suddenly, two heavily armed men wearing black coveralls and black hoods scrambled down his side of the dune. As they confronted him, one stood behind him, and one in front of him, pointing their M-16s toward him.

"You are trespassing on military property," the man in front of him said.

Todd, knowing that he was on a public beach began to protest, saying, "No, I'm not. This is a public beach."

The guard standing behind Todd took his rifle and hit him on the back of the head knocking him to the ground. The two men then proceeded to drag him back into the storm drain. The larger guard carried Todd over his shoulder while the other guard carried on a conversation over the walkie-talkie, saying, "we've got a new prisoner from the beach. Scott's bringing him down the tunnel now. Meet him at the steel door."

"Yes, sir. We're ready to accept the new prisoner," was the response from the inside.

"Over and out," said the guard.

Once Todd was carried unconscious into the basement brig, he was quickly stripped and roughly pulled into a set of black coveralls and combat boots. His civilian clothes were given to the duty sergeant for close inspection.

Todd was fitted with an electronic collar device and locked up in the isolation cell. He would be kept away from the remaining five civilian miners who had survived the most recent series of cave ins.

1630 HOURS

Duty Sergeant Archer from the basement brig called Sergeant Miller on the Chief's yacht.

"Yes, Sergeant," said Sergeant Archer, "Tell the Chief that we have captured a man on the beach near the storm drain entrance. He was knocked out and has been outfitted and is currently in the isolation cell."

"Very good. Have you identified the new prisoner, Sergeant?" asked Sergeant Miller.

"Yes," said Sergeant Archer, "His name is Todd Tasselmeyer from New York City."

"Fine, I'll tell the Chief when he's awake. I'll call you back shortly."

"Thank you, Sergeant Miller," replied Sergeant Archer.

* * *

Janet, carrying several clothes boxes, her purse and her note pad got onto a city bus marked *Hotel Del Coronado*. Due to the heavy traffic, the trip across the toll bridge took about twenty minutes. After about four more stops, the bus came to a stop close to the *Hotel Del Coronado*.

"What a beautiful place," she thought to herself looking around at the immense, hundred-year-old, white painted clapboard Victorian building.

The old hotel had many levels of red shingled roofs.

Palm trees swayed in the gentle afternoon breeze, and there were many beautiful multi-colored flower beds near the entrance. Janet proceeded onto the huge front lobby and approached the registration desk.

"Hello, Miss, may I help you?" said the friendly young man behind the desk.

"Yes. My name is Tasselmeyer. You have a reservation for two nights for my husband and me," she said convincingly.

"One moment, please," he said as he entered her name into the reservation computer.

"Yes, here it is, Room 406 on the ocean side. That's two hundred and sixty-five dollars a night," said the desk clerk.

Shrugging her shoulders, she said, "Sure, put it on his credit card number that we used to make the reservation."

"Here's the key. Enjoy your visit," the clerk said with a smile.

She passed the palm trees and ferns in the lobby and waited anxiously for Todd while seated on an overstuffed leather sofa. After about twenty minutes, she decided that he must have been delayed by the Navy somehow and that she was ready for a hot bath and a change into her new clothes. She walked over to the reception desk and said to the desk clerk, "When my husband arrives, tell him I'm in the room freshening up."

"Certainly, Mrs. Tasselmeyer," the young man responded with a wide smile.

* * *

* 40 *

Chief Sheppard began feeling stronger and decided he needed to call the Captain.

"Hello, Sir," the Chief said weakly.

"Chief! I'm so glad to hear your voice. How are you feeling?" asked the Captain trying to show his concern for the Chief.

"Better, Captain," replied the Chief feeling almost jealous of his now-civilian partner. "Sir, Sergeant Miller just informed me that our boys picked up a beachcomber this afternoon near the storm drain entrance,"

"Fine, we need all the help we can get. Any I.D. reports on him?" the Captain asked.

"Yes, his name is Todd Tasselmeyer," replied the Chief.

"Oh, shit! Chief, we've picked up the architect of Herbert Hall!" bellowed the Captain.

"So that's where I had heard that name before," said the Chief.

"Chief, he designed our brig!" explained the Captain.

"He must not find out who the fuck we are...under any conditions," said the Chief now realizing the seriousness of the problem.

"You're right, Chief. Where's he now?" asked the Captain.

"They have him in the isolation cell," replied the Chief.

"Excellent. Call Sergeant Miller back and tell him that we'll conduct a special fake mast tonight and sentence our trespasser to work for us in the mine," the Captain told him.

"That's sounds good to me," replied the Chief.

"But Chief, are you up to it with your shoulder wound?" asked the Captain.

"Yes, let's do it after dinner," said the Chief. "I'll meet you there about 2100 hours."

"Would it be all right if Cheryl and I spend tonight aboard your yacht?" asked the Captain.

"Certainly, Sir. I was going to suggest that anyway. I don't think you two are very safe in that house with Gartez's men possibly making a return visit," said the Chief.

"I'll see you later, Chief, and thanks again for a brilliant rescue," said the Captain.

When he had hung up the phone, Stan called Cheryl saying, "Darling there's been a slight change of plans for tonight."

"Oh, what is it?" she asked impatiently.

"A Mister Todd Tasselmeyer has stumbled onto the entrance of the storm drain off the beach. My men are holding him for trespassing."

"Oh, Stan!" Cheryl cried. "That girl Janet Derr that we dropped off downtown is his girlfriend!"

"What the hell!" said Stan in disbelief.

"Yes," said Cheryl, "she's planning to meet him in the lobby of the *Hotel Del Coronado* around five today."

"Shit! You call the hotel and tell her that he's been delayed, and I'll send someone around in about an hour to pick her up and take her to him," ordered Stan.

"All right, dear. I'll do as you say," Cheryl lovingly told Stan.

After Cheryl called the hotel, Janet was very relieved to hear her voice. "Oh, Cheryl. Since Todd hasn't showed up I was really beginning to think something terrible had happened to him. I'll be ready in an hour. I'll be wearing my new blue outfit I bought this afternoon."

As Cheryl hung up the phone, Stan grabbed it and ordered Cheryl, "Go! Begin fixing dinner."

"Behave, Stan, you're not acting nice. Ask me nice," requested Cheryl.

Still feeling an internal threat, he ceased his harshness momentarily and said, "I'm sorry, darling. Could you please go to the kitchen and prepare us something wonderful? I really haven't eaten well since last Tuesday night." He kissed her, and she left the room.

Stan quickly picked up the phone and called the marina. "Hello, Chief, listen up. Contact Sergeant Miller and have him and Corporal Lenert drive over to the *Hotel Del Coronado* within the hour."

"What's up, Captain?" asked the Chief.

"That girl, Janet Derr, that you rescued with Cheryl is the girlfriend of our Mister Tasselmeyer!" explained the Captain.

"Oh, brother! Captain. Do you think we can complicate matters anymore?" asked the Chief thinking to himself, "What the hell's next?"

"She doesn't know Lenert but knows Miller and will follow him. Instruct Lenert to wear black and hide in the back seat of Miller's car. Once he picks up Janet, and they've left the hotel's parking lot, let Lenert inject her," said the Captain.

"Like what we did to Mr. Mayhen?" asked the Chief.

"Exactly. Have the men bring her unconscious to the brig. We'll unite the lovers there later tonight," said the Captain laughing in a sinfully manner.

The Chief quickly said, "But she'll sleep for eight hours, Captain."

"That's fine, Chief. We need the time," said the Captain.

"Captain," said the Chief. "I had another call from the Sergeant Miller. It seems that Mr. Tasselmeyer had some sort of roughly drawn map in his wallet."

"So, what's the big deal?" asked the Captain.

"The word *'Dutchman'* was scribbled on the map," replied the Chief.

"Really! Huh. I'll tell you what, Chief. I'll bring the old yellow map from the prospector's trunk with me tonight," said the Captain.

Stan hung up the phone as Cheryl called, "Dinner's ready!"

During the meal of pork chops and gravy with mashed potatoes, Stan asked Cheryl, "Didn't you tell me that Janet had bought her boyfriend that old hourglass that I had sent to New York last July?" asked Stan trying to keep his composure.

"Yes, that's right, Stan. Why?" she asked.

"Oh, nothing, dear, nothing at all," said Stan as he began to eat.

* * *

1930 HOURS

Janet was greeted kindly in the lobby of the *Hotel Del Coronado* by Sergeant Miller who was wearing a dress shirt and jeans.

"Hello again. Miss Derr," he said as he approached. "Your outfit is most attractive."

"Thank you, Sergeant. Is Todd very far from here?" asked Janet.

"No, Ma'am. It shouldn't take us long at all. Please follow me," requested the Sergeant.

Janet and her escort left the hotel and entered the parking lot. The January evening had gotten quite chilly and dark. Janet noticed nothing unusual as they approached the Sergeant's car. He opened the front door, and she got in and buckled her seat belt. Sergeant Miller drove off and turned south along the *Coastal Highway*. As the Sergeant asked her to turn the car radio on, Corporal Lenert raised himself up from the back seat and grabbed her. Startled, she was quickly rendered helpless by the injection put into her neck.

Within twenty minutes, Sergeant Miller and Corporal Lenert arrived at the mine entrance. There they were relieved by hooded guards who carried Janet unconscious through the maze of tunnels and into the basement brig.

She was placed on a cot in the end cell. Closing the cell's bar door, the guards departed.

* * *

2000 HOURS

Stan gathered up the green ledger with the gold safety deposit box key tucked in under its clear plastic cover, and the old yellow map from on top of the dining room table. He then drove Cheryl to the marina and met Chief Sheppard aboard his yacht. The Chief first showed Cheryl where everything was, including a small caliber pistol.

"You'll be safe here. I'll be back in a few hours after I make sure that Janet and Todd are taken care of," Stan told her.

"Thank you, darling. I'll wait up and watch television," said Cheryl.

While the Captain drove to the mine, Chief Sheppard asked about his future.

"I hope Cheryl will soon resign her commission, and we can do some traveling," said the Captain.

"How about the mine, Captain?" asked the Chief.

"I would like us to continue mining as long as we feel it is safe. How do you feel about our latest prisoners, Chief?" asked the Captain.

"Well, I personally think, if Tasselmeyer and his girlfriend begin to work for us in the mine, they shouldn't be set free to tell the world about our operation," replied the Chief.

"Yes, I agree," said the Captain. "But if they don't return to New York, people will probably ask the Navy what's happened to them. That, dear partner, could allow our dear Captain Howerton to have a fucking field day with an investigation of us!"

"You're right," said the Chief. "Maybe we'll just detain them temporarily."

Upon reaching the storm drain tunnel, Corporal Lenert met them and informed the Captain that, "Mr. Tasselmeyer was up and carrying on in his cell, while Miss Derr remained fast asleep in her cell at the other end of the secret brig."

"Well Chief, I'm going to have some fun with this character," said the Captain as he put on his hard hat and together they proceeded past the deflected security sensor light.

Once past the steel door, the Captain carried the ledger and map that he brought from home and placed them on the desk in the records' office. Sergeant

Miller entered and held out his hand saying, "Here's the piece of paper that the duty sergeant found in Tasselmeyer's wallet, Sir."

The Captain took his own old yellow piece of paper and held it close to the paper that Todd had scribbled on.

"Chief and Sergeant Miller! Get a load at this!" the Captain yelled excitedly.

"Sir, it looks like the rest of the map!" exclaimed the Chief who then said, "how the hell did this dude from New York City find it?"

The Captain, looking closely at the two map pieces, said, "I don't really know, but look here. The third tunnel leads to another dead end. At that location, the line angles South and must come around the great room from the other side."

"I see, Captain. There's an 'X' which must mean something really big!" said the Chief excitedly.

"How far are we away from this point now?" the Captain asked.

Sergeant Miller looked at the map and decided that the prisoners were only about a hundred feet away. "If I can use all the prisoners tonight, Sir, we could be at that spot by morning," stated the Sergeant.

"Very well, Sergeant. Assemble your men now, and let me talk to them," the Captain told him.

Within a few minutes the eight guards, wearing black hoods and uniforms, were standing at attention in the secret brig's record office.

The Captain addressed them, "Men. At ease, please. There seems to be about one hundred feet of sand between us and the biggest gold discovery of this century. I need each of you to assist the prisoners to remove this major obstacle tonight. I guarantee each man a share in the profits from this find."

The men signaled their approval and shook each other's hands. The Chief notified them that he and the Captain would conduct a Mast tonight for Mr. Tasselmeyer.

"Sergeant, you and your assistant bring him to the courtroom in about fifteen minutes. Please remove his electro-collar," ordered the Chief.

"As you wish, Chief," the men said as they headed down the red-lighted passageway.

2130 HOURS

Todd had remained seated on the small stool in the center of his cell for quite some time. He had earlier felt the charge of electricity when he attempted to get up. When the two hooded guards swung open his cell door, it startled him. The two approached him, and one removed the collar.

"Who the hell are you people?" asked Todd. "Where are you taking me?"

"Mast, buddy boy, you're going to Mast," was the only reply from the hooded guard.

Todd cursed, kicked and fought his way down the passageway to no avail. He remained handcuffed and in leg irons. He was roughly pushed into the courtroom chamber and stood shaking before a long table.

"Your name is Tasselmeyer?" asked one of the two black-hooded men seated at the long table.

"Yes, so what about it?" asked Todd showing his aggravation.

Suddenly he was slapped across his face.

"Yes, sir, would be acceptable. Understood?" said the other seated and hooded figure.

"Yes, sir," came softly from Todd's mouth, and he again was slapped by the guard standing close by.

"We didn't hear you!" exclaimed both seated men.

"Yes, Sir!" yelled Todd, now on the verge of tears.

The Chief spoke telling Todd, "You've been found to be a trespasser. Is that correct?"

"Yes Sir," spoke Todd loudly.

Now the Captain, using a deeper voice, said, "Trespassers found here are always detained. This Mast finds the defendant...guilty of criminal trespass and sentences Mr. Tasselmeyer...to six months at hard labor. Take him away!"

Todd shouted insults and curses at his accusers as he was taken back and pushed into his windowless cell. As soon as the guard slammed the door, Todd was left in total darkness. He let out an ear-piercing scream. This time, he didn't wake up next to Janet in his bedroom, safely inside of their New York City apartment. He was now caught up in a real-life nightmare!

* * *

* 41 *

Shortly after midnight, Todd and the five other miners carrying picks and shovels and pushing wheelbarrows were led down into tunnel number three by five hooded guards. The red lights glowed along the rocky tunnel walls. Todd had the overwhelming feeling he had experienced this whole scene, since Christmas, through his dreams.

Darkness surrounded him, but he could hear machinery in the distance. The red lights illuminated the passageway. There were shadows of men on the walls. He could feel the tightness of the collar around his neck, but he dares not touch it. He could also have heard some hooded men talking. He tried to listen as he walked.

"Those other finds were nothing to what we've just come across down tunnel number three," said one of the hooded guards.

"Yes, that really must be the 'Motherlode' that everyone's been hoping was here," said another guard.

"Just think of the amount of gold that he's already got," replied the first guard.

"Really, that greedy S.O.B. wouldn't even let us take a single Troy ounce out of here without his knowledge," said the other guard.

After listening to these escorts of conversation, Todd was convinced he was being forced to work in someone's private gold mine. He still believed that Janet was safe somewhere in a comfortable hotel room, and he longed to be with her.

As they approached the end of the tunnel, the leader of the guards yelled, "You, men, listen up! During the next eight-hour shift, you will clean out this area of the tunnel. We have proof that the tunnel leads off in that direction," he said pointing then continued, "the entrance may be blocked by fallen rocks."

"Here it is, sir," another guard called after pushing over some loose rocks."

"Excellent, we'll begin over there," said the leader of the guards. Another hooded guard reminded the prisoners that their collars were activated, and if anyone resisted, they would be stung and shot.

"The sand will not be taken out to the beach tonight. You will pile it along the side walls in this space," the smallest of the hooded guards said.

The leader yelled, "Begin digging, you worthless bunch of assholes!"

* * *

SUNDAY, 0730, JANUARY 6

"Chief, I think you better come down here," the voice on the walkie talkie called. Chief Sheppard had decided to stay in the guard's quarters of the secret brig. He wanted the Captain and Cheryl to enjoy their first night alone onboard his yacht.

"What's up, Sergeant?" the Chief replied knowing who was calling.

"Gold, Chief, more damn gold than you can imagine!" exclaimed the voice.

"All right. Return all the prisoners to their cells and let them eat and rest. I'll call the Captain, and as soon as he's here, we'll come down."

"Very good, Chief, over-and-out," said the voice.

Quickly dressing and going into the record's office, he called the marina. "Good morning, Sir. Good news, the men found a lot of gold!" the Chief exclaimed.

"Wonderful! Cheryl and I'll be there shortly," said the Captain who could hardly wait.

"The Lieutenant, too?" the Chief asked.

"Yes, Chief, I've decided not to leave her alone again during the day light. She's afraid of being kidnapped again," exclaimed the Captain.

"I understand, Sir. Whatever you think is wise," said the Chief.

* * *

Todd and the other nameless prisoners were paraded back through the maze of red lighted tunnels until they reached the steel door. It had some special security features and was hinged on the right side. Todd recognized it from his revision drawings.

"So, this is the basement brig under Herbert Hall!" he thought to himself then continued to think, "that bastard Siegewick somehow discovered this mine tunnel under my building and had the basement complex built. He must have had the topside accesses covered over!"

As each prisoner passed through the steel door, they were ordered to strip. Once closely inspected for any gold items, they were permitted to shower and given clean coveralls and reissued their collar devices.

When Todd passed down the narrow red colored passageway, he glanced into the first cell. Through the bars that faced the passageway he saw a young girl lying on a cot that resembled his girlfriend!

Loudly he called out, "Janet," as his collar stunned him and he fell to his knees. The guards quickly pulled him to his feet and carried him to the end of the cells. There he was roughly unshackled, and the collar removed. Free of the device, he again called, "Janet, Janet." The hooded guard landed a few quick blows before they pushed him into the solitary cell and slammed the door.

The cell had four solid concrete walls. The door had a narrow opening at the bottom where a food tray could fit. That opening was his only way to try and communicate with her.

"Why didn't she respond?" he wondered and feared. Soon all the other occupied cells between Todd and Janet were quiet with sleeping prisoners.

Janet awoke sometime later and called out for help. Todd in his frustration tried to answer her, but stopped when he heard doors open and the guards approaching. He decided just to lie still and keep quiet.

Janet was served a hardy meal of refried beans over rice with a cup of water. She was told by one of the guards that she was being detained under military orders.

"What the hell are you people talking about?" asked Janet confused.

"Sorry, Miss Derr, but we have our orders," said the other guard.

"I demand to see your supervisor, or an attorney!" she yelled.

Quickly the two guards left her and headed out towards the steel door. Todd listened as the heavy door clanged shut. Hearing Janet's defiant remarks made him feel good. He then tried again to communicate with her.

"Janet, it's Todd, I'm in the isolation cell on the end, Todd said hoping she would hear him."

Startled at what she just imagined hearing over the other male prisoner's snoring, she said. "Repeat, louder, if you can."

"Janet, it's Todd," he said louder.

"Todd! Todd!" she cried out pulling on the bars.

"Where are you? I can't see you!" she yelled.

"I'm in the isolation cell down here on the other end," Todd replied.

"Darling, where the hell are we?" she asked.

"Do you remember those architectural revisions I had to make last March for Captain Siegewick?" asked Todd feeling good to be able to tell someone what he found out.

"Yes, I remember," Janet said.

"Well, dearest, we're being held in his private jail, beneath Herbert Hall!" said Todd.

"What!" she exclaimed.

"And guess what else I discovered?" asked Todd.

Shaking her head in disbelief, she said, "I've no idea."

"Outside this jail there are tunnels that lead to a gold mine!" exclaimed Todd.

"Oh, my God! Todd! Cheryl told me about a gold mine, but she didn't mention this jail," said Janet.

"Who's Cheryl?" Todd called to Janet while still kneeling on the concrete floor and trying to talk through the door slot.

"She's Captain Siegewick's girlfriend, a Naval Lieutenant," replied Janet feeling a little surprised he didn't know about her.

"The same Captain Siegewick, former Commandant of Fort Warren?" asked Todd.

"Yes, I believe so. She's also Peggy Finley's twin sister. You know, the girl that sold me the golden hourglass," replied Janet.

"Oh, yes, my favorite Christmas present," said Todd.

"Isn't it truly a small world?" asked Janet forgetting her predicament for a moment.

"Yes, I agree. But again, where did you meet this girl Cheryl?" he asked.

"At noon on Friday, I arrived at Gartez's villa and began my interview with him for the newspaper," said Janet.

"Okay, go on," he called back to her.

"Well, Gartez told me about his political goals, and said he was going to finance himself by taking over some new operational gold mine," continued Janet.

"This one, probably," Todd thought to himself.

"So, while I was talking to him, I noticed a set of dog tags lying in his ashtray on his desk. When I inquired as to whom they belonged to, he became angry and called for his bodyguards. They took me down stairs to the villa's cellar and tossed me into a small room."

"Were you hurt? Todd asked.

"No, but to my surprise, Cheryl Finley was already in that room being held hostage by Gartez!" exclaimed Janet.

"Oh, wow! Please tell me more," implored Todd.

"Evidently, Cheryl had been kidnapped by Gartez's men last Wednesday here in San Diego and smuggled into Mexico. She was taken to his villa on the Baja. He treated her rough. Under torture, she told him the location of this gold mine," Janet said.

"Did Cheryl tell you anything else?" Todd asked.

"Cheryl told me that Captain Siegewick and his Chief Master-At-Arms have been operating the mine since June, and they had found several million dollars in gold," Janet said.

"Where's the gold now?" asked Todd.

Janet began again saying, "well, that's where Cheryl came into the picture. She's a naval accountant and bookkeeper that the Captain had met in Hawaii last July. He fell in love with her and promised to arrange for her transfer to San Diego in August. When she arrived, Stan made love to her and let her exchange his gold ore with some industrialist from Hong Kong she called Mr. Lee. Cheryl also told me that the Captain and his buddy, the Chief, had stolen money from the Navy's building account."

"They probably used that money to build this place," Todd thought to himself.

"Captain Siegewick had Cheryl assigned to the Supply Office, and she straightened out the Herbert Hall account by replenishing the Navy's building fund with some of the Captain's gold money. On New Year's Eve, Gartez's men broke into the Captain's and Cheryl's house on the outskirts of San Diego. They stole her dog tag chain with her safety deposit box key on it."

"Huh! That was last Monday night they were robbed, and she was kidnapped last Wednesday," thought Todd.

"Cheryl remained at the villa for almost three days," said Janet.

"And you were locked up with her Friday afternoon?" asked Todd.

"Right, Todd," she called toward his isolation cell.

"So how did you get back here to San Diego?" he asked her.

"Sometime yesterday morning before sun up, the Chief and some of his men came to rescue Cheryl. They invited me along. The Chief was shot in the shoulder by one of Gartez's men," said Janet.

"Was Gartez killed?" asked Todd.

"No, I don't think he was at the villa when they rescued us," replied Janet.

"You know what that means, don't you, Janet?" asked Todd.

"Do you believe Gartez would raid this mine, Todd?" asked Janet understanding what he meant.

"The whole Mexican army might raid this mine now," he wondered to himself.

Not hearing a response Janet called to him, "Todd, I'm so scared. We know too much about their operation."

"Yes, I agree," sighed Todd as this latest nightmare loomed before him in real time. He then told her, "there isn't much we can do now. I've just spent the night down in tunnel number three. Along with those five other prisoners, we moved enough sand to reveal a huge vein of gold."

"Oh, Todd," said Janet. "Maybe they'll take the gold and leave us alone."

"Don't count on it, dear. Huh, this damn floor is too hard, and I've got to stop talking and stand up now," Todd said feeling sore and very uncomfortable.

"All right, Todd, whatever you say," said Janet sadly.

* * *

SUNDAY, 0800 HOURS

Stan and Cheryl walked down the beach on the water side of the dunes. The Sunday morning sun shone brightly as he said to her, "See these dunes, darling. My people have built them to help stop the beach erosion."

"Oh, Stan, you don't have an environmental bone in your body," Cheryl laughed.

"Now, now, be nice. You're talking to a man who has recently become a millionaire while still on active duty," said Stan proudly.

"Bravo," she said and applauded.

"Come over here," he ordered.

"What is it?" she looked cautiously.

When they approached the entrance to the storm drain, Corporal Lenert was standing the watch.

"Good morning, Sir and Ma'am. Please step this way, I'll deflect the light sensor," said the young Corporal retaining his military posture.

"Why is that, Corporal?" Cheryl asked.

"If the line of light is broken by someone passing by, the alarm sounds inside the Marine detachment barracks back on the Base. The Marines would think that terrorists were trying to get to the base through the storm drain. They are all trained to pile down a manhole in the street and shoot at anything inside the storm drain," replied the Corporal.

"We all wear hard hats for safety down here," the Captain told Cheryl. They each put on black coveralls and hoods.

"We're running a top-secret operation. I don't want your pretty face revealed to anyone," the Captain insisted.

"Now where to, darling?" Cheryl asked.

"Follow me," the Captain replied.

"I'll notify the Chief that you're coming in, Sir," said Corporal Lenert.

"Do that, Corporal," said the Captain.

As they entered the storm drain portion of the project, they walked about a thousand feet when the Captain said, "Stop."

"What's the matter?" Cheryl whispered nervously.

"Listen," said the Captain in a very quiet voice.

* * *

* 42 *

Stan held Cheryl's hand when he heard the low rumble and felt the slight movement of the cement beneath their feet.

"This place gives me the willies," Cheryl told him.

"Me, too, come on. It will be all right," Stan assured her.

They found the hatchway on the wall and proceeded the nearly twenty-five feet to the spot where the four tunnels converged.

"That blackened tunnel over there leads to the workmen's quarters," he said pointing to the left wall. Then turning and pointing right he told her, "Down this first tunnel was where I found the prospector's trunk last July."

"That's when you discovered the golden hourglass that you sent to my sister, Peggy, in New York," said Cheryl expecting conformation.

"Right. This middle tunnel leads down several levels and empties into a large room where we found all of the gold that you exchanged with Mr. Lee," explained Stan.

"Is there any gold left?" she asked.

"Probably," said Stan. "But both of those tunnels have caved in and can no longer be mined. Now we've been working in the third tunnel."

"Have you found gold there?" asked Cheryl.

"Yes, just this morning. Be careful, and watch your head. It's pretty low," Stan cautioned her.

"These red lights make everything eerie, Stan," said Cheryl shivering.

At that location, the red lights were only strung through the third tunnel. The other tunnels remained mysteriously dark and foreboding. They were met further down the lighted tunnel by Chief Sheppard and Sergeant Miller.

"Welcome to the entrance to Hell!" the Chief laughed. "Please, follow me."

Together they all proceeded down through the dim red-colored tunnel. After what seemed like quite a distance to Cheryl, they faced a solid rock wall.

"Over this way, please, and watch your step," the Chief called.

Upon entering through a tight space, the tunnel enlarged enough for everyone to stand upright.

"Well, what have we here?" asked the Captain.

"Sergeant, bring over more light," Chief Sheppard requested.

"Wow," Cheryl said with surprise. "I've never seen such a beautiful sight."

There directly in front of the group lay embedded in the side wall a partially exposed vein of gold. From what they could see, Stan quickly estimated its worth at well over many millions of dollars and said, "This has to be one of the largest amounts of gold anywhere. This makes the legend of the 'Lost Dutchman Mine,' a true reality!"

"It really is an unbelievable find, Stan," exclaimed Cheryl.

"When can we start mining, Chief?" the Captain asked.

"As soon as the prison...er, I mean, the men finish their rest period, Sir. They should be ready to return about noon," replied the Chief.

"That will be fine, Chief," said the Captain as he called, "Sergeant, would you mind escorting the lady back to the beach entrance?"

"Not at all, Sir." said Sergeant Miller.

The Captain turned toward Cheryl and said, "Dear, the Chief and I need to discuss a few brief matters. I'll follow you in just a short while."

"That's fine with me, this place gives me the creeps. Lead on, Sergeant Miller," said Cheryl quickly.

After they had left, the Captain inquired as to the status of Todd and Janet.

"He's in the isolation cell and she's at the other end in a regular cell. I don't think they realize we have them both, Sir," said the Chief.

"All right. Leave them both alone in their cells today. Have the guards doubled at the storm drain entrance, and let the remaining prisoners work down here this afternoon and evening," ordered the Captain.

"That shouldn't be any problem, Sir," the Chief responded.

"Cheryl and I will return about 1800 to help move the excavated gold into the records' office. Then together we can sort it and split up the packets," said the Captain smiling that peculiar smile.

"Understood, Sir. There should be no problem getting some of this exposed part of the vein excavated..."

Just then they each heard and felt a low rumbling.

"What the hell!" the Captain said in a panicky voice.

"It's just our daily earthquake. You get used to them," said the Chief trying to reassure the Captain that everything was normal.

In a few places overhead, sand slowly filtered through the rocks, falling on the floor around them.

"How long has this been going on?" the Captain asked.

"This place is quite unstable. The small quakes have been increasing more since the New Year began," replied the Chief.

"You're not kidding, Chief! Let's get out of here," exclaimed a nervously perspiring retired Captain.

The Captain carefully followed the red lights back to the storm tunnel. Then he ran the one-thousand-foot distance and met Cheryl near the entrance.

"Stan," Cheryl asked, "Where's Janet and her boyfriend?"

"After I got them reunited, they caught a late-night flight back to New York," said Stan, hoping Cheryl believed him.

"Oh good. I do hope they enjoyed themselves here in California. It was really something to run across an old family friend like her so far from home," said Cheryl reminiscing.

"Yes, I suppose it was. Come on, let's go home for a while. That bed grows mighty lonely without us in it," requested Stan.

"Oh, Stan, you're such a romantic," Cheryl said coyly.

Chief Sheppard returned to the secret brig's steel door. As soon as Janet heard his footsteps approaching, she stopped talking to Todd and laid back down on her cot.

Glancing over into Janet's cell, the Chief commented to the guard who met him at the door, "Looks like Miss Derr's injection worked very well." They walked past the sleeping prisoners and went into the guards' living quarters. Once inside, the men removed their black hoods and hard hats.

"Ah, that's better. What's the status of the new prisoner in isolation?" asked the Chief.

"He worked well with the collar, Chief, but he did see and recognize the girl in the end cell," said one of the men.

"Damn, those two will remain here in the brig today. The other prisoners can be taken into the third tunnel after their lunch snack," ordered the Chief.

"Very good, Chief. I'll tell the other guards," said the one guard obediently.

"One other thing, double our sentries at the storm drain entrance this afternoon. We may have some visitors from Mexico," advised the Chief.

Chief Sheppard then gathered up his clothes, replaced his black hood and left for the marina. "I'll be back around 1700. I need to go back to the yacht for my pain pills," the Chief said as he left the secret brig.

* * *

SUNDAY, NOON, JANUARY 6

Miguel notified His Excellency, Señor Gartez, "Our yacht is well stocked and tied up for us in the harbor of Ensenada."

"I want us to arrive under the cover of darkness. Have the crew assemble by mid-afternoon. These Gringoes will pay dearly for my losses," said Gartez angrily.

"How many men, Your Excellency, shall we take?" Miguel asked.

"General Herandes will bring nine others with him," replied Gartez.

"Si, wonderful!" exclaimed Miguel.

Gartez said "That should give us enough to handle any security force we meet in the mine. We don't know of the Commandant's strength."

"The General's men are tough fighters, yes?" asked Miguel.

"The best he has," Gartez said with an evil grin.

"Your Excellency, do you suppose that the Gringoes will be expecting us so soon?"

Gartez replied, "I am sure the Commandant is mining his gold this very minute. If we act quickly, there shouldn't be much problem."

"Si, Your Excellency, we'll take them out quickly and get their gold and return home in a little while," said Miguel trying to show his confidence.

"Si, in a little while, the Gringoe's gold will definitely become, My Gold!" exclaimed Gartez.

Gartez, sitting at the window table in the local cantina, stared out at the vastness of the Pacific. He was an excellent fighter, but he had some reservations about sailing. He ordered several more rounds of Tequila while waiting for the general to arrive. He continued to ponder what Cheryl had told him about the mine being under the Naval Base.

"I don't want a fight with the whole U.S. Navy," he told Miguel. "All I need is the Commandant's gold to allow me the money to win the next Presidential election. After that, I will use Mexico's own wealth to control everything from drugs to oil."

"Si, Your Excellency. The gold will do that for you," Miguel assured him.

"See that it does!" ordered Gartez as he downed another shot glass of Tequila.

* * *

1500 HOURS

General Herandes and his elite militia arrived and were escorted onboard the waiting yacht. Once the anchor was raised and the vessel cleared the harbor lighthouse, Miguel figured it would take his craft five hours to reach San Diego. The trip became quite rough, and Gartez remained below feeling lousy. The men topside didn't fare much better.

"The ocean, she is not cooperating with us tonight, Your Excellency," Miguel said trying to be somewhat cheerful.

"Huh, go away, leave me alone in this cabin until we are in sight of the city lights," demanded Gartez.

"Can I get you something, Your Excellency?" asked Miguel.

"Only the Commandant's gold," replied a pale-looking Gartez. With waves of three to five feet and a strong head wind, the trip took longer and longer. Gartez finally made an appearance above deck and was told by his General, "by the charts we are nearing Imperial Beach. Fort Warren is not much further."

"Gracias, general. How are your men?" asked Gartez.

"Most are feeling better and are ready for a good fight," reported the General.

"Well, I expect the Commandant will not want to give us his gold too quickly, so we may have to convince him it would be in his best interest to do so," said Gartez trying to inform the General that this mission may not be an easy one, but a profitable one.

"Si, Your Excellency, oar's too!" exclaimed the General.

* * *

"Todd, Todd, can you hear me?" called Janet. "They've taken all of the prisoners out and I didn't see you leave."

"Yes, I'm still here. Are you, all right?" he called through his bottom door slot.

"Yes, dearest, I'm fine. I was hoping we would sightsee some of San Diego today, but I guess that will have to wait," she laughed, then began to cry. "Oh, Todd, I really am afraid for us. No one knows where we are, and our expensive ocean view room sits empty."

"How expensive, may I ask?" came faintly from the other end of the room of jail cells.

"Two hundred and sixty-five a night," she grimaced.

"Janet!" was his response. "I don't even have my wallet anymore. They took it yesterday!"

Hoping to sooth him, she innocently said, "The receptionist already had your credit card number."

"Wonderful. Call him and see if we can sublease for tonight?" asked Todd trying to relieve the tension.

"Oh, behave yourself...What's that?" she asked nervously.

"What's what?" he inquired.

"Shhh, listen," whispered Janet.

Together, and yet alone separately, they listened to a low rumbling and creaking sound. The brig lights flickered for a moment, and Janet felt the floor sway very gently.

"Oh, no, I think we're having an earthquake!" Janet screamed.

In an instant everything was calm, but she continued to sob.

"Are you okay?" he yelled out through the door slot.

"Yes," she cried, "Please, Todd, get me out of here!"

Todd also was extremely concerned over their dilemma. He paced back and forth within the tiny cell and hit on the walls many times in frustration.

* * *

* 43 *

SUNDAY, 1800 HOURS

The Captain and Cheryl arrived back at the storm drain entrance and were greeted by Corporal Lenert, his associate, Lance Corporal Scott, and Chief Sheppard.

"How are you feeling, Chief?" the Captain asked.

"Those pills that Corpsman Thomas gave me are really great," replied the Chief.

"You men be extra alert tonight," Stan told the two guards.

"We'll all be down tunnel number three. Notify us if anything or anybody bothers you tonight," said the Chief.

"Certainly, Sir, but there is one problem," Corporal Lenert reminded the visitors. "Sir, our walkie-talkie's signal only can penetrate into the basement area, not the mine tunnel."

"I see," said the Captain in a bit of anger. Then turning to the Chief, he asked, "What do you suggest?"

"Corporal, if there is any trouble, just trip the light sensor and let the Base Marines deal with the problem. You men should have enough time to escape into the connecting tunnel and close the hatch," ordered the Chief.

"As you say, Chief," said the young Corporal saluting.

"Carry-on, men, you're doing a fine job," said the Chief proudly.

"Thank you, Sir," the two guards replied.

The trio donned their hard hats, coveralls and hoods, and walked carefully through the darkened and damp storm drain. Sergeant Miller met them inside the connecting tunnel and guided them through the red lighted third tunnel. As they approached the silently working prisoners, Cheryl commented, "Why do they look so miserable?"

"Any ideas, Chief?" asked the Captain.

From beneath his black hood, he commented, "They aren't paid as much as we are." Both he and the Captain laughed.

"Please, follow me closely," Sergeant Miller told the group. They moved around the tunnel and gathered up many small gold ore nuggets that the prisoners had dislodged.

"This could take all night, Stan!" Cheryl told him sternly.

"Yes, darling, but just think how much wealthier you'll be by morning," replied Stan.

* * *

Todd and Janet remained alone in their basement cells, able to communicate only occasionally. Except for the two on watch, all the rest of the guards and prisoners remained concentrated in the third tunnel mining the gold.

On the dark ocean off shore from Fort Warren, Miguel's thirty-six-foot yacht dropped anchor.

* * *

* 44 *

"Excuse me, Corporal, I see the outline of some sort of yacht there off shore," said the young Marine Lance Corporal to the other Marine on tower watch at Fort Warren.

"They're probably just fishing," replied the Marine on watch in the tower.

"I...I don't think so. Here, take a look for yourself," said the Lance Corporal.

As the other Marine looked through his night binoculars he could clearly see framed in the green lens the figures moving into two rubber rafts and rowing toward the shore.

"Well, I'll be damn. It looks like a mini-invasion of some type," said the Corporal on watch in the tower.

"Shall we notify Base Security?" the young Marine asked his superior.

"Not yet. If they set off any alarms, then our boys will be waiting for them. Make a note of it in the log that we had visual contact with two rafts approaching from the southwest," ordered the Corporal.

"Yes, Corporal," he said dejectedly.

Once the first raft washed ashore, the men quickly pulled it up onto the steep slope of the dune. Within five more minutes the other raft was placed next to the first. General Herandes and Raul Gartez stood on the American beach and briefed their assembled men.

"On the other side of these dunes there is a storm drain entrance. We must enter it and follow it into the gold mine. If anyone is standing guard, take them out," said Gartez.

"We must proceed with extreme care. This place could be booby-trapped somehow," added the General.

The first man to the top of the dune reported seeing three guards. Gartez ordered his best shots, "to the top of the dune and take out the Gringoes."

Three quick bursts of automatic fire sent Corporal Lenert and his two assistants reeling backward and falling to the ground with mortal wounds.

"We...we've been hit...help...hel..." was suddenly heard over the walkie-talkie sitting on the table near Janet's cell.

"Todd!" Janet screamed, "Someone's been hit. What does that mean?"

"Oh, God, Janet. That must have been one of the guards. This place could be under attack!" exclaimed Todd.

"Oh, no! Could it be Gartez and his army?" Janet cried. "Now we're really in deep shit, Todd!"

* * *

Gartez, his General and their men moved silently over the dunes toward the storm drain's entrance. They roughly kicked and spit on the bodies of Corporal Lenert and his young assistants.

"Dirty dead Gringoes!" They all said as they passed them.

As the first soldier entered the storm drain he broke the beam of light. Immediately, an alarm sounded on base in the Marine Corps' barracks.

The Mexican soldiers cautiously moved through the drain tunnel. The men felt the walls for a doorway. Within a couple of minutes one man signaled that he had found an opening. Quickly all the Mexicans disappeared into the connecting tunnel and closed the hatch just as the Base Marines scrambled down the ladder of themanhole from the street above. The Marines stared blankly down the one-thousand-foot empty tunnel.

"Nothing, Sergeant. There's nobody down here!" exclaimed one of the Marines.

"I can see for myself, Corporal it's quite empty. All right, men. False alarm men. Return to the barracks," ordered the Marine Sergeant.

Moans and groans arose from the assembled Marines who were called away from their *"Sunday Night Football"* for this so-called security breech. The Marines climbed back up to the street and returned to their barracks.

* * *

Once the Mexicans reached the point where all the tunnels converged, they naturally selected to move carefully down the red lighted third tunnel.

* * *

After about two hours of working in the pit, Cheryl told Stan, "I've had enough of this and I want to leave and go home."

"We'll leave in just a little while," he told her in a harsh tone. Then turning towards the Chief, he asked, "How's it going, Chief?"

"Huh, I'm ready for another pain pill," replied the Chief.

"All right!" the Captain yelled throwing down his shovel. "Why the hell don't you take Cheryl topside and go back to your yacht. Take your damn pills and get her pretty damn drunk!"

"Stan! I don't believe what I'm hearing. We've been down here for nearly two hours with all your sweaty men and their big guns, and I'm just tired, and the Chief's shoulder is hurting him. That's all. We're tired. I didn't mean to upset you," cried Cheryl.

She hugged his neck and then handed him another beautiful gold nugget weighing several pounds.

"Go on, you two. I'll be along shortly," insisted the Captain.

"See you later, darling," she said as she kissed him. Together with Chief Sheppard she turned and headed out of the larger tunnel into the smaller section. After they emerged and walked a few hundred feet, they suddenly met Gartez, the General, and all his men.

"Señorita Lieutenant! And Señor! Buenos Noches, and Adios!" said Gartez in a most evil manner.

With that his men opened fire. Defenseless, Cheryl and the Chief fell backward, mortally wounded against the rocky tunnel walls.

"Forward, men!" Gartez laughed sadistically as he pushed their lifeless bodies aside with his boots.

*   *   *

* 45 *

"Todd, I heard shots!" Janet yelled.

"Calm down and listen very carefully to my instructions," ordered Todd.

"All right, I'm calm," Janet yelled back to him.

"Janet, I just remembered how the revised electrical schematic drawings of this place goes. Those ceiling wires run to the pulsator," explained Todd.

"Fine, tell me what to do?" begged Janet.

"Move your cot to the center of the cell. Stand on it and unhook the ceiling light covering," instructed Todd.

After pulling and pushing she managed to move the iron bed and reach the light fixture. "I have it off," she said proudly.

"Now look at the wires. Do you see the red one?" asked Todd.

"Yes, it's here," replied Janet.

"How about a yellow wire?" asked Todd.

"Yes, that one is here also," replied Janet.

"Good. Pull on the red wire until it breaks," requested Todd.

After some difficulty she succeeded saying, "I've broken it."

"Now wrap it around the yellow wire, and stick the light cover up to touch them both. Now, don't look at it," said Todd.

"Wow!" she said as the shower of sparks flew. Suddenly all the cell doors swung open! He instantly ran to her and grabbed her. They hugged and kissed passionately.

"Oh Todd, you are such a terrific...What's that! Listen," cried Janet.

"It sounds like more gunshots!" he told her. "Let's move!"

"Wait!" said Janet. "All of our stuff is here somewhere. Let's find it quick." Together they hurried down the passageway and into the records' office.

"Here are your things, look!" she said pointing toward the desk. He quickly grabbed his wallet, his gold watch, her purse and the hotel room key. "Take these too," she said as she handed him the green ledger with the safety deposit key underneath the plastic jacket cover. Since every door had swung open, he found his civilian clothes and, together, they ran towards the open steel door.

"Something sounds like running water," she kept saying as they soon approached the convergence of all the tunnels.

"Holy shit!" Todd yelled as he suddenly saw a huge wall of water rushing and cascading through the third tunnel. She screamed as he quickly pulled her with him up through the connecting tunnel to the hatch.

"Open it! Or we'll drown!" she screamed.

He struggled with it as the wall of water rapidly approached. Finally, almost in a state of complete panic, Todd pushed open the hatch. The couple ran for their lives through the storm tunnel. The solid wall of water crashed through the hatchway and emptied instantly into the storm drain. It flowed quickly right behind Janet and Todd on its downhill course toward the beach.

They ran faster and faster until they finally saw the end of the storm drain tunnel. Passing over the light sensor, they tripped it. Over on Base, the Marine detachment was again alerted to another security breach and came running with their weapons drawn.

Todd and Janet jumped over the bodies of the three dead sentries at the drain's entrance. The bodies were instantly washed towards the ocean. The two survivors scrambled over a nearby sand dune and collapsed.

Opening the manhole, Fort Warren's Marines peered down and saw water running through the storm drain.

"Looks like another false alarm, Sergeant," said one of the Marines.

"Very well, a little running water would set off the sensor. Men, return back to the barracks," ordered the Sergeant.

"Yes, Sir, right away, Sir," was the uniform response.

* * *

Todd and Janet lay totally exhausted on the safe side of the dune as the water continued to gush from the storm drain.

"Those gunshots you heard must have caused another earthquake. Maybe this quake let water into the mine from the bay," said Todd still breathing hard.

"They're all dead, aren't they?" she whispered in his ear and tenderly kissed him.

"Yes, I suppose everything just caved-in on them," replied Todd returning her kiss.

"Oh, how horrible! Poor Lieutenant Finley, Captain Siegewick, and Chief Sheppard," said Janet nearly on the verge of tears.

* * *

Once they felt totally recovered, Todd and Janet gathered up their treasures. Under the cover of darkness, they climbed over the dunes and up the steep earthen embankment. Soon, they stood on the edge of the deserted *Coastal Highway*. Crossing the road, Todd told Janet, "Wait here on the bus stop bench while I go back on Base to get my belongings from the room."

"Don't forget to turn in your transit barrack's room key," she reminded him.

They kissed and he entered Fort Warren's Main Gate.

"I've come back to check out of my room in the transit barracks," Todd told the Marine sentry.

"Very good, sir. You may enter," said the young Marine sharply.

Todd quickly walked the few blocks along Main street and saw no one. He passed Herbert Hall that was illuminated by street lights.

Entering the brightly lighted lobby he got the elevator to the seventh floor and collected his bag of clothes. He returned to the lobby and dropped the room key in the slot of the manager's door.

* * *

Within twenty minutes, Todd was back hugging Janet. He told her, "That ought to keep things straight and eliminate us as suspects in their future investigations."

"Look, a bus marked *Hotel Del Coronado* is coming. Let's get on," said Janet anxiously.

The lights of San Diego twinkled and reflected on the bay as the transit bus slowly moved north along the Coastal Highway. Around ten o'clock, they entered the lobby of the Hotel Del Coronado and Janet, seeing the same young man who had checked her in the day before said, "This is my husband, Todd Tasselmeyer."

He nodded his approval as they passed and entered the elevator to the fourth floor.

* * *

Janet waited until she and her lover finished getting cleaned up and were lying in the king-size bed before she began reading the green ledger.

"Dearest, according to this ledger book, in safe deposit box number 1849 inside a vault of the San Diego Bank and Trust Company there is one large sum of cash."

"How much cash?" he inquired.

"Oh, several million," she said with a big grin. "And here's the gold deposit box key!" she said proudly displaying it to him.

"Oh, God, Janet! Do you think you and I are the only ones living who know about this?" asked Todd.

"I'd bet you a million!" she said as they both let out a midnight scream of joy!

*　　*　　*

* 46 *

MONDAY, 0800, JANUARY 7

The nearly four-hundred young naval officers assembled in the courtyard of Herbert Hall stood at attention and saluted as the National Anthem was played over the base public-address system. They proudly watched as the American flag was raised and flapped in the gentle morning breeze. Each ensign returned his or her salute and then headed to their assigned classrooms. Captain Howerton watched the proceedings from his office window at base headquarters. Commander Wilkins entered his office and said, "Old Siegewick would have been proud of this accomplishment. I hope he's happy out there in the civilian world."

* * *

0930 HOURS

Todd signed the credit card receipt for their room and together with Janet, who still had wet hair, caught a local bus into downtown. After carefully studying and copying Cheryl's signature found in the ledger book, Janet realized that Cheryl had not been a blonde. Janet decided she needed to buy some dark hair color in the hotel's cosmetic shop. She told Todd, quickly dressed, left their room, and went downstairs.

He patiently had waited for her to finish coloring her hair before they checked-out. Janet still carried enough money in her purse to buy them both a light breakfast of coffee and rolls. She then bought herself a pair of dark sunglasses in a shop next door.

"Now when we enter the bank, just act very casual," Todd told Janet, as they walked across California Street and entered the bank.

"Good morning. May I help you?" said the receptionist.

"Yes, I want to close out my safe deposit box. I've been wondering if I could have the money transferred electronically to my account in New York City," said Janet in a calm voice.

"Certainly, Miss..."

"Miss Finley, Cheryl Finley," Janet told her from behind the dark glasses and dark auburn hair coloring. *"Box 1849, please."*

"Yes, Miss Finley just sign here on your card and follow me," said the receptionist.

After she carefully signed the card she was directed to the vault area. When Janet emerged from the vault, she could barely lift the box. Todd quickly gave her a hand getting it into the small room.

Sofia Wilkins was ill that day and a new assistant, Maria Townsend, helped Janet. She failed to recognize that Janet was pretending to be Cheryl. Todd and Janet spent nearly an hour counting the stacks of money and tallying the total.

They placed the stacks of money into a satchel that Todd had brought along. Once they emptied the drawer of its fortune, they closed the room door and began to exit the bank.

"Excuse me. You can't leave yet," an authoritative female voice echoed through the lobby.

"Oh, shit!" Todd thought to himself. Both Todd and Janet stopped and looked at each other.

"Please sign here, and return your key to the receptionist," said the teller.

"It's been a pleasure banking with such wonderful people as you," commented Janet from behind her sunglasses.

"That's why we're here, Miss Finley. Good day," smiled the teller.

Janet and Todd quickly left the bank and kissed right on the sidewalk. They boarded a city bus to the airport. Once seated, they sighed a sign of relief while Todd clutched the satchel tightly.

"Well at least we have return trip tickets," replied Janet.

"Yes, we millionaires do plan well in advance," laughed Todd.

* * *

* 47 *

SAN DIEGO INTERNATIONAL AIRPORT
MONDAY, 1 P.M. JANUARY, 7

Todd watched their plane bound for New York, taxi to the terminal and unload its passengers. He carried the bulging satchel of money as Janet kept eyeing the crowded terminal.

When they were seated on-board, the new millionaires began to unwind and relax. Both Todd and Janet were exhausted from their weekend ordeals.

After the plane was airborne, blood returned to Todd's white knuckles and he requested a double Scotch and soda from the flight attendant. Upon finishing the drink, he settled down and became very sleepy.

Janet looked on with pride at her sleeping boyfriend who had come to her rescue in the nick of time inside the flooding mine tunnel. Her thoughts then drifted to the different ways they could spend their newly found fortune.

Todd's sleeping thoughts, on the other hand, became a doorway to the past:

TENOCHTITLAN, MEXICO, 1534 A.D.

Climbing to the top of the stone temple the Spanish Conquistadors had a full view of the spectacular Mexican city below. Many fires still burned out of control throughout the region. The wide streets, where festivals and processions were held, were now littered with dead and dying Aztecs.

What had been a thriving civilization now lay in smoldering ruins. Faint voices of the captured Aztec Indians begging for mercy from their European tormentors could still be heard. Soon, even the surviving natives would be killed for the glory of Spain.

The Spanish soldiers entered the most sacred part to the temple shrine. Inside the bodies of the murdered high priests were pushed aside.

One mortally wounded high priests in a hidden outcove managed to struggle to his feet and call out:

"Curse on those who possess or own you, oh great god Huitzilopochtli. This sacrilege will be avenged! No matter what form or shape you're in, or where you are. Bring much suffering down from the heavens and under the earth to these infidels who so much as touch you!"

After hearing the priest speak, he was shot with a musket. The soldiers moved through the gun powder cloud into the sacrificial room. There, they defiled the altar of sacrifice by pushing over the intricately carved stone wheel causing it to break in half.

Another pulled down an overhead shelf down. One Conquistador grabbed the squatting gold statue of the god, 'Huitzilopochtli.' He yelled as his hands began to burn and roughly tossed it into a saddle bag as if it were an item of cookware.

The lead soldier motioned to the others and the men quickly left the dark humid room for the sunny stone balcony. That interior room was where human sacrifices had been conducted for several centuries.

* * *

After a several hour horse back ride through the steamy jungle, the soldiers returned to their base camp and presented the looted Aztec treasures to Cortez and his henchmen. The gold and jewelry were dumped into wooden trunks. Hundreds of these trunks of gold were loaded aboard a Spanish Galleons destined for Spain.

MADRID, SPAIN 1535 A.D.

Arriving in Spain, the gold treasures were presented to the Spanish King. Realizing the immense value of the items and the dire consequences of possessing golden idols, the King and the Catholic clergy agreed to melt the gold and mint it into gold coins and Church sacred vessels such as chalices, patens and ciboriums. The King requested the golden idol statue of Huitzilopochtli be re-cast as the frame for a new golden hourglass. The resulting action was that those who handled the hourglass were stricken with illness and death for defiling the Aztec god.

COAST OF SOUTHERN CALIFORNIA, 1860 A.D.

A man from the Dutchman Mining Company found a small wooden crate wedged among a rocky outcrop. He had been walking along a deserted section of Pacific beach near San Diego. The crate apparently washed ashore from a sunken Spanish galleon three hundred years earlier. He took his find to the nearby Company mining location. After entering a mine tunnel in the cliff wall, the prospector opened the crate and removed a golden hourglass.

Disaster struck when a powerful earthquake rocked the region. The man inside the mine tunnel barely had time to wrap the golden hourglass in a quilt and place it into his personal trunk when the mine's ceiling collapsed and killed him. Sand filled the space and preserved the location until modern day when it was rediscovered again by the backhoe excavating the foundation for Herbert Hall.

Todd woke up suddenly as the plane's wheels touched down jarring him in his seat.

EPILOGUE

RIVERSIDE APARTMENT, NEW YORK CITY
MONDAY, 10 P.M., JANUARY 7

Arriving home from the airport, Todd and Janet entered their darkened Riverside apartment. She turned on the lights and quickly ran over to the golden hourglass sitting inanimately on the mantel in the living room. Leaning over, she kissed it and said, "Oh! Hourglass! What good fortune you have brought us. Thank you!"

Walking into the room, Todd placed the heavy satchel down by the sofa across from the fireplace, and said, "Janet! What are you doing?"

"Oh darling, I'm so happy tonight," she replied twirling like a ballerina.

"I don't think you should have kissed that thing."

"Oh. Don't be such a party pooper tonight. We're rich beyond measure! Thank you! Thank you! Thank you!" she said as they kissed. The large gilded mirror reflected everything. Shortly thereafter, the weary couple retired to their bedroom and closed the door.

"Good night, darling. Sweet dreams," whispered Janet.

"Oh, Janet. It seems like this whole weekend was a dream. Never have I experienced such an adventure," replied a yawning Todd.

"And never have we been so rich!" Janet said as they kissed each other again. Various clocks throughout the spacious Riverside apartment softly chimed as the couple fell asleep.

* * *

Whaling sirens of police cars and ambulances sliced through the morning fog. A commotion of people gathered in the lobby of the luxurious Riverside Apartment house. City Police Detectives and Police Officers began interviewing pajama-clad and robed tenants.

Two of New York's top Detectives were talking in the doorway. The first saying, "Joe, from what the neighbors told me, the victims were nice people. Last night, no one saw or heard anything. No signs of forced entry and nothing seems to have been stolen."

The second Detective studied his notes and told the other, "There's no explanation as to where the Aztec masks that covered the victims' faces came from and absolutely no evidence that either one of the two victims was involved in any cult activities."

Just then a NYPD Officer approached and announced, "Excuse me, gentlemen. The coroner is here and is ready to examine our victims."

The two Detectives approached the coroner and one said, "You know, Frank, this is a real bazaar double homicide. It's as if the architect guy and his girlfriend's hearts were surgically removed without disturbing anything. Wait'll you get into this one."

* * *

As the alarm clock buzzed, Todd and Janet woke up screaming from their parallel dream! They then heard an unusual crackling sound. Shaking from fear, they quickly put on their robes and left the bedroom. Standing in the hallway they looked in horror at their beautifully decorated living room. Out of the roaring fireplace stepped a skeleton figure clad in high priest garments of the ancient Aztecs.

It quickly reached out its bony fingers and picked up the golden hourglass from the mantel. It held the object over the flames. The hourglass began to melt and transformed itself back to the original gold statue of Huitzilopochtli.

Todd and Janet screamed as a violent whirlwind appeared and pulled all the flames directly into their living room!

The wind opened the satchel causing all the money to fill the room like confetti. All of their expensive furnishings, along with the thousands of one hundred dollar bills immediately burst into flames!

In an instantly, everything was sucked down into the fireplace along with the skeleton high priest holding the golden idol statue!

All became quiet as Todd and Janet, in shock and disbelief, glanced into their bare living room. Without warning, they began to hear an eerie noise. The walls, ceiling and floor of the living room now trembled and begin to turn to stone! The ancient Aztec temple sacrificial room was being recreated before their eyes. The walls, ceiling and floor began to ooze blood, as a hundred fresh human hearts, from today's sacrifice, hung from the walls!

Janet fainted as Todd cried out in pain and agony, "What will the landlord say?"

*   *   *

TUESDAY, 9:15 A.M., JANUARY 8

Todd's partner, Larry Stevenson, entered his office and in his usual cheery manner asked, "Todd, how was your weekend on the West Coast? Anything exciting happen?"

Todd, still totally exhausted and recovering from shock, raised up from his drafting table. With fear in his eyes, he looked out the window at the gently falling snow. Glancing at the clock on the wall, he thought, "Where should I begin?"

THE END

Lightning Source UK Ltd.
Milton Keynes UK
UKHW011853070121
376641UK00007B/524/J